The
FLORENTINE

The
FLORENTINE

Carl J.
SPINATELLI

New York
PRENTICE-HALL, INC.

◇

"...and the midwife, who knew that my father expected another girl child, came softly up to Giovanni and said to him: 'I bring you a fine gift such as you do not expect.' My father who was a true philosopher made answer: 'Whatever God sees fit to give me will always be acceptable'; and lifting up the cloths he saw with his own eyes the unexpected male child. Clasping his aged hands to Heaven, he exclaimed: 'Oh Lord, I thank Thee with all my heart, for he is most welcome!' Now all those persons who were present most joyfully asked him how he would name the child. Giovanni never answered aught save: 'He is welcome! He is welcome!' and such was the name given me in Holy Baptism ..."

Vita di Benvenuto Cellini,
Firenze: Anno Domini, 1558

FOREWORD

It is perhaps necessary to point out here that the tale which follows is a work of the imagination. Conversely, it must also be made clear that it is less a work of the imagination than may be surmised. A seeming paradox that should be explained.

This narrative is a biographical novel based on the life of Benvenuto Cellini, the Florentine master-goldsmith, swordsman, musician, soldier, lover, and general hell-raiser, who lived in the Italy of the latter Renaissance. It is based, in part, on incidents set forth in his autobiography; in part, on the history of that violent period; and, in part, on recorded incidents in the lives of the various artists and more or less exalted persons who appear on its pages. The vast and almost incredible sequence of tumultuous events that are depicted all actually happened and formed a part, a large and important part, of this ribald and combative Tuscan artist's existence. This is the life he lived, the events which shaped it, the times in which these occurred, and the actions, manners and temper of the individuals with whom he contended in the course of it. The characterizations, while fictionalized, are realistically drawn. A student of that era will perhaps discover that the portraiture is, in the main, accurate. Indeed, very accurate.

For this reason, if some of the subsequent pages seem to you brash, or risqué, or vulgar, or lewd, consider the age and consider the man. Cellini was not one who passed his life in an ivory tower, wrapped up in the glowing mist of creative dreams. He led a violent existence, filled with lusty passion. He was a perfect exemplar of his time. Consequently, what follows is not one of the usual coyly-written, long-haired panegyrics on the life of a Renaissance master.

The world of that epoch was easily the most predatory, licentious, and amoral, to which Man has fallen heir. It was also a period when Man was beginning to understand himself and the world he lived in, a little better than he had understood these things in the past. Hence, the colors used to portray this world, though raw and blatant, are realistic to an age that was gorgeous, reckless, and completely ruthless—dog eat dog reduced to its most elemental equation.

So, then, if you shock easily, I would not bear the burden of asking you to read on. Go no farther than this. You have, alas, made a mistake in purchasing this volume. This is not a tale for the queasy, the squeamish, or the pure of mind. If such you are, it may cause you great mental anguish.

But if you would chance the reading of a lusty, ribald, and somewhat bawdy tale, bartering on the slender hope that you will be repaid in a sometimes amusing, sometimes violent, sometimes horrible, and possibly interesting diversion—if such is tolerable to your taste and inclination, then I would ask you to turn the page and get on with it. Indeed, if such is your bent I do more than ask...I exhort you.

Carl J. Spinatelli

PART I

I

It WAS A LONG, CLUTTERED, LOW-CEILINGED
room, typical of the workshops throughout Italy. A fire blazed dismally
in an open hearth whose chimney did not function too well, and at one
side of it, on the roughly faced, soot-smeared wall, a large leaded window was open slightly, more to let the smoke find some escape than to
let in the cool November air which was beginning to turn brisk. A star
twinkled here and there in the patches of sky visible through the
opening, and in the distance the lofty summits of the Apennines
towered over the rooftops of Florence. Occasionally, a barely audible
street noise was carried into the room on a puff of wind permeated
with odors much less poetic than the moonlit vista the window framed.

The littered benches and tables of the shop were deserted except
for a lone youth working near the front, concentrating wholly and
completely on the task before him. He was perched on a stool, with
his back to the shop's rear door, hunched over the heavy oak work
table. In front of him, near the table's edge, several wide and stumpy
candles set in blackened stands added their fitful illumination to that
of two hanging lamps, while the wavering patterns of their flames
sent wave after wave of weirdly-patterned light shimmering over him.
He was engaged in a delicate operation; chasing, with a slender steel
burin, one of several minute cherubs which peeped from the intricate
arabesque he had carved on a gleaming yellow gold girdle-clasp. The
piece was superbly, exquisitely, done. A discerning patron of the arts
or any person of taste—and there were many such in the Italy of this
year of Our Lord, 1523—would have found it difficult to reconcile such
masterful artistry and skill with such evident youth. For this fellow
was young—had, in fact, barely entered adult manhood. It was evident
from the look of him. His slender figure, partly covered by the leather
work apron, could belong only to youth. It was lean and supple, of
average height—not short but not tall either—and had the effortless
muscular tenseness of a seated cat.

Using the handle of the burin, he stopped to scratch at the week-old stubble on a cheek, and then brushed a stray lock of dark brown hair back behind an ear set close to the skull. The wood handle left a smudge along the tan, almost swarthy skin of his forehead, bringing into prominence a barely visible, faintly bluish vein that softly pulsed its way along the temple. The vein pointed up a fact. It gave notice that the temperament it helped house was quick and passionate and could erupt violently. His eyes gave further proof of this characteristic. They were deep set and limpid brown, and had devils in them that danced a flickering rigadoon in tempo with the wavering candlelight. The cheekbones were prominent and the lips, wide and full, were set in an almost straight line over a determined chin. He had a wholesome face. Not necessarily handsome, but at the same time it would never cause anyone who might look upon it to shriek in dismay.

His name was Cellini. Benvenuto Cellini.

The most fascinating portion of him, as he sat working with the slender, gleaming steel, was his hands—specifically, his fingers. There was magic in them. One could sense it simply from the manner in which they moved and worked. They were fingers whose master could make them do whatever he wished. They were possessed of a wizardry which created with such deft delicacy it scarcely seemed human. They were not the long and graceful digits which one usually associates with creativeness. On the contrary, they were of average length, rather blunt, and already heavily calloused by years of labor on hard surfaces. They grasped with a grip like a vise; and when they moved, bands of corded muscle leaped and quivered like striking serpents. They had become so sensitive they could distinguish differences which varied by no more than a fraction of the thickness of a hair.

At the moment they were putting the finishing touches to the tiny, flowing locks of one of the peeping cherubs. The effect was undoubtedly satisfactory, for Cellini was pleased. He chortled exultantly as he held the piece up for inspection.

"*Per Dio!* not bad at all," he crowed to himself. "This should bring in some credit as well as money; and the credit where it might do some good."

A finger swept in a caress over the modeled surfaces and detected a slight burr, which he proceeded to smooth out.

Absorbed with these final touches he did not hear, or paid no mind, as the door behind him opened to admit the rotund figure of

4

an elderly man with an intelligent, dignified face. The oldster was color-fully dressed in the flamboyant costume affected by an individual of means. He eased quietly into the shop and having softly re-shut the door, he paused, motionless, looking intently at the working gold-smith. He cocked his head, first to one side then the other, appreciating the chiaroscuro effect he looked upon.

"Well then, Neutino," he finally asked, using the familiar diminu-tive of Cellini's given name, "still here I see? How is it coming along?"

Cellini looked up and around. "Ah, it's you, Ser Giovanni? I've just this moment finished."

"So. Let me see what you have accomplished."

Taking the clasp which the young man offered, he leaned toward the candlelight with it. It was a fairly large piece, about the size of a boy's hand, intricately engraved and sculptured, and rich in allegorical figures; the most prominent of which, since the clasp was to be worn by a woman, was a Venus carved completely in the round.

Giovan-Battista Sogliani's examination was keen and critical. While he evaluated, Cellini fidgeted. His trust in Sogliani's judgment was explicit and complete. The man was a distinguished master-jeweler with the experience of a lifetime spent as a professional artist, and a rec-ognized and expert judge of merit in any work of art. Even so mighty a patron as the Cardinal Giulio held him in high esteem and regarded him as well-nigh infallible in matters relating to *le belle arti*.

Ser Giovanni's eyes finally left the clasp and swept over the young goldsmith. He sighed happily, a sure indication that the work pleased him, and pursed his lips thoughtfully. Unquestionably, the youth had talent, great talent. What was more, the fellow was a lad of spirit, a galliard ready to give as good as he got. There was no part of a doubt that he would go far, unless, of course, his rather sharp and ready temper earned him a cut throat before he got there.

"Hm-m-m," he murmured, his eyes returning to the clasp which he turned one way, then another.

"*Gesù, maestro!* Don't leave me dangling this way. Tell me what you think."

"You know, Neutino," the master told him, "when I offered you the facilities of my shop a few weeks ago, I had the thought that doing so would bring me credit and honor. *Caspita!* It has."

"Hah! Then you are pleased?"

"Well pleased. This is exquisite. A true work of art. Incidentally,

5

leave it where I can pick it up tomorrow morning. I intend to show this piece around a bit. And what do you think of it?"

"I'd say I did well," Cellini admitted, extraordinarily pleased with himself. For the old master's words told him that he had succeeded in imparting to his work that almost intangible difference which distinguishes mere craftsmanship from creation. "I think Madama Isabella will be pleased."

"I should think so!" Carefully the master wrapped the clasp in a piece of velvet and returned it to Cellini, who placed it in a small chest.

"That is excellently done, my boy," he beamed. "A superb example of the goldsmith's art. It's a pity that a work of such rare quality will serve no better purpose than to be worn about the fat belly of some high-placed bitch." He shrugged at the vagaries of womankind. "But that's the way of the world. Only tell me one thing: There was no particular hurry for it. Why all this night work?"

Cellini lifted his shoulders in a shrug and waved a hand in a deprecatory gesture. "It's my father. You know that mania of his? Wanting to make a musician of me? A musician, by God!"

"Yes," nodded Sogliani with a smile. "So, then?"

"Of late," Cellini went on, "he's been harping on my progress with that damned flute and cornet. Wants me to study and practice more than I'm doing. So I find things to do. I would do anything rather than get mixed up with that accursed art again." He made a wry face. "I don't wish to offend him, so I stay here and work, or go elsewhere and do other things. When I reach home, he's asleep and that's the end of it."

"I see," Sogliani nodded sympathetically and watched the youth remove his work apron, exposing lean flanks and limbs encased in trunk hose and soft leather boots reaching to the middle of the thighs. "But tell me. This ... this new biddy of yours ... what's her name—Gianna? At the Golden Florin, no? How is it that she never has any trouble getting you to play the flute for her? And for a music-hater, play very well too, I'm told."

Cellini colored slightly. "My dear Ser Giovanni, let me put it thus: If ever you are able to pay out in the same coin as Gianna for my virtuosity on the flute, I shall regard it a pleasure to play for you—any time!"

The jeweler chuckled. *"E perchè no?* One is young only once, why not make the most of it? I remember a time, long ago unfortunately, there was a—but no, that must wait. I wished to ask you ..."

6

Ser Giovanni's face became grave. He had a touchy subject to bring up. He stroked and smoothed a carefully cut beard, while Cellini poured water into a basin and proceeded to wash.

"About these Guasconti," he began, "I'm told you had quite a bit to say about them again. And to a guild member no less! Neutino, when will you learn to leave well-enough alone?"

"You hear of things promptly, *maestro.*" Cellini smiled ruefully.

"Certainly, my frisky gallant! And why not? I am an amiable old goat, intimate with a great many people, and they are constantly inviting me in for a glass. While we drink, they tell me things. I listen. Today, I listened to an account of your recent discourse on the subject of the Guasconti."

Cellini raised a soap-smeared face and sank it into a none-too-clean towel, rubbing briskly.

"I don't know why it should annoy you. You know that for the six months I was with those thieves they consistently over-reached and cheated me, belittling my work so they could push out their own piddling baubles. Why shouldn't I let people know about such underhanded charlatans who masquerade as respectable goldsmiths?"

"Good God!" Giovanni waved both hands in an eloquent gesture that was meant to show how utterly confounded he was. "My dear Benvenuto," he let his voice sink to an even graver tone, "granting everything you say, can you prove any of it? No! Does all this chattering do you any good? Again, no! You know very well that these people are in a powerful position. They own three shops and do a thriving business. And, *carino mio,* they pass for honest and upright men. They have friends in high places, while you are just starting out in the world. They could squash you like a bedbug! That's why you should keep your mouth shut and that warm temper of yours tightly bridled. Let me tell you, they have stated, and no later than this morning, that they intend to make you repent your words—and with a penance too."

"Bah!" Cellini brushed the threat away derisively and slipped a black doublet over his low-necked shirt. "What have they to low about? I'm the one who has been fleeced. What's more, I do not intend to overlook the fleecing."

He strapped a leather belt around his waist, adjusted the purse to one side and shifted a short leather-sheathed poniard, a *misericordia,* to the center.

"God's wounds! Reflect!" exclaimed the older and more level-

7

headed jeweler. "What are you? A reformer? Another Savonarola, perhaps? Do you think that you can undertake to change the universe? There always have been and there always will be men such as these on this world of ours. They are as much a part of it as some of the food you eat. The kind that gives you gas. You have been cheated? Charge it to experience. Now you know better and can take care it does not recur. *Ecco!* That is the sensible thing."

Cellini drew a cloth cap over his hair and picked up his cloak. "You know, *maestro,*" he told the jeweler, "I don't doubt that you're right. But remember this: We are all of us as God saw fit to make us; and from the manner in which He fashioned me, I doubt that I will now or at any time in my life ever permit myself to be so used, and let it go at that.

"I have a great deal to learn of life," he continued, his tone getting warm, "and I try to learn from experience. But I will not be gulled and cheated by those lice without paying them back. I'll give them a penance! One they won't forget too soon either!" The cloak had been thrown back over a shoulder, and with a finger hooked around the haft of his poniard, Cellini glowered while the old jeweler looked on disapprovingly.

"Cool off. For Christ's sake, calm down. And for the love of heaven, at least see to it that you've something with which to back up such utterances before you make them. Isn't that logical?"

Cellini blinked. "I have all I need there, *maestro.*"

"You have? *Sangue di Dio!* What?"

Cellini tapped a blunt finger against his chest. "I have myself," he stated flatly. "Well, till tomorrow, Ser Giovanni, *addio.*"

"*Ah!*" Sogliani shook his head and sighed. "*Buona notta,* my young scamp."

Shutting the shop door carefully, Cellini listened to make certain the servant within took care to fasten the door behind him. When he heard the oily cluck of the lock-bolt and the grinding rasp of the latches, he stepped off the doorway and walked to the center of the street. Patting himself on the chest and yawning widely, he looked about the Via del Mercato. Sogliani's shop was situated in the Mercato Nuovo, close by the Florence branch of the Bank of the Landi. A shrewdly chosen spot since the wealthy clients of the bank invariably became the clients of Master Sogliani the goldsmith as well.

Across from him a gaunt stray dog, scavenging amid the refuse that lined the gutters, looked up, growled deep in his throat and loped off into the darkness. As he disappeared the high-pitched keening whine of fat sleek rats again became audible, as they reappeared to forage for food.

Far down the street toward the Arno, the clear star-studded moonlight glinted off the campanile on the high embattled tower of the Palazzo della Signoria. Within it the huge and celebrated tocsin bell of Florence—*La Vacca,* The Cow—slumbered. Here and there a torch flared as it lighted a doorway along the deserted street. Cellini turned and started in the direction of his home in the Via Chiara, his footsteps sounding dully on the smooth paving stones. For a moment he paused, pensive. Should he stop off at the Golden Florin? A cool glass and a warm joust with the luscious Gianna, who was as frolicsome on a bed as off one, would make a fitting end for a full and fruitful day. But then it had been a long and hard one. He fingered the stubble on his face and decided against it.

Continuing on his way, he reached the Baptistery, crossed the Via dei Ginori to the darkened square of San Lorenzo, and turned into the street leading to his home.

The house of Giovanni Cellini was, as his son expected and hoped, dark and still when he reached it. Letting himself in, he went softly to his room and lit a candle on the table by his bed. The room was filled with models in wax, clay, and stucco. The walls were lined with drawings and designs. Most of them were copies of famous works by Tuscany's many already immortal masters, or of the antiquities collected so avidly by the Florentine nobility, who delighted in seeing young apprentices gather within their halls to study the work of enlightened men.

Cellini looked around at them, muttering a soft reassurance as he gazed. "Some day," he promised himself as he began undressing. "Some day."

The self-assurance had a plaintive appeal. There was in it a touch of pride, a note of fervent hope, and an immensity of unshakable will. It was a challenge flung out at an unborn tomorrow.

II

WITH HIS HANDS CLASPED BEHIND HIM AND his head bent so low his gray beard fanned out on his chest, Master Giovanni Cellini paced impatiently around the kitchen of his house, muttering incoherently while his daughter Cosa set the table for her brother's breakfast. The sun was already high and the younger Cellini had not yet come down for the morning meal.

"Does that young stallion intend to sleep the day through, daughter?" he inquired pettishly. "Perhaps you had better go up again and see if he has awakened."

"He was shaving, Papa. He worked very late—"

"I know that," Master Giovanni snapped waspishly. "It is not necessary to remind me of it. Neutino is forever working late! Every night now these three full weeks—"

Cosa turned and smiled at him sympathetically, shaking her head. She knew what awaited her brother. Every day father and son bickered over the same old theme.

"Here he is now." She smiled again, at her brother this time.

He winked back and faced his father. "Good morning, Papa," he grinned, seating himself on the table bench.

"*Ah, buon giorno, figliolo.*" Giovanni's remarkably lively brown eyes gleamed warmly but he wasted no time in getting to the point. "You worked late again last night." He made a face and waved an open hand peevishly. "What a pity, again to sacrifice your studies on that most admirable flute and cornet. A pity? Nay, a shame, that such a God-given gift must be lost to the world!"

The elder Cellini had played the flute in the court of the Medici. Music to him was a second religion. That his son did not see eye-to-eye with him on its choice as a career was a thing he found as inexplicable as all other inscrutable acts of the Almighty. It made him sad. It made him more than a little bilious too, but he was willing to grant that the latter might be due to the ravages of age. So he let his head shake sadly and sink back on his chest, in order that his son might see just how sad he was feeling.

His son was used to these antics.

"*Vecchietto*," he told him, a little desperately, "I'm doing just exactly what God intended I should do—and paying our way with the proceeds."

The father sighed. This was a point against which he could offer no argument.

"True," he admitted, much against his will. "True. I have almost begun to reconcile myself to that fact."

"Jesus, I hope so," his son fervently muttered to himself.

"Nevertheless, it is a shame!" Giovanni persisted petulantly, venting another long sigh while he covertly eyed his son to see if a proper effect was being produced.

His son had hacked off a chunk of bread, speared a piece of meat, and was eating, paying no further attention to his father's bickering. It lacked three hours to midday. Sogliani would now be displaying the clasp at the Guild of the Goldsmiths, and, it was to be hoped, was being congratulated that so fine a piece of work had issued from his shop. By noon it should be ready, and after delivering it he meant to give over the rest of the day to a celebration he had been promising himself for the past month.

Cellini left the house and strode rapidly along the streets, absorbed in large dreams of future greatness. He had no thought whatever, not the faintest glimmering of an idea, that this day was to be, for him, a fateful one. He turned into the Via del Mercato, still occupied with his fancies, breaking these off occasionally to absently greet a passer-by with whom he was acquainted, or, as absently, to ogle the more comely of the girls who walked by. His thoughts were centered on achieving recognition in his art.

It was near the Via delle Cipolle that he saw her.... And she was something to see! A really entrancing vision, walking along the brilliantly sunlit street, toward him. Straight, slender, round-hipped and long-limbed, delightfully curved, with deliciously full breasts which danced as she tripped along. Cellini abruptly broke off his musing and gaped hungrily and blew out a long frothy whistle.

He whistled again as she drew nearer, and let his eyes wander up and down in careful appraisal. *Caspita!* She could serve, and excellently well, as a—say, a model. The very manner in which she walked was a fantasy. Supple, provocative, an undulant billow, like the movement of a gently rolling wave; a vision with swinging hips and eyes that sparkled and flashed in a languishing way as they threw out an impish challenge. She flounced past with red lips parted in a deliberate smile.

Cellini leaned an arm against the doorpost of the shop beside him and turned for another appreciative look. By Satan's barbed tail, there was a wench! He was on the verge of taking off after her...

"You there! Take your dirty paw off my door! Gutter filth! Remove yourself! You stink up the place!"

Cellini's eyes rounded like the balls on the arms of the Medici. Frowning, he looked around. It was possible that the remark was intended for someone else. He looked, but there was nobody else about. The muscles along his jaw and mouth knotted with stubborn intensity, and as the vein at his temple began its slow rhythmic throb of warning, it came to him that he was leaning against one of the Guasconti shops. That loud, sneering voice belonged to Michele Guasconti. The ill-mannered swine! The whole tribe badly needed a lesson in manners, and, by God, he was perfectly willing to serve as the instructor for it. There had never yet come a time when he wouldn't rather fight than eat. A violent red surge began to crawl up his neck.

Leaving his hand where it was he slowly turned his head, and, sending a red glare of fury at Michele who was sneering abuse, spat insultingly into the shop.

"Go on, piddler! Incompetent drone! Return to your Master Sogliani and cry some more, so that he can clasp you to his bosom! Off with you! Take yourself away from that door before we come out and throw you where you belong—in the gutter with the rest of the dung!"

"You thieving son of a bitch! Come out here and do that!"

Michele disregarded the invitation and shifted his eyes beyond the livid young goldsmith, to where his son Gerardo had stolen after sneaking out the side door. At a signal he loosed a fresh crop of insults, holding the boiling Cellini's attention, while his son waited for the opportunity to move into position. A freight-laden donkey, drooping under a load of brick, was jogging up the narrow street and soon would be opposite the shop door. Gerardo waited impatiently. The beast ambled slowly along, at times obstinately jerking at its lead rope, trying thus to communicate the fact that a few seconds of pause would neither do harm nor be amiss. As it drew alongside the cursing goldsmith, Gerardo rushed forward and gave the precarious load a mighty heave. Cellini went sprawling against the side of the building, with a shower of loose bricks spraying over him.

The startled jackass brayed loudly and began kicking out with its hind legs, dislodging more bricks over the helpless goldsmith. It was some time before it regained a sort of ruffled composure and decided to move off, with a much lightened load.

The fall, and the tumbling bricks, had hurt. But it was the loud, sarcastic laughter of the Guasconti that set the match to the powder keg of Cellini's temper. In a blurred, fuzzy glare of explosive fury he managed to untangle himself and scramble to his feet, trembling with bursting spleen, teeth bared like the fangs of a wolf, that vein swollen and pounding like the hammers of hell.

"Schifoso maledetto!" Clutching at Gerardo's shirt with one hand, he swung the hard clenched fist of the other in a looping blow that caught his tormentor flush on the upper jaw. Gerardo's laughter ceased and he went sprawling in the gutter, limp as a wet rag.

Fuming and red with rage and brick dust, Cellini whirled to face the group clustered just inside the shop doorway.

"Bestia!" His face distorted, Michele turned to his journeymen. "Come, let's deal properly with this miserable bastard!"

Several of the men started forward, then stopped abruptly. With lightning speed the little *misericordia* had been drawn from its sheath and was pointing at them collectively.

"If any one of you whoresons so much as sets a foot past that door," Cellini snarled at them, "the rest of you better run very fast for a priest. By the rood, I swear there'll be nothing left for any doctor to do!"

No one moved. It was known this young goldsmith was a lad who could give an account of himself in a fight. Gerardo remained where he was.

"You craven scum!" Snorting in contempt, Cellini turned away. He strode through the crowd that had gathered and walked off toward the Sogliani shop. The superbly formed wench who had, unwittingly, caused the altercation was completely forgotten. He never saw her again.

In the early afternoon, only minutes after he returned from delivering the jewel piece, the blackleg arrived. A thin, slimy looking husk of a man, dressed in dirt-grayed hose, spotted trunks and grimy doublet partly covered by a long mantle of uncertain color. He threw back the door and entered, so he thought, with a grand manner. The roundlet on his head was too wide and large for the thin, gimlet-eyed face beneath it, and only made him look ludicrous. A sword was belted around his middle and his opulence was attested by a large medallion, presumably of gold, which dangled from his neck. He was a deputy of the Bargello, one of the blackleg breed scurrilously referred to as *"sbirri."* A catchpoll. A sheriff's lackey.

He stomped into the shop, full of the pompous, self-important air common to the civil agent on official business. He stared haughtily down a reedy nose, right hand poised on his hip, the left resting on his sword hilt.

"I am seeking," he loudly informed the room, "one Benvenuto Cellini, who is a goldsmith."

His voice was a nasal whine, into which he attempted to inject a tone of implied authority and the necessity for instant servile obedience.

The object of his quest leaned a leg over a table and let his lip curl insultingly.

"I am Cellini."

Like the rest of the Florentine populace, the young goldsmith did not think very highly of these official street-lice. They were a corrupt and iniquitous crew, available, body and soul, to anyone willing to count out the required number of ducats. More than one tolerably honest citizen had been brought in a badly slashed corpse for resisting these agents of the Bargello.

"The Eight of Florence," nasally continued the officious deputy, "command you to appear before them."

"When?"

"Immediately. I am to accompany you and see to it that you repair there instantly, to answer the charges brought against you by certain of the Guasconti."

By way of reply he received a sarcastic grunt.

"Give me here your arms," ordered the blackleg.

Cellini fingered the small dagger. "I'll give it to you," he sneered nastily. "I'll cram it down your throat."

The shop workmen, who had paused to look on, snickered in appreciation. The catchpoll loosened his sword in its scabbard and glowered.

"Make another move with that oversize toothpick," Cellini growled bluntly, "and I'll rip that scrawny gullet right out of your neck."

14

Accustomed to cringing and whining, the catchpoll was so chagrined by this surly attitude that his hand dropped from the sword hilt he was fingering. Aside from immediate personal apprehensions he had to be careful for other reasons. He was aware that the elder Cellini had been in the service of the Medici and was held in high esteem by that noble family. And Cardinal Giulio de' Medici, even though currently absent, was the absolute ruler of Florence. Caution was indicated, no matter how many political strings the Guasconti had pulled to arrange things their way.

Cellini drew on his cloak, still spattered here and there with brick dust.

"When we walk along the street," he testily announced to the now deflated *sbirro,* "see to keeping a distance. I will not be seen walking with the likes of you."

He did, however, remove the poniard from his belt and place it on his work table. It wouldn't do to appear before judicial authority bearing arms. That would make them frown.

The catchpoll sniffed but made no other comment.

En route to the Bargello, Cellini glumly considered this new turn which his quarrel with the Guasconti had taken. Since the squabble was a personal one, he had not expected a move in which the authorities might become embroiled. The provocation had been ample and he had only done what any man of spirit would do—defend himself. Now that his enemies had laid the matter before the tribunal concerned with the internal peace of Florence, there was only one conclusion to be drawn: They had made arrangements for a judgment against him. The Guasconti, he knew, were politically partial to the faction called *l'Arrabbiati*—the angry ones. He knew also that members of that party were serving on The Eight. It was obvious that palms had been crossed. Clearly his mistake lay in not having immediately run to a few string-pulling friends of his own.

There was only a single glimmer of hope. The Florentine government and all its agencies was completely dominated by top Medicean partisans. In the case of The Eight, the lord Prinzivalle della Stufa was in control. And that nobleman was very friendly with his father. It was just possible that through him the favor-currying Guasconti might be checkmated. Cellini breathed a little more easily, but not much more.

"In any case," he told himself, as he passed through the entrance doors of the Bargello, "I'll soon find out."

15

Thoroughly acquainted with the building and most of the personnel, Cellini knew his way around the Palace of the Podestà. As a young hothead who took abuse from no man, he had been in the place before. Passing into the ancient arcaded courtyard where some guardsmen were watering their horses, he turned right and ascended the wide stair with carved balusters, that led to an open arcade along the second floor level from which entry to the various halls of the *palazzo* was gained.

The Eight held session in a large solemn chamber. The walls were painted in fresco. Sculptured and gilded beams crossed the high ceiling. Ponderous tables, chairs, benches and writing desks, were scattered around. A wide, raised platform ranged down one side of the room. Atop this, seated behind a long and ornately carved judicatorial dock, the eight judges of the tribunal waited in stern silence. To one side, a group of the Guasconti was conversing in whispers.

Having already admitted to one tactical error in not having contacted the right people, Cellini entered the room and was instantly aware of a second glaring blunder. His adversaries were there, resplendent in mantle and hood, the formal dress of the Florentine. On the other hand, like some ill-mannered lout, he was making his appearance in cloak and cap. The implied incivility was not overlooked. There were immediate grunts of disapproval.

"Fellow," sarcastically inquired one member of the octave, "are your circumstances so distressing that you lack even one habit of proper dress?"

"Oh no, my lords." Cellini's reply was prompt and politic. "I came as you see me, in answer to your command that I repair here instantly."

"Ah, a fellow with a ready tongue, hey?" Adroitly Della Stufa jerked the reins from the hands of the *arrabbiato* who had first spoken. "Come forward here. Know, then, young man, that you stand accused by these gentlemen," he waved a hand languidly in their direction, "of having, while they were engaged in their lawful and honorable profession, wilfully and with force of arms assaulted them in their shop. What say you to this? Speak up."

Cellini's hoarse screams impressed even the *arrabbiati*. Purple-faced with passion, he bit out a withering refutation of the charge and demanded the immediate summons of shopowners near the Guasconti who had witnessed the affair. This was Florence—where truth prevailed! The tirade he loosed was so supremely virulent, even the clerks perked up.

"These witnesses you speak of may or may not be necessary," Della Stufa soothingly averred. "We shall see. Meanwhile, see to telling in your own words your version of the affair."

Giving his active imagination full rein, Cellini embarked on a version of his own devising, into which he injected some nicely colored distortions of his own. Two could play at that game. He was doing well. The Guasconti were squirming. He reached the point where, as he naïvely put it, "... it became necessary to give Gerardo a little box on the ear."

"A little box on the ear!" howled another of the *arrabbiati,* snorting in disgust. *"Santa Maria!* Will you but look at the poor fellow! His face is swollen to twice its natural size. Tell the truth! That was no box! It was a violent blow!"

The young goldsmith sent a black look at Gerardo but held his ground. Opinions to the contrary, he pointed out, were the affair of those who voiced them. It had been a light slap and nothing more. He went on with his story, ending with the comment that this trivial but righteous action of his scarcely merited the treatment to which he was being subjected.

Since both sides had been heard, the chief clerk rang a bell and herded petitioners and accused out of the room so that the tribunal could deliberate and arrive at a verdict.

"I say punish him." One judge had finished deliberating before the doors were fully closed. "That Cellini is a troublemaker. He's been in it up to his ears before, and often. I remember him and his younger brother in one fracas where they cut up a half-dozen men. Nearly killed two of them. They were banished for six months because of it. I say punish him. Send him to prison. He needs cooling off."

"My dear Antonio," suavely interjected Cellini's temporary guardian angel, "why not say also that their opponents, in that *fracasso* you allude to, were found to be guilty and were sentenced to a period of years?

"However, my lords and gentlemen, we are here engaged in the consideration of this present affair. Look you, sirs, would a guilty man request that witnesses be brought forth to prove his guilt? Yet this youth has so demanded, and more, has shown where such witnesses are to be found. Consider also his simplicity in insisting that he struck his adversary a box on the ear; whereas under the law, the penalty for a light blow administered in the Mercato Nuovo is twenty-five ducats, while that for a violent blow is little or nothing. The lad is headstrong and short-tempered, granted, and this should be brought home to him. But he is also a virtuous and talented youth who supports an indigent family by his labor. Would to God there were more of his kind in our fair city. Heaven knows there is a great need of them."

A certain amount of hedging followed this declaration, to which Della Stufa listened with ill-concealed impatience. The real point of issue involved was that for some time now his colleagues had displayed a tendency to balk. In fact, the backsliding had reached a point where it was necessary to show the dolts what could and would happen if they continued to stray from the path. He let his face set into grim lines and pointed out that unless the matter was settled properly, he would be constrained to bring this deplorable inability to agree to the attention of certain interested persons who would be certain to take a very dim view of it. That rattled more than one member of The Eight. Who wanted to see political heads fall over such a triviality? A penalty of sorts was quickly agreed upon, and the interested parties were ordered back into the chamber.

The sulking and muttering Cellini was commanded to come forward and stand before The Eight, and to stop that jabbering at once under pain of their instant displeasure.

"Because of your penchant disposition to stir up trouble," the spokesman intoned pompously, "you are sentenced to a fine of four bushels of flour. The said to be bestowed by you as alms to the Convent of the Murate."

"Both parties will repair to the Chancellor and arrange bail," sang the chief clerk, again ringing his bell to signify the end of the proceedings.

It wasn't that the amount requested for bail was high. It was that the young Florentine didn't have the money. The clasp had not yet been paid for. And there was no point in sending for his father. Giovanni didn't have the money either. Mouthing imprecations and calling down the wrath of God on his sneaking adversaries, Cellini sent word to a maternal cousin, a surgeon, requesting that the doctor and distant kinsman please repair to the Bargello to give surety for him.

When, an hour later, the messenger returned with the report that Messer Librodori did not choose to concern himself in the affair, Cellini received the undivided attention of everyone in the room through sheer rhetoric. And to top off the whole, the smirking faces of the self-satisfied Guasconti, as they were leaving, all but gave him a fever. He knuckled bloodshot eyes. The eyeballs burned as though they were being roasted in the hottest fires of hell.

Time passed slowly. As the afternoon wore on it began to appear likely that he would have to spend the night in jail. This, in lieu of the celebration he had planned. By the time the dinner hour arrived he was writhing. A glance around the room showed that none of the remaining officials was paying the slightest attention to him. He slipped quietly and unnoticed out the door and dashed to the Sogliani shop to grab up his little dagger. From there he ran to the house of his sworn enemies.

III

THE GUASCONTI WERE AT TABLE, SMUGLY LIS-tening to Gerardo, who was having difficulty in enunciating properly because of his badly swollen face, when the frothing Cellini, livid with rage, burst in on them.

"You lying rats!" he screeched, waving the poniard wildly. "Today, right now, I intend to settle accounts with all of you!"

The diners stared in open-mouthed astonishment at the snarling, red-faced apparition. The elder Guasconti, grandfather Salvatore, turned as white as the pitcher of milk the maid dropped on the table.

"This is the Day of Judgment," he gasped.

"Madre addolorata! Aiuto!" screamed his son's wife, clasping her hands and calling on Heaven for aid.

The swollen-faced Gerardo spat out an oath and flung himself, arms flailing, at the intruder.

As he sprang, Cellini aimed a vicious thrust at his breast. The poniard pierced Gerardo's jerkin and shirt. By a happy mischance the blow caught him between the arm and chest and did not so much as scratch the skin. But Cellini, feeling his hand sink into the body of his adversary and hearing the ripping sound of the clothing, thought he had killed him. Gerardo was of exactly the same opinion. A startled, unbelieving expression quivered across his face. His jaw went slack and his eyes rolled in his head. He uttered a strangled sob.

"Oimè!" he gasped in an agony of fear, as his legs gave way beneath him. For the second time that day Gerardo fell over in a dead faint.

Everyone stared hypnotically while the supposed victim went through these contortions. Seeing him fall and lie still and inert as one dead, all of the family, swearing frantically, hurled themselves at Cellini. In a brawling, compact, snarling mass, they sprang, jumped and pushed out of the room, down the stairs, and out into the darkening street.

"Kill him!"

"Watch out!"

"Grab him! Hold him, while I give it to the whoreson!"

"Oh-h-h! You fool, that's me!"

"I'll cut the heart out of every one of you lying bastards!"

"Hit him, Peppino. Break his head!"

Fortunately, neither the berserk goldsmith nor his more numerous opponents were capable of performing effectively, beyond some clothes-tearing, clawing, and pushing. They were packed too tight to do any real harm. When the more ample space of the street provided the room, the exhausted and panting mass thinned out and separated. Looking about carefully it was noticed that no dead or dying littered the street and that Cellini, somewhat bruised but still unbowed, had drawn slightly apart. The Guasconti armed themselves, one with a shovel, another with a hammer, others with iron pipes and cudgels, and again sprang forward. But by then Cellini's choler had given way to some display of reason. Realizing that such odds made defeat inevitable, and believing that he had killed Gerardo, he thought it time to get away from there. This left the Guasconti with only his cap, which had been knocked off in the scuffle and lay near the gutter. They contented themselves with showering blows on it till it was reduced to a shapeless pulp.

Cellini ran off in the direction of the Church of Santa Maria Novella, knowing only too well that the Guasconti were already en route to The Eight with the news of his latest outrage. His position was grave. Turning into a side street, he stumbled headlong into a cowled individual who, with head bowed, was walking along the street.

Though momentarily startled by the panting, sweat-smeared hulk that had fallen into his arms, the benign Fra Alessio Strozzi quickly regained his composure. He had known the Cellini family for a long time.

"What has happened, Benvenuto? Speak frankly. Perhaps I can help."

"I beg you, Frater Alessio," Cellini panted earnestly, "for the love of God, save my life. I have just committed a grievous crime."

The information did not excite the white-robed Dominican. These were times when grievous crimes were nothing very unusual. His eyes, peering from within the folds of his cowl, were gentle and held no reproach.

"What is it you have done, my son?"

Cellini told him. This time accurately and truthfully.

"Have no fear. Come. We will go to my cell in Santa Maria. There you will be safe though you had committed every crime in the world."

Thanks poured out at him in a series of rattled gasps.

The Eight was seething—burning with indignant fury.

And why not? The dignity of their high office had been grossly insulted. When they commanded, by God, their command was to be obeyed, especially by ordinary citizens. Now open and flagrant contempt for their authority had been flung into their august faces by a young squirt who, as Messer Antonio bitterly put it, "is still capable of wetting his breeches." It was more than anyone could expect them to bear. Even the formerly partial Della Stufa was in a lather in righteous indignation. Like his seven colleagues he determined to make of that onerous renegade such a public example as would amply demonstrate to all other misguided fools what could be expected for any similar act.

Within the space of an hour after convening in special session, they directed the publication of a drastic edict against one Benvenuto Cellini. While they were about it, and in the proper mood for it, they also subjected to horrific bans and penalties *"any who shall harbor or know this said malefactor, without regard either to the quality or station of such persons, be they whosoever they may."*

Hearing of the edict, old Giovanni ran to the Bargello, flung himself on his knees before the fuming octet and tearfully begged for mercy

21

on his son's behalf. He was petulantly told to take himself away quickly, ere he too was conducted to a gallows. As for his son, his fate was a closed issue. With that, Giovanni was ordered from the room.

The frantic old man left the palazzo behind him, fully realizing that only prompt and spirited action would save his son from the ministrations of a hangman. But what to do? Where to turn?

A shadow blocked his path. He raised a weary head and stared unseeingly at the austere face and figure that had halted in front of him. It was Fra Alessio. Undaunted by the ban, the monk had calmly waited for him. Taking his arm, he led him toward the Ponte Vecchio. As they walked together, he told Giovanni that his son's close friend, Piero Landi, was waiting for them at the Old Bridge. Arrangements were already in motion to effect an escape from the city.

They found Piero pacing impatiently. Time, he told them, was short and there was much to do. With hoods drawn low over their faces the trio crossed the Arno, chose a deserted route and doubled back across the river to Santa Maria Novella.

While Giovanni embraced his son, Landi was stripping off his voluminous mantle. Under it he wore a suit of chain mail and a long sword. He removed these and laid them aside, together with a purse containing ten gold ducats.

"There's no time to waste, Neutino," he told his friend as he undressed. "The Bargello has alerted the watch and armed catchpolls are already out searching the city for you."

Giovanni, weeping unashamedly, helped his son don the chain armor. The world, he felt, was rapidly going to the devil. How else explain these goings-on? Here was his son—the son whose unexpected birth had given him such joy he had bestowed on him the name of "Welcome"—about to be torn from him and hanged like a felon. And why? Because he had defended himself and his rights as a man. It was true that Benvenuto was rather warm-tempered . . . hot-headed even. But it was also true that he never went about looking for trouble, as did his younger son, for example. There was a holy terror! But *he* was a professional soldier—and everyone knew what these soldiers were. And yet, in one sense they were identical. Neither would lift a finger to avoid trouble. It was positively uncanny, how, despite his own peaceful nature, both of them loved a good rough brawl. It was this mad world! What else? He blew his nose on the rim of his shirt.

22

"My son," he sniffed, as he placed the sword belt around Benvenuto's waist, "it is with this weapon in hand that you must find life or death."

His son was not particularly impressed. He was in something of a hurry, but nothing more.

"Don't worry yourself so, Papa. It's not good for you. This won't be as difficult as you think. Take it easy. All will come out well."

He was thinking of another matter as he buckled the sword belt around himself. The image of Gianna crossed his mind. If normal circumstances had prevailed he would be with her now, instead of where he was. He wondered if she missed him. He didn't, couldn't, know that she had already been told of the fate awaiting her paramour. The news made her magnificent bosom swell and heave impressively as she raised brimming eyes toward the ceiling of the Golden Florin's public room. Piteously, she permitted everyone there to witness the extent of her anguish. But the despondency was momentary. After all, a girl had to live! Pouting prettily and dabbing at her soulful eyes, she began a careful inspection of the group who waited the opportunity to soothe her sorrow. A replacement...

"I wonder what she's doing," Cellini mused to himself. "Thinking of me?"

"You know what you're to do?" Piero broke into his friend's reverie. "Head for the Prato Gate, keep along the wall to San Gallo, then ascend Montui. Benedetto Varchi is taking care of that end and will have someone there ready and waiting."

Cellini nodded. Varchi, he knew, would perform as stated. He could be depended on for anything.

Embracing his father again, he turned to his friend, and, following the Italian custom, they kissed each other on both cheeks. Words were unnecessary. They understood without them. Cellini turned to the kindly Fra Alessio, who silently handed over one of his coarse habits, complete to rope cincture and crucifix. Quickly the goldsmith transformed himself into a somewhat young but authentic looking monastic.

"All ready, Frater. Let's be off."

"Patience, my son." The Dominican's serenity was a benison. "Remember our old Tuscan proverb: 'He who goes slowly, goes safely and goes far.' Before you leave there is something we must do. Come!" He beckoned to all of them.

He led them out through the cloister into a bare silent room, a

23

small chapel with a small stone altar surmounted by a cross. A taper burned before its tabernacle. He knelt and crossed himself.

"Brothers," he told them, "let us pray."

Bowing his head and shoulders, the priest clasped his hands in silent prayer. Then crossing himself again, he rose.

"Now, my fine cockerel, we are ready. Let us go and contend with Caesar."

Again he led them out, this time to a small side door in a corner of the cloister, where a lay-brother of the order waited, holding the halter of a saddled ass who snorted in exasperation at being disturbed at such an hour.

Vaulting into the saddle Cellini waved a final farewell. The brother, nodding to the *"benedicti..."* of Fra Alessio, started slowly along the street. He took his time. At the Porta al Prato the guards looked them over in a bored, dejected fashion and let them pass unchallenged and unmolested. In Italy a man-of-God was practically inviolable.

Skirting the outside of the city wall as far as the piazza before the Gate of San Gallo, they turned off and ascended the slope of Montui. It was as simple as that. The slow, ambling donkey eventually stopped near a house where two saddled horses waited, pawing the ground impatiently.

A bulky shadow detached itself from a clump of bushes and moved out into the road, hissing a signal. Cellini squinted sharply at it.

"Fatso!" He thumped a burly shoulder familiarly. "Are you going to accompany me on this madness?"

The large shadow was the brother of Benedetto Varchi. Like most men he was known to his familiars by a surname. In his case, being on the corpulent side, it was *Grassuccio*—Fatso.

Fatso's voice, in volume and timbre, matched the rest of him.

"Olà! you damned troublemaker!" The boom of the greeting startled even the phlegmatic donkey. "Can't you choose a better time for these escapades? But what the devil—it's done. Let's be off quickly before some of those dogs down below start sniffing around."

The lay-brother, hitherto very silent, was shocked into staring terror by the harrowing resonance of Grassuccio's voice.

"Holy Saint Andrew! be off quickly. And for the love of heaven," he implored the large man, "keep your voice low. They can hear you in Venice."

Doffing the costume that had disguised him, Cellini returned it

24

with profuse thanks to the semi-monastic. Then, swinging into the saddles, the two riders turned southwards and tore away at a gallop. Early the next morning they sighted the walls of Siena.

Cellini had made good his escape. He was beyond the reach both of the Republic of Florence and of The Eight.

IV

"WELL, NEUTINO? WHERE TO NOW?"

Grassuccio was feeling hearty and expansive. He looked inquiringly across the table to his companion while he licked at the gravy-smeared fingers of one hand and raised a beaker of *alicante* with the other. A refreshing seven hour sleep had restored tone to tired muscles and had evened out the edges of ragged nerves.

Cellini finished with a mouthful of roast meat before venturing a reply.

"Where else but Rome?" he shrugged. "There's no point in my hedging around. If I'm ever going to amount to anything in my profession, Rome is the place where I'll have to do it."

His portly companion nodded. Since the reign of Leo X, Rome had become the hub from which the masters of the arts radiated out into Italy and the world.

"Right enough," he agreed. "As soon as you're settled there, send word and we will forward your belongings."

"When are you starting back, Grassuccio?"

"Ah-h-h!" Grassuccio thumped the empty beaker on the table and wiped his mouth with the back of his hand. "Excellent *alicante,* this. When? Tonight. In an hour I'll be on my way. Your father will be waiting for news, although it's certain that by now he knows you are safe."

"That's true. I would have been hanged, drawn and quartered, by this time, if they had caught me."

The immense Grassuccio leaned back and belched. Contentedly he patted his paunch.

"Shall I leave you a horse, Neutino?"

25

"Ma che! He'd just be in the way. Take them both back."

"How do you intend to travel? By post?"

Cellini nodded. "That's best, I think," he told his friend. "It will get me to Rome as quickly as possible. I have just ten ducats and they must last until I'm established and working. Then, too, it is madness to travel alone in the south. Bandits are thicker than fleas along these roads and they would flay the hide off anyone for much less than ten ducats. With no horse or baggage to encumber me, I'll travel faster and more safely with the post. I have already talked with our innkeeper. He says the fast post to Rome comes through here about three hours before dawn. I'll make arrangements with the postmaster after I see you off."

Cellini was waiting in the post room when the courier galloped to the station and dismounted. Hostlers quickly transferred the saddle-bags to the waiting relay mount. One of them explained to the courier that he was to have company south, and jerked a finger in the direction of the mail-clad goldsmith. The courier, a tall and broad husky dressed in leather clothing, looked him over noncommittally, without expression. His face was weather-beaten and brown as a nut, and was set in a perpetual squint. He had cheerful eyes, with little laugh wrinkles spreading out from the corners. A stable boy handed him a pewter tankard of mulled wine, from which wisps of smoke curled. He accepted it without a word and leaned a shoulder against the halter post as he gulped. He stayed there, silent and relaxed, for the brief rest period allowed him. At length, he took notice of the younger man. He smiled.

"Name's Cellini? Mine is Rocca. You look toughened up enough to stand the ride. It's a hard one. We eat where we can; good hot meals at Orvieto, Viterbo, and Castellana. From there, you can practically spit into Rome. At all other post stops, we change horses only, like here."

He looked him up and down again, sizing him up. "If you lag behind, I have to leave you. *Hai capito?"*

"You won't be leaving me," Cellini assured him dryly.

"Ah? In a hurry to get to the big city, eh?" Again, with complete affability, the squinting eyes ranged appraisingly up and down the goldsmith. "Very well, Iron-Pants, lift your ass up into that saddle and we'll see."

Though the speech was coarse it did not disturb the inflammable

26

Florentine. It was not meant to be offensive. Cellini said nothing. He smiled grimly and lifted his iron pants into the saddle.

Trotting smartly out the south gate of Siena, the pair spurred their mounts and galloped swiftly into the darkness. For an hour they went along at this pace, then slowed to a walk to breathe their horses. Cellini thought it time to start fishing for information.

"How's Rome doing these days?" he asked, to start things along.

Rocca smiled wryly. "Last time out, all the thieves and whores were doing marvelously."

"When was this?" Cellini queried.

"Eight days ago," Rocca told him. "It's unsafe to walk the streets by yourself, even in daylight. At night it's as much as your life is worth to go out alone."

Cellini nodded understandingly. Some two months before, the scrupulous and pious Pope Adrian VI had died—of a "fatal Roman fever." He had been poisoned. On his death Rome lost its civil head as well as spiritual father. Until a new Pope was elected, there was no one with sufficient authority to enforce law and order. The interim period, lawless and bloody, was one which every thief and cutthroat was quick to exploit to advantage. Anyone bearing a grudge knew that this was an ideal time for effecting a vendetta.

"It's a ratty world we live in," Rocca remarked reflectively.

"Hm-m? Yes ... nasty." Cellini agreed out of politeness. Actually he was much too lively himself to care very much how ratty the world was.

"And the election of the new Pope? How is that coming on?"

Rocca snorted. This was his favorite topic.

"The most foul conniving ever to be imagined! God help us all! For the past two months, all I have heard talked about is the wheedling, the promises, the threats and the arguments that have been made. Our magnificent Conclave seems to be working for everything but the Church. It's all talked about in the open, you know. They don't care one *carlino* who knows it. They are interested in only one thing— themselves, their personal gain and advancement.

"That Englishman, Wolsey," he went on bitterly, "has done everything but stand on his head to win votes over to himself. When I left Rome, I heard it was a three-way duel between Wolsey, the Medici, and Farnese. The first two have the greatest part of the vote, and Farnese was said to have the idea that he could not beat either without gold. It is said he offered two hundred thousand gold ducats to either side in return for its vote. I guess he is pretty anxious. Christ!"

"And our Giulio, what's he doing?"

"Playing a cagey game, I understand. One thing you can say for the Medici, he at least makes a pretense of maintaining dignity. A clever little starling, your Giulio."

"Who do you think will win?" Cellini's question was noncommittal.

"Hell, I don't know. Or care, for that matter. Those three are all of a stripe. Pope Adrian was different. He was sincere and a man of God. He tried to make those red-hatted lords toe the mark. Have you ever observed, Cellini, that only lords and noblemen get to be appointed bishops and cardinals? Peculiar? There are cardinals who are not yet twenty years of age; and all of them gut and squeeze every ducat they can from benefices they've never even seen. Yet, when a man comes along who recognizes the wrong and undertakes to do something about correcting it, what happens? He dies—" Rocca snorted again "—of a fever!

"You know," he continued, "I'm just a simple man. A post courier. I like my dishes plain. It's my opinion that the Church of God should be left in the hands of men of God, men who are devoted to Christianity and to its Church. The ruling of the world can be left to the *lazzaroni* who control it now. The two don't mix well. They should be kept far apart. And all this is nothing more than chatter, so let's get on or we will be late."

They galloped forward, Cellini idly wondering how much truth or wisdom there might be in Rocca's bitter observations. He shrugged. His concern was art, not the morality of men.

They reached the next post station, where the horses were quickly changed. They were allowed a brief rest period before galloping off to the next stop. They were crossing the Paglia when Rocca signaled to slow down. He pointed ahead, into the distance.

"A courier! And not the post. He'll be bearing special news of some kind."

They drew rein and at Rocca's wave, the speeding courier, recognizing the post, slowed to a trot.

"What news, friend?" Rocca called out when the man came within hailing distance.

The courier from the south was gray-faced from fatigue.

28

"A new Pope," he wheezed. "Elected yesterday. I'm hurrying the news forward, as far as Florence."

"Who? . . ."

"The Medici," called back the courier. "Cardinal Giulio has become Pope Clement the Seventh." He waved an arm, sank spurs into the flanks of his foam-flecked bay stallion, and tore away.

"Well, that's that." Rocca gazed at his traveling companion, who appeared smug and elated over what he had just heard.

"You look like a cat in a bird cage," he told him. "I got the impression you didn't give a damn one way or the other."

"I don't really care." Cellini was frank. "But I'm a goldsmith. A Florentine Pope could do me more good than any other kind. Besides, my father has known Giulio de' Medici for a very long time. They were always friendly."

From there onward the grueling ride was uneventful. By evening a torpor of exhaustion had settled over both riders. As time and the rules of the post permitted, they rested or ate mechanically, then continued southward. Below Castellana they rode southwest to the Flaminian Road, which wound its ancient way between mountainous slopes straight into Rome. They passed through the Porta del Popolo shortly after midday.

Cellini stopped at the first inn he sighted within the walls, tumbled across a bed and slept, motionless, till the next morning.

V

To THE EVER-IMPRESSIONABLE FLORENTINE, the world, as he stepped out into the dappled sunlight of the Corso, had just been created. It might be true that the sun above was the same warm sun that shone over Florence. That the air, though warmer and more dry, had something of the same crispness as the breezes that swept down from the northern Apennines. The sky was the same; and the clouds, after all, were merely arranged a bit differently, nothing more. But to the fascinated Cellini, the world had just begun its motions. This was Rome! The great, the triumphant, the eternal!

Rome, where an artist of talent became a prize sought after by lords, princes, emperors, and pope. He walked on air, and, as usual, with his head high in roseate dream clouds, which he only occasionally lowered back to earth to watch the movement all around him. *Corpo di Bacco!* here was fast-paced, colorful living that was something like it.

Enthusiastically he ambled aimlessly down one tortuous street and across to another, gaping like a country bumpkin on his first visit to town. Actually it was all rather like Florence. As a matter of fact, it was pretty generally conceded that Florence, where the enlightened era of learning and the movement in the arts were born, was superior in many respects to the Eternal City. But Rome was vast! It had . . . it had size!

A tangled clutter of buildings reared up everywhere. Straight ahead of him the partly paved, partly cobbled street led to the ancient forum of the Caesars. The Palatine—the hill on which Romulus, over twenty-two centuries before, had traced a perimeter with a plow, designating the site for a city—was now no more than a small section within Rome.

And everywhere one looked—bustling activity! Street hawkers drove pack animals loaded with wares, and frenziedly screamed prices and claims of perfection whenever he paused to listen. Peasant farmers led strings of donkeys and groaning ox-carts laden with produce for the insatiable maws of the Roman markets. Frequently he was forced to one side as horsemen cantered by; once by the retinue of a rider clad in damascened half-armor—a *condottiere* of the Papal armies, stern and rigid in the saddle, with head held high and the plume crest atop his morion fluttering behind him.

Gallants walked elegantly by. Bravoes strolled with the most recent of their frilled and perfumed conquests from the *bordellos,* parading arrogantly and disdainfully eyeing the beggars sprawled against building walls as they whined for alms. There were a lot of beggars in Rome.

Wine peddlers with straw-braided jugs suspended from both shoulders, howled singsong calls and offered cups of muscatel and the sparkling wine of Orvieto. Everywhere yells, barks, harangues, laughter and hoarse shouts. Rome was a seething caldron into which was funneled a continual potpourri from every corner of the Italian peninsula and from every nation in Europe. It spewed vigor and virility. Cellini gaped. This was the modern world, a world for the spirited and the young of heart!

But in the midst of all the movement, one detail stood out. Knowing that a lawless surge of anarchy and violence always followed the death of Rome's civil head, the young Florentine had expected brawling and disorder. This in spite of the fact that a new Pope now was in office. It requires time to take over control. There was all the noise and motion one could ask for, but it was ordered bustle.

Pausing at a street fountain, Cellini let his inquiring eye linger on a man who had just finished drinking. A retainer of some sort, the fellow was dressed in the colorful livery of his master, complete to the arms of the house he served blazoned on his tabard. He stood to one side, casually wiping his hands dry on the bottom portion of a short cloak. Noticing the Florentine's inquiring look, his eyes slanted obliquely toward him. He smiled tentatively. It was more an uncertain grimace than a smile, but it served.

"*Porco cane!*" he blustered. "That was as cold as a dead whore's teat."

Cellini smiled appreciatively, then looked around questioningly.

"Rome seems to be pretty quiet," he commented. "Not much hell-raising going on, is there?"

"Not any more." The voice became complacent, more sure of itself. "It has been anything but quiet around here of late, and there was plenty of hell-raising going on for the past two months. They took care of all that yesterday. Yes. See—" hands and arms waved in a large gesture that encompassed the street. "No more daylight brawling and cudgeling. No more hard boys looking to give you the business at the slightest provocation, or if your purse held as little as five *soldi*. *Ah, sì,* young man. This new Pope Clement handled the matter very efficiently, with speed and despatch. *E perchè no?* It's as a great prince should!"

"How was that?" Cellini was casual but interested.

The man looked askance and seemed very surprised.

"*Ostia!* What a question to ask. And here, too!"

"Ha?"

"Where do you come from, young man? The other end of the world?"

"Not quite. I've just arrived from Florence."

"Ho! Then you were not here yesterday?"

"Yes, but I slept all day."

"I see. *Bene,* just take yourself a short stroll up the street there. The message is written very clearly."

31

The goldsmith shrugged and walked on. He was going in that direction anyway.

A short walk brought him to the end of the street which looked out on the Campo di Fiori. He paused, looked around—and gawked. The message was written *very* clearly. In the center of the large square, three double scaffolds of bright newly-cut timber reared up against the blue sky. From these gibbets, six already shapeless forms dangled, swaying and turning slowly in the light breeze. Above and all around them, an angry flapping and the shrill, strident calls of rooks, gulls, and myriad smaller birds, served to better effect than a squad of trumpeters. They circled, alighted, and pecked voraciously at the tattered, gruesome cadavers. As long as they dangled there they served their purpose. People passing through the busy piazza would see and understand. It was mute and grisly evidence that law had returned to Rome.

Cellini shuddered. It came to his mind that he had but recently escaped a similar end. He walked quickly away toward the Tiber. It was time, he told himself firmly, to end his dawdling. The ten ducats, what with the expense incurred by riding post, plus this, that and the other, were reduced by more than half. The drain had been swift and severe. It was necessary to stop wasting time.

A section of Rome along the west shore of the Tiber, known as the *Banchi,* served as the artist colony of the Eternal City. Here one found most of the shops kept by the best of the numerous artists, sculptors, painters and goldsmiths who had migrated from all of Italy and Europe, in quest of fame and fortune. Quite naturally Cellini headed for this quarter. Arriving there, he peered carefully into each shop he passed, finally pausing before one of the larger goldsmith's shops, his attention drawn by a display of finished pieces placed on a table before a large window. A discreet but eagle-eyed scrutiny of the shop's interior revealed it to be large, airy and well lighted. It seemed to employ a half-dozen or so journeymen goldsmiths. Most of the men were working in silver rather than gold, but this meant little or nothing since the pieces were all large—vases, ewers, basons. One man was engaged on the silver inlay of an engraved shield. It was the kind of enterprise which exactly followed the pattern Cellini had in mind. No trivial, gimcrack commissions for a shop such as this. In there, when payment was made, the ducats were no doubt told down in quantity.

A man writing at a table near the window kept raising his head to peer at the pensive-looking youth who appeared so interested in the shop's work. He was short and stocky, about forty, with hair just beginning to gray at the temples. He had a heavy face, smooth-shaven except for a short beard cut in the Venetian fashion. In time his curiosity got the better of him. Laying down the quill he was using, he walked to the door and looked into innocent, bland eyes which stared directly and disconcertingly straight back into his.

"Well, young fellow," he asked, "you seem pleased? Find the results to your taste?"

Cellini pursed his lips thoughtfully and pinched his chin. It was necessary to show the man that the answer to his question was receiving profound thought. Also, at this point of the proceedings, it would not do to seem especially impressed.

"Oh, I don't know... *non c'è male*. Not bad—but I've seen better."

"You have, eh. *Merda!* Where?"

The answer came smoothly, dropped with a casual flirt of the hand.

"To speak the truth, I've done better myself."

"Oh-ho? And what sort of work do you do, my young loudmouth?"

"Hm-m, a little of the same as you."

"So? A goldsmith are you? What do you call yourself?"

Cellini told him.

"I've never in God's world ever heard of you!"

The younger of the two goldsmiths shrugged and drew down the corners of his mouth. "You will," he told him shortly. "And your name?"

"Stefano Santi," came the complacent answer. "From listening to you, you would be a Tuscan?"

"Florentine," nodded Cellini. "Your shop?"

"Yes. It belonged to my father, Giuseppe Santi. He had a wide reputation as a master goldsmith. Since he died I have taken over and look after things. The shop work is handled by my partner, that fellow over there." He pointed to a short, well set-up man who was busy on a large silver trencher. "Like the place?"

"*Sì.* Nice little shop."

"And you're a goldsmith?"

"*Ecco.*"

"Name of Benvenuto Cellini?"

"Just so." The man was becoming a little monotonous. Cellini was beginning to think he had wasted more time. His lips wrinkled.

"Well..." Thoughtfully the shopowner scraped his upper lip with a hard thumbnail. "We could use another man...but he has to be a good one." His eyes were doubtful as they swept over the face and figure of the youthful Cellini. "You look so damned young," he told him plaintively.

To the Florentine this was tearing the skin off the live dog. He straightened, gave the shopowner a haughty look, and spoke tersely.

"Look you, Master Santi. I've been looking over the work your shop turns out. Some of it is excellent. Much of it is good. None of it reaches such heights that it could be said you are harboring another Ghiberti in your shop. *Hai compreso?* I said I have done better. It won't take very long to prove that, one way or the other."

There was a pause.

"True," the reflective Santi admitted. The direct approach had broken down his defenses. "Suppose you step in here and show us how *welcome* you can make yourself."

VI

"HE HAS BEEN HERE ONLY A WEEK," LUCA DA Jesi was telling his partner, "yet I tell you, Stefano, he's head and shoulders above anyone in this shop. Have you seen that bason for Salviati? Matchless!"

Santi listened gleefully, nodding wisely to himself. In the week since Cellini started working at their shop Master Stefano had been, by degrees, skeptical, surprised, impressed, and now, smugly jubilant.

"Excellent," he purred, giving his partner a broad wink. "We have made a find. A discovery which can be turned to advantage. Here's opportunity. We stand to gain much—in credit as well as in ducats. Keep him busy, my dear Luca...and, er, on the more important commissions. He's at his best on gold work. Put him to work on that Bracciano cup. And not too much praise to his face, eh! Why spoil him...or give him ideas? Are we not paying him a good salary?"

Santi did not yet know whom he was contending with. But he soon learned. His exuberant plans for exploiting the ability of his new journeyman exploded in his face two weeks later, when Cellini cornered the complacent shopowner and broached a plan of his own.

"You are probably aware, Ser Santi," he began in a serious voice, "that I have no intention of being a laborer for hire all my life. I lack the temperament for it. I mean to make my way in the world."

"Very commendable," gushed the shopowner. "Very commendable! A few years in an established and well-known shop such as this and I have no doubt at all but that you will have amassed the necessary experience and money to open a little shop of your own."

Cellini's smile was just a little sarcastic. "My dear sir," he told him dryly, "for a long time I have completely understood that a man rarely achieves fame or acquires wealth by working for someone else. That's my point. I have no intention of wasting a few more years. I cannot spare the time."

Santi winced inwardly. "Heh? I don't think I understand you."

"I intend to secure my own commissions," Cellini explained, "and, if possible, handle the working of them here in your shop. In return for the use of your facilities I will turn over to you a portion equal to a full third of the sum paid me for the work I do here. That is my plan. I would enjoy working here. It's a pleasant shop. But if not here, then somewhere else."

The shopowner looked rather bleak. He hadn't really expected anything like this—and so soon. The lad was still so young.

"Well, Ser Stefano?"

Scowling, Master Stefano chewed over the proposal. There was nothing unusual about it. It was fair, reasonable, the usual agreement entered into between a shopowner and a free-lance artist who lacked a shop of his own. He knew it. Cellini knew it. And now each was aware that the other knew it. He had simply underestimated the young man.

"Very well—" Santi sighed regretfully. There would not be so much money for him under such an agreement, but it was still worth while. This Cellini was really first-rate. "We'll go along that way," he told the Florentine sourly.

In those brief three weeks Cellini had not been idle outside the shop. He had made connections. There was a mass of Florentines in the Holy City. Many of them he had known in Florence. Others he met now. In the loose informal camaraderie of the artist colony, his circle of acquaintances swelled daily. He met people of all stations, active in all sorts of professions including that of idling. It was through one of his

35

new friends that he met his first patron and secured his first commission. Gian-Franco Penni, *il Fattore,* a former pupil of Raffaello Sanzio, presented him to a Spanish patron of his, recommending him highly as a master-goldsmith.

The Spaniard, Don Francesco de Bobadilla, Bishop of Salamanca, was a grandee of ancient and noble family, who had arrived in Rome six years before to attend the Lateran Council. Captivated by the charm and luxurious living of the Capital City, he had remained there. He possessed, in full measure, all the qualities deemed necessary and important to a modern nobleman of parts. He was well educated, accomplished in the social graces, incredibly haughty, and indescribably arrogant. His tastes were impeccable. He was an informed and competent connoisseur of literature and the arts, and, to be truthful, the liberal patron of any artist whose talent succeeded in pleasing his eye, his mind, and his sense of the beautiful. He was enormously rich.

On the strength of Penni's recommendation, the Florentine received a lucrative commission: two large candelabra, to be wrought entirely of silver. These were to be completed quickly, in order that Salamanca might derive some slight pleasure from viewing their grace and beauty. Only one condition was stipulated; they must be exquisite, both in design and execution.

Cellini advised the nobleman not to give the matter another thought. He would bring him the finest silverwork that ever was seen.

Other commissions came along. Slowly at first, then at less frequent intervals. Most of them were small and unimportant, but all paid well. Thus the winter passed, and as spring with its blooming Maytime came to Rome Cellini was busy on various works. The candelabra had been finished to the complete satisfaction of the supercilious Spaniard, who forthwith engaged him in a continuous series of projects.

This initial success, however, was soured by Salamanca's attitude. His disparaging and insulting manner toward anyone of inferior station to himself drained all the joy of accomplishment from the fiery spirit of the Florentine. It left the impetuous goldsmith, who had a full share of the typical artist's scorn for the moneyed patrons who employed him, frustrated and limp with impotent rage. Time and again he was at the point of telling the Spaniard to go straight to the devil. And as frequently he clamped his teeth on his tongue and kept back the flow of angry retort.

In leisure moments, on the other hand, life in Rome was exciting.

36

There were suppers, parties, gatherings in the studios and homes of famous artists, and now and then an invitation from some noble whose favor was worth cultivating. Most charming of all, to the not over-experienced but actively libidinous Cellini, were the liaisons possible with the wenches who served as his models. They were readily accessible, these delightful nymphs, and possessed of a nature that was liberal and understanding.

Since nearly all of his designs depicted human forms, it was necessary for him to employ models of all kinds. The need arose with the first Salamanca commission, for the base-post of the candelabra had been designed in the form of a chained Andromeda. That brought Sabina to the little studio he had fitted up in the rooms he rented for living quarters. Voluptuous and rounded, she posed against a stone pillar, with her wrists chained to the stone. She had large smoldering eyes that said things, and the witchery of her contours was matched only by her soft, sighing surrender.

A cup designed for a lesser member of the Montefeltri family brought Elena. She posed for a Diana poised in action at the height of a chase. Hers was a slender, flat-muscled body. Tall, leggy, high-breasted and rangy, with all the fluid athletic grace of the classic pagan deity she was substituting for, she possessed amorous inclinations to suit. She was unchained lightning.

And somewhere between, the regal Aurora had come to pose for a Venus. In appearance she completely personified that seductive goddess. But in bed she was ice. Utterly placid and unresponsive, she had the goldsmith biting his nails, appalled at what he regarded his failure as a man. Then one evening while visiting in the studio of the painter, Giulio Romano, the conversation turned to this same Aurora and he spoke of his dilemma.

Giulio smiled understandingly. "It's not due to any fault of yours, my dear fellow," he told him, grinning. "You can stop worrying about that. You've missed out there by well over a year. At that time she was all you could wish for. But for some reason she was insatiable. No man could satisfy her. So she became a professional. Six months in a *bordello,* with all these soldiers here, and she turned to ice. Just as she is now, willing but unmoved. A few months ago she left that crowded profession and returned to modeling. The worst of it is that she's putting on weight, growing fat. In a couple of years she will have grown a rump that will shame a broodmare, a breast like the udder of a cow, and a pair of legs that will look like two ham-hocks standing side by side. Here, I'll show you..."

The painter took up a scrap of paper and a piece of charcoal. Quickly and precisely he drew a series of lines and exaggerated curves which resolved themselves into an unmistakable caricature of a porcine Aurora. The portraiture was so realistic that merely contemplating such an end for a creature so divinely formed made Cellini shudder.

And so the weeks moved along. Of money there was actually a surplus. In a time when an income of fifty ducats a year sufficed for all necessities, and a hundred or so made for easy living, the Florentine's skill was supporting him in what, comparatively, was next door to luxury. The money left over and above his personal needs Cellini sent to his father. The delighted Giovanni wrote to thank and assure him of the joy that was in his heart for progress so rapidly made. He had also one little request:

> ...My son, I beg and implore you, for the love of God and for the love you bear me, to practice oftentimes, if only in your spare and lonely moments, that marvelous gift of music which I, your father, have taught you with so much labor and difficulty, and in which you have always displayed such excellent talent. It would be heartbreaking to me were you to lose so fine an accomplishment. Do you, therefore, for love of me, take up your flute or your cornet—which I did not neglect to forward with your belongings—and render up a tune betimes, with the thought in mind that I, your father, am listening...

If up to that point the letter had brought tears to Cellini's eyes, the reference to music brought a volley of heartfelt curses directed at the inventors of wind instruments generally, and flutes and cornets particularly. He hadn't touched either since their arrival from Florence the previous winter, and it was only the thought of pleasing his father that made him unwrap the instruments and play a bit. His new friends were delighted. He was a competent musician, even if he did thoroughly hate the art.

And there was this to be said for that music. In its own perverse way it helped to satisfy Cellini's passion for action. On the occasions when he performed at affairs that were held in taverns or inns, there was certain to be on hand a number of impudent bravoes, brazen soldiers or sarcastic gallants who were spoiling for trouble. What had they to fear from so puny an adversary as a musician? A goldsmith! A damned metal scratcher! Amid such tempers and ideas there could be only one result—innumerable brawls. In time the word got around that this young Florentine was a lad to reckon with. Six duels, from each of which Cellini emerged an unscathed and scornful victor, brought him a reputation—even in Rome.

VII

IT WAS HARD, ON SUCH A GLITTERING JUNE DAY, to work on the copy of the Jove and at the same time eye the lovely Lady Portia as she stood beside him, watching silently. Cellini's eyes slanted over to her every now and then, even though doing so distracted his attention from the copy. His admiration for the wife of Gismondo Chigi increased with her every successive appearance.

He had gone to the Chigi palace in the Trastevere, as he frequently did on feast days and holidays, to pursue his studies. Today he was intent on copying a Jove from the ceiling piece of Raphael's immense frescoes which depicted the entire fable of Galatea and of Psyche and Cupid—or at least such had been Cellini's intent until the approach of Lady Portia.

As always, she was gracious and charming. He noted with pleasure how her gown of purple brocade formed an alluring oval around bare, creamy-pink shoulders. He approved its selection. It showed taste and an eye for proper effect, pointing up as it did her outstanding physical attributes, superbly fleshed shoulders and bosom. It fitted snugly to her small waist, then dropped like an inverted V to the floor. The fillet of seed pearls woven into the braids of her dark hair also was tastefully and effectively managed. Gismondo had a beautiful and youthful lady to wife, he reflected. She looked, and was, delectable. He always enjoyed sketching the more when she was near. And who knew but that one fine day he would be able to serve her in some way.

Ignorant of the train of thought she inspired, Lady Portia continued to watch him sketch.

"What are you, young man," she asked, when he paused to critically eye the flow of a line, "a painter or a sculptor?"

"Neither, *madonna*. I am a goldsmith."

"You are? I should not have thought so. It's unusual. You draw much too well for a goldsmith."

The goldsmith was enslaved. "Not so, *madonna*. An able goldsmith must be able to draw very well. In Florence, nearly all artists—painters, sculptors, engravers, architects—all begin their apprenticeship in the shops of goldsmiths."

"Why so?"

"Because the practice of the goldsmith's art requires study in all the arts. A goldsmith must learn to work in precious metals, to cast, to forge, to hammer, to chisel. He must learn the qualities of precious stones and how to set such jewels to best advantage. He must become proficient in enameling and *niello*. If a large piece is commissioned of him, he must work like a sculptor. In the case of caskets and chests, altarpieces, tabernacles, and such, he must be versed in the principles of architecture because such pieces are identical, in conception and design, with that of a building or a monument. And in order to design properly he must be an expert draftsman, study anatomy and learn to model from the nude. A goldsmith must learn to use almost every tool known to all the other arts, Madonna Portia. Such famous Florentines as Donatello and Ghirlandaio, to name just two, first learned their art in goldsmiths' shops."

Milady Portia smiled. "Were they as absorbed in learning their art as you?"

"Much more, *madonna*. Very much more. All I can ever hope to do is equal their genius. No one can surpass them. Someday, I will equal them."

"That is well said." Lady Portia smiled again, looking at him thoughtfully. Drawing aside she beckoned to a maid and sent her to fetch a certain diamond brooch. When it came she handed it to Cellini.

"Tell me its worth," she requested.

The valuation was careful and precise.

"Eight hundred crowns, *madonna*," he told her, returning the piece.

"Well done, my young gallant. You are very accurate. Tell me, do you think you could reset these stones more effectively in a design of your own?"

The delighted Cellini assured her that such a task would be an enchanting one and in a forthright manner put his words into action.

40

Before her eyes, a rough color sketch of a lily, sparkling with diamonds, took form on a corner of his sketch paper.

Lady Portia gave him the brooch and sent for twenty gold crowns, to be used for making the setting.

"Preserve for me the old gold in which it is now set," she requested as she left him to finish the copy of the Jove. *"Addio,* my young master."

In the shop the next day, Luca da Jesi was unimpressed when Cellini told him of the new assignment he had taken on. Luca had just begun work on a large silver vase ordered expressly by Pope Clement, for use in the disposal of gnawed meat bones, fruit rinds, and other such debris of the Papal dining table. It was an article made more for ostentatious display than for any real necessity.

"You're wasting your time, Benvenuto," he told him flatly. "There's no money to be made by puttering around with such gauds."

"Gauds!" Cellini's professional pride was stabbed to the heart. Shocked almost beyond words, he turned to the wall. "The man is mad!" He turned back, glaring evilly at Luca.

"God's blood and bones!" he yowled. "You have the gall to call this commission a gaud! While you spend your time on a garbage pail? *Merda!* Listen, friend, I can fashion trash such as that any time I wish; but works of a quality equal to this don't come along every day. What's more, there is as much money to be made from a *work of art* such as this, as you will ever get for that—that oversize chamber pot!"

This brought Luca to his feet. Garbage pails! Chamber pots! *Porco diavolo!*

"We will see, my great master," he sneered. "By the time you've finished with the embroidery of that whorehouse trinket, I will have finished this piece. We will then compare payment and see who has done better for himself. Agreed?"

"Agreed? . . . Naturally!"

The next two weeks were busy ones for both grim contestants. Cellini fashioned a lily in the manner of a stylized *fleur-de-lys.* Clusters of diamonds formed the petals; the whole was ornamented with color-fully enameled masks, cupids, and miniature animals. The result was so effective that Luca forgot a portion of his rancor and congratulated him.

The Florentine did no less when he viewed the finished vase. It was excellently done, and his artist's soul would not let him disparage, even in anger, any well-wrought work.

"We will now see," Luca pointed out, "the difference between the two."

The vase was carried to the Pope who examined it carefully and declared himself pleased. That piece would eliminate an eye-sore which offended him every time he sat to eat. Now the table refuse could be hidden within the bowels of this exquisite container.

"See to the payment for this work," he ordered one of the chamberlains who waited at his elbow.

Madonna Portia was enchanted. The brooch, she told its maker, surpassed anything she had ever seen. So beautiful was it that he must set his own price. If it was in her power to bestow, it would be paid.

"Lovely lady," the artful goldsmith answered, "my only desire lay in the accomplishment of such a work as might please you. That also is my greatest reward and I seek no other."

Bowing, he took his leave. Not, however, without overhearing milady's statement that he deserved and certainly would receive something more tangible than that.

Luca was waiting, a fat little purse in hand, which jingled as he tossed it up and down.

"Come. Let's compare your jewel and my plate. Now!"

"Wait till tomorrow," answered his opponent with a scowl. "I don't have my money yet.... And you better wait till tomorrow before you do any more of that grinning too!"

Madonna Portia's steward came the next morning. He handed over a flat little paper packet, mechanically recited the adulatory phrases he had been compelled to commit to memory, and left. Luca, afire with the desire to prove himself and belittle his rival, burst into the workroom. Everyone else was already there, waiting. The workmen, various neighbors who had been advised of the contest, Santi, everyone.

Luca raised his purse high. "Ho-ho!" he exclaimed triumphantly, pouring his fee on the table. It made a nice merry clatter. The coins were all *scudi di giulio*. Twenty-five of them.

The audience looked on—and smiled derisively. Cellini was stunned. Twenty-five silver crowns for two weeks' work! Little beads began to form along his forehead as he withdrew to the other end of the table, tore open his packet and peeped inside.

His eyes looked upon a soothing yellow luster.

Without a word, but with his mouth set in an insufferable smirk, he casually poured the golden equivalent of forty silver crowns across the table.

The onlookers started in surprise. "Luca, my dear fellow, Benvenuto's pieces, being all of gold and half again as much as yours, make a much finer effect!"

Luca all but dropped dead.

It was not avarice. As a partner of the Santi shop he was to receive a third of the Florentine's reward. It was professional jealousy that gnawed like a canker at his vitals. A torrent of abuse poured out of him. He cursed his art, those who had taught it to him, and his imbecility for wasting time on such rank foolishness.

"Never again," he vowed, "will I work on large plate. From here on I intend to devote myself entirely to these whorish gewgaws."

Cellini was outraged. Who did this poltroon think he was?

"Look you, *amico,*" he flung out grandly, "every bird warbles its own tune. I'll tell you again: I can work on your garbage cans any time I have a mind to; but as for you, you will never be able to successfully turn out one of these whore's gauds!"

"And, by God!" the indignant goldsmith squalled, as he stomped out of the shop, "I'm going to prove this to you!"

It took a full week's conniving with Gian Penni to work out a suitable scheme involving two "garbage cans." It was no longer enough for Cellini to prove he could fashion refuse containers at will. He intended to prove he could do it better than his rival.

At the end of the week's scheming Penni made a call on Salamanca, described the altercation between the two artists, and cogently pointed out that such professional rivalry had its points. It could and should be used to advantage. The astute Salamanca grasped the intended idea immediately. He was charmed with it. It was so simple. Two superlative craftsmen striving to outperform each other would bring him two excellent works. He called in both goldsmiths and expressed a desire to commission two large ornamental ewers, such as were used on sideboards for holding drinking water. Two of equal size he wanted. Each of the men was to be entrusted with the working of one. The designs, he waved a hand toward Penni, would be forth-coming from *il Fattore*. Quickly, please.

Bursting with eagerness, Cellini started work immediately. He moved to the shop of Piero della Tacca, a Milanese, who offered him a better financial arrangement. Luca didn't like that, for technical reasons. Santi liked it even less, for reasons evident every time he opened his account books. But Cellini had other fish to fry. He worked.

To the excellent basic design supplied by Penni, he incorporated patterned groupings of foliage, animals, masks and figures. As one of the more subtle qualities of the overall design, he introduced a handle operated by a delicate mechanism and a hidden spring. When the latter was touched, the handle sprang upright, opening the mouth of the ewer. All of this worked out in a manner calculated to draw attention to the virtuosity of treatment and skill of execution.

Then at the insistence of some friends he took on an assistant, a little lad of about thirteen, by the name of Paulino, who functioned as a shopboy. Cellini didn't really need him, but anything for his friends. The lad was handsome and well-mannered, altogether charm-ing, and had a passion for listening to his master play on the cornet. He did not think much of the flute, only the cornet. He had a way of smiling as he listened that led Cellini to play rather more than usual, and to model a head capturing the boy's exact expression.

All in all, things were moving along splendidly. The ewer was beginning to show promise. Madonna Portia had recommended him to the Chigi and several orders followed. His contacts were expanding daily. Cellini was feeling so pleased with himself that when Paulino entered the studio one evening to let him know that a caller waited below, he preened a bit before descending. Another commission, perhaps.

"Who is it, my lad? Did he say?"

"His name is Gino Credi, Master Benvenuto. You know him, I think. He plays the viola."

A musician! What the devil did a musician want with him?

He went down and greeted the man, wondering what it was that had brought him. It was clear that the call was not social.

"I am here as an emissary, my dear Benvenuto. You know I am a member of the Papal band? Well, our bandmaster, Giacomo da Cesena, has heard you perform on the cornet and is so enthusiastic over your ability and talent in our art that he sends me to request a favor. He would like you to play with us on the occasion of the Pope's *Ferragosto*. We have made a fine selection of motets, with portions ideally suited to the soprano cornet. What say you?"

Cellini frowned and wrinkled his lips disdainfully. An emphatic "No" was on the tip of his tongue. There was that ewer. But even as the word formed, the image of his father crossed his mind. To perform before His Holiness! Old Giovanni would regard that as the fulfillment of all his dreams, the answer to all his prayers and supplication. And then there was the Pope himself. For months he had been vainly trying to catch the Pontiff's eye. This might be the means of storming that rampart.

"I don't have time for it, really," he told Gino, still frowning. "But I know my father will feel great happiness if I do this thing. So I suppose I can only accept your kind offer. Please convey my thanks to Master Giacomo. There will be rehearsals, I suppose? When?"

"We start two days from now. Two a week for the time being. More frequently later on. I am glad you have accepted, Benvenuto." Gino rose. "I know Master Giacomo will be much pleased."

Unfortunately for Cellini, when he attended the first rehearsal two days later, Salamanca selected the same afternoon to send one of his gentlemen around to the Della Tacca shop to see how that ewer was progressing. The courtier arrived, looked around, and reported back that Cellini was off gadding about somewhere and the ewer was not being worked on.

When he hurried to the Spaniard's palace after the rehearsal, the goldsmith caught the full impact of the spasm that resulted. If Salamanca ordered a commission, Cellini was testily informed by the irate Bishop, it was to be attended to, and promptly! Who the devil did he think he was, presuming to interfere with such projects? Music practice? The Papal band? His Excellency did not care a damn about either. What he was interested in was a ewer! And unless Cellini looked to his work, the commission would be withdrawn and turned over to a more compatible artist to finish. Was that entirely clear?

"That damn music again!" Cellini grumbled bitterly, as he drooped homeward.

There was no possible way out either. He had promised to play, and so he must continue with the rehearsals. The ewer he pushed forward day and night, even neglecting other work. In an attempt to placate Salamanca, who waited with a tongue sharply honed and

45

ready whenever Cellini was summoned, he submitted the piece for a progress inspection. Another mistake! Unfinished as it was, the ewer brought purrs of satisfaction. The Florentine, gushed the Bishop, was a master without equal. A genius unsurpassed. And if he didn't get right to work and finish it quickly, he would never, *never* again receive another commission!

VIII

Bᴙ THE TIME THE FIRST OF AUGUST HOVE INTO sight Cellini was near the end of his tether. What with trying to appease the raving Salamanca, who regarded the Florentine's acts as open rebellion to his wishes and an insidious plot to defraud him of the ewer, and hold to his promise to play with the Papal band for his father's sake, he had been rubbed raw. In all of Rome it would have been difficult to find a man who sighed with greater relief when the first day of the month of the harvest dawned bright and clear. It was the Feast of August—*Feriæ Augusti* of pagan Rome—the first day of their year.

The band, and Cellini, went to the Papal palace.

The Pontiff was to celebrate the *Ferragosto* in the garden pavilion of his palazzo. This was situated to its rear and side, rising out of a carefully tended slope of ground. It was a classic and formal Roman garden, framed by long straight lines of tall slender pines and evenly tapered cypresses that reared up into the sky. Around the edges of flagged walks, deep yellow yew, trimmed into the appearance of Grecian urns, alternated with statuary that had been old when Nero burned Rome. Bright green box hedges connected the spaces between, with every twig, leaf and stem tonsured to perfection. Oleander shrubs were spotted at points along the walks, lending a splash of color.

Toward the rear a large formal pool glistened in the sunlight. A wood nymph, gracefully poised on the shoulder of a lewdly grinning Pan, held a conch shell from which a jet of water spurted among schools of fantastically colored fish and purled along groupings of water lilies. The gurgling of the stream mingled with the occasional trill of a bird set the mood for the flower gardens which overlooked the fountain. There were a million flowers. Great multicolored beds held captive by red-veined marble walks and rows of potted olive and fig trees filled the air with a scent that was carried to the outermost reaches of the terraces. The *giardino* of the Papal palace was a wedding of nature and art that had borne graceful fruit.

In its center stood the pavilion, a large structure that surged like a pink jewel amid a garland of emeralds. It had a red tiled roof, supported by slender fluted pillars of pink and white marble. Rose-red marble flags covered the floor. The long banquet tables, supported on trestles, were laid around the sides, forming a three-sided square. The bandstand was on the fourth and open side, facing the raised dais which was to seat the Pope. Cellini waited there with the other musicians, eyeing the covered terrace which led to the palace proper. Its paths were filled with bustling pages, stewards, waiters, kitchen and wine purveyors, all scurrying to attend to last minute details.

Suddenly, and seemingly from nowhere, a trumpet blared a signal. All commotion ceased, and as each servant silently took up his position, the Pope led his court and guests to the pavilion.

Cellini gawked unashamedly. Giulio de' Medici had been a familiar sight as a Cardinal and a Florentine, but he had not yet seen him at close range as Pope Clement.

The procession drew closer and the murmur of voices grew. There were cardinals in flaming crimson, bishops in deep purple hues, a mass of courtiers and guests in varicolored splendor. With all this gorgeous color surrounding him, the white-robed Clement stood out. He wore a white gown reaching to the soles of his slippers. His shoulders were covered with a *mantelletta* of white silk. A small skullcap, also of white silk, was set on hair still raven black. A gem-encrusted, golden crucifix hung from his neck, partly covered by his right hand. On the middle finger of that hand gleamed Clement's symbol of office, a simple, almost plain gold band. Its face was cut with the device of a fisherman in a boat; the signet of St. Peter and of the Popes—The Fisherman's Ring.

As Clement mounted to the dais and sat, Cellini got a clearer and unobstructed view of the straight nose, the firm well-formed mouth, the fine eyes keen and piercing which the half-closed lids made seem a little sly. He was not handsome, but this was not unusual. Except for one hereditary feature, exquisite eyes, the Medici were not a hand-

some family. There had been only one exception to this peculiarity—
the exceedingly handsome Giuliano, brother of Lorenzo the Magnificent, who had been assassinated during the Pazzi conspiracy. He it
was who had left behind an illegitimate son who had been taken in
by Lorenzo and reared as befitted an offspring of his beloved brother.
The bastard's name was Giulio de' Medici—now Pope Clement VII.

The Clement whom Cellini saw was still lean, although his face no
longer had its former thin, ascetic, ferret look. It had filled out. He was
smooth-shaven, the cheeks tinged with the bluish shadow of a heavy
beard. Except for his late uncle, Lorenzo, he was the most intelligent
and clever of all the Medici. He was a learned scholar. His sagacity
and acuteness were extraordinary. He was an accomplished statesman and
administrator, and a cunning politician ruthlessly bent on one secret
aim—an end to which he had years before devoted his life. In 1494
Giulio and the Medici had been forced into exile by the Florentines. For eighteen miserable years they had wandered over the face
of Italy and Europe, men without homes, without funds, without
country. He never forgot that, or forgave it. It was his life's work
to carve a state— a Medici state—out of the Florentine Republic, with
his family so firmly entrenched on its throne that no power on earth
would ever succeed in unseating them. For this purpose he had maneuvered himself into the Chair of St. Peter. To this end all of his political
jockeying, intrigues and cabals were dedicated, with no thought whatever to the undeniable fact that with such motives and with such an
attitude, he made a singularly bad Pope.

Clement made a signal. Giacomo da Cesena raised his arm, brought
it down, and the music started simultaneously with a procession of
table servants bringing dishes for the feast.

With speed and precision the multitude of attendants carved and
served food in incredible quantity and fantastic variety: lamb, mutton,
goat, veal, beef, venison, suckling pigs broiled whole and delivered up
to the whims of the diners on enormous trenchers covered with fragrant
laurel leaves. Smaller fare such as pheasant, doves, plovers, ortolans,
and the more lowly chickens, were brought in golden and dripping and
still sizzling on the spits used to roast them. With knife, teeth and
fingers, some three hundred guests gouged and tore at whatever portions pleased them. Pages waited silently with basins of scented water,
so that hands might be cleansed between courses. Other servants offered
side dishes of vegetables, highly spiced stews and ragouts, and steam-

ing sauces racy with aromatic herbs. Wines flowed as freely and as endlessly as the Tiber, mingling their heady scents with the tang of the spices and the aroma of flesh and fowl.

Clement had his own personal serving staff, separate from the rest. One of these presented a gold flagon and a matched goblet, ringed with precious stones. At the Pontiff's nod he poured an amber stream, filling the cup. He raised this to his lips, sipped from it, reset it on the table, and quietly stepped back behind the Pope's chair. He repeated this office with every dish for which his master expressed a preference.

While the assembly dallied and bantered and leisurely stuffed itself, Cellini played the cornet. He played for three solid hours. By then the main dishes of the repast had been replaced with a variety of desserts, and the wine stewards were serving full-bodied sweet wines to wash down these delicacies: malmsey from Cyprus, muscatel from the Italian southlands, malaga from Spain, and muscadine from the Greek islands.

Sipping a favorite vintage, Clement directed the table chatter to a discussion of the music the company had listened to while they dined. Never, he protested, had he heard music more delightfully or harmoniously performed.

Since everyone within hearing distance servilely agreed, Clement requested that the bandmaster be summoned before him.

"We were much pleased with your performance, *maestro.*" The Pope beamed as Giacomo bowed in acknowledgment. The dinner had been excellent. Clement, pleasantly stuffed, was at ease and in a jovial mood. "We were particularly impressed by your cornet. A new man, is he not? We do not recall having heard him before. Tell us, pray, how did you succeed in procuring such a master? Who is he?"

Giacomo bowed again, joyfully. This sort of appreciation meant a substantial bonus. His mouth watered.

"Most Blessed Father, your humble servant is honored above all fame by these kind words which express your pleasure. Know, then, that this man whom Your Holiness has deigned to seek out is a citizen of your own Florence—Benvenuto Cellini by name."

"Cellini?...Cellini! We know the name well. Then this fellow must be the son of Master Giovanni?"

"And it please Your Holiness, that is so."

"In that case, *mio caro Giacomo,* you must see to his being enrolled in our service, with the other bandsmen."

"Supreme Holiness, as to this I cannot undertake to state with certainty that it shall be so, for this man practices the profession of goldsmith. In this he is wondrously skilled and earns far more than he would by playing music."

It did no harm, thought the music master, to point out to the Pope how sorry was the musician's lot.

"So much the better, my dear fellow! We do but desire him the more, since there is in him an additional talent which we did not expect. Allow him, then, the same salary as the rest, and tell him, on our behalf, that he must serve us and that we shall find him all the labor he desires in his other profession."

Extending his arm, Clement handed over a sheer cambric handkerchief in the folds of which there reposed a hundred gold crowns.

"It is our wish," the Pope informed Giacomo, "that you divide these in such wise that he may have his equal share."

Expressing unctuous thanks, the bandmaster bowed and withdrew. Clement reverted to his wine and chatted with his guests.

When Giacomo returned and recounted the Papal conversation, Cellini frowned thoughtfully. He was undecided and worried.

"I'm going to have your name inscribed on the roll of our company immediately," the delighted bandmaster told him.

Cellini's mouth wrinkled sourly. "Let's not be so hasty, Master Giacomo. Let today pass, so that I can think about the matter. Tomorrow I will give you an answer."

But meditating on the move made a decision doubly difficult. Badly as he wanted the Papal favor, he knew that the music would cut deeply into his time and his work as a goldsmith. Could be afford to let this happen? The problem was solved for him that night. Cellini went to sleep thinking over the vexing proposal and had a dream that became a nightmare. His father appeared and tearfully supplicated him to accept the exalted offer. The son sneered at his sire, telling him that on no account would he do anything so foolish as to become a musician. His father assumed the fearsome aspect of an avenging specter and screeched at him: "If you do not do this thing, you will receive a father's curse! Forevermore will you be accursed in all you attempt. But do as I ask and you will be blessed by me forever."

The goldsmith awoke in a cold sweat, with half the blanket stuffed in his mouth, and the fear of God weighing heavily upon him.

The next morning he went to the Vatican and had himself enrolled among the honorable company of the Papal musicians. In the back of his mind he nursed the thought that his father would cut capers for a month after the news reached him.

With that out of the way, he got on with his work. Days went by, made horrible by the ranting of Salamanca. Weeks. There were some calls for music practice. There was one performance, at a small supper. But there were no commissions from the Pope.

IX

AT LAST—IT WAS FINISHED!

The graceful silver arcs were sculptured and wrought with matchless artistry. Eyeing them critically, Cellini whistled out a long sigh of satisfaction. He was pleased. "By God," he muttered, "that's the finest bit of work I've ever done. If it doesn't put a stop to all that Spanish yowling, then nothing will."

He sighed again, happily, and called Paulino. The ewer was finished!

"Little master, this is ready for you to deliver to His Excellency the Bishop. But first I wish you to take it to the Santi shop and show it to Master Luca. Now, when you get there ..."

Paulino felt a certain pride as he walked off on his double errand. He had grown fond of Benvenuto and meant to do full justice to his request that he give a proper performance. He entered the Santi shop and looking neither to the right nor left, approached the table where Luca da Jesi was working. With the covered work clasped in his arms, he stood straight as the bolt for a crossbow and orated like a Cato.

"Master Luca," he recited by rote, with a gravity that had Da Jesi twinkling expectantly, "my master, Benvenuto, herewith sends to you this demonstration of his promise to fashion your garbage pails and chamber pots. He now awaits from you the sight of one of his whore's gauds."

Luca gave the boy a long up-from-under look and took the ewer in hand. He sighed a little enviously as he studied it and realized that

51

he had been beaten—definitely and fairly beaten. What a piece of work! How could anyone feel anger toward a master who could create something such as this out of a lump of silver? Shaking his head in silent admiration, he looked across to the naïve Paulino.

"My pretty little man, I have a message which it would please me for you to take back to Benvenuto. Tell your master that he is a brilliant artist. The most brilliant I have ever known. And that I beg him to accept me as a friend and nothing else. Will you do this?"

Paulino brought out that smile of his. "Most willingly, Master Luca," he sang out cheerfully, taking back the ewer. Paulino liked happy endings. "I promise to repeat your message just as you gave it."

With that part of the comedy finished, he carried the ewer to Salamanca.

His Excellency was in a petulant mood.

"Finally here, is it," he growled, snatching at the piece. "By the eternal cross, it's high time!" He examined the ewer with discerning care. *Vaya,* here was something really choice. Superb! He turned to his chamberlain and gave him instructions.

"I wish to have this work valued. See to it. Have several masters come in, so we will know its true worth. And, yes—be certain one of them is Luca da Jesi. I particularly wish to know his opinion."

The various goldsmiths and jewelers who were called in for the appraisal were loud in their praise. To Luca the ewer was outstanding and he admitted frankly that it far surpassed the companion piece he had made. Like the others he set a high value on the work. The ewer was estimated to be worth a hundred and fifty crowns.

Salamanca nodded solemnly as he listened to the comments, well pleased with the prize that had come to him. "So be it!" he told them, slapping the table by way of emphasis. "One hundred and fifty crowns it is." He beckoned his chamberlain forward. "Go and tell that laggard of a Benvenuto the result of the valuation and the price set upon the work. And tell the lazy varlet also," he continued in a nasty tone, "that I intend to make him await the payment of it for as long as he made me await the sight of it. Go."

Cellini's hackles rose straight and stiff while he listened to the sneering chamberlain repeat Don Francesco's intention. He'd not had enough trouble with that damned ewer, he needed this too! Keeping his teeth tightly clenched, he brooded while the chamberlain rubbed salt in the open wounds.

"By Christ his cross!" he spat out bitterly, when the man finished, "I merit better treatment than this! But then there is no denying facts that stare you in the face. You Spaniards are all alike. Dogs, every last one of you! Scampering out of that kennel that is your Spain! Why it is that creatures like yourselves are permitted to enter our civilized states, I will never understand. By God, you belong in cages!"

Ser Chamberlain's tail feathers were ruffled. His ears grew red, and he glared at the goldsmith, making threatening motions with his head.

"*Merda!*" jeered the Florentine, by now spoiling for trouble. "Wave your head and look as mean as you please, my bravo! That won't jar any of the plaster off the walls. Get out of here, and a pox take all of you!"

Not quite a week later, Salamanca was showing off the ewer to some nobles recently arrived from Spain, when he was called out to attend to a personal matter. Left alone in the room, one of the *caballeros* took up the piece and began operating the handle. He was fascinated by it. But being somewhat over-rough in the manipulation, he was no little chagrined to suddenly find himself with a broken handle in hand. Abashed at the mischief, he called in the head butler in charge of the plate and begged the servant to take the ewer to the master who had fashioned it and have it mended.

"Tell the fellow that I will pay whatever price he asks," he implored, "so that he set it to rights immediately. Now, for God's sake, hurry!"

Cellini smiled evilly when he saw the piece again. He listened to the obsequious major-domo's fervent request and nodded emphatically.

"I'll attend to it right away," he promised. "*Subito!* On my honor, it will be repaired as good as new by the time nones are rung."

True to this promise he had the ewer finished by twenty-two of the clock. He was locking it in a cupboard when the Salamanca butler, in a sweat from having run the whole way, dashed up to the house and pounded on the door.

The Florentine opened the wicket set in its center.

"Quick!" the domestic cried desperately. "His Excellency is asking for it! Bring the ewer. It's ready, is it not? You promised! Bring it here. Quickly!"

Cellini pushed both hands through the air. "Easy, *amico*," he

53

cautioned. "Relax a bit and take things more calmly. Let us talk about the matter."

"The ewer!" screamed the butler. "Bring the ewer out..." He saw the bland look on the goldsmith's face, and gulped.

"Oh no. No!...You can't..."

"I can—and will," nodded Cellini quietly.

Such sweating as the chief domestic had done was as a grain of sand on a seashore. He decided to get angry.

"Open this door and bring out that ewer instantly!" he bawled, aping his master's tone. A hand dropped suggestively on the hilt of his sword.

Cellini swung open the door, drawing a long dagger as he did so, and showed the butler what a long, sharp blade it had. It pointed at his belly all the while he looked at it.

"I am not going to give up the ewer," the goldsmith told him flatly. "Go and tell my lord, your master, that I want the money for my work before I let it leave this house."

Since bluff obviously would avail nothing, the major-domo fell back on supplication. "Give it to me," he prayed as to the rood. "I'll see to it that you are paid. I swear it. I've got to bring it back. He'll flog the hide off me if I don't."

Cellini revolved the ball of a thumb over the middle and index fingers of his hand. "Bring the money," he curtly informed the suppliant. "No money, no ewer."

Despair made the butler revert to anger.

"Very well, you whoreson! I'll see to it that you are attended to! I'll come back with enough of the servants to take this house apart. We will see how you like that!" He took to his heels and disappeared down the street.

The goldsmith smiled evilly again, got out an arquebus, loaded it with care and laid it on a table, and settled down to wait.

A group of Salamanca's Spanish servants arrived, led by the major-domo, who now was mounted on a smart little jennet.

"You men," he ordered importantly, "burst in the door, secure the vase, and then give that ill-mannered lout a sound thumping to teach him manners. Quickly, we are pressed for time!" He waved them on impatiently.

Cellini pulled open the wicket and showed the group the muzzle of the gun.

54

"You skulking bandits!" he howled fiercely. "Do you think yourselves free to act thus, breaking into the shops and houses of our Rome? Thieves! Robbers!" The shouting was making people stop and take notice, exactly what he desired. "As many of you barbarous renegades as move a step closer to this wicket, so many will have their brains strewn in the street with this gun!"

The Spaniards stopped, skeptical and unwilling to advance further.

Seeing the hesitation, Cellini turned the arquebus on the major-domo. "You thief!" he shouted. "Since it was you who brought these pigs here, I mean to kill you first."

He lowered his head and sighted along the barrel.

The butler did not wait. He spurred the jennet and tore away at a gallop.

By then the street was crowded. The neighbors had all come out to see what was happening. Tempers flared at the insufferable affront being put on Italian dignity by these foreign dogs. Several ran off to summon the watch, while others ran back to their shops and homes for weapons.

"Kill the filthy bastards, Benvenuto!" called out Pietrino Crocci, a candler who kept the shop next door. "We will help you!"

Salamanca's Spaniards turned tail and scampered off. They could not press the matter further. It would have been disastrous. They were foreigners. The city guards, aided by the aroused citizens, would have cut them down mercilessly.

Leaving the field in such a manner stung their fierce native pride and sense of valor. But that was nothing to the blow that came when they were forced to tell Salamanca of the incident. He drew them over the coals with a raking that withered them with its scorn. Not that he was concerned with the violence of the attempted assault. What vexed him was the fact that these craven skulks had allowed themselves to be turned away without the ewer.

"Aye! A fine stalwart band of valorous men," he shrilled at them, "that's what you are! Completely worthy to bear the name of valiant and invincible Spaniards who daily prove they fear nothing in the world. You do the Emperor, and me, great honor. What a display of courage! The bravery of it! All of you turned back by one man!" His voice rose to a shriek. "Out of my sight, you drones! Go and change your *bragghette!*"

He beckoned imperiously to Gian Penni. "Go and tell that Flor-

55

entine whoreson that if he does not return the ewer immediately I will arrange things so that the biggest pieces left of him will be his ears! Mark you, master, I said immediately!"

He went on muttering threats while Penni bowed and withdrew.

Knowing the Cellini temper, Penni was concerned over what might happen if the goldsmith continued to oppose the influential Spaniard. He arranged for several of the neutrals who were present to accompany him, knowing that it would look more impressive that way. The combined weight might make the goldsmith see reason.

They called and gave Cellini a word-for-word account.

"Neutino," warned Penni, "you must absolutely bring the ewer back. Otherwise things will go badly with you."

The goldsmith's lips had curled back over his teeth. "That overfed Spanish bastard! Who does he think he is? God! I will go and petition the Pope and have the whole matter brought before the *Podestà*. Tell your precious Don Francesco to go cock his leg up against a pole. I don't get frightened this easily!"

Which was nothing more than bluster and bile, and the goldsmith knew it. Threats from a major-domo were one thing. From Don Francesco de Bobadilla they were something else again. His Excellency was a mule of different breed. The courtiers who had called pointed this out. And as for petitioning the Pope, they made it clear that there wasn't time. The way Don Francesco was burning, by then the biggest pieces left of the goldsmith would be his ears.

"Bring it back to him, Benvenuto," one of them soothed. "Salamanca will pay you for the damn thing, after you return it. He cannot allow you to act in this manner. His honor is involved."

"All right, all right, all right!" snarled Cellini, furious at being held on a string. "I'll bring it back! But not tonight. Tomorrow!"

That, at least, was by way of being a moral victory.

The first crow of chanticleer the next morning found Cellini out of bed. He bathed and shaved carefully and sat to a hearty breakfast before laying out his finest clothing and arms. Much depended on this morning's meeting. His insolent altercation with the haughty Salamanca, he knew, had reached the point where all of fashionable Rome soon would hear of it. It would be discussed by important people. If he managed to carry himself in a manner which would reflect to his credit, the discussion would react to his favor. Nothing impressed the noblemen in the capital like a show of bold bravado. Thus he must cut a proper figure during the coming interview. It demanded special care and special attire.

Stripping down to the skin, he began by covering his rump and loins with a pair of drawers. Dark velvet trunks, brightly slashed with silk, followed. Long white hose were laced to these, and soft black doeskin boots slipped over the hose. Next he donned a fine linen shirt which displayed fringes of lace at neck and cuffs; and then came the focal point of his costume—a richly engraved and gilded cuirass. It was a piece of fighting armor really. A steel corselet which protected the body from neck to girdle. But it was all the fashion just then, and simply by being worn would lend an air of expensive dash, an added fillip of bravado, to the wearer.

A fine damascened sword and dagger glittered against the dark trunks. His *berretta* was flat, foppish, set at a jaunty angle, and held a brilliant plume that knifed back over his ear. A gold chain, thrown over the shoulders and clamped to the armor, had a studied casualness that lent an additional touch of splendor. A short cloak was clasped around his neck and flung back over the right shoulder, exposing the red silk of the lining. Finished!

With his right hand poised on the dagger hilt, Cellini pirouetted before the glass set in a pier between two windows and looked himself over with an appraising eye. Very good! Definitely the air of a man of parts.

"All ready, little master," he informed Paulino, directing him to take up the ewer.

Together they stepped out into the street and walked off, never stopping till they reached the pillared courtyard of Salamanca's palace.

Guards and domestics looked on stonily as they entered and climbed the stair to the reception rooms above. The antique gilding of the doors and doorways shimmered and danced. Room followed room filled with an unbelievable treasure-trove of the arts: frescoes, tapestries, paintings, statuary in marble and bronze, and smaller pieces cut from more precious and exotic materials. Cellini never passed through these rooms without being overcome with a feeling of awe. The masters represented there spanned the period from the glory of ancient Greece to the present. He looked about appreciatively as he walked along.

Salamanca waited in a *sala* usually reserved for large gatherings.

Spacious, enormous, it was bright in the dappled beams of sunlight streaming through deeply recessed, floor-to-ceiling windows. All around the room and at spaced intervals in the corridor leading to it, the irate Bishop had caused his household staff in full livery to take up appointed positions. They were all there—stiff, somber, and silently resentful.

Monsignor too had dressed for the occasion. He was resplendent in various shades of purple, as was seemly in a prelate of the first rank. The rochet, the wide cincture which held it around his ample paunch, the fine wool *mantelletta,* the small skullcap, all purple. And except for the flush of bitter passion which distorted the serenity of his visage, he was not without a certain ponderous dignity.

Apprised that the goldsmith had entered his house, he stalked belligerently around to a heavy, ornate table. Its surface, delicately modeled in intarsia, was bare except for a ewer of wine and a goblet. The sight of the ewer sent an additional spurt of blood to his already livid face, but he made no comment as he seated himself in a high-backed throne chair. The gentlemen of his suite silently grouped themselves behind him.

A page, waiting with a footstool, moved this into position as his master raised a foot, and backed silently away, obliquely eyeing the Bishop for signs of storm. The master had been very testy of late, as he always was when anyone crossed him.

Cellini reached the corridor and paused to look over the array of domestics drawn up for his reception. Their faces reminded him, unpleasantly, of the zodiac. This one looked like Scorpio, that one Leo, another Cancer, and so on as he paced along to where Taurus, the bull, waited with a convulsed countenance on which no rapture was visible.

Reaching the table, the goldsmith uncovered and swept the floor with the feather in his cap, voicing a pleasant greeting as he did so. Then, replacing the *berretta* and tilting it rakishly, he stood waiting silently, left hand idling on the hilt of his sword, a sunbeam glinting off the gleaming surface of his cuirass.

"E bene? ..." Salamanca snarled resentfully. Whatever else there might be on the odious face before him, traces of fear were manifestly absent.

"The ewer, Your Magnificence," Cellini motioned to Paulino, who

58

teetered up to the table, keeping his mouth opened wide so that he might breathe without making any noise at all.

"The ewer!..." Don Francesco blew the cork that was keeping back the flow and began spouting. The stream of invective that rolled off his tongue had the fuming quality of a raging fire that consumes everything in its path. His hands clawed vicious arcs in the air for added impetus.

The goldsmith answered nothing at all. Eyes discreetly lowered, he was staring—interested or bemused, it was impossible to tell which—at the marble flagstones of the floor.

The Bishop went right on rasping. Glaring like a Fury, he ordered paper, ink and quill to be brought in and set before the artist.

"I command you to write out immediately an acknowledgment stating that you have been amply paid in full and are completely satisfied!"

Cellini raised his eyes.

"I shall most happily do as my lord commands," he told the prelate quietly, "after I have received the money that is due me."

The reply sent Salamanca into a new and higher pitch of frenzy. This incredible maggot!...this worm!...daring to make such open defiance! If this were Spain! A new series of imprecations flew through the air, all but leaving spark tracks behind. The Bishop's face was rapidly turning the color of his clothing.

"Cristo," mumbled Cellini as he watched this desperate transformation. "He's working himself into a convulsion. *Gesù, Giuseppe e Maria.* If that happens I'll never get paid."

The angry recriminations and abuse continued to fly, to no avail. Beat him, scourge him, crucify him, the Florentine would write out no notes until the money was told down.

Salamanca was worn out. He was old. The weight of his exhausted emotions told on him. Waving a weary arm, he gasped out an order to bring the money, and slumped back in his chair.

Cellini wrote out a receipt, handed the bag of crowns to Paulino, expressed a polite farewell as he again uncovered and bowed, and departed in high spirits.

Pope Clement smiled when he learned of the affair, but made nothing of it beyond mentioning that he had heard the youth perform musically. He did express a desire to glance at the ewer that had caused all this tumult. Better still, having heard a great deal of comment regarding the quality of Salamanca's art collection, he invited himself to the Don's palace for a look at it. He got around little now that he was Pope.

Salamanca's already inordinate pride climbed to infinity. The Pope calling on him! His thoughts swung to Cellini. Regardless of what had passed, he meant to remain a patron of an artist whose work could create this sort of interest. On the morning that His Holiness was to call, he despatched Gian Penni to the goldsmith with overtures of peace.

Shortly afterward the Pope and a large retinue arrived. They wandered from chamber to chamber, expressing polite admiration, and finally reached the room where Cellini had so recently paid court. Refreshments were served and the ewer sent for, and Clement took it in hand studying it with increasing interest. He was impressed and he let Salamanca know it.

Swelling like a peacock, the Bishop began to prate of the works he intended to commission from this same master. Penni walked in as he was talking.

The Pope knew him well. Gian Penni and Giulio Romano had completed the Raphael frescoes in the Vatican after the untimely death of their master. He nodded to him and smiled in friendly fashion.

Penni acknowledged the greeting with a formal bow, and kept quiet.

"Ah, Your Holiness," cooed Salamanca, *"il Fattore* here is just returned from a call I bade him make on this same Cellini." The complacent Don turned his haughty eyes on Penni, who started to perspire. "Well, *Maestro Penni,* how went things? When is Benvenuto to call on us and receive our orders?"

"Oh, Christ," groaned the painter. And louder: "Why ... er ... Your Excellency ..."

Clement looked on, watching Penni's floundering. There was some sort of *buffa* in the offing, he was certain of it. Gently but firmly, he prodded him on.

"Get on with it, my dear fellow. Speak up. We're all old friends here. What did this Cellini say?"

"Blessed Father ..." Penni bowed and turned to Salamanca. He was trapped. *"Magnifico,* Master Benvenuto states that he will gladly undertake to carry out whatever commissions Your Excellency may have a mind to bestow." The Spaniard chortled smugly. "However," the moist Penni went on in a whisper, "he wishes it to be understood that he will undertake these only on the condition that payment be made in advance."

While Clement roared, Salamanca writhed. His face ran a gamut of colors. Clement went right on laughing—as did the court—as did all Rome, when they heard of the impertinence. The Pope turned to one of his gentlemen-in-waiting, a cardinal.

"It behooves us to give this spirited youth some work for the palace," he ordered. "His talent is great and should do us honor. See to it."

It started then, a rain of work. Innocenzio Cardinal Cibo sent for the Florentine and placed an order for a large vase. A veritable tempest of commissions followed. Cardinals Ridolfi, Cornaro, Salviati, practically the whole of the College bore down on the delighted goldsmith like a locust plague. Madonna Portia, hearing of his success, gave sound advice as well as commissions.

"Things are all yours now, Benvenuto. You are well on your way to fame. What you should do is open your own shop. Why don't you?"

He did so. A large shop, in the Banchi. Within a month he had to employ eight journeymen to handle the mass of work.

Meanwhile orders kept pouring in.

The lord Gabriello Cesarino, Gonfalonier of Rome, commissioned a medallion, cut to order, and received a boldly engraved, erotic masterpiece which depicted a seductively beautiful reclining Leda, contorted in sublime ecstasy while being ravished by Jupiter in the form of a swan. The striking effect of the Leda, cut from a pink stone, contrasting beautifully with the gold of the swan and the background, created a furore. The Gonfalonier basked in the glory of ownership, and Cellini rode the crest of the wave. He had not only become popular—he was the vogue.

And still more work came in.

The Florentine had climbed to the top rung of the ladder by straddling the shoulders of the haughty Salamanca. He had arrived.

X

Busy AT HIS DRAWING TABLE, THE GOLDSMITH looked up impatiently, frowning at Paulino. He was deeply involved in an intricate design and resented all interruptions.

"Well, little master? What is it?"

"A caller waits below, Master Benvenuto. A gentleman, very grandly dressed. He gives the name of Messer Giacomo Barengario da Carpi."

"Giacomo da Carpi? Here?" Cellini straightened. "Bring him up at once, *ninno*. Run!"

Laying down his pencil, he leaned back in his chair and cocked an eyebrow. He had heard a great deal about this ex-professor from the University of Bologna. The man's arrival in Rome had been preceded by a reputation of the highest renown. An eminent doctor and surgeon, proclaimed everyone who knew or had heard of him—a specialist who undertook the cure of the French disease, no matter how desperate the case. Men spoke of poisonous unguents and other wondrous fumigations he had discovered for these cures, for which he charged exorbitant fees.

Paulino opened the door of the well-lighted and appointed studio and bowed in the visitor.

Cellini rose and greeted him with unction. The leech was known to be a great connoisseur of the art of design. That made him a potential client.

"Welcome to my poor shop, Messer Giacomo," he murmured, bowing. "You do me honor."

"Ah, *Maestro Cellini!*" His Erudition was serenely grave. "Know that I have long desired to make your acquaintance, but the press of duty has prevented. Now, at last, I am come to view with my own eyes the man and the works which have acquired so much honor and renown."

Messer Giacomo was a busy man, with a high opinion of the value of his time. He did not believe in wasting it on inanities. As he spoke his eyes wandered around, taking in the pieces on display. They stopped on a pile of drawings lying on a corner table.

"*Permesso?* ..." he inquired, pointing.

Cellini acquiesced by waving a hand toward them, and when Messer Giacomo seated himself and began to leaf through the sketches, he eyed the medico with interest. If the report did him no injustice, here was the leech who had been accused of cutting up two men, to advance certain studies in muscular anatomy. In itself this was not unusual except for the little detail that the two unfortunates were alive when cut apart. Just so! Messer Doctor had wished to view living reactions! Well, he certainly looked the part. He had the face of a vulture. Thin and dried up like a raisin, with keen jet eyes, straggly white beard, great beak of a nose, and the flat cold look of the natural killer. Ruthlessness was written into every seamed line of it.

"My decision to call on you," the Doctor explained as he examined the sketches, "resulted from a pleasant visit of yesterday. I spent the evening as the guest of His Excellency, my lord Salamanca ... a charming man!"

The goldsmith grunted.

"We discussed many different topics. The arts—and other things." Messer Giacomo paused and waved the other things away. "He showed me some of your work. That ewer ... Magnificent! You are a master of the first rank."

Cellini bowed in acknowledgment and in full agreement.

"It struck me then and there," the caller went on, "that it were well you be represented in my own collection. Ah! ... what have we here?"

He pulled out some drawings of several small, fancifully designed vases, rather different from the usual run of such pieces.

"The illustrious Don Francesco," the bemused surgeon, engrossed in the drawings, absent-mindedly began to discuss the "other things," "was extremely confused and somewhat irked over the doings of His Gracious Holiness—a fellow-countryman of yours, I believe. I did what I could to soothe him by directing the conversation into more pleasant channels. Tell me, Master Benvenuto, do you follow the course of modern politics?"

63

"No, *messere*. Not at all. I devote myself to my art. I am a gold-smith, not a politician."

"So." Giacomo da Carpi's lips puckered thoughtfully, his eyes, almost closed, were intent on the drawings. "No doubt you are right. Who is there that can follow such an intricate skein? My lord Sala-manca was upset by his inability to comprehend the pattern of Pope Clement's policy with Spain. It appears that our Pontiff is jumping back and forth—an ally one day, an enemy the next. Have you formed an opinion of this?"

"None, Messer Giacomo. To me statecraft is but another name for confusion. I take no interest in such matters."

Cellini shrugged off the question. It was one he had heard before. Many men wondered at the political intriguing of the Medici, exclaim-ing over a policy which appeared to be entirely without direction. It turned like the wind. When he became Pope, Clement had sided with France. Shortly thereafter, for no apparent reason, he switched to Spain. Recently he had turned again toward France. These were not matters which concerned a goldsmith. To hell with them.

But Messer Giacomo had completely forgotten politics. The words he spoke were just sounds made while absorbed in the study of some very interesting designs.

"Benvenuto," he looked up, "you will execute these for me in silver?"

"I shall be honored to do so, Your Worship."

"Excellent. *Ma però,* you must see to it that you hold exactly to this magnificent sweep of line you have captured in your cartoons. Here—," he pointed, "—and here. Do the work well, in your usual manner, and I promise you will have no cause to grumble over the compensation. Agreed?"

"Agreed, *messere.* Be assured that the finished pieces will please you. I shall create something novel and unusual. I warrant your satisfaction."

"Good!" The Doctor nodded affably and leaning back, looked around the studio again. "An agreeable workroom you have here, master. One is at ease in it, and this permits the processes of thought and imagination to have full rein. It reminds me of my study in Ferrara, where I now live. I long to return there." The leech shook his head and frowned. "I fear I do not think very highly of this Rome, my Benvenuto. I find it oppressive...and so much French sickness!

Also, I have seen things here—peculiar things—which I do not like."

"Indeed, Messer Giacomo?"

"Quite so. For example, all the dead rats one sees in the streets. For the past week I have seen nothing else. Every time one steps out of a house, one must kick their repulsive carcasses aside. Pah!"

Cellini nodded. For the past few days this strange occurrence had been much in evidence. There were dead rats in nearly every street of Rome, lying in the gutters amid the garbage, with legs and snouts stiff in the air.

"Very peculiar," maintained the Doctor. "During my walk to your shop I counted nine of them. Nine!"

"What do you make of it, *messere?* Some here maintain it is an omen. Do you think this is so?"

Giacomo da Carpi shrugged and arose. "Frankly, *maestro,* I know not. As like as not it could well prove to be some Devil sign or other. Who can say with certainty? Well ... I must leave you and be off about my work. *Arrivederci.*"

Cellini accompanied the Doctor to the door and bowed the leech on his way to a tour of the moneyed syphilitics of Rome.

Making the little vases suited the Florentine's fancy and he put them in work immediately. The commission did not use up much time. Ten days later the shop handyman delivered them to Messer Giacomo and returned to the shop with a pleased smile on his face.

"He raved when he saw them, master," he called out as he entered. "He was highly pleased. He bade me say that you performed exactly as you promised, and that he will send a purse of seventy-five crowns this afternoon."

The goldsmith beamed. *Caspita!* Seventy-five crowns was little short of munificent.

The handyman walked back to the shop door and stood there snickering.

"Come and have a look at this, Master Benvenuto," he invited, nodding at the street. "Here's a sight."

"What is it, Davido?" Cellini came up beside him and looked out. There was an elderly man staggering along the street, stumbling and reeling from one side to the other, drunk as a coot. He came to a stop against a building wall and leaned his flushed face against the cool stone, clutching at the wall for support. Abruptly he turned and began to vomit.

65

"Why, it's Ser Renaldo!"

"Yes," laughed Davido. "The mercer who keeps the shop down the street. Look at the old dog! His face looks like a boiled carrot. I swear he's filled to the ear lobes."

"Go and help him to his home, Davido."

The handyman started out but just then two of the elderly mercer's neighbors came along and dragged him off between them. The old fellow was babbling incoherently.

Davido came back to the door, shaking his head. "He'll vomit his guts out before he gets there. Which is just as well. I'll wager he catches a merry time when he gets home. I for one would not relish facing that wife of his, in such condition." Davido whistled. "What a harpy!"

The mercer, Ser Renaldo, didn't much relish facing his wife either. She was a shrew who gave him no peace. And as he expected she nagged and scolded him to great length over the disgrace he had put upon her. For an honorable shopkeeper to appear on the streets in broad daylight so disgustingly drunk, she squalled as she angrily rattled pots and pans concocting a brew of bitter herbs, was shameful. What would people think—and say! How could she face the neighbors!

Too sick to argue with her, the mercer drank the horrible tasting mess she forced on him and went to bed. He was not drunk. He'd had only two mugs of wine and could not see how he was at fault if these had made him ill. His face felt very hot. His head ached so it made him dizzy. And he was still retching from the stomach disorder that had come upon him and made him vomit in the street.

That herb remedy, whose efficacy his wife swore by, proved utterly worthless. By evening the mercer was delirious, and large inflamed lumps were swelling out all over his body. A doctor was sent for, but when he arrived he took one look and ran out of the house without saying a word.

Renaldo died the next day. His wife mourned him in approved fashion, and after the funeral complained of feeling very feverish and upset. There were others in the Banchi suffering from this same complaint. In the more densely populated Capitol district there were many more. How many no one could say, because there people were so poor they were always sick with this or that disorder. Before the week was out there were at least a thousand victims of the malady and it was

66

evident that an uninvited and unwanted visitor had stalked into the city. It was the answer to all those dead rats. It was bubonic plague. The Black Death had come to Rome.

Like the rest of the population, Cellini was terrified. Plague was not a thing you could face with courage and skill—and fight. The pest was a hidden terror, a lurking killer that struck silently and dreadfully, without warning. No one knew how or when it would strike. And if you asked why it came, you were told it was the will of God. There was no other answer. As its virulence increased, the once noisy bustle of the city was stilled until there were only the knelling of the church bells, the wailing of the people, and the creak of the dead-wagons carting off loads of bloated corpses to common graves or blazing pyres that flamed for days at a time on human fuel.

Commissions at the shop dwindled to practically nothing. There was little work to do, and the goldsmith looked for none beyond that which came voluntarily. He and Paulino left the city as often as possible and spent their days in the Campagna, studying the antiquities and hunting the pigeons which nested in the ancient ruins. The once busy shop was almost deserted. Of the seventeen people who had been employed there, only three remained: a journeyman, the cook and housekeeper, and little Paulino. The others had all fled.

He wrote encouraging letters to his father every week, hoping that the old man would not worry himself sick over the danger his son was facing. The days dragged wearily on. The city was gloomy and still, weighed down by a pall of terror and dread. Life was becoming an intolerable burden.

"I swear to you," the goldsmith's friend, Bruno Retti, complained bitterly one morning when he called at the shop, "if this doesn't come to an end soon, I'll cut my throat! What manner of life and living is this? Any beast fares better! Never a day or an hour or a single moment when the terror that grips us all does not overcome every other thought." Bruno sighed deeply. *"Per Dio,* do you remember the old times, Neutino? The gaiety...the cheer...and the jolly companions? Would it not be wonderful to bring that old spirit back, if only for a brief space?" He looked up suddenly, his eyes alight. "Why not? What do you say to a little supper party—and to hell with everything else?"

Cellini agreed at once. "It's an excellent idea. Things are far too glum. I will be your host and promise a tasty repast and some choice wine. When do you wish it to be?"

"Tonight. Why wait?" Bruno chortled with pleasure. "I've just the companion to bring along. Are you going to ask one of the girls over as your partner?"

"No. It's too chancy. You intend to bring company, Bruno?"

"But naturally, old fellow!" Bruno twirled at the stubby end of his mustache. "And a choice bit she is. Just wait till you see her." He snapped his fingers significantly.

"It's a risk, you know. With all this plague."

"The seven devils from the bottom pit of hell take this damn plague!" retorted Bruno. "Life has become so dull it's hardly worth the living anyway. I am desperate. You don't mind if I bring her along?"

"Not at all. Suit yourself in the matter. Like you I will be glad of some company, even if most of the sport will be yours. You can stay the night. I've plenty of room."

Bruno came early, bringing along his lady for the night. She was a sturdy, well-built specimen named Faustina, a professional from Bologna. Tall. Buxom. Very attractive. She had a little servant girl along who was still in her teens.

The supper was very diverting. The roast was hot and tasty. The wine, cool and heady; and the chatter, aimless and witty. Everyone was cheered. The Bolognese bawd was a gay and spritely whore with a one-track mind. An affinity for wine made her bubble a great deal, and she kept the table in an uproar by her ardent ogling and passionate asides to the goldsmith. She was not in the least backward in voicing her desires.

"You know, Neutino," she hiccuped, running a hand down his cheek. "*You* arouse me...make me mad with desire. The passion I feel for you consumes me!" While her bosom heaved suggestively, she vented a maudlin sigh and pouted archly. "Now surely such a warm and cozy little oven deserves none but the best loaf?" Her eyes wandered coyly up and down.

Cellini started to sweat. But for the fact that she was Bruno's guest ...No, it would hardly be right to interfere with his friend's arrangements.

Faustina sensed his indecision. "You aren't really going to allow such an opportunity to pass?" she wailed. "Here I wait, a fiery caldron

68

that wants filling, promising such a time as you have never enjoyed—and you sit pensive. Bah!...*Merda!* Bruno won't mind. Will you, little lamb?"

The debonair Bruno twirled his mustache and elegantly waved permission, grinning at Cellini.

"No." The Florentine's sense of loyalty won. "It is unthinkable. You are here as Bruno's guest, not mine. We will arrange things for another time, eh?"

Faustina shrugged. Oh well, it didn't matter that much. Long experience had taught her that when a room is dark, one man did as well as another. She rose and beckoned to Bruno, prodding him to his feet.

Cellini remained at the table, muttering to himself while he absently shucked roasted chestnuts and gulped muscadine. His vacant stare fell on Faustina's little servant girl. He hadn't noticed her before, but there she was—all plump and rosy and ripe and ready for plucking. She sat straight in her chair, intact and as yet unused, and weighed down not a little by the burden of so monstrous an oversight. Cellini looked—and asked a question with his eyes. She smiled demurely, but the answer was clear. She was more than willing. He lurched to his feet and stopped wasting time.

The next morning he swayed a bit as he got out of bed. He was dizzy and his stomach felt empty and upset. He licked around his mouth with a tongue that felt thick and furry. He was strangely tired, as if he had walked all night. He dressed and went down to the kitchen to take breakfast.

The cook was serving the others when he came in, greeted them a little glumly, and went to sit down. As he did so a crushing headache came on him, so painful it made him sway in his chair. He nearly fell. The others seated around the breakfast table stared blankly, their faces set in puzzled, stupid lines. Faustina gasped and pointed dumbly to his left forearm. He looked. Small fresh sores. Farther down, just over the wrist, a large red carbuncle.

"Plague boils!"

A blind panic seized every inmate. The workman and cook scrambled for the door, leaving every earthly possession behind. So, also, did the pleasant company of the night before. The bull, his cow, her little calf, all fled from the dread affliction. Only Paulino remained.

69

He flatly refused to abandon his master. And Cellini....An icy hand clutched at his heart, freezing his blood, his every breath, stifling him with a penetrating cold. His hour had struck and he was face to face with certain death. He doddered over to a couch and lay there, awaiting the end.

With his master looking so lost and full of despair, Paulino walked sadly to the doorway and stood looking out into the street. Here, at least, he couldn't see the terror on Master Benvenuto's face. He was still idling there, not knowing what to do, when the personal physician of the Cardinal Iacobacci chanced to stroll by. The lad gazed at the doctor slyly, a thought forming slowly behind his eyes. If he could manage to get the doctor inside, perhaps something could be done.

The medico smiled as he came alongside. "Ah there, little master-goldsmith! Taking the air, I see. And how is the older master, Benvenuto, on this dull day?"

"Feeling poorly, Master Doctor," Paulino sang back gaily, giving a little shrug of affected indifference. "He drank too much wine last evening and has a bad headache. Won't you come in and comfort him a little?"

The doctor didn't think. He was completely taken in by the naïvete of a little shopboy standing in the door of his master's shop. He entered and walked over to the goldsmith, chattering with Paulino all the way.

He laid a hand on Cellini's forehead. Very feverish. He looked him over more closely—and saw that which he would rather not have seen.

"God's wounds, I am ruined!" he howled, turning angrily on Paulino. "*Vigliacco mostro!* What have you done to me! Now I can no longer look after my lord, the Cardinal. Having been here, I cannot even enter his presence again. You treacherous little bastard!"

Paulino did not understand. "But Master Doctor," he told him innocently, "this man who is my master is worth more than all the cardinals in Rome."

The leech clutched at his temper with both hands to keep from strangling the lad. After a while he let out a shuddering sigh and turned back to Cellini.

"Since I am here, Benvenuto, I will consent to treat you; but I must warn you of one thing, if you have romped with a woman recently, you are doomed."

70

The doctor held to the prevalent theory that continence was a prime physiological factor, both in the transmission and cure of the Black Death.

The goldsmith gulped in dismay. "B-b-bu-but I did so this very night."

"*Porco cane!* With whom and how often?"

"All of last night," groaned Cellini, "and with a very young maiden."

The medico screwed up his lips and pondered. He did not hold much hope. Plague was plague. "Well... since the sores are fresh and not yet stinking, we will be able to apply our remedies in good time. Do not have too great a fear." He shrugged lamely. "It is possible that we may be able to effect a cure. We shall see."

Poultices and nostrums and physics and purges were administered, all of them worthless. With incredible rapidity the fever increased, as did the lancinating pain from the angry red buboes that swelled out all over the goldsmith. By nightfall he lay shrieking in delirium, the carbuncle on his forearm grown into an enormous white-capped sore, so large that as it pulsed it made his arm jerk. The doctor strapped him down to the bed and lanced the festering mound, cleaned it out, plugged the open wound with lint so that it could drain, and covered it with a plaster. He had done all he could. If Cellini survived the three days which invariably marked the maximum span of life following the initial attack of the pest, there was a chance. From here on it was up to the Almighty.

For two days Cellini raved. On the morning of the third day, the doctor, with Paulino's help, forced some hot milk down the goldsmith's throat. All day long and half the following night, Cellini continued to rant. Then he sank into a troubled sleep which lasted for twenty-four hours. When he awoke the delirium was gone, and the doctor began to have hope.

"By God," he told Paulino as the lad beamed happily, "we will save your Benvenuto, little master. The worst is over and behind us. Keep him warm and give him a cup of hot milk every three or four hours. I will return tomorrow."

Four weary, soul-wracking months of slow convalescence went by. But the battle had been won. The goldsmith had survived the contagion of the Black Death. Within the city the fury of the plague had abated and a show of order was returning.

71

Shut in and ostracized as he was, Cellini heard little of what went on in the world outside his door. Occasionally a friend dropped in and passed on a little gossip. Giovanni Rigogli spoke of a rumor filtering into the city, circulating the report of a terrific battle fought between the armies of Francis and Charles, outside the walls of Pavia.

"Everyone is talking about it, Neutino. The way it's told, this plague was nothing to that slaughter. France is said to be crushed. King Francis has been taken prisoner by the renegade Bourbon. Most of the French nobility and ten thousand foot of the French army were slain; and those who survived were captured. What do you think?"

Sitting up on a couch and starved for news of any kind, Cellini shook his head. "I don't know. These rumors ... you never know what to make of them. They're always enlarged and distorted as they pass from mouth to mouth. It will probably turn out to be nothing more than a sally, or a skirmish. What are they saying at the Vatican?"

"That's where I heard it, my dear fellow. It is said that Clement is mad with anxiety over the news. He was embroiled with France, you know. He's in a lather, not knowing whom or what to believe. Some say he ordered Salviati to send out men and ascertain the truth at the source."

"That sort of thing," remarked Cellini, "is going to take time."

"It will take weeks. Yet what else can he do if he wants the facts?"

The goldsmith shrugged and motioned these complexities out of the way. "I too have news. I'm going away tomorrow. *Finalmente!* You know the painter, *il Rosso?* He has invited me to a villa of the Count Anguillara's, where he is staying. A place called Cervetera. It's on the shore of the Tyrrhenian. There I can complete my recovery. I've bought a pony to ride on for the journey. Go and have a look at him before you leave. He's a wild little fellow, covered with hair four fingers long, and looks like a bear. Paulino is mad about him. Went riding on him this morning."

Warmly greeted by his friend, and well received by his patron, Cellini passed a delightful month at the elegant seaside villa near Civita Vecchia. The Count set a splendid table. The weather was sunny and not too chill. Every day he went riding along the shore, filling his pockets with curiously shaped shells and never tiring of looking at the unbelievable blue of the Tyrrhenian Sea.

But after a month the place began to bore him, and he returned

72

to Rome. The holiday had completely restored his health. He was as hale as ever and more than eager to take up where he had been forced to leave off. In the Eternal City the plague had died out and things were near to normal again.

XI

AS A GOOD AUGURY FOR HIS NEW BEGINNING Cellini took up a commission ordered months before by Pope Clement, a large silver and onyx cup intended as a gift for one of the chancellors of the French king. The design for it had been started but never completed because of the plague, and now his mind buzzed with an entirely new conception. The old sketches were put aside in favor of a new theme, drawn from his recent sojourn by the sea. A mass of preliminary drawings, which represented two weeks' labor, were scattered around, and the frown of concentration on his forehead deepened as he studied these for possible changes. His pencil moved in quick sure strokes.

The new conception of the cup was sharp and clear in his mind and came easily to his pencil point, the various parts merging into a smoothly integrated whole with a pleasing flow of line. He liked, particularly, the superb contrast that was achieved. The new base and stem were fashioned in the form of a silver sea dragon which held in its gaping maw and taloned claws a shallow onyx bowl carved with curling seaweed. Schools of fishes, sea horses and snails played among the curving tendrils. The rim of the bowl was a wide silver band worked with an interlaced pattern of shell fish, and the cover rose in a series of waves that lapped about the tail of a silver mermaid rising out of the sea in an arched movement that carried the eye over her superbly modeled, dripping torso. The finished cartoon was perfect, certain to please. He yawned and flexed his back. Tomorrow morning he would take it to the Pope for approval.

The streets of Rome were quiet and deserted, but the usually placid Vatican, when he entered, was buzzing with excitement. Clerks and pages, even courtiers, were running around with intent frowns on their faces, speaking in subdued whispers. Only the Swiss guards were calm

73

and serene. In their parti-colored uniforms and gleaming half-armor, they mounted guard with customary aplomb. Upstairs in the ante-chamber of the Papal suite he accosted a courtier seated at a table.

"*Messere,* I have here the finished design for a commission assigned to me by His Holiness. Since he is most anxious to see this I have hurried here with it. Please to send in my name and advise the Holy Father that I await his pleasure."

The request made the foppish little attendant start from his perch, his watery eyes rounding in irritation. "Not today, master! Not today!" he yapped sharply, his birdlike hands fluttering. "The Pope has no time to waste on such fripperies just now! Come back another time. Next week!"

The goldsmith stared in surprise at the outburst. He shrugged. Perhaps Clement was occupied at the moment. "If I could have a word with His Eminence, my lord Cornaro," he suggested, frowning at the dandy.

The attendant continued to wag his head obstinately. "No! I cannot disturb the Cardinal either! He is engaged with His Holiness on affairs of State. Come again next week!"

There was that in the perfumed little fop's manner which plainly indicated it would be useless to press the matter. Something of importance was stirring, no doubt of it. Cellini gave the little pipsqueak a sour look—fripperies!—and turned on his heel.

As he was passing through the Hall of the Pontiffs he saw one of Cornaro's gentlemen, young Alfredo Valla, talking with a member of the Papal suite, an Orsini. He knew both of the young nobles and walked over. Now he could learn what was up. They turned as he approached.

"*Olà,* Benvenuto," Valla waved while Orsini nodded affably. "Here, Orazio, is a fellow who cheats death. Nothing can kill him. Not brawls, or duels—not even the plague! How fares the master?"

"In health, excellent," answered Cellini, smiling. "Otherwise, very confused."

"What brings you here, Benvenuto? One would suppose Clement has little time for you at the moment."

"I have just now discovered that fact. There is a perfumed little drone upstairs who made that quite clear. What the devil is going on here?"

Orazio degli Orsini smiled thinly. "You mean to say you don't know?" He showed a palm. "Word has finally arrived confirming those rumors regarding Pavia. The reports were true. France has suffered a terrible defeat."

"More," broke in Valla, "it is also true that Francis was taken prisoner."

"What of it?" asked Cellini.

"What of it!...My dear fellow, look around you! You've been upstairs? You see all this frenzy? Clement is thunderstruck, and well he should be. Not only was he leagued with the losing side, he now must face the fact that Charles has emerged as the most powerful man in Europe. His Holiness is moving heaven and earth in an effort to effect a treaty with him. He, Salviati, and several others including my lord Cornaro, are closeted with the Imperial Ambassador, the Duke of Sessa." Orazio stared out of the window at the Court of the Belvedere. "It appears," he murmured, "that our Clement is about to change sides again. I wish him well, by God! He has managed up until now, but this is just a bit fantastic. How long does he imagine he will be permitted to go on playing this game of his?"

Cellini shrugged contemptuously. "These cabals," he sniffed disdainfully, "they stink to high heaven."

The Orsini laughed at the expression on the goldsmith's face. "Then all this is of no interest to you?"

"Less than that! The devil take all of it. Why should it interest me? I am an artist."

"Speaking of artists, Benvenuto," Alfredo turned the subject easily, "are you attending Michele's supper?"

Cellini's nod was a little dubious. "I believe so. I've been invited. Unfortunately I have involved myself in a problem there."

"What supper?" asked Orsini, "and what problem?"

"There is a new society of artists in the Banchi, Orazio," grinned Valla. "Perhaps you have not yet heard of it. The sculptor Michele Agnolo of Siena has formed the group. It is dedicated to the proper celebration of life and living. The male members are all artists who have survived the plague. They meet twice a week and raise the devil."

"He's just the man for something like that. I have never met anyone faster than he at tilting a flagon. What about this supper, Benvenuto?"

"It's an entertainment given by Michele. He has invited all of us to attend, subject to a condition."

"And the condition?"

"Is that each of us must be attended by a suitable crow. The member who dares make an appearance without one will be made to pay for the whole of the entertainment."

"Fair enough. And who is to be your companion?"

"That is my problem."

"Bah! Are you trying to tell us something like that would bother you?"

"It didn't until last night. I had my crow all selected. Everything was arranged. I intended to take Pantasilea."

"Who is she?" Orsini looked inquiringly at Alfredo. "Do I know her?"

"A very beautiful creature," interposed Cellini. "A model."

"The devil she is," laughed Alfredo. "She's a beauty, granted. But she's no model. That whore!"

Cellini waved. "A whore, then. In any case, I was taking her. Last night, Francesco Verdi—you know him? He paints miniatures. He's head over heels in love with the trollop. He begged me to yield her up to him. We are such good friends," the goldsmith grimaced, "I couldn't bring myself to refuse the dolt. Now I don't know where to turn. It damned well serves me right for being such a fool." Shaking his head in disgust, he nodded a farewell and walked off.

All afternoon, while he dabbled around the shop, he mulled over the vexing problem of finding a suitable crow. Of women there were plenty. But the affair called for something out of the ordinary. This was to be a gathering of men of genius—men of taste. To make an appearance into such a company accompanied by just any low-slung, draggle-tailed scarecrow, was unthinkable. There was a point of honor as well as pride involved. Yet go there he must, and properly attended, or appear stupid and unresourceful.

Sitting and musing he watched Paulino tinkering around with a young friend of his, a Spanish youth of about sixteen. The lad was the son of a neighbor and the two were very friendly. An idea—a completely mad idea—came to his mind.

"It might work out," he murmured, selling it to himself. "And if it does, it will cause a riot. There's no harm in trying it out here. Diego! Come here a moment!"

"Yes, Master Benvenuto." Diego came up expectantly, prepared for anything. He was accustomed to the goldsmith's whimsies, having frequently served as his model. "What is it?"

Cellini eyed the youth. He would do nicely. No beard to speak of, except for a slight down. A razor would take care of that. Marvelous complexion. Excellent figure . . . masculine, but graceful. Fill it out properly, and by the girdle of Venus they might carry it off!

"Look you, Diego, I wish you to dress like a young woman. Clothes, stuffing, paints, jewelry, everything. What say you?"

"If you wish," Diego shrugged.

The goldsmith worked carefully. The padding and the cosmetics were applied with judgment, and the clothing selected with caution. The biggest problem was the earrings. All women wore them, and Diego's ears were not pierced. He solved that by cutting through the thin gold rings of a pair he had on hand and clipped these to the youth's ears. The effect was perfect.

When he had finished he drew the lad before a mirror. "Take a look at yourself," he invited proudly.

Diego looked and whistled at the vivid transformation. He really looked like a girl. A pretty girl. "But why all this, Benvenuto?"

"Listen, my young friend, I want you to do me a big favor—come to a dinner with me, dressed just as you are. And remem—"

"You're mad!"

"No, no! How mad? It will be a simple thing. Look in the mirror! It can't fail. Just remember to act like a girl. Be demure. I promise you the time of your young life."

"*Sei matto spolpo!*"

With a sigh, the Florentine rooted around in his purse and brought up a crown. "Well? How about it?"

Diego gulped. "All of it?"

"All of it."

"Let's go," the youth told him, reaching for the coin.

Gian Penni spotted them as they entered. "Look at that!" he yelled, pointing with his wine cup. "Look! Now *there* is a piece!"

Cellini lifted the veil from the painted face of his beauty. The pack howled gleefully.

Diego, in some confusion, blushed and began to fumble with the laces on the bodice of his dress.

77

"Not yet! my lovely one! Not yet!" bawled the lusty Michele Agnolo. "Wait until we are alone. Save those for me!" He turned to his guests. "Boys, we can't call *her* a crow! This is a swan. A peacock! Ahhhhh, my friends. See—" engagingly he patted Diego's buttocks "—what awaits us in paradise! What's her name, Neutino? And don't look so worried. No one is going to steal her from you!"

Cellini's face went blank. "Er...name...Oh, her name! ...Why, it's...it's Pomona!" he cried, his frantic gaze falling on a bowl of apples. "Yes," he sighed, "Pomona."

Since Diego had the good sense to keep as quiet as possible, and the others were already busy eating and drinking, the deception was palmed off. All through the supper, to the serving of fiery *rosolio,* no one suspected.

Diego was having a wonderful time. He was seated between Pantasilea and another even sexier-looking doxy named Alma, the crow of Giulio Romano, and was thoroughly enjoying the conversation crossing back and forth between the two wenches. The topic was an absorbing one. Each was acquainting the other with the diverse circumstances involved in her entry into the ranks of their profession.

Pantasilea's history was the more prosaic. Her mother had been in the business when her daughter was, so to speak, born into it. She had early in life been well instructed and initiated in the mysteries of the art.

"With me it was pure chance," maintained Alma. "It came about as the result of an accident which befell me when I was a young girl. Fourteen years of age, in fact."

"All this happened some time ago, then?" queried Pantasilea.

"What I like about you, honey," retorted Alma, "is that you can be such a nasty bitch in a very sweet way." She let her eyes wander up and down. "You should talk!" she sniffed. "You look like something the cats play with in the streets at night!"

"Never mind her." The enchanted Diego prodded her on. "What about this accident of yours?"

"Well..." mollified, Alma went on with the tale of her initiation. "I was born and raised in the country near Camerino, where my people have a farm. And as is the custom on a farm, a portion of the household chores fell to me. At the time every day during the afternoon I had to walk to a nearby thicket and gather fagots for the fire. Now on this particular day I had gathered together a large fagot of dry wood, and

78

having lifted this atop my head, was returning home with it. I was walking along a little lane when this youth came up behind me—all red in the face he was—and began to rub my rump. I was so surprised I could only stare at him like a ninny. What with that bundle I was carrying, there was little I could have done anyway. After a while he told me that he had watched its movements as I walked along and this had caused him to be overcome with desire."

"And what did you say to that?"

"By that time I had found my tongue. *Naturalmente,* I told him to stop doing that and go away. But what was there I could do? He stroked very pleasantly, let me tell you—and I was beginning to like it. A nicely set-up young man, he was." Alma smiled reminiscently.

"And then? . . ."

"Without wasting another moment he lifted the fagots off my head and had me on my back with my skirts flying before I could utter a word of protest."

"I'll wager you didn't particularly wish to utter it," Pantasilea broke in dryly. "How did you find the experience?"

"Well . . . *di certo,* that first time I did feel some slight annoyance. But it was of a most agreeable sort." Alma sighed and reached for her wine cup. "And that is how it happened with me."

Pantasilea was puzzled. Diego, in the role of Pomona, was frankly bewildered. "I don't see how that made a professional of you," he told her.

"You don't? Well, it did—in a manner of speaking. You see, that stupid clown didn't keep quiet. He spread the word around. Within a few days there was a line of men in that thicket, waiting for me to pass by. It was rather tiring, I can tell you. Still, in a short time I was earning a bit of money. But as for that first one, he was a dolt! Do you know what he did, after he finished satisfying himself of me? Calmly lifted those fagots back on my head and sent me on my way. The wretch! After all that work, expending all my energy, he didn't have the grace to carry those fagots for me. Oh! . . . all men are dogs!"

Diego was so overcome he nearly rolled under the table. Squirming and twisting in his chair, he tried as best he could to keep a straight face. The resulting grimaces gave him the look of one afflicted with acute indigestion.

Alma looked on with concern. "What's the matter, dear? Don't you feel well?"

79

"No...I'm afraid not." The rogue in skirts sighed heavily and brought up a sorrowful expression. "I have a confusion and turmoil in my belly that is most annoying. I fear I am with child. That devil of a Benvenuto, of course!"

"You poor thing! Here, let us try to ease you." Tenderly, Alma and Pantasilea began to knead the supposedly aching portions of the spurious Pomona. In the course of the massage, first one hand, then another, wandered down a bit lower than was perhaps necessary.

"Corpo di sangue!" screamed Pantasilea, grabbing excitedly. "What have we here? This is the first wench I've ever seen carrying something such as this around!"

"So that's the way of it!" yelled Alma. "Traitor! Trickster! Why should you wish to keep that a secret!"

The room was in an uproar. The girls circled the howling Diego and were attempting to pull off his skirts.

"What are you going to do with this knave of a Benvenuto, Michele? After all, he didn't bring a crow!"

The sculptor chewed over the question. "My friends," he adjudicated, "we must act with wisdom and with justice. Neutino has not, as you point out, brought a crow. Yet he did bring something better —imagination. I congratulate him. We must all congratulate inventive talent of this kind. Here comrades...ladies...a full cup for all ...a toast to our Florentine and to his creation of the evening!"

All of them drank, and cheered the two to the echo.

XII

IF CELLINI HAD HAD A SON, AND THAT SON WERE leaving him, he could not have felt worse. He wept. Paulino—little Paulino who had refused to desert him all through the plague—was leaving, returning home. There was no help for it, the thing had to be. An older brother had died suddenly, and the lad's father came to take him back to the family circle. It was necessary that he now shoulder the duties and privileges of a first-born. The goldsmith loaded his little shopboy with baggage, clothing, money, and for a parting gift gave him what he knew would be appreciated beyond anything else on earth—the shaggy-haired pony. That set Paulino to turning handsprings. He was sorry to have to leave. Life had always been lively and full of surprises with this young goldsmith he'd been apprenticed to. Things were never dull. But the pony filled his cup to such a level that happiness was the only emotion he was capable of feeling. Even so there was a tearful farewell; and many times afterwards he reflected on all those happy times with his Master Benvenuto. What a hell-raiser! What an education for a young man!

Work at the shop was picking up by leaps and bounds. The silver cup was well along. A series of fads came into vogue and set business to jumping. The first of them was brought into fashion by all the battle talk and interest in soldiering. Every gentleman in the city was ordering damascened armor. The armorers and goldsmiths of Rome reaped a harvest. Cellini worked mainly on the cuirass and hat of the ensemble, especially the hats. He designed armets, morions and sallets, until he was sick of looking at them. The requirements were always the same: a steel shell fancifully crested with some ferocious beast or dragon poised in a crouch and waiting to spring at its prey.

A fad for inlaid poniards followed. It started when some little Turkish daggers came into the Florentine's possession. All of iron—hilt, blade and sheath—they were engraved with foliage patterns done in a Turkish style and neatly filled in with gold. The mere sight of them stirred Cellini to action. If an infidel Turk could do that, then he intended to do better! He did. The canny Florentine merged crude utility with a delicacy of design that delighted the eye, and was rewarded with a slew of commissions as soon as he began exhibiting the weapons he had made. These surpassed the Turkish samples by far. His poniards were made of tempered steel, with a quadrangular blade that rang like a bell and gleamed blue as the twilight sky. The haft fitted into the curve of one's hand as smoothly and snugly as the joined lips of two lovers. And, of course, there were aesthetic considerations. The arabesques he designed swirled and waved around the dagger hilt and sheath in weaving patterns of bryony and ivy and acanthus. Flowers and miniature animals intermingled in an endless diversity of curling forms. There were grotesques and monsters no one ever saw before or would see again, since they were figments of an active imagination, supreme craftsmanship, and unsurpassed skill. As Cellini's friend and patron, the Florentine lord Giovanni Gaddi put it: "One might say it would almost be a pleasure to be stabbed by a poniard of such graceful line and exquisite beauty. You have proved yourself anew, my Benvenuto."

The rollicking society of roisterers broke up and scattered with the winds, business taking many of the members out of Rome. Michele Agnolo left to begin work on the monument of the late Pope Adrian. Of the others, one went this way, one that, each looking to his affairs. Even Giulio Romano was gone—forced to fly from the city.

The forced flight came about as much for Giulio's artistic ability as for an ode written by that most unconventional man of letters, Pietro Aretino. Pietro had written a panegyric composed of sixteen sonnets, each of them refulgent with the mood and method of that most thrilling of all congresses which occurs betwixt the sexes—physical love. The openly and self-acknowledged son of a prostitute, Pietro was not one to be sparing in his choice of words. He had written with an inspired quill.

Giulio was captivated by the charm of this doggerel, aside from the theme of which it treated. Accordingly, it had required but little urging by the poet to induce him to immortalize this heated verse by illustrating each sonnet with an appropriate drawing. He achieved a graphic delineation that was spectacular to a degree, and very definitely on the realistic side.

As such things usually did, news of this erotic tour de force eventually reached Clement. He was distressed. When the copies he ordered were brought in for a personal inspection, he was horrified. Here was gratitude! Not only were these obscenities the work of a man he had aided to eminence as a first-rate painter, the ode itself was penned by a lazar who had received his first pension from him. This because of a laud Aretino had written, extolling the virtues of Clement VII. A laud in doggerel. A sonnet of fourteen lines! The relationship was revolting! He ordered the Bargello to apprehend both of these miscreants. He'd see how a taste of the cells in Sant' Angelo suited their artistic tastes.

But the elfin Aretino had already flown to Reggio and the protection of another Medici—the invincible Giovanni delle Bande Nere. As for Giulio Pippi, otherwise known as *the Roman,* he wasn't around either. Advised by his friends at court of the Pontiff's reaction and orders, he was off to Mantua and the service of the Marquis of that

Principality, the valorous and perhaps more liberal minded Federigo Gonzaga.

On the other hand, there wasn't too much time which Clement could devote toward exacting a just vengeance for these doings. There was a matter of far greater moment which needed his attention. His on-and-off ally and King of France, Francis I, had finally secured his freedom from the Emperor.

The Frenchman, vaunted monarch that he was, had been hard put to bear up under the hospitality provided by the royal Charles. The terms to which he had to agree in order to win freedom were onerous, but after what he had been through he was ready to accept any terms whatever. He had to agree not to attack Milan again, to restore Burgundy, to reinstate the renegade Duke of Bourbon in the estates shamelessly robbed from him at the instigation of Francis' own rapacious mother, the doughty Louise of Savoy, and other things. He promised. And why not? Jail, even in a castle, was still jail! Insufferable to a gentleman whose life was dedicated to three noble pursuits which he always took great care to list in the order of their importance: love, the chase, and war.

He couldn't very well engage to wage any wars when he was incarcerated. There was too little freedom of movement. Nor could he go traipsing gaily about the countryside, tracking down game. Those jailors of his nasty bastards, every last one—wouldn't even hear of it.

As for making love—there he was about ready to shriek. This was the one point in which the lecherous boors who had the keeping of him had shown a spark of gallantry. They had, from time to time, passed in what they referred to as "select gentlewomen." He was speechless! These Spanish jades were positively beyond description. They didn't make love. They assaulted you! Lunged at you in a frenzy of action, like tigresses. It was as though they had never before known of what manner of pastry a man is made. *Foi de gentilhomme,* he could thank that one lucky star which shone for him that he was a ruggedly-built specimen of a man. There had been several occasions when he could have sworn his ribs had been cracked in the onslaught. It was an unbelievable experience. Here was none of the sweet and tender fondling so characteristic of the ladies of his own wondrous France. Instead, the violence of a baker kneading dough! None of the gentle "Oh's" and "Ah's" from moist red lips, which brought a man back with renewed vigor and unslaked thirst. He'd had enough!

83

He agreed to everything, gave over his two sons as hostages in token of agreement, and rushed back to his France.

No sooner did he again tread on the beloved soil of his homeland than he peremptorily repudiated everything he had agreed to. He sent representation to Clement, offering that the treatment to which he had been subjected more than justified this.

Clement, who didn't relish the ever increasing power of the Emperor, speedily absolved him of any taint for so doing.

All of this may have been amusing up to a point, and the talk of Rome, but it elicited no more than a ripple of interest from the busy Cellini. He had other things on his mind. Another fad, which he had carefully nursed into being, was growing in popularity: rings, iron rings inlaid with gold, which formed a talisman that kept the wearer of one free from insanity.

In his busy shop he displayed a selection of these, made for various patrons, to Aurelio Bellardi. The nobleman was enraptured.

"They are matchless, Benvenuto. Incomparable! You are without peer in your art. Certainly they are vastly superior to these ancient models you show me here. Whence came these originals, master?"

"They were found in some little antique urns which I came upon while journeying in the Campagna, my lord," Cellini answered gravely. "The vases were filled with ashes, and when I emptied them these rings tumbled out. As you see they are simple iron rings inlaid with gold, each set with a tiny cameo of shell. A pity the iron is so badly corroded."

"Indeed, yes," agreed Bellardi. "And what is this you say about their cabalistic value?"

"Curiosity prompted me to discover what purpose such simple rings served," sagely murmured the goldsmith. "So I applied to men of learning in these matters, scholars wondrously wise in the knowledge of ancient lore. They have stated that these rings are potent amulets, once worn by folk who desired to abide with firm mind, unshaken by any extraordinary circumstance or calamity, either of good or evil fortune."

To doubt this interesting allegation never occurred to Cellini or his caller. Witches were condemned to the stake daily. Astrologers and mystics were consulted by everyone. Why, then, doubt the efficacy of such a talisman? Everyone wore a charm which warded off the Evil Eye. Why not a ring that kept madness at a distance?

"Upon displaying these rings to some of my patrons," continued the goldsmith warmly, "I was commissioned to fashion some for their own use. I did so, making mine of tempered, refined steel. These, when engraved with exactly the same configurations seen on the originals, produced so fine an effect that I am now engaged in making many such."

"Hm-m-m. You are perhaps too fully occupied to oblige me, Master Benvenuto? I hope not." Messer Aurelio saw fit to use an imploring tone. "I would see you well satisfied in the matter. Forty crowns, so you achieve a fine work. What say you?"

"Eh, my lord. Could I dare refuse a gentleman of the stature of Your Excellency? Done, *messere.*"

Few if any commissions were coming from the Vatican. Clement was too fully occupied with his intrigues. He was tremendously busy just then on a political something called the Holy League, which he intended to use as a bridle for Charles V. The Emperor's reaction to it was a foregone conclusion: nobody likes a halter.

All that summer Cellini worked on rings—and then, medals. Another fad entered the epoch. It became the fashion to wear a medal in one's hat, the face of which was cut with whatever fancy was decreed by the person who ordered it.

Clement was still deeply involved with his cabals. He was very upset that August. The Emperor Charles had countered his Holy League by issuing a manifesto which systematically set forth all of the perfidy and devious manipulations practiced by the Supreme Pontiff. Nor was that all Charles did. He sent orders to his Viceroy in Naples, commanding him to proceed to Rome as his special representative to the Holy See—with a plan.

Don Ugo de Moncada came to the capital and began to amuse the cunning Clement with negotiations, advice, and a multitude of reasons which made an immediate withdrawal from the Holy League advisable. At the same time, the *hidalgo* was secretly aiding and stirring up the rankling resentment of the powerful Colonna. That Roman family's regard for Clement—who had excommunicated the lot of them and annexed many of their possessions, for reasons purely political—was the purest distillate of hate.

That was in September. On the twentieth day of that month, the vogue for ordering little fancifully engraved medals ended abruptly.

It was a clear, sunny morning. The merest touch of the approaching autumn was in the air, giving it a wine-like zest. The Romans had started about their daily affairs, when suddenly the city was overrun with the soldiers and followers of the Colonna; all acting in clock-like concert under the banner of Pompeo, former cardinal and chief-captain of that ancient Ghibelline House.

Cellini immediately buried all articles of value and was donning armor, when Alessandro del Bene rode up to the shop with an offer. His father, the illustrious lord Piero, wished to employ the goldsmith for the defense of his palace. Was Cellini interested? The pay was good, and there was the prospect of some spirited action.

The offer was delightfully accepted.

But the Colonna were interested only in Clement. While bands of their soldiers held the city gates, and others paraded through the streets to prevent any surprise counterattack, the main body calmly and lei-surely sacked the Vatican, St. Peter's, and the palaces of the more hated of Clement's faction.

The Pope and cardinals of the court fled to the refuge of Sant' Angelo, the fortified circular tomb of the Emperor Hadrian which was connected with the Vatican by a stone corridor. The Colonna promptly surrounded the place, listened heedlessly while the enraged Pontiff thundered his wrath at this despicable affront to his holy person and to the dignity of the Church, and went right along with their looting. It was all very orderly. Cellini watched it from the roof of the Del Bene palace.

Clement swore he would never bow to the demands of such scoun-drels. Never would he give in to such unmitigated villainy! Within two days the food supply in the Castel Sant' Angelo gave out. The Medici Pope had to revoke the excommunication decree against the Colonna; restore all their former possessions; withdraw all Papal troops from the vicinity of Milan—this at the behest of Moncada; promise to withdraw from the Holy League; and give over hostages as a sign of his good faith and intention to carry out these conditions.

The Colonna withdrew their troops and Clement withdrew to lick his wounds and quietly begin hiring mercenaries. He wasn't through with the Colonna by any means—hostages or no hostages. When his troops reached sufficient strength they swooped down on the Signories of the Colonna in a concerted and devastating attack. Four-teen of their castles were razed in the general massacres that resulted.

In Rome Moncada paled at the thought of his royal master's

reaction to this murderous vendetta. In point of fact, he did right to feel concern. This was just the sort of thing that would give the Emperor Charles something to think about.

The rest of the year was tranquil and serene, and Cellini spent the period in a sustained effort to further his reputation as a master. Toward the end of January, Alessandro del Bene dropped in and asked him to attend his father as soon as was convenient. The Del Bene were on Cellini's preferred list of patrons, so with the thought that an interesting commission might be put in his way, he called on the nobleman after dinner.

The erect and elderly lord Piero smiled a greeting and waved him to a chair.

Cellini bowed. "I gathered from Your Excellency's message that I might have the honor of being of service," he remarked courteously, accepting the goblet of wine presented by a servant.

"In a sense that is true, master." Piero del Bene frowned and fingered his pointed beard. He was a man of lively intelligence. He had seen much of life and men and had long ago learned to tread cautiously and with careful thought. Sudden disaster, like sudden death, was a distressingly common occurrence, and he preferred, whenever possible, to plan ahead. "Benvenuto, have you perchance heard anything of a rumor to the effect that a Spanish army is marching south from Milan?"

Cellini looked at him without expression. "No, my lord. Not a word."

The nobleman pondered, gazing out the window into his garden. "There may be nothing at all to what I have heard, you understand. A report has reached me and several others here in Rome, including His Holiness. It may be sheer fancy. Womanish imagination. However—" he paused, pursing his lips, his fingers curling into the gray of his beard. "However, I have deemed it best to discuss certain precautionary measures, even though they may seem totally unnecessary at the moment. I have requested you to attend me in order to ask that you hold yourself ready to again enter my service for the defense of my palace and household."

"Defense, Messer Piero?" Cellini raised his brows. "Defense against what?"

The elderly Del Bene sighed softly and sank into a chair. "Perhaps nothing," he admitted. "I most sincerely hope so. I have received word that the Duke of Bourbon has collected a powerful force and is marching south. My fixed opinion is that if Bourbon is moving at all, it is with the intent to march on Rome."

Cellini stared, round-eyed and skeptical. March an enemy army down central Italy and attack the Eternal City? Idiocy!

Del Bene saw and interpreted the look. He smiled wanly. "I am well aware that all this sounds rather foolish. As I have pointed out, I am merely discussing precautions. I may count on you?"

"Always and at any time, Excellency. But frankly—" The goldsmith shrugged.

"My thanks, Benvenuto. That is what I wished to learn. We will leave the matter thus, with the hope that we shall never have to pick up the thread of it. Still," the keen old eyes clouded, "to speak frankly, I cannot shake off my concern.... And, oh yes...I very nearly forgot. Here...I received various papers from my associates in Florence. This letter for you was among them."

Cellini excused himself and broke open the seal. If the lord Piero's fears had caused him any concern, this vanished from his mind as he read. The letter was from Benedetto Varchi. His boyhood friend was coming to Rome on business, he wrote, and he was sending advance warning of that fact so that Cellini would know what was in store. Here was news!

XIII

THE VAGARIES OF TRAVEL WERE SUCH THAT nearly a month went by before the goldsmith embraced his old friend outside the inn next to the post station, where Varchi paused to wash off the stains of the journey before making his way to the Vatican and Clement. Feeling great joy, they clouted each other's shoulders. The eyes of both were glistening.

"Benedetto! You old rogue! You're looking famously—and that beard!" Cellini whistled. "You are in good health?"

"Eh, old fellow..." Varchi's dusty shoulders lifted halfway to his ears as he raised a hand in one of those Italian gestures which defy description. *"Così-così.* And you, my Neutino? It has been so long. Too long! How are you getting on?"

The goldsmith motioned to the moon-faced innkeeper who stood by beaming, and ordered refreshment. He turned back to his boyhood companion.

"You don't need to answer, *compagnone,"* Benedetto grinned at him. "I already know. Word of your fame has traveled, you see. Here you are a master! Hah!" The historian grasped his friend's shoulders and shook them. "In Florence we are told that you work like a Vulcan, love like an Adonis, and fight like a Mars. Knowing you, I would say the description is precise. *E bene?"*

"What would you, old friend? Remove what you have named and what remains of this comedy that is life? But my father, Benedetto? What of him? You left him well?"

"Well and happy. Age serves only to increase his wisdom. Of necessity, his pride has increased out of all proportion. It's the one fault to complain of—his constant boasting of the genius displayed by his progeny. Your sisters are also in good health and send their love. As for your brother, Cecchino, he's doing splendidly. He has won honor in the service of Giovanni de' Medici. He was in Florence when I left, lording it over us poor stay-at-homes, and strutting about in the gray-black armor of Giovanni's Black Bands." Varchi looked around and wrinkled his nose disdainfully. "Rome hasn't changed, has it? Pfui! What foul air! What a stench!"

They were standing in a yard between the outbuildings and the inn, a stink hole reeking with heavy smells.

"That's your pride talking," laughed Cellini. "You never could see any place but Florence, and there it smells just as badly as here. Let's go inside. You can do with a glass of wine."

News from home! Intimate and reliable news. Attentive ears absorbed it greedily. Varchi imparted all manner of gossip. It didn't matter. It was all welcome.

"How long will you be here, Benedetto?"

"Only a few days. I came at Clement's order, to discuss certain documents relating to the affairs of the Medici. I shall have to stay at the Vatican."

Benedetto flung the towel he was using to a corner and finished dressing. Since he would probably be called into audience as soon as he arrived at the Papal palace, he clothed himself in the somber, scholarly robes befitting the dignity of his calling. His long, dark-red doublet showed a white ruff at the neck. Its plainness was relieved by a heavy gold neck-chain and medallion. The comparative simplicity of the costume emphasized the sensitive, intelligent face beneath the close-cropped black hair. Varchi looked, every bit of him, the historian and distinguished man of letters.

Cellini looked on, voicing approval. "Very good," he nodded. "Excellent taste and sound method. No one can say you lack guile, my friend. You cut a proper figure, *per Bacco.* Dignified as a Bishop. But what's this about staying at the Vatican? You mean we won't be seeing each other?"

Varchi chuckled. "I'll not have much free time, I fear. Remember, my Neutino, I'm at the orders of Pope Clement. However, I promise to spend this evening with you if I hang for it. We'll talk all night." Varchi paused and looked at his friend. "What is it, gossip?"

There was a bemused expression on the goldsmith's face. "Heh? Oh, nothing much. I just this moment thought of something. Tell me, Benedetto, have you heard any of this jabber about an Imperial army moving south?"

"Jabber? That is not jabber, *amico.* It's the truth, verified by the government in Florence. Bourbon is moving south. They're greatly worried, at home. It means trouble. That horde isn't walking down Italy just to take some air."

"*Dimmi,* you know something of all this?"

"Something of it, surely. But—" Varchi stopped as knuckles rapped against the door. A servant called out the information that a page waited below to conduct *il signore* to the Palazzo del Papa.

"I'll come down directly," the historian called back. "Bid the fellow wait. You see," he looked at Cellini and made a face. "There is no time. I carry letters to His Holiness, so I'd best be off quickly. In this way I will finish the sooner." He picked up his round, low-crowned hat and a black cloak. A flat bag full of documents and letters lay on the bed. "I will see you this evening."

"I'll be waiting, so don't fail to come. If you must, tell Clement you're ill with the pox. That will release you."

Varchi chuckled again and picked up the flat bag. "Until then, *addio.*"

The supper that evening was Lucullan—good food, fine and mellow wine, interlarded with reminiscence and talk on more current doings. When it was over and the platter of fruit, the bowl of nuts, and the flagon of sweet wine that marks the termination of the Italian's ritual to the cult of the belly, were placed on the table, the goldsmith and his guest eased their belts and sat back in a mood of contented and reflective passivity. Varchi's eyes were closed and his fingers toyed idly with the stem of his goblet.

"An excellent supper, Neutino," he murmured. "I'm much the better for it. It has served to reassure me. You remember your question about the Imperial army? Do you know, I've had to answer that same question a hundred times since this morning. There is a tension here, an undercurrent of fear pulling at the sleeve of every man that has asked it. It's as if they had to keep glancing around a room in order to prove to themselves that someone or something they dread has not silently entered."

It was no more than the truth. In Rome, the citizen in the street was contemptuous of any danger. The merchant class was indifferent. They didn't have time to bother. Among the haughty nobles, the only class who more or less knew what was going on in the world, a tension was beginning to make itself felt. One couldn't define it. There was no imminent danger. Bourbon, if he was marching at all, was marching on Florence, or Urbino, or some other city in the north. Not Rome. He couldn't possibly push that far down into Italy. Besides, who would dare attack the Apostolic See? Sacrilege! Still, the tension persisted. It was so real it almost seemed tangible.

"It is the opinion of one man I conversed with," continued Varchi, "that a terrible retribution is about to be visited on Italy. He is a worthy and very devout Cistercian, who sees little good in this depraved city. For which reason he is regarded as an ass. He maintained that this modern Sodom and Gomorrah—those were his very words—will someday be subjected to a visitation of Divine wrath. I wonder?"

"That Bourbon," Cellini drawled lazily and sat up straighter. "I still think it's nothing but jabber. If he is intent on war, then why move south? Why not stay in the north, where there is plenty for any army to occupy itself with? There are some here who believe he has designs on Rome. I was even approached by the lord Piero del Bene, a clever man, who requested my service if the danger should grow. It's ridiculous. What it will boil down to, if anything, is probably

91

nothing more than a move based on some strategy or other. They're applying pressure on someone. I'll wager on it."

"As to that, I don't know," Varchi answered soberly. "I do know that he is on the march."

"I don't see why that should bother Rome, or Clement for that matter. Unless he's concerned for Bologna."

"You don't? The error in your reasoning, Neutino, lies in the fact that you have never been interested in these things. You have never raised your head to see what is going on all around you. Clement is indeed involved. He's involved up to his ears."

"Another wager I would make is that you have every little detail of this cabal stored away in that brain of yours, Benedetto. Well, tell me about it. But first—moisten your tongue a bit. Drink up."

Varchi raised his goblet. "There isn't much to tell, really," he told his friend. "Examine the thing thus: Whatever plans Clement makes, whatever direction he takes—this jumping back and forth with his alliances—has but one motive, the security of the Medici. And there aren't many Medici left—on his side of the family. There's Catherine, the only legitimate heiress; and two males, Ippolito and Alessandro, both illegitimate. They're all in Florence, under the care of Passerini."

Cellini laughed. "The baton sinister. There's nothing unusual in bastardy, my friend. It happens in the best of families—particularly in the best families."

"True." Varchi smiled. "But about those two males, Ippolito is actually who they say he is, a natural son of Clement's late cousin, the Duke of Nemours. As for Alessandro . . . It was given out that he is the offspring of Lorenzo. The Lorenzo who was made Duke of Urbino after Clement and his uncle, Leo X, stole the duchy from the Della Roveres. But this is not so."

"No?"

"No, my friend. When first he was seen at home, everyone remarked his woolly hair, dark complexion—very dark, Neutino—in short, his negroid appearance. They also wondered why the Medici waited until Lorenzo had died, before claiming that this unknown boy was his bastard. Well, old fellow, there are people in Florence who make it to their interests to look into things. They looked very closely into this certain thing called Alessandro. It took time, and a great deal of gold, but the answer was found. He isn't Lorenzo's son. Mark this well, Neutino. *He is the son of none other than Giulio de'*

Medici! The spawn of a union between Giulio and a mulatto-Moor he bedded in Spain, during the Medici exile. Some say she was a slave; others, that she was a whore."

"What? Nonsense!"

"Not nonsense, my friend. Fact! It is the exact truth, just as I have stated it. For some reason, Giulio, now Clement, wishes to hide that fact. That's why the lad was reared in Naples and kept hidden until a suitable father could be found."

"And what do they say of Alessandro in Florence?"

"Say? In the beginning, he was well received. Like Ippolito, who is much admired. But as time went on, his true nature began to show. The youth is a sadistic monster, an abomination of God. He is easily the most inhuman, bestial creature ever to enter our city. These traits, plus the fact that Clement is his true father, give many cause for concern."

"And so?"

"And so—nothing. He has been elected to office. Up until now that is as far as he has gone. *Dunque,* so much for what remains of the elder Medici line." Benedetto's voice had thickened from the well-aged muscadine. Cellini was feeling drowsy and his shining eyes were acquiring a blank, vacant stare.

"Now, consider Clement's politics," Varchi swallowed and went on. "Not for nothing is he known as the 'Master of Craft.' Ever since he attained the Papacy he has kept the balance of power in Italy, and in Europe, in a state of continual upset. Playing one ruler against the other with truly remarkable adroitness, all for just one end—the glory of his House."

Cellini smiled dryly. "Here in Rome, there was a great deal being said about all this jumping back and forth. Everyone wondered why."

"The answer actually is simple. It was done to keep both Francis and Charles off balance. Doing so, you see, takes care of most of Europe, which must then choose a side or remain strictly neutral. Charles has tried everything in his power to counter this policy, and has been growing steadily stronger. This so worried Clement that he created the Holy League—an alliance between himself, France, England, Venice, Florence, and the ousted Sforza of Milan. The avowed purpose of the League is to stop Charles. It has an army of thirty-five thousand men, commanded by the Duke of Urbino—the same Della Rovere who was kicked out of his duchy. He regained it after Leo's death, which in no way assuages his hatred for anything connected with the name of Medici. His efforts at stopping Charles have been conspicuously unsuccessful. That's why this move by Bourbon can be so dangerous. There's no one to stop him." Varchi stretched and yawned. "Ho—it grows late, Neutino."

"What do you think the Bourbon's up to, Benedetto?"

"Ask the devil, gossip. He's about the only one who knows for certain. You wish to know what I think? I think the Emperor is gorged with Clement's duplicity and intends to pay him back for everything he has had to put up with from him. I think he is sending Bourbon to capture and sack Florence. And it could easily be even more than this—much more! Bourbon could continue south, even here to Rome, and afterwards hole up very comfortably in Naples. As I say, there is nothing and no one to stop him."

"*E bene!*" Cellini's eyes began to gleam from more than an excess of muscadine. He screwed up a thoughtful brow and noisily emptied his goblet. "*Via!* It's jus' as well that the lord Piero spoke of using my services. Who knows? Perhaps we'll see some action." He lurched unsteadily to his feet. "C'mon, friend Benedetto, I'll walk back to the Vatican with you." He eructed. "Y'might get lost, by yourself..."

XIV

STANDING NEAR A WINDOW OF HIS PRIVATE study in the ducal palace of Milan, Charles, Duke of Bourbon, clasped his lean hands behind a straight, stiffly erect back, and unconsciously squared his shoulders. His piercing eyes roamed thoughtfully but coldly over the narrow, dirty streets of his prize city, a city he would soon be leaving behind him. His Milan! His head lifted so high his black beard jutted straight out in front of him. Two years ago, after the seizure of his archenemy King Francis, the Emperor had invested him with the duchy. It had been lost and rewon since, and he idly speculated if this would ever recur.

The thought of Francis flashing across his mind made him snort scornfully, while the cold look in his eyes changed to a blaze of fury.

Dear, ratty, cousin Francis! The incredible fool who was responsible for all this travail. And that royal mother of his—Bourbon's eyes smoldered anew at the mere thought of that calamitous female! She it was behind all his troubles. Louise of Savoy! The Queen Mother! How long ago was it that she began her underhanded tactics? Five years? Six? He scarcely remembered. But it was no trouble to recall the episode that had started her off. That came back vividly and effortlessly. It happened shortly after his wife's death. It had been requested that he attend Francis and his mother in private audience; and he had done so, as was expected when a king made a request that was tantamount to a command.

And what had been demanded of him?

Marriage to the Queen Mother!

Marriage, mark you! as though he, a Bourbon and every whit as royal as the ruling House, were some churlish lordling pawn to be moved about at whim. A long thin lip curled wolfishly as he recalled the look of surprised consternation and anger that twitched at the Queen Mother's face, when he laughed and spurned the proffer of her hand. It had been the wrong move, of course. He knew it then, and he knew it even better now. The rankling venom in Louise's tender bosom flamed into a bitter implacable hatred for the man who had forced upon her this new role of a woman scorned. From that moment she and her son made his life in France one mounting impossibility— a relentless persecution which ended in his desertion and the offer of his services to the Emperor Charles.

Now, after four years of war, here he was in the ducal palace of Milan, looking down on the filthy, tatterdemalion ruffians who made up his army. They swaggered about, Spaniards, Neapolitans, Germans, Swiss, Flemings, English, Scots, thieves and cutthroats from every nation in the world—the scum of Europe for the most part. All of them with empty bellies, ragged backs, scowling faces, and rage-filled eyes. *Sang de Dieu!* one could scarcely resent their anger and restlessness. Any man has the right to expect payment for his services. Even soldiers. Especially soldiers! These men had not been paid for months. Here he was alone, too. Pascara dead; Lannoy in Naples; only Del Guasto and De Leyva on hand to help control this angry rabble. All of his jewels were in pawn, as were those of his two chief aides and a few of the higher-ranking officers. The money they'd brought in had not gone very far. Those arrears were too large.

95

And to further increase his difficulties, the Lutheran reinforcements from Germany—fetid dregs of the peasant uprising there—had been swarming in for two months. Sixteen thousand sons of the Devil, commanded by the iron-handed George von Frundsberg and the youthful Philibert, Prince of Orange. Bourbon smiled grimly. To his mind a more unholy alliance was never joined. Catholic Spaniards and heretic Lutherans banded together to war on the Pope! The Germans hadn't been paid either. Why? Was this madness...or some subtle finesse? He had given the matter much thought and had come to the conclusion that if it was madness, it was of a sort in which considerable method was evident. It was all too pat, too carefully planned. It achieved just exactly the effect desired. The men growled and demanded action. Pillage, loot, food!

The Spaniards were not choosy. They didn't care where the loot was to be had, so long as they had the getting of it. But the German lansquenets wanted Rome—and Pope Clement, the Antichrist! Frundsberg even carried a length of silken rope, reserved for the special use of hanging Clement high.

The Emperor, as is the way with emperors, was forwarding despatches by the bagful. They arrived daily, tersely written orders which always resolved themselves to one specific command: Bourbon was to march on and invest the Papal States as soon as the German allies joined him. Letters and despatches aplenty—but no gold. That detail was always overlooked; Bourbon's demands for it, always ignored.

A knock sounded on the door. Bourbon turned as it opened and watched Antonio de Leyva stride into the room. The Duke looked inquiringly at his chief aide.

De Leyva nodded briefly, tugging at the short skirt of his embroidered doublet. "All is ready, Your Grace. You can lead out the men whenever you have a mind to. Have you decided on the time?"

"As quickly as possible, my dear Antonio." Bourbon sighed deeply, shaking his head. "If we do not act quickly, this rabble will be about our ears. Best to offset that by letting them exert themselves elsewhere, eh?"

De Leyva nodded agreement. "That is true. With a long march ahead of them, there will be less time for complaints."

"I don't know about that, Antonio." Bourbon turned and looked out the window. "It's a cold January. Crossing the mountains will be anything but warm work."

96

The chief aide's hard smile was grim. "They'll listen to you. They'll march too. That scum is hungry—for loot as much as for food. Yet, God grant you find food. Else you will have an uprising on your hands. The men are in an ugly mood. You do right to move quickly."

"Tomorrow, then. All is ready, you say?"

"Everything, my lord. Your Grace has but to don armor and mount."

"Very well. Tomorrow. Give orders."

The army set in motion. Things went tolerably at first; then they took a bad turn. Food was short. Hunger gnawed first at bellies, then at tempers. At Piacenza there arose an ugly muttering and considerable squabbling. Bourbon didn't stop. He continued down and over to Bologna, intending to sack that fat city in order to take the edge off his men. But when he reached its vicinity the clamor rose so violently, he had to stop and take hold.

While he was thus engaged, Clement, alternately thundering and quailing, forwarded a frenzied Papal Nuncio to his staunch friend and ally, Francis I. "Come forward with your valorous troops, as you have promised us," he exhorted. "Achieve glory now, lest the Emperor triumph, to your eternal disgrace ..."

At that particular moment Francis was busy with the building of another palace. This one at Chambord—a beautiful place. He lacked the time to give much thought to glory. Who was it that had been compelled to suffer through that nerve-racking imprisonment in horrendous Spain? Had it been Clement?

His answer to the Pope, such as it was, contained a bright new set of promises. These, at most, required but the ink used to set them to paper. After which he set out on a gay hunting and whoring party into Champagne.

Bourbon, on the other hand, had a full-fledged mutiny on his hands. His scabrous, gaunt scarecrows were cold, hungry, and bitterly savage. It was something that he managed any semblance of control over such out-and-out cutthroats bent solely on personal gain. Only for this were they ready to fight, and, if necessary, to chance being killed. What they wanted was loot, and at the moment—food! With both lacking they were not an army but a ravening horde of bloodthirsty murderers.

That was what Bourbon faced.

97

But the regal Charles was a man of quality. His personal bravery was beyond question, and the men knew it. He was a gifted soldier—they knew that too. He'd proved it often enough. More than all this, he was a man of noble stature. He had presence! If he made a promise his men instinctively relied on its being kept. So he made them a speech, painted a glowing picture in the rich colors of gold, jewels, clothing, of loot and food and women—waiting in the south. The plunder of some rich city was what he promised.

For that, they would continue. But let him receive help from heaven if he didn't perform as stated. They made that clear, and started south again.

That sermon held them in check for a month, till the latter part of March. By then the Imperial army was in rags and its sorry-looking members reduced to venting their anger by aimlessly slitting the throats of such peasants as were too slow or dim-witted to move out of their path. They were eating grass—like cattle. And if that wasn't enough! God Himself had to take a hand in their misery by sending bitter torrent after bitter torrent pelting down on their weary heads and threadbare backs. The rain sloughed off them to mingle with the earth and create a swirl of sticky ooze through which they could drag their rag-covered feet.

They blamed Bourbon for it. Undoubtedly, it was their commander who had, somehow, offended God! It made them so mad they looted his tent, and, just then, would have taken him apart joint by joint, had he not been a little beforehand of them and taken refuge with Von Frundsberg and his Germans.

The Lutherans had confidence in Bourbon; as much and more than in their own captains. But they were no better off than their Spanish and other companions in arms and in misery. Their bellies growled just as loudly. The pelting rains soaked them just as thoroughly. They sickened and died just as miserably, as quickly, and in about equal quantity. They surrounded the commanders and made demands—gold, food, clothing. They had been promised their arrears in pay when Bologna was sighted—and they had passed Bologna!

"Patience!" screamed the purple-hued Von Frundsberg. He was as hungry, as wet, and as miserable, as any. "Patience, you gutter rats! And continue the march south! Everything you want is there! Gold, all you can carry; food, as much as your dirty bellies can hold; fine

98

clothing and women, soft and warm—all this in the south is waiting. *Schweinehunde! vögelde Ratten!* Get back into ranks!"

The men refused to listen. The tumult rose higher. Frundsberg raved and cursed and screamed himself into a fit of apoplexy. He died of the seizure.

That cowed the men. This undoubtedly was another sign! Muttering darkly, but tolerably manageable, they once again turned south, gorged with their venomous hate and an unholy lust for the blood of Pope Clement—who was responsible for all this misery.

As the relentless pressure mounted, Clement reached the height of his frenzy. He summoned Lannoy from Naples to a Papal audience and offered a hundred thousand ducats for a truce of eight months' duration. Even the Duke of Urbino became resolute. His own duchy now was in peril. Vigorously he pushed west to cover Florence, knowing full well that if that city fell, Urbino was doomed.

Lannoy brought the money north to Bourbon's camp, but he didn't dare enter it. The Lutherans got wind of the purpose of his visit and became so viciously bitter, they openly threatened death if he so much as spoke of a truce. Bourbon himself had to ride out to meet his old co-commander. He listened to the offer, took the money, then shook his head sadly.

"It's a futile attempt," he told him. "I require three times this amount for arrears in pay alone. And it would avail nothing if you had that much with you. The situation at my camp is such that I am listened to or obeyed only so long as I continue south. I can do nothing. This is the will of God!"

And Clement, who had stripped his treasury to make up that ransom, was already disbanding his mercenaries. Economy necessitated this move. He flattered himself, however, on having purchased the right to continue with his own plans. With that gold he had provided for the safety of his Florence, and had brushed away any possible threat to himself here in Rome.

The irresistible surge pushed south into the Apennines. Mountains, storms, rivers swollen into rushing torrents—these were as nothing. Like the hordes of that other scourge of God, Attila the Hun, the Imperialists swept forward, gutting everything in their path. By April the ragged, hate-filled army emerged beneath Arezzo. Now the plan was evident to all. There was no longer any doubt of the Bourbon's intent. The goal had not been Florence, nor yet Urbino. It was Rome!

Clement was beside himself. The frantic cries of his appeals could be heard on every side. Don Ugo de Moncada, still in Rome as Imperial Representative, rode north to meet Bourbon and try to reason with him. He didn't really expect to accomplish much, but for the sake of appearances, he thought to go through the motions. It would look well, and the Almighty would no doubt reckon it a good deed.

"Your Grace must not proceed farther south," he told the haggard Bourbon. "A treaty had been entered into between His Holiness and His Imperial Majesty. It guarantees the city. You must order your men back."

Bourbon held up a weary palm. He was feeling bitter. "I cannot, Don Ugo." He shook his head at the royal emissary, much as he had done to Lannoy. "I would not be obeyed. I no longer have any power over this human trash. They do as they please."

The next day, with fatal relentlessness, the march was resumed. The progress of the slavering riff-raff was so swift, they reached Viterbo before it became known in Rome that Bourbon had quitted his encampments in the territory of Siena.

In the Roman Campagna the birds were caroling, the olive groves were a sea of silver petals, and the blooming fruit trees, gay as the plumes on a gallant's *berretta,* towered over the surrounding fields. On the second day of May, the heretic hordes and their non-heretic allies spilled out into it, pressing ever onward toward Eternal Rome.

XV

WHEN THE PATTERN OF EVENTS FORMED AN unmistakable outline of what was coming, Cellini wasted no time in futile worry. He closed his shop and withdrew to a little cottage hidden behind the Banchi. There it was peaceful and quiet and one escaped the attention of the roving bands of disbanded mercenaries whose pleasantries created such a disturbance it was unwise to maintain a public shop.

By April all the work on hand was finished and delivered. By then the intent of the Imperial army also was clear. The Florentine began making arrangements. Personal funds were placed in the hands of bankers outside the troubled areas, and all business affairs were terminated. In two weeks' time Cellini was ready to devote full time to the matter at hand. He called on Piero del Bene.

"*Signor mio*," he began, after the servant closed the door of the nobleman's study, "I have called to take up the thread of the project Your Excellency discussed with me last January. It is now fairly certain that there will shortly be some fighting to do. I place myself at Your Lordship's command. What is your will?"

"Well said, my Benvenuto," answered the courtly Piero. He fingered his gray beard and leaned forward. "That which I suggested at the time you speak of, I order now. It is my desire that you enlist the services of fifty brave comrades, to be used in the defense and protection of my household. These lances will serve alongside my own guards. Further, I appoint you their captain, with pay and appointments equal to those we agreed on during the attack of the Colonnesi. Are you content with this arrangement?"

"Completely, my lord. I shall begin on the *impresa* immediately."

"Good. See to it."

Fifty select and tough *bravi* were enlisted in short order. The goldsmith's brawling had brought him wide acquaintance in such circles. As a consequence, his selection was careful and particular. The compact troop was quartered in the Del Bene palace, where it awaited developments. The pay was good, the accommodations excellent, their appointments the best available. The Del Bene were a rich family and this was no time to be niggardly.

Meanwhile in the sumptuous grandeur of the Vatican's chambers, a highly distraught Clement paced the floors. The situation which confronted him was a critical emergency that could easily prove to be the end of everything he had planned and worked for. Apparently there was no stopping these harrowing barbarians from the north. And he had, in a rash hour, been so unwise as to disband his three thousand Swiss. The only possible solution lay in a swift rearming. Every available man—craftsmen, shopkeepers, pages, servants, even the lowest dregs that infested the city—all must be impressed in a hasty levy. He ordered so.

A motley ruck of four thousand was thrown together, incised into artillery and foot, and placed under the orders of the Papal captain, Renzo da Ceri.

"You must see to using these men to best advantage in our behalf," Clement plaintively told his captain, who stood straight and stern before him.

"Your Holiness makes far too much of the danger," Renzo coolly assured the Pontiff. "Certain it is that in a moment of emergency, should any such arise, our Rome can quickly muster a force of thirty thousand men." He flicked out a hand. "More than enough with which to exterminate a roving horde of foreign marauders. Moreover, the walls of the city are in themselves a sufficient defense against an army that has no artillery. Let the Bourbon come, Your Beatitude. Let him approach! Within the space of a few days he will perish of starvation in the wastes without our walls."

"Think you so, indeed?" Clement was clutching at every straw.

"Aye, I do, Most Blessed Father. Another point, surely Your Holiness must know that the army of the League is afoot and should reach here shortly after Bourbon?"

"Yes, this fact is in truth of some small consolation to us," agreed Clement, without much heart. "But to return to this meager army on which we shall be compelled to depend for an immediate defense. You will require assistance in the command and ordering of these men, will you not?"

"A suitable officer to act as my aide would be of great service, Your Holiness."

"We have been giving some thought to his selection . . ." Clement paused to ponder. The man he had in mind was ideal. A professional soldier of the first rank, who, at the moment, happened to be incarcerated in one of the dungeons in Sant' Angelo for disturbing the peace—of his own signory. In spite of this, there was not a doubt in the Pontiff's mind but that the man would prove amenable and devote himself with zeal to such praiseworthy projects as the defense of Rome and the protection of his jailers.

"Summon here before us the lord Orazio Baglioni," he ordered.

That Perugian nobleman did not, of necessity, think very highly of the Medici Pope. It could not be expected that the victim of such a trap as he had fallen into would kiss its perpetrator on both cheeks.

On the other hand, Orazio Baglioni was a resilient and clever man. He knew enough of the world's rash ways to prepare against or take advantage of any sudden whimsies of fortune. For example, he himself had with laudable foresight seen to the efficient murdering of several much-too-closely-related kinsmen, in order that the rule of Perugia would fall to him alone. And had he not done so, one of those wretches would undoubtedly be ruling there now! Accordingly, he understood the gist of these matters. Understood that the modern man of affairs must be possessed of a temperament sufficiently elastic to withstand sudden shifts in policy. And he was a first-class *condottiere,* there was no doubt on that score. All the Baglioni were. They had to be—to live! In short, recognizing a piece of buttered bread when it was offered, he lauded the lenity being displayed by Clement and came to terms.

It used up the better part of the afternoon and evening to scrub the muck and filth and vermin off himself; but at the end of that time, Da Ceri could congratulate himself on having acquired a canny aide and useful co-captain.

Clement, however, still labored under considerable uncertainty. He had a dread of that French renegade and all those ragged, famished heretics of his, and voiced a desire to leave Rome until the whole vile mess was over and a thing of the past.

His cardinals wouldn't hear of it. They were implacable. The very idea! It was most supremely necessary, they baldly insisted, that the Pontiff be on hand to witness the annihilation of his enemies. Also, money was needed. And who but he himself could raise this? It could not be expected that the Supreme Pontiff would act in the manner of sundry merchants who, with appallingly misplaced prudence, had embarked their goods and themselves on barges, in order to effect an escape via the Tiber. These misguided imbeciles had been stopped and ordered to return to their homes. It was pointed out to them—a certain amount of persuasion was required to drive the point home—that such ridiculous precautions served only to raise the spirits of the invader and encourage him in his hopeless emprise. They must remain in the city, where they might better serve the community by contributing the ducats so badly needed for their defense.

The merchants of Rome looked askance, and held tightly to their purses. Why contribute gold? All was safe. There was nothing to worry one's brain over. The heretics did not have a chance. Why, all the sages and astrologers in the city were predicting victory.

In vain did a thunderbolt from on high dash the Infant Saviour from the arms of the beautifully sculptured Virgin that stood so proudly in the Church of Santa Maria in Traspontina. Utterly disregarded was the hapless fact that a mule-mare had dropped her foal in the Palazzo della Cancelleria! Not even when a consecrated Host leaped from the tabernacle in the very chapel of the Pope, did anyone take awesome alarm. All this, despite the unquestioned certainty that any one of these ill-starred omens was a dire portent, sufficient unto itself, to foretell that doom—disaster—impended.

Then came the news that the heretics had reached the Campagna. Cellini and his men gave their weapons a final, careful honing. Four days, at most, he told Alessandro, would suffice to bring the devil to the gates of Rome.

He misjudged by one day. On the evening of the fifth of May, Bourbon drew up in the meadows alongside the walls of the Trastevere and made camp. From there the greedy eyes of his men could feast on the rich palaces, churches, buildings, all filled with loot that was theirs for the taking.

A trumpeter and a herald carrying a pennon rode out of the camp and approached the section of wall where Renzo da Ceri waited. Bourbon had a message, a simple request. He was desirous of securing permission for the passage of his troops through the city. He was of the mind to go to Naples—by that particular route.

To such insolence Da Ceri could only answer in kind.

"Say to my lord Bourbon," he savagely spat out at the herald, "that he and all his rabble can go to the Devil—by way of Hell! Get you gone!"

The die was fully cast.

XVI

EARLY THE NEXT MORNING A THICK WREATH-ing mist began to form over the ground. As the dawning day cast its grayish light over the contorting tendrils that writhed in the soft spring breeze, the main force of the Imperialists waited impatiently for the signal to move up to the attack.

A vanguard of German lansquenets, covered by Spanish arquebusiers, had advanced in the dark and were already nearing the walls at Santo Spirito and the Borgo. The weather favored them. The low-lying fog provided such excellent cover that the attackers remained hidden until quite close to the positions selected for the assault. Slowly they crept nearer, dragging heavy scaling ladders along. They flinched momentarily under a sudden rain of crossbow bolts and the scattered fire from the defenders' arquebuses, which poured into them as soon as they came into view. Holding their shields over their heads and shoulders, they leaned over and pressed on, leaving the Spaniards behind to send up an harassing counterfire. The nearer they approached, the better targets they made. The dead and wounded lay where they fell; those who survived the hail of metal continued the advance until they reached the wall abutments. The heavy ladders were moved into position, and with ringing cries the first shock troops began to ascend, holding their wicked looking assault weapons—long, halberd-like pole-axes—ready. Their yells turned to shrill screams of agony as vats of blazing pitch, flaming oil and quicklime, poured down over them, making blazing torches of ladders and men alike. But when the last feeble moan died out and the stench of seared human flesh had blown away, there were ladders still in position and men already mounting them.

The trumpets blared an order. They were instantly answered by the fierce war whoops of the Spaniards. *"A muerta! Amazza! ... España! España!"*

The main body of the Imperialist army hurtled forward into battle and the attack against the walls of Rome was under way.

At the Del Bene palace, Cellini had been up before dawn for a final inspection of the defenses. He had just completed this when Alessandro approached.

"Look you, Benvenuto. Let us ride out as far as the walls at the Campo Santo and see for ourselves how the battle is progressing."

The goldsmith had been gnawing at a lip for an hour, vainly trying to think of a plausible excuse for doing that very thing.

"Fine idea," he answered, nodding gravely, as if the suggestion was receiving his most profound consideration. "We'll take one of my boys along for company, just in case."

Well armed with swords and firearms, the armor-clad group rode out of the *cortile* where they were joined by a young fire-eater, Cecchino della Casa, who was bound for the same place.

They trotted silently through the Via Lungara and the deserted streets of the Trastevere, past the barricades erected in the streets leading to the bridges that spanned the Tiber, until they reached the old cemetery of Santo Spirito. The din was terrific. Climbing to the ramparts of the city wall, they found that they must tread carefully, stepping over the bodies of fallen defenders. Close by, just to the right of where they stood, the deafening crescendo bespoke a raging battle which mounted ever fiercer. The mist was dense, but beginning to dissipate a little. The dim halo of the sun peeped gingerly over the horizon behind them, and it was now possible to see for short distances.

The growing light permitted the artillery in the nearby forts, including Sant' Angelo, to open fire. Smoke, flame and scrap iron belched out of the muzzles of swivels, falconets, culverines, and murderous bombards. Anything and everything on hand was being fired at the enemy. The swirling mist hampered the gunners, who were firing more by ear than by eye. Their cannonades tore lanes through the compact masses locked in combat, killing and maiming as many of their own men as enemies.

Till now, the battering assault against the walls was being contained. Four onslaughts had been hurled back, with terrible losses to both sides. At about the time Cellini and his companions reached the walls, a mixed company of Spanish foot, probing outside the walls, chanced upon a small building in the garden of Cardinal Ermellino's palazzo. The side of this house formed a part of the wall. It contained a porthole which had been made over into a window and an even lower opening which served to light the cellar. Two small holes— overlooked! The Imperialists crawled through like ants; one portion coming up on the defenders from the rear, the other fanning out into the Borgo.

While this was taking place, Cellini, looking out over the wall and not liking what he saw, turned to Alessandro, shaking his head.

"We had best get back home," he advised. "As you can see, we can do nothing here. Before very long the walls will be won. Good Christ! look there! Our cannons are slaughtering more Romans than Imperialists!"

Alessandro was shocked into panic by the sight all around them. "Would to God we had never come here," he cried. "You're right. Let's get back as quickly as God will let us." He scrambled down towards the horses below. The soldier and Cecchino della Casa scampered after him.

The goldsmith hung back, scowling. To turn tail in such craven fashion was more than his conceit and spirit would allow.

"A moment!" he snapped out sharply. "Since you have brought me here, it is necessary that we perform some action worthy of men before we leave. For myself, I mean to get at least one chance at these whoresons!" Cradling his gun in his arm, he walked carefully to the wall's scarp and looked down.

From among a packed group milling around one of the nearer ladders he selected for his target a man whose dress and aspect made him stand out from the others. Clearly this was an officer, and from the look and bearing of him, an important one. A white cloak partly covered but did not hide the damascened armor beneath it. His helmet was shaped in the form of a springing dragon whose wings swept down, protecting the ears. He was shouting and waving a sword which flashed weakly in the dim rays that were beginning to penetrate the mist. His boldness and spirit bespoke authority. As Cellini watched, the man grabbed at the ladder. The goldsmith raised his arquebus and sighted carefully. Slowly, tenderly, as the man began to mount, a steady finger squeezed the trigger.

The flash of the prime, the loud report of the charge, a spurt of orange flame, and through the acrid smoke he saw the sword drop from the man's hand as he clutched wildly at his chest and toppled to the ground. Instantly, men ran to him.

Cellini didn't know it then, but he had selected none other than the mighty Bourbon for his first target.

The goldsmith's fire drew wasps. A sporadic, ragged volley sprayed around the section of wall on which he stood. A whining *zinnngg-g-g-g* hissed past his ear, forcing him back behind the protective scarp. Turning he called to the others. They came over and methodically fired into the churning masses below. To miss was an impossibility.

They reloaded and fired three volleys before the answering enfilade compelled them to abandon the wall and return to the horses.

"This goes badly," offered the goldsmith as they descended. "The defense is crumbling and falling back. I fear it will prove impossible to save this side of the Tiber."

Things were going badly. Although the raw recruits were fighting well, the massed flow of the attackers could not be stemmed indefinitely. When the attack on the rear came it caused consternation and panic. The ranks broke and the men began to withdraw as best they could, dragging the cursing Da Ceri along with them. They slowly fell back to the barricades, while Da Ceri and Baglioni took to slashing those who turned away from the battle. It didn't help. One after the other the barricades fell, the defenders hacked to pieces by the enemy already inside them. The Borgo region of Rome, where stood the Vatican, St. Peter's, and many of the palaces of the noblemen-prelates, was lost. The retreating Romans fell back to the vicinity of the Ponte Sisto, leaving the streets lined with bodies and red with blood. The Imperialists spilled over into the Trastevere, butchering as they advanced.

The mounted quartet tried desperately to reach the Del Bene palace. They couldn't make it. The infiltrating enemy was at their heels and all around them. The only partly open route to safety lay toward Sant' Angelo. If they could reach that haven, some means might be found for returning to the Del Bene house, which stood on the east side of the river. And if the brutality already being evidenced by the Emperor's hordes was any indication of what could be expected from them, it was plain that the Del Bene household would need all the protection it could muster.

Galloping into a small court that opened on a piazza already in enemy hands, the four had to hack a bloody path through Spanish foot soldiers before they could turn into the narrow street which connected the Villa Barberini with the Porta Santo Spirito. The iron-shod hoofs of their mounts rang on the cobbles. Alessandro del Bene's horse had been wounded in the neck and was almost mad with terror.

"Croce di Cristo!" Della Casa panted, pointing, "look at that inhuman swine!"

A Spaniard who was with a company of lansquenets had caught sight of a heavy ring which glinted on the hand of a wounded officer lying in the street, his hands tightly clenched and beating the ground in pain. With the battle raging all around, the fellow dared not pause overlong. At the same time his avaricious eyes made it clear that he had no intention of passing up the ring. Coming up to the wounded man, he leaned over and grasped the fist, raised it, and with a swift stroke of his sword severed the hand at the wrist. The hoarse screech of pain that rose in the air meant nothing. The Spaniard had already turned away, cramming the bloody stump into his cuirass as he ran after his comrades who were heading toward a church.

The cursing Della Casa was on the verge of taking off after the man when Cellini, in front, pulled up quickly and brought his horse rearing to a sudden halt. The others did the same. Directly in front of them another pack of howling, blood-crazy lansquenets had turned into the street.

"They're too many for us," he shouted, looking wildly around. "This way, quickly!" They wheeled into another court, leaped a low wall and dashed out into a side street which led to the Piazza San Giovanni.

The lansquenets did not bother to follow. They turned off and joined the group headed toward the church. The desecration of churches was the special province of the Lutherans. All through the march south they had never passed one they did not gut and burn.

At the entrance of the building a monk stood resolute, holding up a heavy crucifix while he cried for mercy on behalf of the people locked within. The first of the Lutherans to reach him tore the cross from his hands and with demonic fury used it as a bludgeon. The thorn-encircled head of the metal Christ extended on the cross slammed and tore at the priest's head and face. Flesh ripped off his bearded cheeks in strips and furrows. One terrible blow clove his skull and a trickle of slimy gray pulp began to ooze slowly out and down over the sightless eyes.

The soldier's comrades had already set fire to the building. The blaze licked up and enveloped the old wood structure in a matter of minutes, while the shrieking within rose in a cacophony of dread. Soon the doors flung open and the people who had sought refuge in the house of God streamed out, stumbling blindly around the street, begging for mercy.

The lansquenets worked with smooth precision. All but the girls and younger women were cut down mercilessly. The handful of women who were spared were stripped and herded off under guard to a temporary prison. Later on, they would provide entertainment.

One of the girls caught the fancy of her guard, a burly German whose long mustaches curled straight out and up from both sides of a thick nose. He fingered these as he eyed the wench and, finding her pleasing, pulled her out and ran a greedy hand over the curve of her stomach, ending the gesture by cupping and squeezing one of her breasts. The girl became hysterical and clawed at his hand. The startled lansquenet rumbled out an oath, staring at the blood oozing from the scratches. It crazed him. He knocked the girl sprawling and kicked her senseless, tearing open a gash which extended from her neck to her hip. Her thigh and shoulder was a welter of bloody bruises. Appeased, he reached down and wound a hand in her hair and dragged her off after his comrades.

As he was doing so he ran into a squad of the Spanish allies who were now overrunning the Borgo. He greeted them with a fierce yell, pointing proudly to his swooning captive.

The officer commanding the squad held up a hand, signaling a halt. An obscene leer twitched at the corners of his eyes as they took in the dirty heretic and his prize. Beside him, tugging at their chains and snarling through bared fangs, were three gigantic mastiffs, held in leash by soldier lackeys. The dogs were powerful beasts, clad in steel armor and chain mail, the special pets of the captain, who had reared and trained them with loving care. The smell of fresh blood whipped them into a frenzy, and the sight of the bleeding, faintly moaning girl, her back and side ripped and flayed, sent them straining upright, forepaws clawing desperately at the air.

The captain's brow arched thoughtfully. Here, after the hard fighting on the walls, was a chance to catch one's breath and watch some sport. He signaled to the lackeys, who immediately loosed the dogs.

Two of them tore into the girl. Her thin scream of fear gurgled into a bubbling silence as the fangs of one ripped open her throat. The remaining mastiff streaked for the German lansquenet. They clashed and fell, the dog biting and tearing, the soldier stabbing and hacking desperately as he screamed for help. He won, but not before his arm had been laid open clear to the bone from shoulder to wrist. The mastiff fell on his side, whimpering, gagged by a slashed belly.

The Spaniards gazed in spellbound fascination as the dogs ripped and gorged themselves on the warm flesh of their kill. This would be something to tell the folks back home! Like their captain they stared open-mouthed, with a primordial gleam in their eyes.

Not till his pets were sated did the captain move. Then he crossed to the wounded Lutheran who sat whining in the street, and calmly ran him through—for having dared harm one of the dogs.

The mounted quartet rode madly through the streets, fighting a way through bands of the enemy when they were small, or detouring to other streets when they faced too-great numbers. They twisted and turned in one street and down another, hacked and fought all the way to the St. Peter Gate, around to the Church of San Angelo, and from there almost to the castle portal.

They made it. Just barely made it and no time to spare. The great portcullis was falling, sealing off the entrance from the castle bridge, as they galloped toward it. Badly rusted from disuse, its descent was slowed to a lumbering, shrieking drag that set one's skin to crawling. Its fall was slow enough to permit their flipping nimbly under, but not slow enough for several cardinals who were struggling amid the terror-stricken stream of fugitives that jammed the bridge.

Cellini was given no time for a breathing spell. No sooner did he dismount in the castle courtyard than he was collared by one of the Pontiff's distant and lesser known kinsmen, the Captain Pallone de' Medici.

"You there ... Cellini!" he called out, "I claim you for the service of His Holiness. See to—"

"A moment, my Captain," the goldsmith interrupted. "This cannot be. I am already engaged by the lord Piero del Bene, father of Alessandro here, for the defense of his house. I must see to returning—"

The impatient captain waved him silent. "Have done!" he rasped at him curtly. "What idiocy is this? His Holiness is your patron, is he not?"

"True, *messere.*"

"You are, then, in his service! ... and spare me your comments! I've no time to listen." Captain Pallone's terse sharpness halted the Florentine's words, leaving him standing with his mouth half-open. "These others can leave by the north postern and reach the Del Bene house from there. The route is open, I believe, and there are barges to take them across the Tiber." Pallone was openly irritated by the ugly look being cast at him by the artist. "I tell you again," he ordered angrily, "see to finding a position from whence you can best aid with the defense. Quickly! if you please!"

It did not please him, but the Florentine was compelled to abandon Del Bene and the others. There was no arguing with Pontifical authority.

He climbed to the keep at the same moment when Clement, who had refused to leave the Vatican, finally bowed to necessity and allowed

III

himself to be led stumbling through the stone corridor which connected the palace with Sant' Angelo.

On the lower keep a gentle breeze blew soothingly. The sun had broken through the mist and was clearing it. Cellini paused to look around for the commanding bombardier, Giuliano Fiorentino, meaning to attach himself to this artillery unit. He spotted the man near an abutment and walked toward him. The fellow was leaning helplessly against a battlement, staring in agonized silence at the sacking of his own home and the torturing of his wife and two children. He was stiff and still, stunned into immobility. The burning fuse he held fell to the ground. All at once, as the goldsmith watched, the tautly corded neck muscles went limp and wailing sobs burst from him, racking through his body in great retching gasps. His fingers dug into his face. Here he was—and there they were—and the gap between could not be bridged. Others among the men were no better off, for by now all of the Borgo was overrun.

Not so, Cellini. This was action! And action was what set his blood to singing as it coursed through him. He grasped the fuse from the limp hand of one of the men, and bellowed for assistance from the few still capable of movement.

"You, there," he yelled fiercely to two gunners who stood glum and submissive near their cannon, "what are you waiting for? A direct order from the Pope? Turn that cannon to the San Spirito Gate and lay it on the bastards! Be quick, god-damn it!"

By sheer lung power he sent them scurrying, moving and loading the guns. Both the Borgo and the Trastevere were exposed to the fire of this keep. Swivels and falconets were turned on points where the greatest havoc could be wrecked and the fire laid on. Charges of iron and stone ball, chain links, chunks and scraps of stone and metal, anything that could gouge and tear was sent hurtling into streets overrun with Imperialists. The cobbles and paving stones, already littered, became crowded with bloody corpses. Dismembered remnants of human forms were splattered against walls and festooned grotesquely over railings and casements. The cannonading became an interminable, relentless volleying. It finally compelled the enemy to post sentries who directed the marauders along safer routes.

The three thousand souls who had crowded into the fortress castle showered praise and called down benisons on the head of their new master-artillerist. The fire belching from the castle keep was so withering, it actually kept the enemy from the vicinity. They had no choice —and no artillery either.

Meanwhile Renzo da Ceri had left the Borgo and raced to the Capitol region in inner Rome, where the populace waited expectantly. He commanded, yelled, cajoled and begged them to make some effort to stop the Colonna, who were mounting an attack from the east side of the city. The Romans refused. Why keep out the Colonna? They were fellow-citizens!

"Well then," howled the harassed captain, "hear me! The main body of the enemy is contained in the Borgo and the Trastevere. Both of these regions are, as you know, on the west shore of the Tiber and both are separately walled. The Borgo is lost, and I am off to the defense of the Trastevere. If you cut away the bridges which span the Tiber, these sections of the city can be held and saved. Will you do this, at least?"

What! Hack down their fine bridges! This *condottiere* was not only an ass, he was insane! The heretics were suffering terrible losses, were they not? Well then, the few who survived could be cut to ribbons before they even reached the bridges. Again, they flatly refused to take action.

In the Trastevere the defense was even bloodier than it had been in the Borgo. But there were too many Imperialists, and too few Roman defenders. Soon this defense too was shattered. By midafternoon the inner gate leading to the bridge of San Sisto was stormed and taken. In solid companies, the Emperor's army crossed the undamaged and undefended bridge which traversed the river and swarmed into the densely populated boroughs of the city. Organized resistance ended.

Rome had fallen. Only the Castel Sant' Angelo and a few of the better defended palaces still held out.

XVII

LONG BEFORE THE ENEMY SWARMED ACROSS the Ponte Sisto, the sweating Florentine had won official recognition. The Chief-Captain of the castle defense, the venerable Antonio Santacroce himself, came up to the keep and called to him.

113

"I am come here to offer congratulations, my dear Benvenuto. Well and excellently done." Santacroce's voice was as calm and un-hurried as if the holocaust all around were nonexistent. He turned to Guido Benardini, who had been second in command under the still helpless Giuliano Florentino. "Master Guido," he ordered, "you will assume the charge of this keep until Giuliano has recovered from the shock of his grief. Master Cellini here is needed elsewhere." The corners of Messer Antonio's eyes crinkled and his lips bent slightly. He was smiling. "I have come to raise you up higher, Benvenuto. Please to follow me."

Cellini followed the nobleman to the highest eminence of the castle, to the tower crested with a bronze statue of the militant Arch-angel Michael, and called "The Angel."

"You will be in command here and have the charge of these five cannons, my friend. As many men as are needed will be sent up directly, to serve under your orders. And...here—" Santacroce handed over a purse. "Your salary, in advance. I will see to it that food is brought up. Meanwhile, see to continuing your valiant efforts. God be with you."

The goldsmith was in a rapture of excitement. The high keep commanded sweeping views all around the city. All afternoon he poured salvo after salvo into the Trastevere. About an hour before sunset, one of the men called him over to the battlements facing the Borgo.

"They're mounting an attack on the Vatican and St. Peter's," the man pointed excitedly. "The Swiss have held them off thus far, but look there! Whole companies of reinforcements. Can we do nothing?"

"We'll do what we can," Cellini answered grimly. "*Olà,* you men, run all the guns over here! Aim at the Square of St. Peter's and the streets around the Vatican. And don't stop firing as long as there is light to aim by."

At the Papal palace and St. Peter's church the Swiss guards, who since the reign of Julius II had the charge of protecting the person and possessions of the Supreme Pontiff, were engaged in a feat of arms so heroic it was almost without parallel. To a man they had refused to leave their posts, and since early dawn they had contested every foot of the avenues leading to the palace and the church. Not one Imperial-ist had succeeded in setting foot inside the doors of either building. But the end was at hand. The guards were exhausted and spent from the day-long fighting; and with all Rome now in their hands, a horde of Lutherans were approaching from every side.

The cannon on The Angel began to thunder and hurl destruction into the surrounding streets. The Lutherans changed direction and passed through better protected avenues. In groups and squads, the Swiss guards fought their losing battle. They piled up mounds of enemy dead, over which they, in turn, fell. Except for the handful, forty odd, who had been ordered to Sant' Angelo as a personal guard for the Pontiff, they were wiped out. None survived. A squad of lansquenets was busy all the next day, hauling bodies out of St. Peter's. Not that the action was inspired by humanitarian motives or idealistic piety. They didn't bury the dead, only dragged them out and flung them into the streets. They emptied the church because they wished to use the most celebrated basilica in Christendom as a stable for their horses.

Night began to fall, and with its encroaching darkness the flaming pyres of gutted and burning buildings began to flare against the darkening sky, throwing an eerie light over the tortuous, corpse-filled streets.

From his position on The Angel, Cellini leaned cautiously sideways against a parapet and looked out over the vast, almost unbelievable spectacle of the first city of the world being ravaged and torn asunder. Tumult raged and conflagrations sputtered into being everywhere, lighting up all of the city. The whole of it trembled and simmered. Waves of fearful sound swept from wall to wall, rising and falling to swell again higher than before. The Imperialists were pouring across all the bridges, trampling over the more than ten thousand dead and dying who lay in streets which ran red with their gore. The tally kept rising higher as the kill-crazy soldiers swarmed in and chased the hapless inhabitants through the streets, butchering them mercilessly as quickly as they captured and stripped them. When they wished to enter a house, they tore down its door. If the house was defended, it was surrounded and set afire. Those who came out were hacked down as they ran from the blaze. If any chose to remain inside—it saved time and trouble.

In the darker streets the night was alive with death shrieks and the shrill, wailing screams of women already making payment of themselves. In the west sections, the roistering was loudest. There the women set apart since morning had been parceled out and were being made to provide the entertainment expected of them.

The men on the high keep looked in fascinated horror at the sub-human devastation taking place wherever they turned.

"Look over there! That house just off the Traspontina." One of the gunners, a young fellow, leaned out of an embrasure, gesticulating.

The building to which he pointed had a high belvedere set off from its upper floor. Lights flickered behind the tall windows and there was a great deal of yelling and screaming going on inside. The long doors opening on the columned balcony had burst open and a slender girl—she could not have been older than thirteen or fourteen—ran out, her long dark hair streaming behind her. She was entirely naked and hysterical with fear. There was something of madness in her movements. A shouting, frowsy looking hulk of a man shuffled up to the door and paused there laughing, as he raised what looked like a large crock to his mouth. He drank deeply, laughed again, and lurched forward. The girl's screams tore into the night. She moved wildly right and left, like a frightened animal, as the soldier closed in slowly, enjoying the effect he had created. Behind him an older woman, probably the girl's mother, also naked, had pulled to the door. She was being held by a comrade who had won her fairly by a lucky throw at dice. She did not scream, but her face was wet and, even from The Angel, it could be seen that there was a deep, almost inexpressible agony on it.

The soldier reached the girl and put an arm around her, drawing her to him. He blubbered a comment of some kind and lifted her bodily to kiss her bare shoulder. She shuddered violently and began to pound at his face with her clenched hands. It angered him. Releasing her he stepped back and swung the earthenware crock at her head, sending her toppling over the railing. The older woman's breath seemed to freeze as the thin wail floating upward ended abruptly. She pulled herself free from the momentarily stunned soldier holding her and ran to where the other man was leaning over the railing, chuckling drunkenly at the sight below. It seemed to the men on The Angel that they could hear the patter of her bare feet as she ran. She collided with the soldier and heaved him bodily over the low rail.

For the briefest instant the man hung suspended in space, clutching wildly for a hold where there was nothing but empty air. He uttered a hoarse cry as he fell, splattering down beside the body of his last victim. The woman turned calmly, thinking to meet death at the hands of the soldier's companion. But the remaining comrade laughed loudly, clutched her around the waist and dragged her back into the room.

"Al buon Cristo in cielo!" choked the older of the two men next to Cellini, turning hurriedly away. "God in Heaven! have you ever seen the like of that! May Heaven help her! Heaven help them all!" He crossed himself and walked off quickly.

Cellini unhinged his locked jaws. His fists had clenched so tightly the fingers ached. He looked around bitterly. There was nothing that could be done. All this was nothing more than the grim aftermath of a city's fall—any city. He shrugged and stepped toward the gunner who was leaning out of the embrasure and tapped him on the shoulder.

"Move back away from there," he warned. "These fires all around make one stand out in as fine a target as any marksman could wish for."

The gunner straightened up and smiled derisively, remaining where he was. "Nonsense," he scoffed. "Where's all this courage and spirit you're supposed to have? Surely you can see that those animals down below are not concerned with Sant' Angelo tonight. They are otherwise engaged." He started to smile again, just as the clear, snapping, bell-like sound came.

Ping-g-g-g-g-g!

It happened so quickly Cellini froze with his mouth open, staring at the gunner. The smile withered as the fellow tried to speak. He opened his mouth, but only a faint gurgle wheezed out. He made a mighty effort—but the words would not come. A look of unbelieving surprise spread over his face. With an infinite weakness he lifted an anguished hand in a vain attempt to pull out the squared shaft of the crossbow quarrel that had cut right through his corselet to protrude grotesquely from his back. He never reached it. As his arm rose with such painful slowness he breathed a spent sigh, his knees buckled and a bright arterial ooze started to stream from his open mouth. He kept trying to speak as he pitched forward on his face, quivered slightly, and slowly relaxed into stillness.

Cellini stared down at him, stunned. He snorted and shook his head. These over-smart gallants! Be a fool and pay the price for your folly! That had been the way with this dolt. *Requiescat in pace!* He called dully to the men and gave orders that the body be taken below.

Savagely he told them he would have the ears of anyone caught standing before an open embrasure.

The next morning the grim business of sacking the city began in deadly earnest. Nothing and no one was spared. Shops, homes, churches, public buildings; Rome, section by section, street by street, was pressed through a fine sieve. Bags of plunder were dragged along the streets by delighted soldier-bandits, gowned in the flowing robes of cardinals, prelates, and great lords. Prisoners were now being taken, insofar as these were known to possess the wherewithal with which to redeem themselves; and the palaces whose defenses had withstood the initial hurried assault, now received ample attention. The soldiers of the Emperor went about the business of collecting loot with an impartiality, a lack of discrimination so absolute it left many a victim agape with astonishment.

The palace of Cardinal Colonna—he was with the army that captured the north and east districts of the city—was one of the first to be sacked. The Marchioness of Mantua, lady of a house closely allied to the Emperor and very much active in the present campaign, was compelled to pay over fifty thousand ducats as a ransom for her palace and the nobles and merchants who had sought refuge there. It was that, or total pillage. Rumor had it that her son, Ferrante Gonzaga, received a fifth part of the sum as his share of the spoil.

The Cardinal of Siena, devoted to the Imperial cause, had come to an agreement, a golden one, with the Spaniards. None the less, he was seized by the lansquenets and driven bareheaded through the streets, with lusty application of the *bastone,* until he agreed to redeem what remained of his august person with another five thousand ducats.

The Ambassador of Portugal, with the ensign of his sovereign waving proudly from his window, saw fit to assume a rather high and haughty tone. His palace was sacked from top to bottom. Stripped of loot that was valued at five hundred thousand ducats. And Isabella d'Este, sister to the Duke Alfonso, cousin to Bourbon, and leagued with the Emperor by signed articles, had to watch helplessly the looting of the Este palace in Rome. More, she herself was commanded to tell down the additional sum of sixty thousand ducats as a personal ransom, or face the consequences.

She paid over the gold. There was nothing else she could do. Bourbon was dead; fatally wounded by an arquebus ball while valiantly leading his men to the attack against the walls. The Prince of Orange was his logical successor as Captain-General; but he had not yet been able to exact any semblance of obedience from the men. He tried, heaven knew, but had got nowhere. The men did as they pleased. And he didn't dare push too hard. In their present exuberant state it would take little for them to turn on him. He had to move slowly, with delicacy.

It was to be expected, of course, that when the rabble soldiery made their curt demands for ransom, there would be those who balked at the payment of it. It is hard to pay over thousands of ducats to scum that had never before seen such sums. It was bad reckoning for they were dealing with impatient jailers. The Spaniards especially were expert in the arts of persuasion.

They would take such a recalcitrant fool and hang him by an arm or leg from one of the upper windows of his house, and leave him there until he became docile. There were the boot, heated pincers, hot baths—very hot!—and the dental treatment. The last was very popular. If you worked with abandon on a man's teeth, using a hammer and chisel, your patient invariably and quickly would see things your way.

For those really misguided simpletons who thought to disclaim any knowledge of where they had hidden their wealth, there was a special treatment. An ear or nose was cut off and roasted over a slow fire until cooked to a turn, and the unhappy owner of the appendage was then forced to eat it. Under these tender ministrations they babbled everything one wished to learn.

As usual, the clergy was the special prey; and also as usual, the comedy more often than not took a macabre turn. A German bishop who was unable to produce the ransom required of him was stripped, his head decorated with fresh green boughs, like a bullock, and whipped through the streets to the cattle market where he was put up for sale along with the other animals. It became a common sight to see mules and asses dressed in cardinal's robes being ceremoniously paraded around the piazzas. The altars of the churches served as gaming tables where sacerdotal robes were put up as stakes against the favors of courtesans who were reaping large profits from self-sale.

One poor monk died a martyr's death for refusing to administer the Holy Sacrament to a jackass dressed in a bishop's gown. Many clergymen were beaten till they died or made open confession of sins of the flesh to confessors who insisted on literal demonstrations of the manner and method of their commission. And the cellarer of a monastery, a lay-brother who was slow in filling wine cups, was strapped down across a bench and stoop after stoop of wine forced down his gullet until he burst.

XVIII

In A FEW DAYS THE PRINCE OF ORANGE MANaged to take hold and knock together a troop strong enough to invest Sant' Angelo. The activity around the castle began to pick up. In itself this was something of an achievement, for the men selected had to forego the delights of raping and looting and return to the far less intriguing business of conducting a siege. It took two exemplary hangings to make the men see reason and knuckle down to being soldiers. They dug a trench around the castle and the investiture progressed, languidly and halfheartedly.

Some artillery from nearby fortifications was brought up and artillery duels began to break up the one-sided advantage of the *castello*. But soon it was evident to the Imperialists that they remained at a disadvantage in these barrages. They lacked precious powder. Their stone balls and iron charges crashed against immensely thick walls. With considerable bitterness they learned that it is much easier to shoot down on an open target than up at a hidden one.

Clement never left off intriguing. Even while the battle had raged he continued to treat with the representatives of His Majesty. The day after the city's fall he switched to the army and sent for the Imperial Commissioner. That brought Don Juan di Gattinara, a bulky, hammered-down Spaniard, dark-skinned as a Moor, with a tendency to waddle, and more than a match for anyone in the castle when it came to discussing exorbitant terms in polite language. From then on there were consultations every day.

Not that these stopped any of the fighting. If anything the artillery duels gained in intensity whenever such a meeting was in session. During one of these Cellini was knocked unconscious for over an hour by a ball which crashed against an angular crenel and ricocheted off, striking him on the chest. His steel cuirass buckled like paper and only the fact that the ball had spent its force saved him from instant death. As it turned out he recovered in time to continue the barrage.

That same afternoon Santacroce sent for him. The nobleman smiled gravely as the artist entered the room.

"We are all happy to see you none the worst for your experience," he said pleasantly. "You are certain you suffer no ill effects, Benvenuto?"

Cellini reassured him.

"That is well." Messer Antonio nodded seriously. "There is an important matter which I mean to entrust to your hands.

"You must know, my Benvenuto, that our Blessed Father is counting on an early deliverance by the army of the Holy League, which is intent on this very purpose. His Holiness has seen fit to appoint a Pontifical lieutenant and envoy, the illustrious Francesco Guicciardini, whose mission it will be to press the need for relieving our Eternal Rome and this Holy See. Messer Francesco has stolen out of this castle during the night and is even now speeding to the encampment of the League's forces, to present and uphold our Holy Father's case.

"Now Messer Francesco also carries the intelligence that a signal has been settled on, which will show our friends that this fortress continues to be valiantly defended and has not yet yielded. It is this: every night, three beacon fires will be lighted on our summit, and three cannons will be fired thrice. The signal is to be made at the first hour of the night, and you, my Benvenuto, will see to it that this duty is properly discharged."

"Since it would be pointless to waste powder needlessly," the matter-of-fact Cellini pointed out, "I take it these nine rounds were best put to good use?"

Santacroce gave another of his grave smiles. "I did not expect you would overlook the opportunity," he answered. "Do your will, in whatever manner seems best to you."

Day and evening there was always plenty of company on The Angel. The Pope preferred the larger keep directly underneath, but many of the other lords would come up and pass the time watching the goldsmith and his gunners work the guns. Cellini didn't object to the company. But there were thirteen cardinals in Sant' Angelo, and the clothes they wore were like flags. Everytime they appeared in their bright-red caps and gowns, snipers began loosing bolts and musket balls. He politely asked them to stay away. They ignored him and returned when they pleased. It had to be stopped, so one day when Cardinal Gaddi drew near to ask more of his inane questions, Cellini tartly told him not to come any closer. Gaddi flushed in instant anger.

"Why!...Why curse you and your impudent tongue, knave! You would be best served by having it torn from your throat! Why should I not draw near you, or any other vermin I choose?"

The goldsmith temporized with difficulty. He returned the angry red-cock's savage stare with one of his own and snapped crisply:

"Because, *my lord Cardinal!*" he gave the title the inflection of a curse, "the scarlet robes and hat you wear are conspicuous and draw enemy fire. Look!—" He pointed to the nearby Torre dei Bini. Several crouching bowmen had already leveled their arbalests.

"If you and the other cardinals here," Cellini spat out nastily, waving in the direction of Ravenna and two others, "seek to flirt with death, by all means do so! That is your affair and none of mine. However, neither my men nor myself have any wish to be made unwilling partners in such pacts. Wherefore, I intend that you will not stand near me."

Gaddi and the other red-hats glowered at the temerity. The goldsmith shrugged and loudly gave orders that all cardinals were to be locked off from the keep. Should any attempt to force the way, the matter was to be immediately laid before the Pope.

Orazio Baglioni came up as the flustered princes were leaving. He had become friendly with Cellini, recognizing in him a kindred, fiery spirit. A professional soldier, he walked casually but carefully to the battlements and stood there with his hands clasped behind him, rocking slowly on his heels. He lifted his head and inhaled hungrily. After a while he turned and raised an eyebrow at Cellini who was standing nearby.

"From what I overheard as I came up, I take it you were having words with my lords, the red cockerels," he said with affability. "It's time someone ruffled their tail feathers a bit. By the beard of Christ, those churls know no more of soldiering than they do of the calling they profess to dress for." He turned back and breathed deeply. "I've come up for some air. There is another session with the enemy taking place below. I prefer not to become entangled in the affair."

"You were outside yesterday, Signor Orazio?"

"All day," Baglioni answered. He was engaged in carrying out certain of the negotiations. "And let me tell you, the stench in the streets, with all those decaying bodies lying about, is enough to make you vomit your guts out. Why do you ask? Have you something in mind? Speak freely."

"Yes, my lord. I have already explained to you how I was compelled to abandon the illustrious lord Piero. I am most interested in learning what has happened to him and his household. I have many friends there."

Baglioni frowned. "Piero? . . . Piero del Bene?"

"*Sì.*"

"Ah, yes. I know him well," Orazio nodded. "Yes, I have heard. Everything considered, he did well. His palazzo was attacked that first evening, but its defense was strong and it held. Del Bene had not been caught napping. He had a strong troop on guard—some excellent fighters who held off the enemy for all of that night and most of the next day."

"Hah!" Cellini exclaimed proudly to the smiling commander. "My boys, those! What then?"

"When the business of looting began, the defenses of that palace were remembered. It was deemed advisable to extract a suitable ransom from lord Piero and leave it. Not that the enemy could not have stormed and taken it, you understand? It was simply felt to be easier and more convenient to secure a ransom and go on to other things."

"What came of that?"

"My lord Piero is an astute man. He entered into negotiations immediately and thus secured the safety of his house and family. I heard the sum he paid over was fifteen thousand ducats." Orazio turned toward the Prati and smiled tightly. "His burden was an easy one. In any case, he had the intelligence to realize that Rome had fallen and was lost. Tell me, Benvenuto, did you ever know a certain rich merchant in the Strada Lungara, who bore the name of Ser Domenico? He is, or was, a trader. Owns a fleet of barques engaged in trade along the coast."

"Slightly. I seem to recall setting some jewels for him. Long ago— long, long ago—before all this." Cellini waved toward the city.

"Just so. *Dunque,* this Ser Domenico, for all his wealth, contributed the magnificent sum of one hundred crowns toward the defense of the city. On Monday his palace was stormed and sacked, and all within made prisoners. It was known that he was a very rich man so none of the house was killed. Instead Ser Domenico was ordered to pay a huge ransom. I don't know the figure, but it was large. He refused. *Ignorante!* They brought in his daughter, tied her down on a table, and while her father was forced to look on she was raped by forty-two soldiers. It killed her. She bled to death. The sight drove the father mad. The next day he and his sons were put to torture till they paid over everything they had hidden away. Ser Domenico destroyed himself that night. One son no longer has a tongue—" Baglioni waved a lean, hard hand disdainfully. "These bourgeois merchants are all of them imbeciles. Grasping poltroons! When their gold is in danger they are unable to see beyond their ridiculous noses..."

The Perugian nobleman had been looking out at the walls as he spoke. He stopped and pointed with his face.

"Do you see that place out there—that house—it looks like an inn or tavern of some sort? Just outside the Porta Castello."

Cellini looked. It was an inn where he'd had many a gay time. "I know it well, my lord. It's a hostelry called the Baccanello. Look closely and you will see it has a sign showing a bright-red sun, hanging between the windows."

Baglioni thrust out his lips thoughtfully. "There's something going on in there. Too many officers entering and not coming out."

"It's a nice enough place," Cellini pointed out, "and barely damaged. The host serves good food and wine. The accommodations are of the best."

The Perugian was frowning in concentration. "I've recognized three of them," he mused. "Look you, Benvenuto, if you give your attention to firing that demi-cannon within an arm's length of that sun yonder, you will do a fine bit of work. There are men of importance in that house."

"My lord, I can undertake to hit that sun in its center, but that vat full of stones standing in front of the gun will be thrown off the wall by the blast. It might do damage."

To question any order he gave always irritated the lordly Orazio. He waved impatiently. *"Fuoco! Fuoco!* Don't waste time chattering. In the first place, it cannot fall. It's too heavy. In the second place, if it did, and were the Pope himself beneath it, it would be less serious than you think. Get on with it. Fire, I say!"

124

Cellini shrugged, aimed with his usual care, and touched off the charge. As he predicted he hit the sign squarely and knocked in the front wall of the inn. As he further predicted, the blast lifted the tub of stones and knocked it over the wall to the keep below, where its contents crashed down between Jacopo Salviati and the Cardinal Farnese.

That the two were not crushed like a pair of roaches was due, not to Divine intervention, but rather to the fact that Cardinal Farnese was engaged in furiously upbraiding Messer Jacopo, whom he blamed as the cause for the sack of Rome. Jacopo had persuaded Clement to disband those Swiss mercenaries. In hurling insults at each other, they stood apart to give space to their violent gesticulating. The heavy tub fell with such resonance that both turned white as sheets and gulped audibly. The courtiers standing around enjoying the tirades set up a loud chatter.

Baglioni listened to the commotion below, smiled his tight little smile, and ran down to see what had happened. Cellini forgot precautions and snaked out through the embrasure to look down. A heavy swirl of dust was rising, effectively blocking out everything. He could see nothing, but he did overhear a comment being voiced by one of the nobles.

"By the rood!" someone exclaimed with a great deal of passion, "it would be a very good thing to kill those damned gunners!"

The Florentine did not wait for further details. He pulled back, saw to the loading of two light falconets, and turned these on the stair leading to The Angel. A lighted fuse burned in his hand. He was ready.

The servants of Cardinal Farnese began to stream up the stair. At its last turning they came to an abrupt halt. The barrels of the two pieces glared down on them like twin tunnels leading straight to hell. The steel-capped Cellini, poised over the guns, sneered at them.

"You skulks! Get back down to the cesspools that spawned you. By the cross of Christ! if there is a whoreson among you who dares set foot to the next step, I'll pound all of you into jelly. Back! And tell my lord Cardinal that I have but done as my superiors ordered— for the safety of the many here, not their injury!"

Somewhat crestfallen, the drones withdrew, giving place to Baglioni who came bounding up the stairs.

"Stand back, there!" thundered the goldsmith.

The Baglioni bridled like an angry bull. He stopped and called out sharply: "Cellini! This is the lord Orazio! I come as your friend!" The goldsmith sniffed. "Excellent!" he called down. "In that case, my lord, mount alone—and come up in any manner you care to."

Orazio bridled again. By temperament he was as vindictive as a viper. His pride smarted under the flip tone being used to address him.

"I have a mind not to move another step and do exactly the opposite of that which I intended," he snapped at the Florentine.

Cellini shrugged. "My lord," he told him, "I have been set at this post to defend others. I am equally prepared to defend myself. Do as you please."

Orazio was silent for a long moment, then called out that he was mounting alone. When he reached the top Cellini took one look at his angry white face, and let his hand drop with elaborate calm to the hilt of his sword. His legs slid out slightly, putting him in a defensive stance. The movements were deliberate, not made to be overlooked.

They were not. Color returned to Baglioni's face and he burst into laughter.

"By the beard of Christ, you are a man of spirit! You please me. I have returned to have a word with you regarding this accident. The thing is delicate... and my position here—" Baglioni shrugged. "It would have been best if you had squashed those two rogues, instead of merely frightening them half to death. One is the cause of this great disaster, and the other is apt to be the cause of something even worse. But as regards the two of us," he went on evenly, "if you are asked, do not say I was up here with you when the accident occurred. For the rest, fear nothing, I'll take care of things from below."

The affair made a great stir, but no one disturbed the goldsmith. The Perugian was keeping his word. An invisible mantle of protection was being extended over Cellini, from below.

When His Most Catholic Majesty, Charles V, received word of the fall of Rome, together with a little something of the manners being displayed toward the inhabitants and the sacred person of the Pope, he uttered a howl of protest. He professed to be indescribably shocked. He issued a royal command ordering his entire court into mourning, as a token of sympathy for the treatment being accorded the Holy Father. He commanded that prayers and masses be offered up before the altars of all the churches in Spain, that solemn processions throng the aisles of the cathedrals, in the hope that Heaven itself might be moved with compassion and see fit to bring about the speedy deliverance of the Pontiff. That a simple order, duly signed by him and forwarded to Rome, would instantly accomplish this end never seemed to occur to the anguished Emperor; and his numerous councilors knew enough of royal ways and whimsies to keep any such importunate thoughts to themselves.

They commiserated with His Imperial Majesty when he proclaimed against the sacrilege, and the appalling horror and disgrace being perpetrated by his men, but they offered no sage and unwanted advice. They managed to look quite as grief-stricken as their monarch when he ordered that full explanation be sent to all neighboring princes and allies, disclaiming all knowledge of Bourbon's horrendous intentions. They applauded his virtue when he disowned and condemned the acts of his troops in central Italy. But the Imperial army remained where it was, its license and its actions unchanged and unchecked.

XIX

THE NEGOTIATIONS WERE NOT GOING ANY TOO smoothly for the besieged in Sant' Angelo. The demands were exorbitant. Three hundred thousand gold crowns; possession of Sant' Angelo; the ceding of Civita Vecchia, Ostia, and Civita Castellana; the cession, in perpetuity, of Parma and Piacenza; etcetera, etcetera, etcetera.

Clement asked for time to consider. Gattinara contemptuously agreed and left, to return the next day with further codicils. As he waddled pompously across the Ponte San Angelo, an arquebus ball wounded him in the right arm. The codicils had to wait. In their place another Imperialist commission called to demand the head of the would-be assassin.

"A most dishonorable act, Reverend Sir," howled Juan di Urbina, lieutenant-general to the Prince of Orange and officer in charge of the delegation. "Why, such a thing is unheard of! To fire on a negotiator is contrary to all the established rules of chivalry and war. It is not to be expected that such a thing can be permitted to pass by. On behalf of His Highness and of the Imperial armies, Your Eminence, I demand the head of this knave!"

Cardinal Cornaro, the Papal delegate who received them, pursed his lips and looked around at the angry faces with bland eyes. He was a testy old fire-eater, but he knew how to control himself when he had to. "Oh, I agree," he answered in an exceedingly dry tone. "You are quite right. To permit such an act of inhumanity to go unpunished is unthinkable. Indeed, is there anyone better fitted to know that than you gentlemen? It is, of course, necessary to punish the man responsible." Cornaro sighed. "Will you tell us, Messer Captain, who it was that dared to violate the rules of war and fire on the Imperial Commissioner? Where did the shot come from?"

The Imperial deputation was considerably abashed by this query. No one, it seemed, knew for certain. The soldiers who accompanied Gattinara were of the belief that the shot came from the high keep—was thought to have been fired by a steel-crested, cuirassed individual, young and of imposing aspect. Such a knave had been observed to look down and grin maliciously, after the event.

Only one man up there answered that description. Cornaro sent for Cellini.

With magnificent élan the goldsmith looked around the conference table while he listened to the charges being leveled against him. His men, he knew, could be trusted, and that arquebus would be very hard to locate. Seeing the anger stamped on the faces of the Imperial officers, he let his own darken with a fierce scowl.

"Who the devil is this Gattinara?" he snapped irritably. "I don't even know who he is, much less that he has been wounded. Who is he?"

One of the officers choked out an answer, giving Cellini a black look the while.

"And who are your witnesses to this trumped-up charge?" glared the Florentine, staring with proper offended frigidity down his nose. "Some of your Lutheran heretics, I'll warrant! Or are they Catholic Spaniards?"

"Ah... there were no witnesses, Master Benvenuto," Cornaro broke in.

Cellini turned to the Cardinal with a new expression on his face, this one full of wounded pride.

"I marvel that Your Eminence permits me to be so used," he

murmured in a hurt tone. "This is a shocking thing! Finding myself accused of harming a man who, after seeing our Rome sacked and gutted, comes to dictate peace! I am horrified at the implication. My lord can send for my men and question them if he so desires. But it will avail nothing. None of us knew of the occurrence. Is Your Reverence at all certain that this is not some new stratagem? A new trick? The shot could have been fired by one of their own men, to prolong things so that they can gut the more. This..." he waved around contemptuously. "This is idiocy!"

Cornaro gave him an expressionless look and turned to Juan di Urbina. "Well, Messer Captain?"

"Where were you when my lord Commissioner was wounded?" the lieutenant-general snapped harshly at Cellini.

"Where it pleased my convenience, *messere!*" snapped back the goldsmith, bristling like a wild boar. He had no intention of budging by so much as a hair's breath. "Who the devil are you to ask me to account for anything?"

"Er, you have leave to answer, *maestro,*" suavely interposed Cornaro. "Perhaps by so doing it will clear the matter up."

"When was this Gattinara wounded?" The goldsmith's eyes blazed into those of the ranking officer.

"Not three hours ago. This morning, one hour before midday."

"Pah! I was engaged with the Captain Orazio Baglioni. My lord Cardinal can ask him."

Cornaro pursed his lips, waved the goldsmith out and ordered his secretary to request the lord Orazio to appear.

The secretary made it a point to advise Baglioni on the subject. The Perugian entered, bowed to the Cardinal, nodded to Juan di Urbina, whom he knew, and swore by everything he held dear that the lie told by Cellini was as true as gospel. They had been engaged in a private discussion when the unfortunate Gattinara was shot.

Proof was lacking, and without it the only way Cellini could be got was by storming the castle. Orange couldn't order that, with the Pope inside. The world had been shocked enough as it was.

Clement continued to ravel out the negotiations as long as possible, having fair grounds for expecting relief from the army of the League. What he overlooked was the fact that Francesco Maria della Rovere, Duke of Urbino, commanded that army. The hatred within that Urbinian was comprehensive enough to cover anything connected with the name of Medici. It was the Medici—Giovanni as Leo X, and Giulio as his then advisor—who had robbed him of his duchy. That score remained to be settled. His march to Rome was, to say the least, a leisurely one. The Papal envoy sent advices to the Pope, pointing out that he was getting nowhere in his attempts to press for speed and forthright action.

Clement thundered denunciations. Francis, badly worried by the turn of events, sent word to the League commander urging all possible speed, while he assembled an army of his own. Venice rushed peremptory orders commanding Urbino, who was the Captain-General of that Signory, to proceed instantly, with all speed and at whatever risk, to the rescue of the Holy Father. Meanwhile, the Signory decided it might just as well take advantage of a golden opportunity, and seized Ravenna and various other Papal fiefs.

Everyone clamored for speed and action, but Urbino continued his apathetic crawl and let the heretics grow tired of waiting. They did just that. They had had enough of the delay. Gattinara demanded an immediate answer and an end to the dawdling. The Imperial army, he said, would wait no longer. And while he rapped out the ultimatum, word came from Guicciardini that the army of the Holy League at last was nearing Rome. The exultant Clement, having no more excuses to draw on for protracting the parley, pointed out to Charles' mediator that the Confederacy of the League was all but within hail and would shortly decide the issue once and for all. He was a little smug about it all, particularly when he smoothly requested an additional six days' respite, so that this auspicious event could take place. If the heretics were still around at the end of that time, Clement swore he'd come to terms.

The vexed and impatient Gattinara let it be known that Charles' army felt only contempt for the miserable soldiers of the League. They would welcome this opportunity to destroy them.

"Only let me presume to warn Your Holiness on one point," he sneeringly advised. "Our noble captains may interpret Your Holiness' answer as an indication of rupture, and immediately storm the castle!"

More than one cardinal blanched at the threat. They asked for fifteen minutes, for private consultation.

The Conclave consulted, faction wrangling with faction, without result. Clement's request for six days' time was carried back to Orange and his captains. The castle wasn't stormed. That had been a mere flourish, a bluff, of Gattinara's. The delay was tacitly conceded since there was nothing Orange could do about it. It would expire on the twenty-fifth.

On the twentieth, Urbino straggled into Isola di Farnese, nine miles from Rome. He detached Captain Guido Rangone and sent him with a troop to take up a position at Montemario, three miles from the city. The next day, Rangone's welcome banners and streaming pennons were sighted by the besieged in Sant' Angelo. Everyone crowded to whatever openings they could find, for a view of the advance that was now a certainty. The Imperialists were so badly upset they didn't fire a shot at the densely packed windows and keeps. They too were intent on those waving banners. Every officer on Orange's staff knew that it would be next to impossible to hold off an organized attack with the drunken, booty-laden swine that made up Charles' army. Orange was himself violently perturbed.

The Pope watched from his usual place on the lower keep. The Angel was crowded with gloating prelates and courtiers. Renzo da Ceri edged up alongside his aide, who was standing next to Cellini. For a long time he watched, looking out at the welcome sight, making no comment. He turned and eyed Baglioni.

"What do you make of it, my lord Orazio?" he asked quietly. "Can they force an entry and relieve us, do you think?"

Baglioni's lips were quirked down at the corners in utter disbelief. "This is a surprise," he told the captain. "An agreeable one. I was entirely mistaken. I own it. I would have wagered everything I possess that Urbino would never march here. It was my fixed opinion that he was incapable of such resolute action." He smiled and waved to the banners. "There he is!"

He shrugged and smiled again. "To win into the city will require no great effort, my lord Captain. Those beasts below are even more undisciplined and unmanageable than when they arrived at the walls. Orange will not be able to hold back an attack in force. I'll wager he means to retreat as soon as an attack begins. Look at those drunken dogs slink along the streets!"

For several hours the banners of the League waved proudly in the breeze.

"They are grouping," gloated one of the courtiers, chortling excitedly. "Massing their might for a single irresistible swoop. We will re-win the city in one stroke."

131

Cardinal Gaddi called for wine to toast the certain victory. "And why not, my lords?" he sang out grandly. "Are we not about to be freed? A few hours and we will be engaged in exacting a just retribution for all we have been made to endure."

"Look you, *signori!* The banners begin to move! They come! They ... Good God above! It can't be! ..."

Consternation and disbelief followed the unfinished utterance. No one could believe what his eyes saw. The banners were indeed moving —northward! In a matter of minutes they faded from sight. The old score was settled. Urbino had paid back the Medici. Rangone had been recalled.

Clement was beyond consolation. His head shook as if palsied and his bleared eyes wandered wretchedly over the city, horrified by the sight they looked upon. Rome was a ghastly, stinking ruin; a blackened sea of charred, hideous skeletons that had once been houses. Portions of walls stood here and there, like rooted mourners turned to stone. A dread, macabre silence hung in the streets which festered in a convulsed litter of coagulated black pools. The thousands of unburied dead rotted and putrefied under the hot sun. A fetid, miasmatic stench rose from the maggoty heaps. It was sickening, unbearable. The air above them was black with swarms of iridescent flies. Countless, madly buzzing millions of them, feasting on the human carrion. The fear of pollution was so widespread that food no longer was being brought into the city. Famine began to lick out with its tentacles, adding to the misery of the survivors. And here and there among the putrid, swollen cadavers, big fat rats were beginning to roll over and die.

Wearily, all hope of succor gone, Clement withdrew to the seclusion of his chambers. He had let it be known that the terms asked by the Imperialists, most of them, were impossible of fulfillment. Ostia was held by Andrea Doria, who was in the service of France. Civita Vecchia and Castellana, by now, were in the hands of the League. Neither had any intention whatever of recognizing a Papal capitulation which would compel them to withdraw from these tax-yielding possessions. The ransom in gold was equally out of the question. Rome was a ruinous hulk, despoiled of everything that had value. The treasury was bare. There was some plate. There were red hats as well as some other offices and benefices which could be sold. But even so it

132

was doubtful if such a fantastic figure could be raised. He sent for Cellini.

The goldsmith came down and was admitted to the apartment where Clement waited, fretfully pacing the hard stone floor. His personal servant, Cavalierino, stood glumly by. Cellini looked the lackey over, as he always did. The man was a French peasant, a former stable groom of the Strozzi, whom Clement had taken on as a valet. He had proved faithful and the Pope trusted him implicitly in many things. Yet, despite his present exalted position, Cavalierino still looked a dolt, a rustic churl. The handsome clothes he wore never seemed to fit or belong on his ungainly frame. His flat face had an uncouth, stupid stare. He always appeared on the verge of cringing whenever anyone addressed him, and he always answered in a keening whine. He was thoroughly hated. All were jealous of the trust placed in him. He was not stupid. He had become a rich man.

Clement stopped pacing and sank slowly into a low-backed, circular chair. He heaved a heavy shuddering sigh, took hold of himself, and looked at the Florentine.

"We have a matter of grave import and utmost secrecy, which requires the use of your talents." He spoke calmly and nodded quietly to his valet.

Cavalierino bowed, his usual half-cringe, opened a nearby chest and began dumping an incredible array of wrought gold and jewelry on a table. Clement gazed at the pieces pensively for a while, before turning back to Cellini.

"These," he said, pointing, "are the jewels of the *Camera Apostolica*. It has become necessary that the stones be removed and the gold reduced so that it will not be evident that it has served as a setting for gems. The stones we will secrete on our own clothing and on those of our servant here," he waved toward the valet. "However, it is necessary that we repeat to you our admonition regarding secrecy. You understand the need for this?"

"Completely. Your Holiness may rely on my eternal discretion."

"*Ben detto*. Get you the tools of your craft and return here. *Subito.*"

So it was done. The jewels were removed and sewed into the linings of Clement's and Cavalierino's clothing. The gold was dumped into sacks and discreetly conveyed to Cellini's quarters in the high keep. Its total weight was almost that of the goldsmith whose task

133

it became to melt down the intricately wrought works into unsightly yellow lumps of purely commercial value.

The Florentine locked himself in, built a small furnace of brick with a large pan at its bottom to catch the gold as it dripped down through the charcoal, and began operations. In the days that followed he established a new routine. He would throw a quantity of gold on the live coals, and while it heated and melted down, would go out on the keep to see what could be done in the way of annoying the enemy.

Toward the end of this task, one evening a little before evensong, he saw a soldier ambling along on muleback, skirting the bank of the new trench being dug across the outer approaches of the castle. The man was clad in rich rose armor and was talking to the men in the ditch, bandying words with them. That made him important. Only high-ranking officers went in for that sort of puerile byplay. Cellini aimed a charge of scrap iron just a little in front of the ambling mule and let fly. As it happened the beast bore the brunt of the charge. The poor animal was torn to pieces. The rider escaped with a face full of the metal. Possibly his armor protected the rest of him, but his face was badly gashed. The men working in the trench were in a dither. Cellini was wondering why when Baglioni came dashing up the stair.

"God's blood and bones!" he yelled. "Who fired that shot?"

Cellini looked at him inquiringly. "I did. Why?"

"Why!" he cried, waving frantically. "Beard of Christ! Do you know who that was? That was Orange himself!"

The Florentine, elated beyond words, gave what passed for an indifferent shrug. He flipped a hand.

"Just another target for our guns up here," he told Baglioni, with the casual manner of one to whom such things as killing off enemy generals is nothing at all. "Look! They're leaving the trench to get him. Men! Over here!"

The Angel's cannon sent the enemy scattering back into the trench. One courageous, or idiotic, soldier refused to be swerved. He braved the barrage and dragged the wounded Orange back to the diggings, where he could be safely carried. They hauled him, limp and bleeding, to a nearby inn. His officers hurried there to see what was what.

Orazio flew to inform the Pope, who had already been informed. Such news travels fast. Clement had sent for Santacroce.

"My lord Antonio," the Medici was excited, "you have heard of this most recent exploit of our Benvenuto?"

Messer Antonio bowed and nodded, as courtly and grave as ever.

"We have at hand an heaven-sent opportunity," exulted Clement. "See to it that all bombardiers train their cannon on the house where they have carried Orange. When the lord Orazio here fires an arquebus, it will serve as the signal to discharge all guns in unison." He turned proudly to the cardinals and gentlemen-in-waiting thronging around him. "In such wise, my lords, we shall with a single blow slay all their leaders. The heretics, left thus without a head, must inevitably be put to rout. And then!—" Clement licked at the words, so sweet and savory they were "—then we shall at last be free of all these impious knaves!"

Santacroce bowed and withdrew to give the order. Every gun in the castle was aimed and waiting for the signal. And while the gunners waited, the lord who was carrying out most of the negotiations with the enemy, Cardinal Orsini, got wind of the plan. He stormed and ranted at Clement for even considering so impolitic an action. Did not His Holiness realize that a treaty of accommodation was at the point of being completed? Was it not clear that if the leaders of that rabble were slain there would then be no one to stop them from storming the castle and completing the ruin of everyone within it? That signal must never be given!

The despairing Clement, worn down by these hot and cold flashes, washed his hands of the matter and left the decision to the Sacred College. They could, he told them, do as they liked.

The order was immediately rescinded. Better to be besieged than garroted!

Baglioni writhed at the selfish stupidity, but followed orders and sent to advise the gunners of the new decision. Cellini turned green when he heard it. With his usual brashness he accidentally allowed a lighted fuse to touch off a demi-cannon—and to hell with the consequences. The blast reverberated through the castle. It ripped away the pillars supporting a wall of the building, which began to sag dangerously. Those inside scurried out like rats, carrying the bleeding Orange along with them.

Orsini was quivering like a reed in a high wind. That ... unspeakable Cellini! First the Farnese incident, then Gattinara, now this!

"This infamous scoundrel must be severely dealt with," he bawled to the Pope. "Everyone in the castle is aghast at his insolence. Your Holiness must at the very least have him hanged instantly, lest he end by bringing on the ruin of all of us!"

Clement was of a different mind. Some high words passed back and forth, but the Pontiff had his way. Cellini was glowered at a great deal, but no one molested him. He finished with the gold and carried it to Clement, who said not a word, but gave him a quiet smile and directed his valet to bring in twenty-five crowns for the goldsmith. He was gone when the bucolic churl returned empty-handed. In place of the twenty-five crowns the goldsmith received a sneer. How did he think the Papal drudge had become rich?

Cellini scowled and muttered angrily at the swindle, which was about all he could do. That valet was too solidly entrenched. He went back to his quarters and relieved his feelings by kicking the furnace apart. When he came to sifting the ashes, however, a measure of cheer returned. He amassed a neat double handful of little millet-like grains which had become mixed with the ash. Cheerfully the goldsmith poured the gold into a soft leather pouch. That it was nothing but barefaced stealing—and from the Vicar of Christ, no less—was no deterrent to the Florentine. To him the gold represented a self-payment of salary. And certainly he had a right to expect payment.

News of the fall of Rome reached Florence four days after it occurred. Commotion and rioting were instantaneous. The lowing boom of *La Vacca* resounded over the city, summoning the populace, who streamed out toward the great piazza. There and in the Via Larga around San Marco, the rabble-rousers were waiting. They screamed at the citizens. Here was the opportunity again to cast off the ever-tightening yoke! Who was it they feared? A broken prisoner? A spent old man who cowered behind the stone walls of a Roman tomb! The revolt spread quickly. The turbulence mounted, became irresistible. Passerini and his two Medici charges were unable to cope with it. They sneaked off to Lucca just as the Florentines were tearing down the statue of the Pope and began to sack the Medici palace.

The Signoria again banished the Medici permanently. Within a week the Papal authority over Florence was abolished and Niccolò Capponi elected to the office of Gonfalonier. A jubilant Grand Council once again proclaimed Florence a Republic of the people and forswore all earthly rulers by solemnly declaring that henceforth the sole lord and king of Florence was Jesus Christ Himself!

The despots were still in power. It was merely another, a different group of noble politicos who took over. Taxes remained just as high. Oppression was just as widespread. Justice was as readily purchasable a commodity as ever. Life went on, not one bit different from what it had been.

The six days' grace came and went on into the bottomless abyss of eternity. In Rome nothing happened. The besiegers now were as fully aware as the besieged that the League had failed utterly. There was no longer any tendency to hurry things along, except for the fact that a small matter had cropped up and was causing some concern at Imperialist headquarters. Plague had broken out. The festering corpses in the streets had nurtured it, and now the pest was beginning to lick out at the remaining population. This in itself was not anything to worry over. What caused concern was the indisputable fact that the plague made no distinction whatever between victors and vanquished. It had a deplorable and total disregard for such details. The day before there were something over a hundred deaths from it, and many of the victims were members of Charles' army. The toll was mounting by the hour and there was the thought that it would get worse instead of better.

As Orange's wounds, if not his looks, improved, he sent Gattinara back to the castle for a resumption of negotiations. The bickering over terms began anew. Clement was deeply engrossed in this travail when the news from Florence got through and was brought in to him.

It was as deep a thrust as he could receive—and live. It rocked him, shattered him, stunned him into the immobile silence of a dotard.

All the bitter cups he had been compelled to drain were nothing to this. The news tore at his body, his mind, and the deepest, most secret parts of his being. Rome had been bad enough—but Florence! Florence meant more to him than a dozen Romes. For its possession he had abased himself continuously, suffered humiliation after humiliation. All this, that the most important, the greatest city in Italy—the Florence of the Medici—would remain just that!

Bitter, scalding tears rolled down his face. He lifted himself out of his chair and faltered to a window—a man suddenly grown very old and very weary. No one in the crowded room bothered him. He was not annoyed with unwanted petty demonstrations of sympathy. He pressed his hands against his throbbing head. Where now, his life-long dream of a Florence that was to be the unassailable Medici State? All the soaring optimism that had sustained him through the years collapsed, bursting like a pricked bubble. Everything he had worked and connived for had been wiped away; burned out of the world by this terrible holocaust that had descended upon and engulfed him.

He could take no more. Clement capitulated. He promised to sur-render Sant' Angelo, agree to all terms. He asked only for a few days in which to rest. For better or for worse, the Emperor Charles had won. He had broken the back of the political power of the Pope.

On the day that Gattinara withdrew and the Papal jailer, Don Fernando de Alarcon, entered, the smooth-shaven Clement began to grow a beard. A symbol of mourning and of self-penance. To the last day of his life, he never shaved it off. And out in the world, in the courts of the mighty—even in Sant' Angelo—the Medici was already being referred to by another sobriquet he had earned for himself. The "Master of Craft" now had become the "Deceived Deceiver!"

In THE WIDE SPACE OF OPEN GROUND BETWEEN the inner *cortile* of Sant' Angelo and the earthen redoubt of the out-works nearest the Porta Castello, the compact mass of men fidgeted with nervous impatience. It was still dark and the sky full of stars, but in the east a faint flicker of gray was beginning to edge out of the horizon. Whenever someone clanked his armor or a horse snorted, those nearest hissed for quiet while the man himself took to cursing volubly. There were some three hundred men and as many horses, all armor clad and geared for battle, waiting for another quarter-hour or so to pass so that a plan could be put into execution: a last sally made by volunteers who hoped to win their way out of the castle and the city of Rome before the final capitulation of Sant' Angelo.

In front of them some soldiers were busy oiling and greasing the winch that raised the grate of the portcullis and the chains on which it hung, together with the hinges and the iron rollers of the doors. The element of surprise was of the essence. They were three hundred against some fifteen thousand enemy troops remaining in the capital. At best the chances for success were slim.

Off to a side Renzo da Ceri was going over final instructions with his co-commander and seven acting captains. Cellini was one of the latter. He had been among the first to volunteer for the sally, having absolutely no desire to see himself handed over a prisoner when the Imperialists took over the castle. On Baglioni's suggestion he had been put in charge of forty men. The other squad captains were all professional soldiers.

"Mark well the importance of following the order of our plan exactly," Da Ceri repeated in his quiet voice. "All depends on surprise and precision of movement. There must be no avoidable noise. The horses will make a great enough clatter as we leave. I will lead out two hundred men, commanded by you four captains." His steel gauntleted hand made a division in the group. "We turn to the left, toward the bridge, as soon as we are outside the doors, and create as much havoc as possible in that quarter. The enemy expects nothing since the surrender of the castle will come about at any moment. It is hoped they will not divine our true intent until it is too late to prevent it. Any counteraction should be directed entirely on the Ponte San Angelo.

"Ten minutes after we leave, my lord Orazio will lead the remaining hundred to the right and take and hold the Porta Castello. Orazio, you are allowed a brief twenty-five minutes in which to accomplish this. For a soldier of your parts, this is sufficient time."

Baglioni nodded affably. War and battle were his handmaidens. Five minutes to reach the Gate. Twenty-five to take it. All the time he needed.

"*Bene*," Da Ceri turned back to the others, "one-half hour from the moment my lord Orazio and his men leave, a cannon will be discharged from the keep. This is the signal for us to turn and fly to the Porta Castello—and freedom. Caution the men not to lag or they may be left behind. And harken, my *bravi*, I repeat again, this sally must be timed to perfection. It must be dark enough to give us needed cover while in the city, yet light enough, by the time the Castle Gate is won, to assure that we do not miscalculate the road. Else we will be helplessly mired in the bogs and marshes around the Sposata. So, then, is all understood?"

A series of curt nods and guttural affirmatives answered.

"*Allora, cavalieri,* the time is come. Extinguish the lantern. I will give the order to raise the portcullis." Da Ceri's eyes flashed as he sent a final reassuring glance around. "Good fortune to all, and God go with you."

A flip of his finger and the steel visor of his armet snapped down over the lower part of his face. The others followed suit. Cellini was wearing a morion, a steel hat which covered head and ears and the back of the neck, to which he had fitted a broad nasal with slits for the eyes. He reached up to make certain it was secure as he walked to his mount. He and his squad were to act under Baglioni and help capture the Castle Gate.

The portcullis began its slow ascent. At one point it shrieked and a ripple of oaths rose from tense lips while a soldier frantically ladled olive oil over the winch chains. It moved again, slowly, lumberingly, and with comparative quiet, up the well-greased runners.

On the ramparts a guard turned and waved a signal. Thus far the enemy suspected nothing. The mounted men squeezed back in their saddles and hunched forward for a charge, their lances remaining upright because of the confined space. They were ready.

"Open," called Da Ceri.

The doors swung smoothly in and the horsemen, five abreast, poured through, bringing their lances to rest as they filed out. Imperialist guards in the trench set up a shout of alarm. Crossbowmen posted along the ramparts answered with a rain of crossbow bolts and quarrels. In a remarkably short time the two hundred were gone and the doors reshut.

Outside, an uproar was rapidly rising above the rattle of the horses' hoofs. The noise was reassuring. The first part of the sortie seemed to be coming off as planned. The clamor followed Da Ceri to the San Angelo bridge. Above it could be heard the war cries of the assailants. "*Da Ceri! Roma! Patria!*"

The hundred still within the fortress waited. Cellini gripped his long spear tightly, adjusted his shield and felt along the saddle bow for the heavy mace looped there, before grasping the reins. His horse pawed and tossed its head. A soldier near the doors kept his eyes on

a clock lighted by a covered lantern. Nine minutes...eight...five...
two. He signaled.

The doors swung silently in again.

The remaining horsemen cantered out into the darkness, veering
to the right. With the first shouts of the Imperialist sentries in the
nearby trench, Baglioni lifted high in his saddle. "Form your lines,
comrades—and forward! *Avanti!*"

Cellini kicked the rowels of his spurs into his horse's flanks and
tore away with the rest. Beside and behind him were his forty men,
half of whom had an arbalest strapped down on their saddles. They
rode straight to the trench, mowing down the guards on duty there.
There were few soldiers. The horses climbed up the other side and
galloped to the second, newly dug ditch. This one was entirely empty.
The horses clambered down and up and they were in the Borgo.

Baglioni pulled in his mount. "Reform quickly. Hasten!" Lines of
horse were forming as he yelled. "Cellini, Berglino, remember well to
see to your tasks when we reach the Gate." He waved in the dark.
"Avanti!"

The troop dashed down the deserted streets of the Borgo to the
Castle Gate. The element of surprise had been complete. The empty
streets attested that the enemy was confining its attention to what
appeared like a sally directed at the San Angelo bridge.

The Porta Castello, however, would be under heavy guard, as were
all the city gates. Platoons were kept on constant duty at all the en-
trances—crossbowmen, arquebusiers and halberdiers.

The Gate guards heard the horses thundering down the street but
had no way of knowing whether the cavalry was friend or foe. It was
too dark to make out the silent riders. Certainty came when the Italians
were upon them, cutting them down.

At the Gate Cellini and his squad wheeled to the left toward the
barracks leading out to it, riding down a trio of startled lansquenets
before they could bring their weapons into play. Only one of them
succeeded in leveling his halberd at the Florentine. Cellini turned the
thrust on his shield and skewered the man on his spear. The impetus
tore the shaft from his hand, leaving it impaled in the dead soldier.
Catching another pike thrust on his shield while he loosed the mace,
the goldsmith swung in the dark. The large steel knob, bristling with
spikes, crunched against metal and bone, hurling the victim a full five
paces, his helmet and skull crushed like two eggshells.

Rearing and prancing, the horses swept into the soldiers pouring out of the barracks. Trained for battle, they were in themselves a match for startled foot soldiers. They reared and kicked out with steel-shod hoofs, sending men sprawling under the hoofs of other mounts or making them easy and helpless targets for the weapons of the riders. But it was not all one-sided. Steel armor was no protection against an arquebus ball or a crossbow bolt. It was still dark but there was some light from the flaming torches in the Gate house, and this served to light an occasional tall target.

Berglino and fifteen of the cavaliers had quickly cut a path to the winch that worked the portcullis and formed a ring around the shed raised over it. Damage to that mechanism would mean that the grate would stay closed and the attempt fail.

While they guarded the windlass the main body of the cavalry was slashing and hacking down the foot soldiers milling around helplessly in the tangle of choking dust and horses. Buildings were beginning to stand out against the graying sky. The horsemen could now be seen in outline, and the enemy arquebusiers and crossbowmen were using their weapons with greater effect. Mounted riders toppled more frequently. A horse screamed frightfully as a ball tore into its neck and sent it crashing to the ground.

"Cellini!" roared the Perugian. "Beard of Christ! get after those swine on the rampart!"

The Florentine was already so engaged. The twenty men armed with arbalests had dismounted and were picking off the rampart guards like pigeons, while their captain and the rest of the squad circled around and protected them.

Another five minutes and the fighting ended as abruptly as it had begun. The few remaining foot soldiers capable of doing so turned and ran.

"Quickly! Damn it!" Baglioni's horse pranced as its master shouted. "Raise the grating!"

The winch handles were turning as he spoke. Slowly the portcullis rose. A half-dozen men dismounted and stooped under the sharp, tine-like points of the grate rods and slid the heavy cross bar of the doors out of the way.

Horsemen erupted out of the gateway as the doors swung, swooping on the bewildered Spanish soldiers on the other side. The Spaniards had been enjoying an all-night carouse in the nearby Baccanello when the clamor broke out. In various stages of drunkenness and indecision they had grabbed their swords and left the inn, to be hacked down like so much pork as they blindly staggered around looking for cover. The sally was successful. The Porta Castello was taken and stood open.

Baglioni dismounted and flicked up his visor as he walked back to the Gate, kicking the limp body of a dead Spaniard out of his way. His face streamed with sweat. "Cellini! Post two sentries on the rampart. Dante! See to it that all wounded men are tied to their horses. Let me know what losses we suffered. Hasten!" He turned toward Sant' Angelo. The furious clamor was loud in that direction. The sky was lightening and one could begin to distinguish details.

"How much longer before the signal, I wonder?" the Perugian mused, wiping his face with a scarf. "Well, Dante?—"

"Nine dead and badly wounded, *messere,*" reported the Captain. "Seventeen others less severely wounded. They are being strapped to their saddles."

"Good. Less than I imagined. Mount and stand by."

For several minutes the troop waited in a tense silence, recovering breath and shifting in their saddles. All at once faces became even tenser. Heads cocked and ears strained to catch a new sound that reached them dimly. A low rumbling that slowly increased in intensity. Galloping hoofs! coming, not from the direction of Sant' Angelo, but from the south side of the city.

"Cavalry!" shouted one of the men posted on the rampart. "Coming out and around the Porta Angelica!"

"Another troop moving up inside the walls," called down the other.

The purpose of the last sally was by then known and the Imperialists were moving to check it. This was to be expected. It was also to be expected that the enemy would move on both front and rear and so crush the assailants between them. But had they realized that the diversion at the bridge was part of the whole plan? On such short order how many men had the enemy been able to pull away from drink and revelry? Baglioni would have given much to know. Whatever the odds he would do best to engage them outside the walls, where there was room for maneuvering. He was about to speak when a bright flash and a loud report boomed from the castle keep. The signal!

"Hah! At last! You wounded men start off immediately. Berglino, take two men and lead them. Mind you hold to the road. Head north toward Castellana for two leagues and wait for us. You men—form ranks on me. Two lines—with some twenty paces between. Dante, you and yours on my left. Cellini, on my right."

The lines formed facing the oncoming Imperialist cavalry.

"You sentries! How many are there? Can you make out?"

"About fifty horses, Excellency," came the answer. "No more than that outside the walls. It's impossible to tell how many on this side. Here come Da Ceri and his men!"

"Come down and mount, both of you. Then stand by and direct them." Baglioni raised his arm. "Forward, cavaliers! Forward to victory!"

Once more spurs bit into the flanks of the horses and the troop of sixty-odd horse charged straight for the galloping enemy. *"Baglioni! Roma!"*

"España! Sant' Iago!" came the answering shout from the charging Spaniards.

The thundering hoofbeats were shattered by a crash that seemed to shake the earth beneath them as the two opposing troops crashed headlong into each other.

For Cellini the next few minutes passed in an unreal blur of parries and slashes, of horse against horse and rider against rider. He was dimly aware of vivid colors, or armorial bearings emblazoned on cuirass, shield and crest, of the plume-crested horseman he smashed against in the first impact. The man gave way and then disappeared— whether by his hand or because of the churning mass of men and animals, the goldsmith never knew. He could hear the triumphant yells of Orazio Baglioni, who was alongside fighting like a madman. Once he swung his mace at a *caballero* about to slash at the commander. The cavalier dodged the blow and in the next instant was pulled away by the press of the battle.

The Italians, with freedom as well as life at stake, fought with a savagery that was unequaled. The advantage of slightly superior numbers was increased by the fury of their initial assault which unhorsed nearly a fourth of the enemy, while they themselves lost only six men. The Spaniards were slowly giving ground. Their ranks were thinning out and small openings appeared.

Baglioni's experienced eye was quick to see the cracks. His horse reared and wheeled while his yell split the air. "Dante, Cellini! by me!" He slashed and hacked at an opening in the direction of the enemy Standard, near which the trumpeter was blaring the order to rally.

"The banner," squalled Orazio, pointing with his sword. "Victory is ours if we take it. Hah!—" With the speed of lightning he turned a sword thrust on his shield. "By the beard of Christ! It is you, Don Estaban! Well met! Here . . . I repay in kind!—" Cheerfully the Perugian swung his battle sword in a cut that would have cleft the lordly De Soto from crest to loin, had he not been just as agile in turning the blow.

The milling swirl of men quickly separated them and the three Italians inched toward the Standard.

The goldsmith and the commander reached the trumpeter together. Baglioni's sword flashed on one side as the Florentine's mace swung from the other, hitting the man full in the face and silencing him permanently. A jerk of the reins and Cellini's horse wheeled on its hind legs and charged the Standard bearer. The mace crashed down but was stopped by the soldier's shield. The diversion was enough. Baglioni pounced before the Spaniard could turn. His sword hacked relentlessly downward like a cleaver, and the man tottered and began falling as the commander yanked the pole from the limp hand.

He was tearing the banner from it when a new roar and another smashing impact hit the fighting mass. Da Ceri's men had arrived!

Demoralized and without a rallying point, the Spaniards scattered in panic-stricken disorder.

"Cut the bastards down!" yelled Baglioni. "Don't let up for an instant!"

The fighting, however, was over. The enemy was scurrying back to the Porta Angelica.

One of the Italian captains drew rein alongside the Perugian, to receive a clap on the shoulder from a steel glove.

"*Porco diavolo!* I am glad to look upon your face again, Milio." Flicking up his visor, the commander wiped his face with the enemy banner. "You came in good time. I take it you threw back the troop coming up from inside the walls?"

"It was easily done, my lord," panted the soldier. "We engaged them briefly before they turned back. We were too many for them."

"How went things at the bridge?" asked Cellini, coming up to them.

"We left some thirty men on the field, Benvenuto." Captain Milio turned again to Baglioni. "Including our valiant commander, *messere.*"

"Da Ceri! Killed?"

"No, my lord. He was unhorsed and taken prisoner. He shouted to us to carry on with honor."

"Bravo! Ho, men! Pick up our wounded—and back to the Porta Castello."

"Your Excellency will have to assume full command."

"I know, my Milio. And we had best move before the enemy assembles a more than sufficient number of hornets. We have been uncommonly fortunate thus far." Baglioni started. "What was that?"

The clap of a loud explosion and a cloud of debris rose from the vicinity of the Castle Gate.

"The winch working the portcullis," answered Captain Milio. "One of our men brought back a keg of powder. They've blown it up. There will be no pursuit through that door!"

"Well thought on. Let us be off. Forward, men!"

It was the matter of a few minutes to arrange the order of march. In the full light of day scouts dashed ahead to reconnoiter. A vanguard galloped after them. The main body, with the wounded, came next, and was followed by a strong rear guard. A matter of a few leagues would find them in Civita Castellana. The last sally from Sant' Angelo had been a victory. A small and personal victory—but a glorious one.

PART II

XXI

"Bᴜᴛ...ʙᴜᴛ ᴛᴏ ʙᴇᴄᴏᴍᴇ ᴀ ꜱᴏʟᴅɪᴇʀ, ᴍʏ ꜱᴏɴ!"
Giovanni Cellini made an effort to keep the dismay he felt from showing. "I am amazed to learn you wish to do this."

It was early evening. The goldsmith son of old Giovanni had
arrived in Florence that morning. He had entered the city openly, in
excellent health, superbly clothed and mounted, with a pouch full of
ducats and a servant at his back. The least his father had expected
was the news that he either had perished in that great battle for Rome,
or had been ruined in the horror that followed. It was a miracle, nothing
less. And now, this last detail—

"I don't see why not, Papa," his son was telling him. "The only
reason I didn't accept the captaincy before was the ban still in force
against me. We can take care of that now."

"Tell me about it from the beginning, my Neutino, that I may
understand the case fully." Giovanni made another effort and looked
up brightly. The years had gnarled him, their weight had bent him.

His son leaned back and gazed at him fondly.

"*E bene,*" he began. "In order to win out of that fortress prison
in Rome, before the Imperialists came in and made real prisoners of
us all, Orazio Baglioni and Renzo da Ceri led three hundred of us
in a bold sally. A warm hour's work it was, believe me, my old one. We
fought like demons. Some sixty fell in the fighting. Da Ceri himself
was surrounded and taken prisoner. The rest of us hacked a path
through the enemy and fought free. We went on to Perugia."

"Well done! And then, *ninno?*"

"In Perugia, my lord Orazio wished me to take over the command
of that band, in his service. I declined the offer explaining that I would
gladly have accepted but for the fact that I was interested only in
finding a means of returning home to you—" the goldsmith drew

down the corners of his mouth "—without being hanged when I arrived. I explained about the ban.

"My lord assured me he could be of use since he had just been made Captain-General of Florence and placed in command of Giovannino's Black Bands. Piero del Lotto, the envoy from here, was then at hand and I was highly commended to him by the lord Orazio. Naturally, Ser Piero was impressed—as one would expect. He let me know that I could come on whenever it pleased me, and that all arrangements would have been made by the time I arrived. And so, *vecchietto mio,* as soon as you can you will go to The Eight and buy off that ban."

"Most willingly, my son. Tomorrow, the first thing. And having removed the ban, *caro,* you are certain you wish to become a soldier?" Giovanni's face clouded. This was wrong, all wrong.

"Bear in mind, *figlio,*" he prodded, "that my other son, your brother Cecchino, is a valiant soldier. One in the family is enough. It seems to me right and sensible that you pursue the noble art in which you have won fame and renown." Giovanni was so intent on dissuasion he even forgot music. "Tell me you will think more on this before you arrive at a final decision?"

After Cellini had half-promised to heed his father's words the old man did not press him further. The thing to do, he reasoned, was to get Benvenuto out of Florence before Baglioni arrived to take up his new duties. He had already formed a plan.

The ban was bought off. The tribunal redeemed it with indifference and passed on to matters that were causing them more concern. Plague was raging in the city. Florentines were dying by the hundreds every day. The plague figured prominently in the old man's scheme to get his son out of Florence. Adroitly he waited a few days before opening his mind to his goldsmith son.

"*Figlio mio,*" he told him one morning, concern showing on his face, "the plague here is terribly violent. Whenever you leave the house I always have a dread that you will return with it upon you. I have been thinking," his tone became livelier, "when I was a young man I remember journeying to Mantua, where I stayed for several enjoyable years. A fair city it is. Rich and hospitable. You would like it immensely. So I pray you, my son, for love of me, that you remove yourself there, today rather than tomorrow, so that I may regain a little peace of mind on your behalf."

Cellini wasn't worried about contracting the plague. He'd already had and survived it, which brought a measure of immunity. Second attacks, though not unknown, were uncommon and rare. Still the idea of travel tickled his fancy. He had never been to Mantua.

Two days later Giovanni sighed with satisfaction and mouthed a prayer of thanks as he watched his son ride off. This should put an end to all his nonsense about captaincies and soldiering.

The journey was somber, difficult and dangerous. The land was so darkened by the twin scourges of pestilence and war, that Cellini was heartened when he sighted the spires of a thriving city which had managed to escape both calamities. Two hours after he put up at the Tavern of the Red Cock, he had come to an arrangement with a Master Niccolò da Milano, goldsmith to His Excellency, the Marquis. Several days later, on a Sunday, he called on Giulio Romano, and the gay days of Rome lived again.

"Why the devil did you wait so long, you drone?" Giulio affected to be slighted and hurt. "And why put up at a scurvy inn?"

"Ah, my friend. I've come here to work, you know."

"Bah! Come, let's ride out to the country for the day, so you can inspect my present project." Giulio fingered his beard. "You know, I think you will like it. I'm living in it, like a lord."

"Just like Rome?"

"Better, Neutino. Far, far better."

"*Per Dio,* then let's go," Cellini told him. "I mean to see what you've been up to all this time. *Andiamo.*"

They mounted and rode out of the city gate.

"What are you engaged on, Giulio," Cellini asked as they paced along the road, "more of those little gems for Aretino's sonnets?"

"No, no." Giulio laughed at the memory. "No more of those. I'm working on a vast project. A palace. The Marquis tells me it is a fit monument to my genius." Giulio Romano was proud of this work. He nodded gravely to himself. "It is, indeed, my masterpiece."

They ambled along, chatting and enjoying the rolling countryside till Giulio stopped and flung out an arm to his left.

"*Eccolo!*" he exclaimed, pointing with pride, "*il Palazzo del Te.*"

A fantasy of architectural splendor emerged gracefully from the surrounding hills in a massive upward sweep. There was a blending of color, a combining of textures, a subtle harmony that was enchanting to look upon. The Florentine was captivated by the quiet charm it radiated. Dismounting, he and the painter paced slowly through the villa, pausing in each room. There was spaciousness, comfort, flawless appointments of flamboyant elegance. There was wall after wall of voluptuous frescoes by this Roman master who had been the favored pupil of the immortal Raphael. Cellini turned admiringly to Giulio.

"Master!" he sang out. "This is a triumph! The great Raffaello Sanzio has nothing to be ashamed of in having taught you your art. This is a Paradise."

Giulio was enthralled by the praise. Cellini had a reputation for telling the truth when he criticized.

"Let's go out, Neutino. I want you to see the gardens with the sun on them."

The gardens were terraced and screened by rows of ancient conifers, through which the cool *tramontana* whistled and sang an accompaniment to the croaking of the bullfrogs and the chirping of crickets. Satyrs, Pans and nymphs dominated walks and little arbored nooks. Spraying jets from the fountains formed a background that sparkled and dissolved into multicolored facets as the spray dispersed the sunbeams. It was a dream. Poetry transformed into reality.

"There's no sense in your wasting time in a shop, like some damn lackey!" Giulio shattered the dream. "I will present you to His Excellency."

The next day Cellini bowed before the Marquis Federigo Gonzaga and demurred politely while Giulio praised him to the skies. The ruler did not need the recommendation. He had been advised of the goldsmith's arrival the moment Cellini passed through the south gate. He had a tentative commission ready and waiting.

"We have a project in mind, *maestro,* if you will oblige us. Something suited to your superb talents, which would give us great pleasure to see executed." Hawk-faced, tough as baked leather, the stately Federigo got right to the point. "It is our desire that you fashion a reliquary suitable for holding the phial of the blood of Christ, which was brought to our fair Mantua by the great Longinus. Giulio here will make you the design for it."

"My lord," the painter interposed, "Cellini is a man who has no need for the drawings or designs of others. Your Excellency will be able to judge for yourself, when you have seen his model."

The goldsmith set to work on a wax model of a seated Saviour whose left hand supported His cross, while the fingers of the other

152

appeared to be opening the wound in His side. The sacred relic reposed therein. It was a beautifully designed piece of work.

But if the Marquis was pleased, Cellini was not. He was not happy in Mantua. The place cramped him. Even the air was dank. The city fell still lower in his estimation when he came down with a quartan fever—which came of the foul air of the place, of course. He took on a mistress, thinking to take some of the curse off the city. Her name was Leonora and she was vivacious, pretty, and as eager as a basketful of puppies. Nothing helped. To him the whole of Mantua wasn't worth a *carlino* with a hole in it.

He stopped accepting new commissions and pushed ahead with those on hand. The bouts of chills and fever, fever and chills, were giving him fits. Mantua had a doubtful value in only one respect. News came in every day: war-ravaged Rome was being devastated by the plague; in December, Clement's escape from Sant' Angelo. The Pontiff, said the courier, had disguised himself as a peddler and together with a personal servant had stolen out of the postern on the Vatican side, past the lax and sleeping guards, and had run off to Orvieto. Florence, Venice, Ferrara, and Genoa joined with France and declared war on Charles. England joined them. In Florence the pestilence had subsided. The city was quiet—finding itself anew.

Cellini set out for home.

The Via Chiara was quiet and subdued. All of Florence was, for that matter. Forty thousand persons had died of the plague. Expecting the worst, Cellini dismounted and knocked on the door of his father's house. Only a dull echo answered. He kicked at it until a little dormer-like window overhead was flung angrily back. A hunchbacked old crone pushed her face through the opening, railing out at the goldsmith for disturbing her. Her cackling voice had the shrill quality of a badly rusted hinge.

"Get you gone from my door, you son of a disease!" she shrilled at him.

Cellini's lips curled over his teeth. "Misshapen hag!" he snarled back. "Ill-mannered deformity! Is your ugly face the only one to be seen in this house?"

"None other, you whore's spawn!" she screeched. "May the devils of Hell suck up and wither your vitals before the year is out!" It was late December.

"And may this house be freed from the curse of your mangy face within the space of the next hour!" the goldsmith yelled back, spitting up at her.

A neighbor cautiously put her head out the door and offered the information that the old man and the others who had lived in that house all had been carried off by the plague. The news was not startling. Cellini had expected nothing less.

"Are you of the Cellini?" the woman asked. "A son. Then I can give you some good tidings. Your younger sister Liperata escaped the pest, though her poor baby died of it the same day as her husband. I heard she moved from her house into that of a certain Mona Andrea dei Bellacci. No. I don't know where it is."

The goldsmith turned sadly away. Only a sister left. Everyone else gone. He headed for an inn.

Even the Golden Florin was subdued. A few guests ate or drank amid the somber quiet, the aftermath of wholesale death.

"Neutino, my friend!" It was Giovanni Rigogli. "We meet again!" He rose from a table to clasp the goldsmith's shoulder. "I've heard about your great loss. A pity. Cecchino is inconsolable."

"Eh?"

"Your brother—Say! he thinks you're dead!"

"He's alive, you say?"

"Yes!" Rigogli laughed joyfully. *"Domineddio!* A single bright ray penetrates the gloom. I am happy for you, Neutino. You think him dead, while he thinks the same of you. I will take you to him. Come—"

The meeting was extravagant. Arm in arm the two brothers ran to their sister for a reunion that lasted through the night.

Cellini wanted to go back to Rome. Both his brother and sister were against it.

"What for?" they bickered. "There's nothing going on in Rome. Stay here at home a while."

"What of you, Cechin," the goldsmith asked. "You were in the service of Alessandro de' Medici. Are you going to stay here?"

Cecchino tossed a hand. "For a while. Until Alessandro calls me back to his service."

Piero Landi added his weight to the argument. "Why not stay, Neutino. Surely you can work as well here in your native Florence as elsewhere. Besides, it will be interesting to see what develops here. The

Medici are banished. The Imperial army is quitting Rome and retiring to Naples, which means Clement will be returning to Rome. This will no doubt affect Florence. Stay and see what comes of all that."

Cellini shrugged and set about opening a small shop in the Mercato Nuovo. There wasn't much doing. A great deal of jewel setting—work of no special importance. All that could be said for it was that it paid well. A single exception was a gold medallion ordered by a Sienese. The subject was a Hercules tearing open the lion's mouth, modeled with all the brilliant artistry that was becoming Cellini's hallmark. Michelangelo, who called frequently at the shop, praised it highly.

"The attitude of your Hercules, *mio caro,* the fierceness of the beast. These are superbly rendered. Very masterful."

"It pleases you, master?"

"Immensely. It reminds me of an antique cameo I saw once in Rome. By the way, speaking of Rome, I have received advices that Clement has removed to Viterbo. Closer to the capital, eh?"

Slowly, life in Florence regained its bubbling effervescence. Not even the bad news of military reverses could dull the laughter. The Imperial armies might be inflicting defeat after defeat on the allies; but the season was at June, the warm summer sun sparkling and clear, and it was wonderful to be alive—to sing and laugh and love.

All that summer, into the fall, Cellini worked on settings for precious stones. His brother had been recalled and was off somewhere. Liperata had remarried. He was growing tired of working just for the sake of earning money. Not that he was shy about gathering in gold; he had a high regard for it. But surely there was something more to life than this? He was cursing this futility when a smartly dressed young man, a gentleman by the look of him, entered his shop.

"*Prego.* Am I addressing the master, Benvenuto Cellini?"

"The same, *messere.* Pray, enter. *S'accomoda.*"

The gallant sank into a chair, absently scratching at his crotch while he looked around with lively curiosity. "*Maestro mio,*" he began when the inspection was at an end, "my name is Federigo Ginori. Know that I am sent to you by the great Michelangelo himself. I desired the design for a medal from him and he advised me that if I would be well served, I must seek out the unsurpassed Benvenuto Cellini. I implore your genius, good master. Will you accommodate me?"

Cellini bowed. At last! A work requiring some imagination.

"*Bravissimo!* I wish a medal, fairly large, depicting an Atlas who

155

bears the world upon his shoulders. Certainly one of your high reputation can evolve a splendid rendering of such a theme. *Un disegno classico.* I beg that you will give me your thoughts on this idea of mine."

The goldsmith pursed his lips, frowning in concentration as he sorted the various concepts conjured up by his mind.

"It comes to me thus," he answered, pulling forward a sheet of paper and a stick of charcoal. "The figure of Atlas is best cut well out from the background plate of gold, in a manner showing the full majesty of his proportions as well as his stupendous task ... so, Messer Federigo." He was sketching as he spoke. "The heaven upon his shoulders I envisage as an engraved crystal globe—thus." His hand flew along the paper, while the young patron watched avidly. "Upon the surface of the crystal, a field of lapis lazuli with a zodiac engraved thereon in a deep intaglio ... Hah! *Per Bacco!* The composition produces a fine effect! Blue stone, yellow gold and clear crystal will make for a fine contrast. Under the whole we shall incise the motto: *Summa tulisse iuvat,* in classic Roman characters ... There. *Eccola!*"

"*Bellissima,*" gushed Ginori. "*Per Dio, maestro,* it will go hard, waiting to see your finished work."

Cellini flung aside the charcoal. "You are recently come to Florence, *messere?*" he inquired politely.

"Ho-hum," the gallant stretched and yawned. "But a few days. I have come here from Naples. By way of Rome," he added. "The renowned Michelangelo mentioned that you too have come from that city."

"*Sì.* And how did you find our unfortunate Rome?"

"A shambles, my dear fellow. Ruined, scarred, and desecrated. More than half the populace has been massacred by war and plague. Our Blessed Father returned to the Vatican the day after I arrived there. A pale and dejected Pope Clement he was. *Povero uomo!* An ill man, to my mind. Do you believe in signs and omens, Master Benvenuto?"

"*E perchè no?* Why not, I say? It is well known that such frequently occur."

"So. Then listen to this. At the very moment that His Holiness returned to the city, just as he passed through the Porta del Popolo, a most violent storm broke out. It lasted all the day and night and brought the Tiber to raging flood. A portent, this! A sign!" Messer Federigo crossed himself.

156

XXII

"AND SO," THE PONTIFF WAS SAYING, "I HAVE deemed it wise to bring you here for a discussion of family affairs."

In a small *stanza intima,* set off in a secluded corner of the Vatican's so-called "Borgia Tower," the three surviving male members of the *Ca' Medici's* elder branch surveyed each other across the table.

Clement sipped leisurely from a cup filled with a thick frothy mixture of milk, eggs and spices laced with Marsala wine, and made mental notes as he eyed the two youths seated across from him.

Ippolito was self-assured, courtly and graceful—the gallant courtier and man of fashion. Black hair and short beard accented the whiteness of his skin and that birthright of the Medici, his magnificent eyes. A red velvet hat glittered with gems, and his plain dark doublet, slashed with purple velvet, had a row of carved gold buttons down its front. The jeweled hilt of a dagger showed between his hands as they toyed with the head of his walking stick. He was universally esteemed and showed great promise. Everyone looked on him as the next great Medici statesman.

Tough and slender, Alessandro was more war-like in appearance. There was a touch of the ruffler about him. He wore an engraved corselet over a silk shirt and a loose jerkin over this. Smooth-shaven, his close-spaced features seemed somehow at variance with his swart complexion, wiry hair and heavy lips. *"Il Moro"* they called him—and a Moor he looked. There was a predatory twist to his manner, indefinable, vulpine. The elusive quality of a night hunting animal; cruel, pitiless, bent only on satisfying its needs. He was shrewd without being clever, cunning and ready-witted without being adroit. He lacked subtlety. In whatever he undertook he considered only himself. No one else concerned him in the least.

"Family affairs," added Clement, between sips, "as these relate to our Florence."

Neither of the two young men felt out of place. That they were quite young—Ippolito was twenty; Alessandro even younger, eighteen —was of no importance. Both were expected to think and reason with adult intelligence. They kept their eyes on the white-robed, bearded Clement, and waited.

"*Ascoltatemi,*" the Pontiff requested. "I have devoted long and anxious hours to the matter of our reinstatement in Florence. On this our future, the future of our House, rests. Unless we find the means to return to power there, we are lost. The machinations, the involvements of the plan itself," he waved a hand, "are of no importance. The soul of the matter lies in the result we must at any cost attain. Are we bundles of straw, to be flung about at whim? *Dunque*—" he paused dramatically, "—we come to the problem: how can we regain Florence?" He looked around to his two charges through half-closed eyes.

Alessandro's reply was a stream of invective. He had not enjoyed that forced flight and did not relish thinking back on it.

Clement held up a palm.

"Futile," he told him, patient but curt. "You weave a rope of sand. Tell me, pray, what does anger avail us? Can we gain our objective through a display of it? No. Understand that if we act at all it must be with deliberate calm. How else shall we be able to surmount the obstacles which confront us?"

Alessandro poured out a goblet of wine and gulped it down.

"Something in Your Holiness' manner," Ippolito remarked smoothly, "leaves the impression that Your Sanctity regards as possible the chance of our return to power in Florence. Eminently desirable! *Ma come?* How? The people don't want us."

"*Poveretto!*" Clement smiled indulgently. "Know, then, that I have long ceased to marvel at the ease with which a populace, any populace, allows itself to be led—once a halter has been clamped to the ring in its nose. *Pecore!* However, as you have perceived, I have indeed thought of a possibility. My present position, reduced though it is, will permit its being put into execution."

Clement laid aside the cup of spiced milk and looked from one to the other of the young men.

"Where," he asked, leaning his elbows on the table, "lies the present strength of Florence?"

The question was rhetorical.

"The strength of Florence," he went on, "lies not within herself,

158

but in her allies." Clement made a fist and extended the fingers of it as he enumerated. "France, England, Venice, Ferrara, and Genoa— in that order of importance. With them she is strong and can defy us indefinitely. Remove them and you remove all her potency. *Mi capite?* To go a little further along: how can this power be stripped away? In this manner: let us but secure an alliance with either Charles or Francis, and the rest becomes child's play. Help we must have—and must secure. That, in simple terms, is our problem."

"Simple, you say!" Alessandro snorted. *"Per Dio!* Let me offer the opinion that this is the biggest obstacle which confronts us. If our House is to regain its position we must have the support of either France or Spain. Quite true! And there lies the problem. Secure the assistance of Spain, and France is on the other side of the coalition, ready to neutralize it. Court France, and we court further destruction from Spain. Where are we, then?"

Clement sniffed with delicate calm.

"An elementary deduction, my son," he told him patiently. The filial reference was not an admission of parenthood, merely a form of address. "These things are well known to everyone. One must learn not to waste time in demonstrating that which is self-evident. Such time is better spent in devising a means for surmounting it. *Hai compreso?"*

Alessandro's swarthy features flushed. He nodded glumly and slouched back in his chair.

"As Your Holiness has stated, elementary," Ippolito interjected. "And yet, as Alessandro points out, it remains the most important fact to be considered. To surmount it would be more than a success. It would be a miracle! *In verità,* I confess freely that such a stroke of genius is far beyond the scope of my poor ability. *Caspita!* To maneuver some of the strongest forces, the most important governments in the world! A difficult thing."

"Impossible." Alessandro snorted again. "There, Blessed Father, is your rope of sand! How ..."

Clement slowly shook his head.

"Difficult," he murmured, "yes. Impossible—no!" He sighed with obvious satisfaction. "I will explain more fully.

"As you know, France has been suffering defeat after defeat by the armies of Spain. She is inclined to come to terms, and this Charles also desires. Discussions to that end are taking place at Cambrai. Now the Emperor is also *extremely desirous,"* Clement laid heavy stress on the two words, "to arrive at an accommodation with us here in Rome. He is justly fearful of the censure of the whole Christian world, as well as of the coalition we could presently bring against him. What with being fully occupied in Germany, taxed to an even greater extent by the Grand Turk in Hungary, to say nothing of the embroil here in the north and south, he is most anxious to settle his differences with Holy Mother Church. We have been holding off any such negotiations."

Clement caressed the side of his nose with a finger.

"The thought has crossed my mind," he told his two listeners who were hanging on his every word, "that, in return for certain concessions, we might, haply, be inclined to come to an accord with him."

"By the eternal cross!" whispered Alessandro. That the Medici had maneuvered himself into a position where he was making demands of his conqueror, awed him. "A bold and creditable tack," he admitted. "And the concessions, Your Holiness?"

"Simply stated, our reinstatement to power in Florence, devised thus: *Uno*—the treaty with the French to include the provision that France must forswear all ties in Italy and abandon all interference in Italian affairs. *Due*—Venice and Ferrara to receive lenient terms and so be removed by treaty. *Tre*—armed aid with which to invest and subjugate Florence. You perceive the effect of all this? *Bene!* England can be lulled through the Curia. Genoa has already withdrawn from the war and can be disregarded. As regards the battle phase for the city— there, I confess, a measure of uncertainty exists. Unfortunately, the Captain-General of Florence, the illustrious Orazio Baglioni, was slain in a battle near Naples some months ago. A pity. He was a reasonable man. On the other hand, I rejoice to learn that his successor is another of the Baglioni. His brother, Malatesta. It may well be that my lord is open to inducements. An agent is engaged in a preliminary exploration of this detail. *Ecco!* What remains?"

"*Corpo di sangue!*" crowed Ippolito proudly, pounding the table. "A deft stroke! Masterful and well planned. I hold myself enriched at being permitted to sit at the feet of such a ruler as Your Holiness. Would that I might display such profundity of mind! What statecraft!"

"Perfection!" echoed Alessandro. "It is an instrument fit and worthy of Your Sanctity's ability."

The elder Medici was highly pleased with the acclaim. One little side lane of this tortuous scheme he did not divulge, though it did indeed concern his two charges. That must wait on developments. He did, however, enjoy the adulation. He received so little of it of late.

"Consider well, *figlioli*," he beamed paternally. "At twenty, one must not expect to be possessed of the intellectual scope that can be yours at forty. There are years between. One lives—and if one lives wisely—one learns."

"*Va bene.*" Ippolito bowed. "I shall keep this thought before me, Most Blessed Father. One point, if I may be permitted. How is this project to be broached to His Majesty?"

"A mission leaves for Barcelona within the week. In the meantime, until we know the mind of the Emperor, much remains to be done in other directions. There are affairs to be put forward immediately. Have the goodness," the Pope pushed back his chair, "to attend me tomorrow morning. And remember..." Clement raised a finger to his lips.

In early June the disquieting news reached Florence that a Papal mission was journeying to Spain. No one liked the move. It was well known that once Clement straightened out his troubles with the Emperor he would have time to give to the Florentine problem. Rumors flew about like bats; but it was not till August that the French Ambassador called at the Palace of the Signoria to discuss his country's recent treaty. The galling note came at the end of the talk.

"Excellency," the Ambassador sighed and addressed the Florentine Chief of State, "though it wounds me grievously, duty compels me to imform Your Serenity that as a result of this accord with Spain, my beloved France must withdraw as an ally of this great Republic."

Throughout the city nothing else was talked about. Cellini dined with Varchi and Piero Landi that same evening. He asked for details, but the historian could cast no light on the French move and said so. Piero had his own ideas.

"There's England," he pointed out. "I'll warrant she won't stand by idly when she hears of this."

Varchi shook his head. "You're underrating Clement," he told him. "If I know the Medici, England has already been attended to. Henry of England wants a divorce so that he can lie with that Boleyn bitch. And both of you know that the Pope won't give him one. He won't hesitate to use that as a weapon."

"Oh well, there are other ways," offered Landi. "If what one hears of that monarch is true, he has a way out of that." Piero brought the edge of his hand down against the back of his neck.

"He doesn't dare. The present queen is Catherine of Aragon. She happens to be an aunt of the Emperor Charles."

"Eh, *coglioni,* that is something to think about. Still, if Clement won't grant a divorce, how can he keep England from forcing France to hold to her commitments with us? By all accounts, Henry is no dolt."

"Easily," answered Varchi. "By gulling him. He may not be a dolt, but he is in heat. He wants Anne Boleyn, and, incidentally, an heir to the throne. In that condition, he can be gulled by any smooth manipulator. And believe me, Clement is smooth."

"How gulled?"

"Simply by giving him hope that a divorce may be forthcoming if he takes no notice of what goes on here."

"Politics!" Cellini made a sour face and gave a toss of the hand. "You can have the damn stuff!"

One by one, Florence's allies were lopped off: Genoa, France. A strangely quiet England took no notice of the French abandonment. Venice and Ferrara were hurriedly suing for peace on receipt of extraordinarily moderate terms. The Republic had grossly underestimated the capacity of the Master of Craft. She stood alone. No peace terms were offered her by Spain.

In September Rome issued a declaration of war. Simultaneously the Emperor commanded Orange to accept service under Clement and march on Florence.

While the clouds gathered, the Republic prepared against the coming storm. Fortifications were strengthened and rebuilt. An area half a league wide, all around the city walls, was stripped bare of all cover. Every house, tree and shrub was torn away. A citizen army was conscripted and put under arms. The streets resounded to the usual harangues. From the pulpit Fra Benedetto da Foiano thundered against the ungodly tyranny of the Medici lust for power. The tempo turned to one of fevered exhilaration. Live today for tomorrow you die was translated into lavish feasting and entertainment.

Within a month, while Clement traveled to Bologna to place the crown of Holy Roman Emperor on the head of Charles and to smooth out the remaining fine points of his intrigue, the Imperial army took up positions beyond the bared perimeters around the north and south walls. Attack after attack was hurled back. Weeks, then months passed. The Florentine field army under the Florentine General Ferucci hammered back with a vigor that stopped every attempt to gain a foothold.

Cellini, commandeered in his turn, had joined a company of nobles which formed part of the garrison commanded by Captain-General Malatesta Baglioni, to defend the city proper. His shop became a meeting ground where the war was won every day—orally. It was during one of these verbal jousts, around midday of a bleak March, a caller entered and announced that he had a letter for the goldsmith. A letter from Rome!

The shock of the bald announcement nearly gave the Florentine indigestion. True, a letter from Rome is a trifle, but trifles can be misconstrued.

Nervously he tore open the seal—and blanched as he read. It was from the hand of Jacopino della Barca, an intimate of Pope Clement.

While in Bologna, wrote Jacopino, the Pope had been reminiscing on the battle of Rome and had recalled the valor displayed by the goldsmith. His Holiness had speculated over what had become of him, and on being informed that Cellini was back in Florence, the Holy Father requested that he, Jacopino, who was returning to Rome, write and advise the master to return quickly to the service of the Pope...and when was he coming back?

"From Rome, eh, Benvenuto?" a gallant snickered. "Tell the wench she'll either have to come here or wait a while longer."

Cellini gulped. "Ha-ha...yes."

"Who is it from, Neutino?" another of the youths idling in the shop asked. A letter from Rome naturally aroused curiosity. "Anyone we know?"

"*Ma che!* It's from an old fool who wishes information on a commission I worked on several years ago," improvised the goldsmith. "These Roman lords must think I keep a history of every little piece I turn out." He shrugged. "It's nothing."

With seeming disdain at the imaginary imposition, he crumbled the letter in his hand and casually tossed it into a trivet of burning coals.

That night he dashed off a hurried appeal to Messer Jacopino, advising him—for God's sake!—not to forward any more letters. With a sigh of relief he sealed the note and sent it to the merchant who had delivered the other.

Two weeks later, in the early evening this time, another letter from Della Barca! Never in all his life had the goldsmith been so completely alarmed. His mind projected a horrific picture of himself being torn limb from limb by a ravening mob who screamed for the blood of this traitor, this Medicean tool, they had nursed to their bosoms. He downed a stoop of wine and wiped the sweat from his face before he broke the seal.

There was the usual complimentary opening paragraph, then:

...Esteemed master, His Holiness, on returning to our Rome, has again deigned to inquire concerning your whereabouts and disposition. To such effect that I once more am writing to request that you return with all speed to Rome. Our Blessed Father has commissions of the greatest importance which he desires to entrust to your care. Wherefore, my most excellent Benvenuto, if you seek to prosper, if you would continue in the favor of this Sacred Vicar of Christ, leave all else behind and fly here at once, in obedience to his wishes. Above all, do not allow yourself to act in opposition to the will of the Holy Father by remaining there, in that city, acting in concert with all those mad and senseless rebels...

"Holy Saints!" gasped Cellini. He read no farther. The words blurred on him. *"Che imbecille!* I've got to get away from here before this empty-headed son of a bitch succeeds in getting me beheaded as a traitor and a spy."

He ran to the house of Piero Landi.

"Olà!" Piero greeted, always happy to receive his friend. His smile turned to a frown when he saw the expression on Cellini's face. "What the devil's wrong, Neutino? You're badly upset."

"Piero, my friend," Cellini pleaded earnestly, "believe me, for your own safety it is impossible for me to explain my state of mind. I must leave Florence as soon as possible. Will you see to it that the gems and gold in my shop are returned to their owners? I can get you their names from my account books."

Landi was shrewd enough to guess at the facts. He had been present when that first letter had arrived.

"Where are your account books, Neutino? At the shop? Good. I'll find them myself. Be off quickly, *compagnone.* Don't give another thought to your shop affairs. I'll take care of everything. And harken! I think I understand. Don't wait. Pack some clothing and be off tonight.

Ten ducats will open any gate in the city. And as soon as you can, write to me, my friend. *Addio.*"

XXIII

WONDERFULLY RELIEVED TO BE BACK IN Rome after four nerve-racking months in Bologna, Clement lounged back on a couch and let his shoulders sink comfortably against a pile of cushions. Things were going well for a change and he felt pleased with himself. The last details of his little proposition to Charles had been worked out, with the Emperor in full agreement, and these needed only time to be fully realized. He smiled. Ippolito was in for a surprise. With a contented little sigh he lifted his slipper-clad feet atop a low stool. Officially the Pope was somewhat indisposed and resting in his bedchamber; actually, his health was beginning to fail.

In one of the chairs in the room, a low-backed affair constructed of two semicircular frames, Jacopo Salviati sat and quietly watched the Archbishop of Capua glide across the floor to a window. They were the only gentlemen in attendance and both were silent. Clement was engrossed in a book, a favorite of his—the *Iliad* of Homer, translated into the precise dactylic beat of Latin hexameters by the Italian poet Poliziano.

The Archbishop turned from the window as a Papal secretary entered and approached Clement.

The Pontiff looked up vacantly. "Well?"

"The goldsmith, Benvenuto Cellini, Your Holiness," the courtier said deferentially, "in the company of Messer Jacopino. Your Sanctity will recall having caused Jacopino to write..."

The Pontiff nodded. "Bid them enter."

Cellini strode up to Clement and sank effortlessly to one knee. The Pope shifted his feet slightly and adjusted his long robe. The goldsmith pressed his lips against each of the gold crosses pinned to the white silk of the Papal slippers. As he did so Clement lifted a hand and manipulated a finger in the form of a cross over the bowed head.

"I am most happy to see you returned to my service," he told the rising goldsmith in an informal congenial tone. "And how did you leave our Florence?"

165

"Waging war, Blessed Father," Cellini replied bluntly.

"Yes...eh, well...we must expect that," Clement responded cheerfully. "But that will end, my Benvenuto. It will end."

The Pontiff turned to polite chatting. How was the goldsmith? Doing well? His family? Clement was indeed sorry to hear of his father's passing...

"Most Blessed Father," Cellini spoke with deference. It was Holy Thursday of Easter week, and there was a detail—a little gleaming dagger that had been hanging over his head since the days of Sant' Angelo. Only the Pope could remove it. "I beg a private word."

"Certainly, my son," the paternal Clement assured him. He waved the others to a far corner. "Well, then, Benvenuto?"

"Holy Father, know that since the time of the sack I have been unable to receive Communion. No priest will absolve me! The details are these. Your Holiness remembers the affair of the gold? The instructions issued to Cavalierino for a certain recompense for my hard labor? Well, your servant gave me nothing but abuse, and on returning to my quarters to dismantle the furnace, I discovered among the ashes a handful of little gold grains. Since I had not the means to enable me to live decently, I thought to use this and restore it—" the goldsmith gagged on the word "—later, when the opportunity offered. Now I am at the feet of the True Confessor, requesting such favor as will grant me leave to receive the sacraments. I beg for the pardon of Your Beatitude, that I may regain the Grace of my Lord God."

Clement heaved another little sigh. Oh, well—people, after all, were just people.

"My Benvenuto, I certainly have the power to absolve any improper action. Therefore, see to telling me all."

"That is all, Blessed Father. It amounted to the value of one hundred and forty ducats. So much did I receive for it from the Mint in Perugia. With this sum I was enabled to return home and comfort my poor old father."

"Your father was a good and worthy man, and you are not degenerate from him. Indeed, I am sorry the sum was so small. However, such as you say it was, reckon it a gift from me. Make this assurance to your confessor and when you have taken Communion, let us see you again."

Cellini withdrew, spiritually cleansed of his oversight, shriven by the Vicar of Christ himself.

When he returned after the Easter holidays, the Papal mood remained congenial. From the throng of courtiers that surrounded him, Clement motioned the goldsmith forward.

"If you had returned here earlier," the Pontiff told him, formally this time, "we would have commissioned you to refashion the two tiaras we destroyed in the *castello*. However, we intend to set you to a task of the greatest importance, wherein you will be enabled to display the full extent of your talents." The Pope settled back in his chair and took up a flat jewel case. "We desire a clasp for our Pontifical cope; a morse, round like a trencher, and a span in width. Upon its surface you will represent a God the Father in *mezzo rilievo,* and in the center of your composition," Clement opened the jewel case, "you will set this marvelous diamond, together with these other fine gems. It will be greatly to your advantage, Benvenuto, to finish this quickly, since we would derive some small pleasure from the use of it. So be off and make us a fine sketch model."

Cellini took careful note of the gems, their size, cut, and purity of color, and was off like a shot. Here was a commission any artificer in Rome would give his teeth for. He made arrangements with a jeweler, one Raffaello del Moro, for the use of his shop, and buckled right down to work on a design.

When the word got around, the envious goldsmiths who handled the numerous commissions issued by the Vatican began biting their nails. Among these was Micheletto, the elderly and brilliant craftsman who had been entrusted with the working of the two tiaras. A skilled goldsmith, high in the Pope's favor, it was a part of his duties to oversee all commissions given out by Clement personally. Thus he awaited the call for a consultation with this Florentine, who felt no need to consult with anyone. It became necessary for Micheletto to make an unasked for visit. In something of a pique, he called at the Del Moro shop and asked the goldsmith from Florence what he was doing.

Cellini was busy on a drawing, but he paused to look up at his fellow-goldsmith.

"Oh," he told him, "something the Pope has ordered from me."

"His Holiness has directed me to oversee all work being done for him," Micheletto fumed.

"Is that a fact? In that case I'll ask the Pope, after which I will know what answer to give you."

The elderly master bridled. "Very well," he snapped. "We shall see

167

whether or not you can be made to repent this impertinence. Who do you think you are?"

Cellini casually waved him out of the shop.

The barbed dagger of the Florentine's insolence pierced Micheletto where it hurt most, in his pride. The slight smoldered and flamed into bitter rancor. This lazar, this young hellion, must be taught a sharp lesson.

The scuffle for Papal commissions was a ruthless dog-eat-dog affair, for with the Pontifical favor, success was assured. The fortunate few who skimmed the cream had to be ever on guard, had to be continuously alert against the spiteful and malignant tactics of the many who wanted only to pull them down and step into the vacant place.

In order to keep abreast of this constant plotting, an artist—any artist—made it a point to acquire friends at court. Friends of all kinds and stations, the more the better. These formed the little cliques of supporters and well-wishers who kept him informed of the shifts and conspiracies being set in motion against him by his enemies and their friends. Very often they served as his defenders when he was absent and unable to defend himself.

Cellini had made many such friends. Most of them were also his patrons and it was to their own interests to guard his reputation. And since at court nothing was ever secret for very long, bit by bit, morsel by morsel, the meat and bone of Micheletto's plan was brought in to him as it was being evolved.

First Micheletto called a meeting of the master-goldsmiths serving the Vatican, to discuss ways and means of checking the ascendancy of this Florentine upstart. They deliberated, and started work on some thirty designs for a gold clasp, each differing from the others. While these were being prepared, the elderly Micheletto took counsel with the Milanese jeweler, Pompeo, an artisan who was firmly entrenched at court. Pompeo wanted that commission more than he had ever wanted anything. There was a reputation to be made from it, and he was ready to go to any lengths to discredit the man who had robbed him of it.

Tall, somewhat corpulent, a trifle greasy looking, Pompeo quivered in anticipation as he discussed possibilities.

"Look you, Master Micheletto, you have ready access to His Holiness' ear by reason of your present office. I, in turn, have the good fortune to be high in His Sublimity's favor." Pompeo leered. "It should not be difficult for us to show the Pope how badly he is being served by this Cellini."

Micheletto nodded agreement. He did not see fit to add that the favor Pompeo enjoyed resulted largely from the internecine nepotism practiced by an uncle, Traiano Alicorno, who was first chamberlain of the court.

"It is the just reward for the superior skill evident in all your work, my dear Pompeo." Micheletto's voice held a touch of irony. "It is for this very reason that I seek you out and enlist your aid. Also," he added, as if in afterthought, "I would suggest we make use of Messer Traiano. A powerful man. He can be of service here."

"Just so. I have already discussed this affair to some length with my illustrious uncle." Pompeo's eyes narrowed to slits. "But, mark you, good Micheletto, I shall insist that mine be among the most prominent of the designs, when these are placed before His Holiness for inspection."

"My dear fellow. How could it be otherwise?" Secretly amused, Micheletto was as certain as he drew breath that this pretentious buffoon had no possible chance. The pompous dolt had not the mind, the imagination, with which to conceive such grandeur. Moreover, his own cartoon would quickly point out the indifferent skill of the other— perhaps all the others.

When the sketches were completed Micheletto had no difficulty in arranging an interview with the Pope.

Clement listened quietly. The cultivation of the arts formed an important part of his life. The old goldsmith's words worried him. He spoke of having seen an indifferent drawing for the morse, and pointed out that all this secrecy made it obvious that Cellini was hiding the work to cover up its many faults.

Pompeo backed him up.

"Like my very worthy colleague, Master Micheletto," he insinuated venomously, "I too have seen this Cellini's design for the Papal button. *Un offesa all'occhio!* An offense to the eye, Your Holiness! This piddler is incapable of carrying out a work of such importance."

Clement pondered. It was possible that these two might be right. They were competent men; and his Messer Traiano had touched on this same subject. It disturbed him.

"If this is so," he told them, "then we must see for ourselves. If, as

169

you say, he is unfit to carry out such a project, then we shall cast about for someone who is."

"Most Blessed Father," Pompeo bored in, "Master Micheletto and myself have undertaken to prepare several excellent designs. These are ready for review by Your Holiness."

"*Eccellente,*" remarked Clement. "We are pleased with this mark of your devotion to our service. However, we will wait until Master Benvenuto has completed his model. Then we shall give consideration to all."

"...And that, my good fellow, is how the matter stands at the moment." Annibale Caro, distinguished writer and poet, ended his account of the manipulations projected by the Florentine's rivals and looked closely to see what emotion his words had kindled. Surprisingly, he saw none. The usually volatile Cellini was calm.

"What do you propose to do about all this scheming?"

"Nothing, my friend. Nothing at all. I intend to finish my model; after which, we shall see who is fit and who is not fit. I don't mind competition. If I'm no better than they are, then I don't deserve this commission."

"When will you have finished your model?"

"Very soon ... three or four days."

"Any plans for the presentation of it?"

"At the moment, none. Right now, I am thinking and looking forward to nothing but the pleasant evening in store."

"Ah. You are attending Bastiano's supper and entertainment to-night? Good! I shall see you there. Be certain to come, Neutino."

"I'll be there," Cellini assured him. "From what I have been told of Bastiano's plans, it promises to be an enjoyable evening."

XXIV

I T WAS EARLY WHEN THE FLORENTINE ARRIVED
at Bastiano's house. Several of the painter's guests had already preceded
him and were lounging around the large dining hall. Annibale Caro
waved and resumed his conversation with two other men of letters, the
poet Antonio Allegretti, and the Latinist Giovanni Greco. The host,
Sebastiano del Piombo, or, more simply, Bastiano, seemed deeply involved with Giovanni Gaddi, Clerk of the Papal *Camera*. In a far
corner, Lodovico da Fano plucked the strings of a lute while he recited
an ode extolling the beauty of two ladies, who listened raptly to the
glib, improvised lines.

Messer Giovanni answered Cellini's easy bow with a wave and a
smile. Bastiano, a large florid man of forty-five, hurried over.

"Ho, Neutino! Enter and welcome." The painter fingered his
beard and sent an approving eye over the goldsmith's costume of black
cloth stitched with a large pattern in silver thread. *"Coglioni!* I fear for
the ladies this night. Who among them will be able to withstand the
presence of so finely plumed a peacock?" He grinned as he clapped an
arm around Cellini's shoulders and drew him into the room.

"You know everyone here—*di qua, Remo,"* he called to a servant,
"some wine for Master Cellini ... Make yourself free, Neutino. I return
to settle a point with Messer Giovanni. He insists on a portrait of his
brother, and lacking the time I cannot possibly paint it. You will find
confects on the table."

Cellini sipped his wine and sauntered around the room and hall,
nodding and returning salutations as new guests arrived. For the twentieth time he paused over the paintings hung around the walls, as
thrilled by their mastery as when he first examined them. As he ambled
past the open doorway of Bastiano's studio, his eye was arrested by a
painting barely visible in the dimness of the large workroom. Curious,
to pass the time, he wandered in, lighted some candles and carried them

171

to where the canvas stood propped up on the easel. Gradually, as he drew nearer with the lights, it took on form. It was a portrait—a portrait of a girl with limpid eyes and parted lips that smiled a little smile which was at once tender and somehow saucy as well. She was dressed in an easy-fitting peasant costume of the warm south, an eggshell-colored, loose-necked blouse held tightly around a slim waist by the embroidered band of a full red skirt. She held a tambourine edgewise on the rounded curve of a thigh, and a creamy dimpled knee showed below the gathered-up embroidered hem of the skirt. Bastiano had managed the clothing so that it covered without concealing the supple figure underneath. In the whole of the work the Venetian's justly earned fame was evident. Toying with his wine cup, Cellini lingered over the effective arrangement of mass, the delicacy of the modeling—plane on receding plane—giving an illusion of roundness and depth that was delightful to look upon. The exquisitely rendered flesh tones touched with warm olive tints, so reminiscent of the coloring of Giorgione, contrasted so well with the restrained rendering of the sun-drenched field and serenely clouded sky of the background.

"*E bene, maestro?*" Bastiano had crept up behind the goldsmith and broke into his reverie.

"Eh?" annoyed at the interruption, Cellini whirled. "Ah, Bastiano, my friend."

"Well, what do you think of it?"

The softly strummed notes of a lute and the more langorous tone of a *viola da spalla* fluttered into the room.

"Your usual excellence, master. No more need be said. The model, who is she?"

"Just that, a model. She is a Sicilian dancer of my acquaintance. Name of Angela. You find her pleasing?"

"Beautiful—if she actually looks as you have portrayed her."

"She does. Graceful as a cat, too. She's a bit expensive, but worth it, even ..."

"Even, what?"

"I was about to say, even if it means putting up with her mother, a greedy old bitch who tries her hardest to sink her avaricious claws into every male who displays any interest whatever in her daughter. Her name's Beatrice, I think." Bastiano sniffed. "I had to keep throwing her a few coins now and then, and in the end I had to throw her the hell out of here, else this would never have been finished."

172

"In any case," the goldsmith told him, "you have completed a piece of work worthy of your talent."

"I'm glad it pleases you. But let's get back to the others. They're all here and our dinner waits."

Cellini became aware of her the moment he re-entered the room. There were about thirty guests ranged around the long table and she was seated near the far end, between Piloto, a long-time Florentine friend and fellow-goldsmith, and Marco Cardani, a gem engraver. They were all three laughing and chatting, and as she happened to be facing the door when the goldsmith entered, he recognized her instantly as the girl who had sat for the painting. And in the same instant, as her eyes fell upon him momentarily, he saw that Bastiano had taken no liberties with that face, had added nothing to it. It was fully as beautiful and expressive as the painter depicted it. Seating himself, he examined her with care—what he could see of her.

She was wearing a vermilion gown of stiff brocade, with short puffed sleeves slashed with pink silk. The dress had the usual low cut bodice which tapered in a wide triangle, leaving the column of her neck free. The tightly laced stays underneath emphasized the deep hollow between the upward thrust of firm, rounded breasts. A pendant of gold filigree hung between them like an invitation, and a red stone set in it flashed as she turned from one to the other of her table companions. With a sigh he heartily wished she hadn't been placed so far away.

All through dinner his eyes stayed on her. He turned away only once, to answer a remark made by Bastiano's mistress, Mona Teresa, who was seated next to him. And when he turned back he saw that she was looking toward him with that same slight smile on her lips. She looked and smiled and then turned to say something to Piloto, who looked over and grinned broadly, then made her a long answer. When he finished she looked again at the Florentine and smiled—a big, friendly, inviting smile. Cellini's insides fluttered and he had to take a drink of wine.

After what seemed an age the repast came to an end and the tables were removed. Chairs and settles were arranged around the walls and little groups began to form. Cellini could see all of her now, though she still was at the other end of the room. His eyes told him little more. She was tall, long-limbed and slender. The skirt of her dress swept down to the floor and exposed only glimpses of a small red slipper and the occasional curve of a leg as it pressed against the fabric of the gown. Mona Teresa was pouring a continuous stream of inane jabber into his ear, in which he had to appear interested. He dared not break away lest he slight the mistress of his good friend and host.

It was Bastiano who approached, squeezed Teresa's hand to silence her, and looked smilingly at the goldsmith whose eyes and mind were not there at all.

"Close your mouth, Neutino."

"Ha?"

"You're slavering, *per Bacco.*" Bastiano laughed. "Come—I'll present you. Why the devil didn't you signal, or something?"

Cellini was too far gone to answer. He followed, all docility. His throat felt strangely dry and there was an alarming inner turmoil that was something new. But at the moment there was nothing and no one else on earth but the ravishing, tawny-skinned beauty at the other end of the room.

"Mona Angela Catelli, my sweet poppet. *Prego...*" The painter took her hand and drew her to her feet. *"Il illustrissimo maestro,* Benvenuto Cellini, whom you have enslaved with a glance." Bastiano laid a finger against his nose and appeared to ponder slyly. "You may call him Neutino, my dear," he told her dryly. "I'm certain he will like that."

The goldsmith bowed and Angela curtsied, smiling up at him as she did so. Her movement was full of grace.

He looked at her, close up.

She stood straight and poised, with shoulders thrown back and bosom thrust forward, her arched neck curving outward slightly and the slender oval of her face tilted up, showing a piquant chin, full red lips—so full they pouted a little—and a pert, slightly aquiline nose. Her skin had a lustrous softness with something of the color of a fully ripened peach touched with a tawny olive tint. Her hair was as black as a night of affliction and cascaded in silken waves over neck and shoulders. Her eyes were a trifle slanted, almond shaped. They looked dreamy and had the warm, sheening glow of banked fires. The whites had a milk-blue cast, the irises brown with little flecks of a lighter, more golden color. There was something else in them—a pledge—an assurance that if she to whom they belonged were ever to belong to you, all that you ever longed for or dreamed of or desired of love and of woman would be yours and only yours.

They were like promises whispered in a silvery moonlight.

174

Cellini looked into Angela's eyes and saw all that—and his entrails corded and tied themselves into knots. He pressed the flat of his hands against the skirt of his doublet. The palms were sweating. His fingers quivered. A difficult thing, keeping one's hands off Angela.

Angela chuckled softly and moistened her lips with the tip of her tongue.

"You seem satisfied with what you see, Master Neutino," she quipped. She had a throaty voice. The slightest touch of a lisp slurred her words. It was probably the too full lips which caused this.

"By the splendor of God!" gasped the goldsmith, grinning. "You are well named. *Angela!* Lovely angel! Dream of my dreams! You are a star fallen from a sky that can never again be as beautiful, now that you are no longer there."

Angela's eyes flashed.

"Hah! By the girdle of Venus, *ben detto!*" Bastiano beamed at a compliment so neatly turned. "Our Benvenuto has, as usual, coated his tongue with honey. Beware, my Angela!"

"Alas, Neutino. Are you then so well spoken with all women?" she asked with a pout.

Cellini made a hopeless gesture. He was regaining some consciousness, and with it some wit.

"Never before, light of my eyes. I have never before been able to see beyond the moon; and now I not only see beyond it, I can touch a lovely star that was there—you."

"*Caspita!* This improves as it moves along," Bastiano interposed. "I yearn to hear more, but you must leave off for the present, my dear fellow. *Adesso, adesso,* Angela must hold to a promise she made me." He turned to her. "Well then, my adorable Terpsichore, you will favor us with a performance?"

Angela turned on the full power of her eyes and looked at the Florentine impishly. He went limp.

"Would you care to see me dance, Neutino?"

The goldsmith recalled that Bastiano had mentioned she was a Sicilian dancer. He nodded vehemently.

"Would I enjoy the sight of Venus come back to earth?" he told her. "What a question!"

"Very well. I go to change clothing. But will you be waiting for me? Or must I yield place to one of these lovesome ladies? I don't think I would like that." Her nose wrinkled like a rabbit's.

Cellini breathed deeply and looked carefully around the room, as he took hold of her hand.

"*Dolce mia vita,* there is no one here but you."

Holding her hand in both of his he turned it and kissed its palm.

Angela closed the hand into a fist, caressed him with her eyes, and left to change.

Bastiano was beaming again. "*Al corpo di Bacco!*" he approved. "Superb! Matchless! I stand before you an instructed man, my Neutino."

The painter went to consult with the band and a short while later, called for attention.

"*Attenzione, signori...signore! Vi prego!...*My lords, gallant gentlemen, lovely ladies who would shame the Graces themselves! a spectacle awaits your pleasure. A fitting finale for our pleasant evening together. Mona Angela is to dance a tarantella for us. You—will judge of its merit. So, then, *amici,* the lovely Angela..."

While the guests cheered, Angela glided to the center of the floor and bowed. She had changed into the same peasant costume Cellini had seen in the painting. There were bracelets on her wrists and her hair was combed back behind her pink ears, exposing large hooped earrings. There were no tightly laced stays to distort her contours. The freed, slender figure in the gay costume stood out with a supple gracefulness that was ravishing. Her feet were bare and she stood poised in the center of the floor, one hand on her hip, the other holding a jingling tambourine. The Florentine studied her with undisguised admiration. There were no angles, no straight lines. She was all pleasing curves. His trained eye told him that here was no ordinary, run-of-the-mill, everyday bit of work. This was the product of an inspired hand—and the inspiration had lasted to the conclusion.

Like many another artist before and after him, Cellini was aware that all too frequently when the Creator began the moulding of a lump of clay with the thought of turning out something outstanding, the Hand slipped. A feeling of futility, frustration, or perhaps ennui, seemed to set in. The Potter lost interest and became lax. That had not been so in the present case. Angela was a work constructed with loving care.

With startling suddenness the string band erupted in the rapid, staccato tempo of a Neapolitan folk dance; the treble mandolins predominating, the bi-necked theorbos adding resonant basso notes in rich harmony with the alto tones of lutes and viols. Three tambourines thumped out the triplet time in unison with the one held by the dancer.

Slowly at first Angela began the initial steps of the lively and passionate tarantella. Her legs flashed as she expertly whirled and stepped in the sensuous movements. As the dance progressed the tambourines quickened the tempo, the cadences became faster. The music and the dance grew wilder, more abandoned. The fire of it caught up dancer, musicians, and onlookers alike. They were swept away in the vibrant, seductive movements that were now so swift the eye saw only a flash of motion, a streak of red skirt, white blouse and flying tresses, and the supple muscular writhing of tawny legs as Angela pirouetted and whirled around the floor in an ever-quickening rhythm that ended in a crashing crescendo.

The music ceased as abruptly as it began, leaving Angela in the exact position she held at the beginning of the dance. She poised there briefly, then sank to the floor in a bow, amid a roar of frantic applause.

"You were pleased, Neutino?" Face flushed, bosom heaving, Angela laid a hand on the goldsmith's arm while she worked her feet into the slippers a servant brought her. She looked up inquiringly.

"Lovely one, all the gods on Olympus never saw better. I begin to wonder if you are but a dream. Can it be that you are real?"

Angela smiled saucily. "Real enough, and for the moment, warm enough."

"Here, take some wine."

"No, not now. It might make me ill. Tell me of yourself. I wish to know if what I have heard of you is true."

"What have you heard?"

"That there is genius in you; that you are a master unsurpassed in your art; that you are fierce and reckless—*un uomo di terribilità*—equally an artist, a gallant, and a soldier; and that your path is strewn with the lovely ladies you have spurned and cast aside." Angela's smooth brow wrinkled. "Is that last true?"

Cellini countered with polite deprecation and reassurances, as his companion had meant he should, and proceeded to draw Angela's history from her. She was a Sicilian, a dancer recently come to Rome from Naples. She lived with her mother in a pretty little house near the Banks, not far from Bastiano's home. The painter had seen her dance at an entertainment given by a Roman gentleman and had asked her to model for a painting that had been commissioned of him.

"...And I have a little donkey on which I ride. He neighs every time he sees me."

"I can see why," the Florentine answered truthfully. "Tell me, how is it that a maid as pretty as you is not yet married? Are you promised?"

"Married? Thank God, no! Nor yet promised. Life is much sweeter and freer as I live it." Angela looked up soberly. "I have no illusions of what my lot would be if I were to marry.—A life of drudgery as the broodmare and chattel of some petty craftsman or shopkeeper. No, I prefer to live my own life and enjoy my youth. Besides, I earn nice sums from my dancing. Much more than any husband I could snare. Then there is my mother. She would never allow it. If I married she would then have to depend on my brothers for support." Angela laughed. "She would have no easy arrangement there!"

They became lost in each other, reliving past years and past experiences, until, looking around the room, they saw only four or five guests. The others had all departed.

"God's teeth! Let's be off. I will see you to your home, yes?"

Angela smiled and nodded. "I won't bother to change. I'll just get my cloak."

Cellini lingered only for a farewell glass with Bastiano and Caro before joining her at the door.

"Why not ride with me, pretty one?" he asked, pointing to the prancing barb saddled and waiting behind a little droop-eared donkey, who, as Angela had said, neighed when its mistress came into view.

"I'm not certain I could do it. I've never ridden that way before."

"I will teach you."

Angela looked up, a roguish smile on her lips and in her eyes.

"I don't for a moment doubt it, *carino,*" she chortled. "I'll wager you could teach me things."

Cellini laughed and called to his link boy. "Nuncio—lead my lady's donkey as you light the way."

Vaulting into the saddle, he leaned down and easily lifted her up across the pommel. In the near darkness of the lantern's glow she hooked a leg around it and slipped her arms around his chest while she shifted to a comfortable position. The softness of her breasts pressed into him. The warmth of her penetrated like a brand. Unthinking, without conscious effort, he leaned over and crushed his mouth to hers.

Angela pulled back with a sigh and laid her head against her shoulder.

178

"I fear we run too quickly, you and I, Neutino," she whispered. "Or it may be that I have never before met anyone like you."

"Your lips, *dolcetta*—they are as sweet as ..."

He searched for and found them again.

"I want you to pose for me sometime, my dream. In these same clothes you are wearing. I wish to portray you as you appeared when first I looked upon the loveliness that is you. Will you?"

She squeezed her arms tighter around him. "Of course."

"Marvelous. When?"

"Right now. Immediately," she answered, cuddling against his arm. "Do you live far from here, Neutino?"

"No. Very close."

"Take me there and make your sketch. I'm thirsty and wish a drink."

In Cellini's studio they sipped wine while he worked by candlelight. Angela posed standing, in the peasant costume she was still wearing. The neckband of the blouse had crept down over her shoulder and her hair tumbled down in charming disarray. The goldsmith had thrown off his doublet and was working in his shirt. He was half finished with the color sketch and already thinking of asking her to pose for a wax model. He looked up at her. Her eyes stared back, eloquently.

Just how it happened, neither knew. Without being consciously aware of having risen, he was beside her, pulling her to him. She swayed and pressed close.

"Gently, *mi amore*," she whispered against his cheek. "Gently, or you will break me in two." Her fingers ran a tingling course along his arm. The muscles of it were flexed and tense. "You're strong—and I'm not made of marble."

"That I know, my treasure," he told her through his teeth.

She tossed back her head and laughed softly, her lips parted, her white teeth glistening, and her breath blowing out through them gently. He tightened his hold around her as she raised a hand to his shoulder. The other went around him and began toying with his neck. Angela closed her eyes and pulled his head down, lifting herself up, straining against him. Cellini's mouth closed hungrily over hers, his hand caressing the curve of her back. She sighed tremulously and her tongue pressed against his lips, moving, exploring. He pulled her greedily

179

closer. An anguished little moan blew against his mouth and a quiver trembled through her and made him press her all the harder.

A long minute tiptoed silently past and dissolved itself into memory.

Angela pulled her mouth away and pressed her cheek against his lips. She was breathing heavily, in little shuddering gasps. Cellini lowered his head and kissed her bared shoulder, where the blouse had pulled off. He began tugging at the drawstring in the neck band, kissing her neck and throat.

She moaned feebly. "Careful, *tesoro mio,* you'll tear it."

"I don't care."

"I do," she whispered with a sigh. "I must go home in it. Wait... my love..." She tugged helplessly at his arms. "Let me..." She kissed him lightly on the tip of his nose and disengaged herself.

A little breathlessly, her fingers shaking, she began unfastening the laces of her skirt. She had little to remove.

The goldsmith's fingers fumbled so he had to go for another goblet of wine. But when he returned and saw her in the flickering candlelight, the tingling sensation that stole through him made him gasp. There was a sultry warmth about her that was intoxicating. It changed the room, the world, making it misty and unreal. Angela's fingers caressed his face. She was breathless and trembling, almost swooning. Her arms went about him and he felt her lips and her hot breath on his cheek. He kissed her furiously, desperately. He became lost in the pulsing throb, the ineffable thrill of her. All thought and presence vanished in a rapture that was a churning wave, sweeping away time and present, oblivious to everything but the joy of fulfillment.

XXV

THE CELLINI WHO STRUTTED PROUDLY INTO the Vatican was something of a new and different man. The fluid of life bubbled as it coursed through him. He hummed a snatch of song and bowed cheerfully to acquaintances and friends as he strode down the long halls, the finished model of the morse pressed confidently under his arm.

Arriving at an antechamber he sent in his name and requested that His Holiness be informed that he waited upon his wishes. Traiano came out, lied that the Pope was occupied at the moment, and sent one page scurrying off after Pompeo and another for Micheletto, urging them to hasten with the drawings. He let Cellini cool his heels for nearly two hours. The Florentine didn't mind. He knew the reason behind the long wait; knew that the chamberlain was lying in his teeth. It didn't bother him. Nothing could, just then. He used up the time thinking of Angela. *Angela!* The two hours passed like a flash.

The two goldsmith-conspirators puffed into the antechamber, casting disdainful glances in his direction. He leered back at them. Traiano reappeared, winked surreptitiously at his nephew, and waved all three through a series of rooms, into the presence.

Clement was in his favorite official chamber, the magnificent *Camera della Segnatura,* a room adorned with frescoes painted by Raphael, his first work in Rome. Seated in a massive chair, before a long, extravagantly ornate table, the Pope was talking with some of his gentlemen. He stopped when he saw the three drawing near. They knelt.

"Ah! You are come," he greeted them. "Good! We are most anxious to see what you have accomplished."

Micheletto and Pompeo pushed forward, unrolling cartoons as they advanced. Pompeo slyly insinuated his drawing among the first few to be presented. Cellini didn't seem to mind being thrust into the background. He stood by, silently looking on with a detached air, while Clement began a careful scrutiny of the designs.

In common with his fellow-men, the Medici Pope had to make the most of a drab age. Diversions were few. Entertainment was basic and usually gross. For the opulent, there was one realm which offered escape —the cultivation of the arts. There one could find a vast man-created world in which the beautiful reigned supreme. As was the case with nearly all of the affluent patrons of that age, Clement possessed keenly developed tastes in the arts. The drawings before him were examined with the discerning eye of a connoisseur who knows what to look for. He was displeased. Here he had thought to be diverted by a study of some interesting conceptions and glowing ideas. To find relaxation from the cabals and intrigues that occupied him....And what was he given to look at? The vacuous piddlings of incompetent fools! No creative effort. No feeling. Nothing but poverty of imagination.

181

Cellini looked on silently, his face carefully washed of all expression. He had quickly seen that the designs, though different, all ran to the same pattern. They were skillful enough, but all betrayed a lack of judgment, of understanding, and of sound principles of design. None had grasped the fact that when figures are to be introduced into a design containing large gems, it is necessary to compose with extreme care. None had understood that unless this is done, the two—figure and gem—will clash with each other, and the eye will not know which of the two is the true center of interest. All of the designs had set that large diamond in the center of the breast of God the Father. *Ignoranti!* The hollow conceptions of base minds. *Canagliaccia!* He was bored. He yawned indolently, feeling a little sorry for the Pope.

Clement examined a few more of the designs, leafed through the rest, and hissing out a sigh of exasperation at the cramped imaginations that had created them, flung all of them to the floor. His stern eyes looked at the thoroughly downcast pair before him.

When his eye shifted to the Florentine, a crease quickly appeared on his brow. It arched inquisitively. That impertinent look on the master's face—what did it signify?

"Come forward here, Benvenuto. Let me see if you have fallen into the same error as the rest. Show me here your model."

Cellini moved forward, unclasping the little box. He held it closed, opening it quickly and dramatically before the Pontiff.

Clement's eyes shone.

"As God is my Creator and my Judge!" he gave a gasp of delight, "had you been within me! ... Were you a part of me! ... You could not have done other than you have done! In very truth, these lazars know nothing but how to disgrace and dishonor themselves."

Cellini turned proudly to Micheletto and Pompeo, who were slowly diffusing the purple-green vapor of envy and apoplexy. A smirk curled around his lips, as he leered at them again.

More leisurely the Pope, surrounded by courtiers, re-examined the model. The figure of God was shown in a three-quarter view, seated and leaning forward, His hand raised in benign benediction. A mantle flowed voluminously around Him. Below the figure, the diamond sparkled from a setting supported by the upraised arms of three cherubim—the center cherub modeled in full relief, the others in half-relief. All around them, other cherubs, properly subordinated, held the other

182

gems. The model was executed in white stucco on a black stone, in full scale.

The Pope's smile was back in place. He turned to his first chamberlain.

"Messer Traiano, fetch hither immediately five hundred gold ducats of the *Camera*."

The gold was to be melted down and used for making the morse.

Clement resumed the study of the model. It pleased him immensely. Still—

"Look you, my Benvenuto, we fear for one thing. Stucco is easy to manipulate. The difficulty is to create this in gold."

Cellini waved that away contemptuously. Today he was another Vulcan.

"Most Blessed Father, let it be understood between us that I am to receive nothing for my efforts unless the finished work is ten times better than this model of mine!"

That started an argument. The assembled court flatly averred that the goldsmith could never achieve such an aim. The Pontiff, too, was skeptical.

The Florentine brushed aside all contention, holding to his statement. Proof, he told them, would be forthcoming.

The gold arrived. Clement told him to go straight to work. He was very anxious to see the finished clasp.

Cellini withdrew, impatient to start on the piece. But more than this, he wanted to get back to Angela. It had been four hours since he last saw and held her. Too long!

The days that followed were idyllic, filled with the pleasure of creative work and the glow of the continual warming flame that was Angela. One evening, some eight days after he had started on the gold morse, a shopboy came to the goldsmith's room to announce a gentleman caller from the Vatican. Cellini went down. He knew the courtier, a Bolognese nobleman and Papal chamberlain, but he could not recall his name.

"*Messere*," he murmured, "how can I serve you?"

"*Ah, buona sera, maestro*. I grieve at disturbing your hours of leisure, but His Holiness wishes you to accompany me to the Papal palace, together with the morse, as much as you have done of it."

"Er...some trouble, Your Excellency?" Was it possible that those dull-witted enemies of his had not given up their lost cause?

"Oh, no! Quite the contrary. More good fortune. I will explain as we walk, Master Benvenuto."

En route to the Vatican behind the courtier's retinue of pages and servants, the two exchanged civilities, then:

"So that you will know the mind of the Pope, Benvenuto, be advised that he does not wish to see this work of yours so much as to offer another commission. You will be asked if you will undertake to fashion the dies for the Mint of Rome. For this reason, I advise you now so that you may think upon the matter and have your answer ready."

Coinage! A branch of art he had long wished to set his hand to.

"I have already given a great deal of thought to this very thing, *messere,* and have an answer ready. Yet tell me, pray, what mood is His Holiness in?"

The courtier dandled a hand. *"Così-così.* The despatches from Florence have not held much good news. There seems to be a battle impending. Except for that the Papal army is getting nowhere. It appears that in a recent heavy attack on the walls we were again flung back, and more!" The nobleman smiled. "While the Imperial troops were fighting their hardest, the youths of Florence showed their contempt by playing a game of *calcio* in the Piazza della Signoria, in full view of our soldiers, who looked on from the heights outside the walls."

Although the goldsmith took pains to remain strictly neutral in the war and the political jockeying for power over Florence, he had to laugh. He could picture the surly chagrin on the faces of Charles' Spaniards as they viewed that demonstration of defiance and contempt. A game of football—while under fire—priceless.

"Yes," smiled the chamberlain, "His Holiness, too, laughed when he read that, saying that such a gesture was to be expected from the Florentines. Still...this, on top of that last blow by your fellow-citizens..."

"What blow?"

"Well, it has been kept quiet. Hidden under the rose, so to speak. I myself learned of it by chance. Some weeks ago the *condottiere* Stefano Colonna, who as you may know is in the service of Florence, arranged a sortie. In the dead of night three thousand Florentine soldiers, each wearing a white shirt over his armor so that he might be recognized by his comrades, stole up on the Imperial army and began a massacre. *Come di fato,* but for a misunderstanding on the part of the Florentine Captain-General, the Colonna white-shirts might have routed the whole of Orange's besieging army."

"Misunderstanding?"

"*Sì.* The lord Malatesta Baglioni apparently misunderstood a signal. While the fighting was at its height and the Colonna banner sweeping all before it, the Captain-General caused retreat to be sounded. It was a most fortunate blunder—for Pope Clement."

The Medici had just finished with supper and was dawdling over his wine when the two were ushered in. If the bad news from Florence was causing him concern, the Pope did not show it. He was affable, jovial. But then, it was quite possible that those despatches were telling him more than he cared to say. He called the goldsmith to him.

Cellini made his obeisance and displayed the morse, which had progressed to a roughly cut, sketched-in figure. Even so, it displayed a style superior to the model.

"This is exquisitely done, *maestro,*" the Pontiff told him. "We are ready to believe you will not only reach but surpass the mark you boasted of. But to come to the point of our request that you attend us here, it is our intention to give you another commission. One which, handled as competently as this present one, will please us greatly. Have you ever tried your hand at making dies for coinage?"

"Never, Your Holiness, although I have long studied the art and know how these are made."

"Have you the courage to attempt it?"

The question was not an idle one. Failure in a commission of such importance to a ruler as the coins which proclaimed his reign could well mean irreparable disgrace.

"For such a task, one which I have long desired, I have no lack of courage, Holy Father."

"Very well. You will then make the model dies for a gold doubloon. Upon the face of the coin you will represent a naked Christ with His hands tied behind Him, and the inscription: *Ecce Homo.* The reverse is to depict ourself and the Emperor supporting a cross which appears to be toppling. Around it, this legend: *Unus spiritus et una fides erat in eis.* Go now and show us what you can accomplish."

Everything else—excepting only Angela—waited, while Cellini made two steel dies. He worked day and night, designing, engraving, discarding and redesigning, until he had made a set which showed

185

his adequacy for the task. He quickly stamped a gold coin, and together with the dies and a collection he had got together, took it to the Vatican. It was a warm Sunday afternoon.

"*È una cosa maravigliosa!* A marvelous thing!" chortled Clement, looking up to see the goldsmith fingering a flat box. "What have you there, master?"

Cellini spread out the collection he had brought along, the coins of two former Popes, Julius and Leo.

"Your Holiness might like to make a small comparison, since this is my first coin," he told the Pontiff.

The comparison was careful. When it was finished Clement was bound to admit that his fellow-Florentine had scored another triumph. He proved the point by ordering two other variations for the reverse of the doubloon.

Cellini drew a document from the inner pocket of his doublet. The paper had been prepared a week before. It was a petition requesting the post of Stamp-Master in the Mint.

"Since Your Holiness is pleased with my efforts I beg from you the office of Stamp-Master, so that I may better serve Your Sanctity."

The *maestro delle stampe* drew a salary of six gold crowns a month and in addition received payment for all dies made under his supervision, at the rate of three to a ducat. That made it a lucrative post.

Clement nodded agreement. "In truth," he said, "you have earned it fairly and deserve it." He handed the petition to his Datary. "See to it that this is registered quickly," he told him.

The Papal *Datario,* Messer Tommaso Cortese, was a member of Pompeo's clique.

"Most Blessed Father," he suggested quietly, slipping the document into a pocket, "this is a matter for consideration. It were best not to run so fast."

Clement frowned. He knew the meaning of that. The petition would never be forwarded, unless—

"We understand you perfectly," he curtly informed the courtier. "Give us here that paper."

The Pope signed and returned it.

Cellini beamed. The extra money would do handily. Angela was proving an expensive little kitten.

"Now that you have your answer," the Pope informed his Datary, "see to it that the seal is affixed and the document forwarded at once, for such is our pleasure. The shoes of Benvenuto are worth more than the eyes of all these other clod-pates put together ... Yes?—"

Clement stopped and looked inquiringly at Battista Sanga, who had rushed headlong into the room. The Papal secretary was in a lather of excitement.

"Your Beatitude will forgive this abrupt intrusion when you have heard the news I bear. Holy Father—" he straightened and squared his shoulders "—a despatch has this moment been received from our forces investing the Republic. The army of Florence has been destroyed in battle and the city is ready to sue for peace!"

Clement rose to his feet, his face blossoming in a beatic smile. He clasped his hands.

He had won back his Florence!

XXVI

Another commission, neutino?"

Angela stopped a dance rehearsal and looked up expectantly as Cellini came in. He had spent the morning at the Vatican and was whistling happily as he climbed the stairs.

"Another commission, *dolcina,*" he smiled, taking her around the waist and lifting her to a seat on the table. "Another coin—of the value of two *carlini*. And since its value is low, its distribution will be great. And I have good news! Alessandro de' Medici is coming to Rome. Which means that my brother will probably come with him. It has been a long time since I've seen Cechin."

"When does he arrive?"

"The Pope didn't know, a few days very likely. Why so pensive, *carina?*"

Angela pouted. "It's Mama," she told him eyeing him a little anxiously. "She's at it again."

Cellini sighed. He had come to dread that female. Bastiano had been precise in his description of her—a greedy bitch. The old harridan nagged unceasingly of her continuous needs. She had been milking his purse from the day she'd learned of his feelings for her daughter.

"What does that old battle-ax want now?"

187

"She needs wine for table use."

Not too bad. The last of Beatrice's needs had cost him some twenty crowns—a complete set of furniture for her bedroom.

"Did she say the wine was for her use, or is it for those two lazars you have for brothers? And in any event, does she think I am a banker? I am a Cellini, not a Medici."

"She is difficult," Angela mused reflectively, "but I've never known her to be any different. She's like that all the time. She also says I'm not home enough, that I don't give her comfort."

Cellini frowned. "Ah? I have understood. Tell her to get herself a barrel of wine, if that will quiet her down. Tell her to drown herself in it."

Angela slid her arms around him. There was a new dress she'd seen . . .

Cecchino had news when he arrived in Rome. His master had been faced with the Papal fief of Penna. And since Penna was a duchy, the Medici scion was Duke Alessandro now.

"That's whom I now serve," he told his brother grandly, with an aloof toss of the hand. "A duke, no less. No more of these two-for-a-*soldo* noblemen for your little brother."

"*Ecco!*" Cellini bowed elaborately. "But tell me, *fratello,* is all this doing you any good?"

"And why not, pray? I've come up in the world since we parted in Florence. I've been given a command. A small one, but it will grow. The mighty oak starts its life as a little acorn, remember. I even have an ensign, Bertino Aldobrandi. You remember the family, at home? A nice young lad. Shows promise."

"Ah! In that case I can only regard you as a future *condottiere,* a coming Giovanni delle Bande Nere," laughed the goldsmith. "Drink up, and tell me how long you will be in Rome, Cechin?"

"Who knows? That is not for me to say. From what I gather it may be some time."

"You will put up here with me, of course."

Cecchino looked at his older brother with a large grin on his face.

"My lad," he told him, laying a hand on his shoulder, "I've met your Angela at dinner today. You don't want me here. You don't want anyone here. I have put up at an inn, with Bertino. Oh, don't worry," he added quickly, stopping the protest forming on his brother's

188

lips, "I'll be here every day. It's just that there's a portion of your life I have no intention of interfering with. That belongs to you—and Angela. By the way, where is she tonight?"

"Dancing. An entertainment given by some Spanish lord. She does quite a bit of that. Does very well at it too," he added with a frown. "And she won't give it up. She's a very independent creature."

Cecchino laughed. "Good. That's the way for a wench to be. Self-sufficient. Let's go calling. I'm free until tomorrow. Alessandro is going to the Vatican tonight, to confer with his—" Cecchino broke off, smiled, and went on "—with the Pope. It is not politic to refer to Clement as Alessandro's father. I must learn to stop doing so."

Sitting placidly in the same little private room where he had discussed his plans for Florence, Clement's fingers drummed idly on the smoothly lustrous table top while he waited for Alessandro to be shown in. He sat in the same high-backed chair, gazing unseeingly at the lighted cressets suspended from the ceiling. His secretary, Sanga, loitered silently in the background. He did not know what the Pope intended to discuss with Duke Alessandro, but being a curious man he hoped he would be permitted to remain during the meeting. The golden light from the lamps, which cast such grotesque dancing shadows around the room, showed him the satisfied look on the Holy Father's face. It bespoke high doings—affairs of the greatest consequence.

With no thought of his secretary's inner desire, Clement was mulling over his plans, checking over each salient detail. Yes, he agreed with himself, best to move slowly and surely, one careful move at a time. There was no hurry. Florence could not again be wrested from the Medici grasp. He had made certain of it, this time. The hold upon her throat was firm. Her thralldom to the Emperor—by way of the Medici —was complete. And as for the Emperor Charles, there were plans afoot in that direction also.

Becoming impatient, he frowned and began to fidget. What was keeping Alessandro? Did he have to salute every member of the court? No matter. Such buttering was good policy, and it was high time the lad started showing some political sense. Yes, best to move slowly since there were a number of loose ends that remained to be tied. Valori could remain in Florence for the time being. He was doing well there.

Behind him Sanga stirred. Someone had knocked gently on the

door. The secretary ran to open it, bowing and murmuring a greeting.

Duke Alessandro entered, his swarthy features starkly highlighted by the flickering lights. The shadow pattern flung across his face would have delighted Titian himself. He crossed to the Pope and bowed.

"Finalmente! you are come. *Buona sera* and welcome, Your Grace!"

Alessandro dropped to one knee and negligently kissed the ring on the hand Clement extended.

"May I take this opportunity," he said, rising, "to add personal thanks for the honor Your Holiness has faced me with."

Clement smiled. "Well spoken," he told him. Turning, he waved to Sanga.

The secretary's face fell but he left the room, silently closing the door behind him.

"How did you find things at Penna?" Clement asked the new Duke.

"Most agreeable, Holy Father. It is a comfortable signory. Rich in revenues. Very tolerable."

"Va bene!" Clement pointed. "Sit you down there. We have important affairs to discuss. They concern you."

"Indeed, Blessed Father?" Alessandro lounged in his chair, waiting expectantly.

Clement pursed his lips thoughtfully, looking keenly at the dark-visaged, perfumed Alessandro.

"Yes," he told him, "they do indeed concern you. You must know what is coming. What to expect. What you shall have to do ... and when.

"During my discussions with Charles at Bologna," Clement went on without further preamble, "we arrived at certain private understandings regarding Florence. For reasons of my own, I saw to it that it was clearly understood between us that the rule of Florence was to be the sole province of the son of Lorenzo, Duke of Urbino. He, of course, is you, my dear Alessandro."

The youth gaped stupidly. He had expected a part in the rule of Florence—a small part. Ippolito was a young man of ability, with many powerful friends, and was everywhere regarded as the next Chief of State there.

"Heh?" he wondered if he had heard correctly.

"Sì." Clement nodded quietly. "You have heard correctly; but have you understood correctly? I will repeat: the rule of Florence is to fall

entirely to the *son of Lorenzo, Duke of Urbino."* Again the Pope laid judicial stress on the last words.

Alessandro understood perfectly—and correctly! At last understood why Clement never had and never would openly acknowledge him as his natural son. It was the offspring of Lorenzo who held the preferential claim of dynastic succession in the House of Medici. As usual, the astute Clement had overlooked nothing.

"I ... I had not ... had never hoped to be so favored," stammered the youth, overwhelmed by his good fortune.

"Surely," Clement offered slyly, "it is no more than one of your parts and forbears deserves? But let us get on.

"In order that we Medici shall be closely bound to the Emperor, I have prevailed upon His Imperial Majesty to give you the hand of his daughter in marriage."

"Daughter?" faltered Alessandro. He was not aware that the Emperor had a marriageable daughter.

"Yes. His daughter Margaret."

She was a bastard. But then, so was he. "Isn't she just a child?"

"Quite so. She is now ten years of age and will be unable to enter into wedlock for another five years. When she has reached fifteen, however, she will be joined with you in Holy Matrimony. *Ecco!* I look forward to performing that ceremony myself. Surely a Medici prince with the daughter of an emperor for his consort will prove an impregnable rock?" Clement leaned back, beaming proudly.

"I agree with all my heart, Your Beatitude. Yet, give me leave to put one question?" Alessandro continued without waiting for permission. "I have grave doubts that this will be as simple as it sounds in the telling." He hurled what he thought was a thunderbolt. "What of Ippolito?"

Clement waved a hand. The thunderbolt fizzled out in a wisp of smoke.

"Leave him to me. And heed well what I say to you. Everything we are discussing here must remain a closed secret until each move is ready to be made. You will say, or do, nothing. You understand me? *Nothing!* Until I give the word. And above all else until Ippolito is properly disposed of."

"Disposed of?" Absorbed by the possibilities inherent in this remark, Alessandro selected an orange from a salver on the table and began peeling it abstractedly.

Clement's eyes had narrowed to slits. "I am aware," he murmured, "that practically every noble house in Italy is of the opinion that Ippolito shall be wedded to our little Catherine, in order to perpetuate the elder Medici line. This is an excellent concept. Fundamentally sound. But it happens that I have other plans—better suited to our purpose.

"As regards Catherine, my dear Alessandro, you, as the natural son of Lorenzo, cannot possibly be joined with her. She is, so to speak, your half-sister. Such a marriage would be incestuous. However, your half-sister will make excellent bait for an alliance of our House with that of royal France. If such a project can be made to come about, and I have every reason to believe it can be, it will form a strong bulwark against any possible move by Charles, even though he is to be tied to us by your marriage to Margaret. You perceive the strategy in all this?"

"I do, Your Holiness." Alessandro scowled sourly. The Pope, it seemed to him, was wandering from the most important portion of the project. "Permit me to remind Your Sanctity that we have not yet disposed of Ippolito."

"Ippolito!" Clement again waved a hand. "Do not be concerned with him, *figliolo*. I shall take very good care of him. I shall arrange things so that it will be equally out of the question for our good cousin either to rule in Florence or to marry our little Catherine."

Alessandro flipped a segment of orange into his mouth and arched a brow. There was no fathoming the mind of this man who was his father. Poor Ippolito. He snorted softly. And yet, unless Clement had it in mind to arrange one of those quiet little assassinations, how?—

"Your Holiness will forgive my ignorance but I cannot comprehend how this can be done, unless . . ." leering evilly he left the remark unfinished. That he might be conniving in the murder of a member of his own family caused him no concern. Alessandro was not squeamish.

Clement had no difficulty in grasping the implication. He wiggled a hand violently.

"No, no! My dear boy, learn that if you would rule for long, you must plan wisely and carefully, and far in advance. Sometimes, what you have in mind is necessary, but such drastic measures should never be employed except as an extreme. No, no," the Pope shook his head, "my plans for Ippolito are quite simple—and effective. We shall do him high honor. Elevate him to the exalted dignity he deserves. And why not? He is a Medici, is he not? We are even prepared to exert a gentle pressure, should a misplaced modesty compel him to refuse our noble gifts. We shall," Clement smiled benignly, "make him a cardinal."

It was so artlessly simple, Alessandro giggled. Of course! A cardinal, espoused to the Church, could not marry—but he could rule!

"This would take care of the one, but not the other," he hastily informed Clement.

"True," nodded the Pontiff. "Now if, having been made a cardinal, our Ippolito were to be sent off on a long and urgent official mission to some distant country—Hungary, for example—he would hardly be in a position to offer objections or hindrance to *your* assuming the rule of Florence."

XXVII

THE WORK ON THE PAPAL MORSE WENT STEADily forward. The dies for the new coin were coming along. Some minor commissions were in various stages of completion. These and a medallion currently absorbed Cellini's professional interest. The medallion especially was to his taste. Its face depicted Venus and Vulcan; the Olympian husband busy at his forge, his goddess wife preening and playing with her son, Cupid. Needless to say, the model for the Venus was Angela.

"I think that medallion is turning out exceptionally well, Benvenuto." Raffaello del Moro nodded seriously and went on eating.

It was Sunday. The Del Moro household and shop had gathered for an early dinner.

"Not that it can be compared with the morse, which is by way of being a masterwork," Raffaello went on with pensive gravity. "Still, it has a—a quality, a certain charm, that pleases me. A proficient work." The elderly goldsmith paused to listen. A distant clamor that had broken out some time before, grew louder. "Eh, what is all that noise, Giovanni?" he asked his eldest son, who had gone to a window.

The youth pulled his head back into the room.

"I can't see from here, Papa. Sounds like a fight. I'm going out and have a look."

"For heaven's sake, don't go," Cellini advised him. "These street brawls are all alike. You might end by getting mixed up in the scuffle, with everything to lose and nothing whatever to gain. Stay and finish this excellent dinner."

"Wise counsel, that," agreed the father. "Stay here, *figlio*. Do not concern yourself in it."

Giovanni was already out the door, headed in the direction of the crowd milling in the street up near the bridge. When he got there the fight was over. A young man, little older than himself, was being helped away, his right arm dripping blood. Another youth, more seriously injured, lay in the street. Some men were preparing a litter to carry him to a nearby apothecary shop. Giovanni drew nearer and looked down at the youth. He gulped. It was Bertino Aldobrandi, ensign to Benvenuto's brother. Up ahead, a troop of catchpolls were walking off, dragging wounded comrades with them.

"What happened?" he asked a bystander.

"A brisk encounter, *per Dio!* Between all those blacklegs there and four youths. A dozen of them! picking a quarrel with four young men little more than boys—and they damn near routed the lot of them. Two of the youths were wounded. That one," he pointed to Bertino who was being carried away, "very badly."

Giovanni stayed around for awhile, then turned back to his home. As he did so he bumped into Cecchino, who had come to see what all the noise meant.

"Hello, Giovannino," he greeted the youth briskly. He had met all of the Del Moro family, being constantly in the shop with his brother. *"Che cosa è successo?"*

Giovanni gulped again. "A fight, I think."

"So? Who got it?" Cecchino nodded toward the pool of blood in the street.

"Ah . . . I don't know . . . exactly . . ."

The floundering alarmed the younger Cellini, why he could not say. His face hardened.

"Who? . . ." he asked again in a low voice, taking hold of the lad's shoulder.

Giovanni swallowed hard. "B-Bertino . . . I think he's dead."

Cecchino drew in a deep breath. He paled. A lad of sixteen—butchered!

"Who did it?" he snarled through clenched teeth.

"I don't know," Giovanni whispered. He was scared.

Two hands gripped at his jerkin and lifted him off the street.

"Who, I say? Who killed him?"

"It's God's truth, Cecchino," gasped the youth. "I don't know!"

"I do," piped up a losel who was looking on with interest. "I was right here when it happened. That young fellow was done for by a blackleg armed with a great big two-handed sword. Wears a blue feather in his *berretta*. Look," he pointed to the troop of catchpolls who were now near the bridge, "you can still see the bastard."

"*Gràzie!*"

Cecchino sprinted off after the Bargello guards. The man he sought was at the rear of the band, the blue feather in his cap bobbing as he walked. The heavy sword lay across a shoulder. There was blood on it. He was boasting loudly when Cecchino reached the troop.

Two catchpolls were in the way. One went sprawling on his face in the gutter. The other was lifted by the belt and hurled aside. Blue Feather turned.

Cecchino drew.

"*Provati!* You murdering whoreson! Come, test your skill on me!"

Blue Feather did not wait for a second invitation. He swung the edge of his sword in a vicious downward arc.

Trained in the stringent school of the Black Bands, Cecchino jumped lightly inside and under the arc, falling into a low crouch, one knee resting on the ground. As the heavy blade swished through the air over his head he turned and lunged, ramming his sword straight through the man's guts. The hilt of it slammed against his belly. Blue Feather went limp. The sword clattered out of his hands and he pitched backwards, his eyes glazing and his face freezing in an expression of startled surprise.

Cecchino pulled out the blade. Yelling defiantly he turned on the blacklegs nearest him and began lunging and thrusting. There arose an uproar of hoarse shouting and clashing steel. The inept *sbirri,* whose prowess lay in numbers rather than with skill in arms, crossed swords with the avenger only to be paid off in bloody gashes. Despite the vast difference in number the fight was actually one-sided. Most of the constables were turning away, trying to force a path through their own comrades. One of them, an arquebusier, was caught in the press. He was in a blind panic of fear for his life. He dropped to his hands and knees, and dragging his arquebus along with him, managed to crawl out of the tumult. He found himself behind the maddened Cecchino. Shaking with terror he leveled the musket and fired. The ball went low. Cecchino splayed down on the street before the Ponte San Angelo, blood gushing from a shattered leg. The catchpolls scampered off in disorder.

"The devil!" Cellini swung out of his chair and walked to the window where the shopowner was looking out. "That clamor is getting louder. This must be something serious. Can you make out the cause of it, Master Raffaello?"

The old goldsmith turned. "No. I can make out nothing from here. The crowd seems to be gathering around the bridge."

"I'm going out and see what is happening."

Buckling on his sword, Cellini walked off in the direction of the castle bridge. The crowd was thinning when he got there. He saw a group of men whom he knew and walked over to them. They nodded silently and made way for him as he came up. There was someone lying on the ground, splattered in an ugly welter of gore. The poor devil looked familiar. Cellini peered at him more closely . . . *Holy God in heaven!* A cold sweat broke out over him. He shivered. *"Cechin! . . ."*

Cecchino rolled his head around and looked up. His teeth were clenched hard, locked against the pain.

"Hello, brother," he gasped, making a macabre effort to appear cheerful. It didn't come off. The pain was too intense.

Two scalding tears began to sear the goldsmith's face—and soul. His brother tried to lift a hand. Cellini took hold of it.

"Don't be upset by all this, Neutino. It's to be expected in my profession. Have me removed from here. . . . There . . . there is not much time . . ." He fainted.

Cellini looked up, dazed.

They told him what had happened.

"Shot from behind? Like a dog!" He laid a hand gently on his brother's head.

A squad of the blacklegs was coming back. Their officer, one Maffio, had ordered the craven louts to return for the body of the man with the blue feather in his cap.

Cellini raced forward, wrapping his cape around his left arm to form a shield as he ran. He headed for Maffio and had his sword out of its scabbard when he was pinned from the rear. One of the men had run up behind him and locked his arms around him, holding on desperately.

"Not now, Benvenuto," he hissed into his ear. "Don't be an ass! There are too many, and besides he is not the one you seek."

Others ran up and helped to hold off the goldsmith. One of them called to Maffio.

"Away with you, quickly, or your life ends here and now!"

Maffio looked on blankly. "Who," he pointed, "who is he?"

"The brother of him you see lying there. Get you gone!"

The officer waved his catchpolls back in the direction of the Tower of Nona.

Cellini carried his brother home.

The leeches came and held weighty consultation. They dressed the mangled leg and dutifully prescribed a potpourri of physics, charms, and treatments; but there was little they could do that was helpful. The bones were crushed and splintered. They decided that nothing would be gained by amputating the leg. They could not stop the bleeding. They could only look on helplessly while the patient bled to death.

Duke Alessandro called in person as soon as he heard of the accident, and promised that the Papal surgeon himself would come and see what could be done.

A bad hemorrhage started after he left. Cecchino was delirious when the revered Papal leech, Messer Giacomo Rastelli of Perugia, was announced. The learned physician made an examination and slowly shook his head.

"It is unfortunate, but there is naught that may be done here. All I can hope to do is bring about some small temporary comfort." The doctor drew out a box containing an iridescent powder, which he mixed with an oily liquid. "His Sublime Grace, the illustrious Duke Alessandro, has given over to me a pearl which I have caused to be pounded into powder. Mixed with this distilled essence of potent drugs, the nostrum will help to quiet the young man."

Aided by the other leeches, who nodded vehement agreement to the sage diagnosis and skill of their eminent colleague, the decoction was administered. The Perugian doctor looked at Cellini.

"Have you summoned a priest, Benvenuto?"

"Not yet, Messer Giacomo."

"Do so at once. Your brother has not long to live and must make his peace with God."

197

A monk from a nearby monastery came and administered the last rites of the Church while Cecchino raved. The turbulent delirium lasted through the night, ending abruptly at sunrise. Cecchino turned to his brother and quietly laid a hand on his arm.

"*Fratello,* I do not wish to remain here any longer."

Kicking out with his sound leg, he made the motion of mounting a horse.

"Farewell, Neutino. Farewell . . ." The hand went limp.

At the proper hour, toward the approach of evening, Cellini interred his brother in the Church of San Giovanni of the Florentines. Over the grave he erected an inscribed marble slab. The Cellini arms were incised in its center: a lion rampant on an azure field, with a label of four points in chief, and three lilies. He made one small but significant change in the heraldic bearings of his family. From the dexter paw of the lion he removed the lily it normally held—and replaced it with an ax.

A reminder that his brother's murder waited for revenge.

In a furious burst of activity the medallion and the coin dies were finished. As furiously, he applied himself to the gold work of the morse. Neither his heart nor mind were on the work. He could not sleep or eat—could do nothing that would remove the image of his brother and the manner of his death from his mind. The picture ate into it like a malignant canker, destroying every other thought.

In his eagerness to have the finished morse, Pope Clement was having him over for progress inspections as often as three times weekly. The Pontiff did not, however, have to be the keen observer he was to see that his goldsmith had been plunged into a gnawing apathy of grief.

"Benevenuto," he told him one day, with a worried shake of his head, "I did not know that you were mad! Have you not yet learned that there is no remedy for death? What is it you seek to do, follow him to the grave?"

Morose and dejected, Cellini did not answer. He slouched out and went feverishly on with his work.

Not even Angela's tenderness helped. She tried every love art at her command—and she was a girl who knew how to employ them. All her efforts went for nothing. The goldsmith's nights remained sleepless; a constant tossing and turning, while the torment within ate into his

198

brain. There was no more joy, no more happiness. He had no eye for Angela. He was all taken up with a new *innamorata,* a new sweetheart to whom he was paying ardent court—the man who had shot down his brother from behind.

That musketeer's every move was being watched with a solicitude so fervent it might have been considered touching had it not been prompted by so deadly a purpose. A hundred times Cellini could have challenged and drawn the man into a fight. That was not the way! To allow this sleazy son of many to die in the heat of formal combat—facing his opponent—was intolerable. For him, death must be made to sneak up from behind, unobserved and unexpected. Repugnant though the act might be, the swine must be killed in the same dishonorable fashion that he himself had killed.

Days and weeks of this vigil went by.

One evening, just at that period between sunset and night when twilight begins merging into dusk, Cellini waited, silent as a ghost, watching the house in which the man lodged. It stood near the Torre Sanguigna, next door to the *bordello* maintained by the Lady Antea. Just as the shadows disappeared from the graying street, the arquebusier came out and stood outside his door, sword belt in hand. He had just finished supper and was contentedly sucking his teeth and picking at them with a dirty fingernail.

Cellini's eyes blazed fiercely. Here at last was the opportunity. The street was deserted. He drew a long dagger and let it hang in his hand, heavy and ugly, while he looked around carefully. Lady Antea was one of the most popular whores in the capital and her establishment was certain to be well patronized at this hour. That made it touch and go. If he were recognized the consequences could be fatal. This bastard he had to deal with was a catchpoll, an agent of the Bargello. Given some evidence, the Bargello would have to act.

Warily, as softly as a cat, Cellini crept up behind the blackleg, the long, curved Pistoian dagger ready for use.

"The thing to do," he muttered to himself, "is to strike at an unprotected spot. The son of a bitch might be wearing steel underclothing."

Reaching a point three short spaces from the man, he leaped, swinging the cutlass in a heavy backhanded blow, meaning to cut the head clean off his victim.

Startled by something, the catchpoll whirled and lurched with a frightened jerk. The blow missed his neck and caught him on the shoulder. The impact jarred the goldsmith's arm to the socket. The blade crunched and grated against bone and a blackish, sticky flood began to splash down the arquebusier's clothing. He dropped the sword belt and stumbled awkwardly, shattering the silence with piercing shrieks of fear and agony. In a blind panic he started running down the street. Cellini caught up with him in four running leaps and grabbed him by the hair. Lifting the dagger high he plunged it straight down into the man's neck and back. The blackleg crumbled on the street, making little whimpering sounds. His fingers clutched at the cobbles in a final involuntary spasm, as his lips pulled back and bared his teeth in that horrible grimace that is the stricture of violent death.

Using all his strength the Florentine tugged vainly at the dagger. He couldn't pull it out. He strained desperately, without budging it. The expected happened. Four soldiers, swords in hand, came springing out of Lady Antea's house, advancing grimly. To them Cellini was a bandit stripping a victim. Fearful of recognition, the goldsmith left the dagger behind, drew his sword, and sprinted off toward the Piazza Navona and the palace of Duke Alessandro. At the moment this was the safest refuge in Rome. He entered and asked to be permitted to speak with His Grace.

Alessandro looked at the flushed face as it bowed before him.

"Well, Benvenuto?" he asked, pleasantly enough.

Cellini sketched out the details, laying stress on the fact that he had been compelled to leave the dagger behind.

His Grace pursed his lips, looked at one of his gentlemen-in-waiting and smiled a dry smile.

"Did you kill the bastard?"

The goldsmith drew in a deep breath and expelled it noisily through the nose.

"Sì, Altezza," he nodded grimly, "I killed him."

Alessandro nodded back, and pondered. The homicide—he flicked that away. This fellow had but avenged the murder of his brother, a brother who had been in the ducal service.

"Were you alone?"

"Yes, Excellency."

"And you think that dagger can be recognized?"

Cellini nodded.

"Think no more of it," the Medici told him. "I'll see to the thing. You had best spend the night here. Tomorrow, return to your work on that jewel the Pope has his heart set on. Keep the affair quiet and remain indoors for a few days, until I can give the Bargello a little lecture." Alessandro frowned. "A little sermon on this bad policy of his, of slaying my servitors." The frown deepened into an angry scowl. He hadn't thought of it in that light before. "I'll teach him manners," he added nastily.

Wiggling a finger, he signaled that the goldsmith could withdraw.

XXVIII

THREE DAYS PASSED, FOUR, A WEEK . . . AND there was no summons from Clement ordering the goldsmith in for an inspection of the morse. Not a word despite the fact that Clement wanted the piece finished. The silence was forbidding and boded no good even if there hadn't been a peep out of the Bargello and his blacklegs.

The eighth day came—and joy of joys!—the Bolognese chamberlain came with it, bearing the long awaited order to report to the Vatican.

"I pray you favor me with the answer to a question, *messere*," Cellini requested as they walked to the Papal palace. He still could not remember the man's name. "His Holiness will no doubt have heard of a little *imbroglio* in which I have involved myself. Can you tell me his mind in the matter?"

"You put it delicately, *maestro*," remarked the chamberlain with a grin. "The Pope isn't too happy over the occurrence, but he seems well-disposed toward you. Duke Alessandro has explained the case fully and in your favor, pointing out that as a man of spirit you could not have acted otherwise than you did. My own suggestion would be that you continue with your work as if nothing had occurred and let the storm pass."

When Cellini reached the presence he encountered a look so black it shook him to the soles of his feet. Never had he seen the Pope so grim and full of menace. Sweating, saying not a word, he made his obeisance. In the dead, empty silence he uncovered the morse and displayed it before Clement's stony gaze.

The Medici was always deeply moved by a masterly work of art. By degrees, slowly, the bleakness drained from his face. Eventually, he looked up and gave Cellini an oblique look which spoke volumes.

"You have made vast progress in a short time," he said in a noncommittal voice. "It grows more beautiful each time we see it. Very well done. See that you continue to press forward with the work."

The Pope leaned back and eyed the goldsmith. "And now that you are cured, Benvenuto," he drawled, "give heed to yourself. Take care how you live."

The hint was soft-spoken and casual, but it struck home. Another little gambit like this last one, my Benvenuto, the Pontiff was telling him, and I will have you hanged from the highest gibbet in Rome.

In the hall Cellini encountered Alessandro on his way in. The goldsmith's cap swept the floor as he bowed, murmuring grateful thanks.

Alessandro waved them away in a grand manner. "How went things with His Holiness?" he asked.

Cellini gave him an account of the interview.

"*Eccellente.* And now that this affair is over and done?"

"My lord, tomorrow and the next day I mean to give my weary brain some rest. I'm going on a hunt."

"Ah, so. Where?"

"In the Campagna."

"I wish you a full bag. But wait! I have just the thing for you. A hunting dog. Bred in Penna. You will find him an excellent field companion. I'll have him sent to your lodgings. A gift from me, to help you regain some of the joy of life. And so, *buona fortuna.*"

Toward an artist, one who was not likely to get in his way, Alessandro could be gracious and charming.

Nasone arrived that afternoon—a large, shaggy, friendly dog with a glossy brown coat and a white blaze running down his snout. In the field his pointing, retrieving, and instant obedience to command were such that he quickly wormed his way into the Florentine's affection.

The jewelry and goldsmithing business took an upward turn just then and began booming. Orders came in so rapidly that Cellini rented a two-storeyed dwelling and opened his own shop. On the ground floor he built a large, well-appointed workroom, workmen's quarters, kitchen and dining room. Upstairs, his private apartment, an airy studio, and a room for Angela who practically lived there anyway.

Life again took on a dreamy quality, marred only by the insatiable greed of the cackling Madama Beatrice. Glumly Cellini was forced to the realization that in this world one can never hope to be completely happy and contented. Not that he minded an occasional raid on his purse, even if Angela did keep this fairly empty all by her luscious self. But that calamitous old hellhag's demands were unending, and she was driving him into a nervous frenzy with the loudly voiced threat to take Angela away unless they were met.

"I dislike saying it of anyone connected with you, my little pigeon," he told Angela bitterly, after emptying his purse to satisfy the most recent requests of mother and daughter, "but that old fiend has the disposition and appetites of a werewolf. *Un orco!* New shop or no new shop, this can't go on. *Diàscolo!* I do not have a well of gold!"

"I know, sweet my love," wailed Angela, "but after all is said and done, she is my mother!"

"I know," admitted Cellini with an uncomprehending shrug, "and I cannot understand that. What we should do is run away together." His eyes lit up. "That's it! The answer to the whole problem. We'll run off to Florence, just you and I."

Angela frowned. "I don't know. I am not known in Florence and there won't be much demand for my dancing. I'll not be able to earn anything."

"Bah! I'll have enough for us. Have you ever had to ask me twice for anything?"

"No," conceded the lovely Angela.

"Well then?"

"If you wish, my love. I'll go with you anywhere. But Mama will have a fit."

"Let her," Cellini answered, nodding happily at the thought. "There'll be just the two of us. It will be heaven. *Un vero paradiso.*"

Nasone barked his approval.

But there was the morse to be finished. More commissions came in and kept on coming. Travel, and the preparations for it, were forced aside. Running off to Florence had to wait.

As a matter of fact, the gold work on the morse was nearly completed. It needed only to have the gems placed in their setting and some finishing here and there. The Pope sent over all the jewels except the diamond, which was then in pawn with some Genoese bankers. The shop was humming. Five journeymen toiled on a quantity of commissions. April was approaching. Spring was in the air and the weather already quite warm. During the day the windows and doors stood wide open.

Lounging indolently against a wall across the street, that spawn of iniquity, Isacco Baldo, continued his careful study of the Cellini shop. He was pleased. The shop was good-looking, busy as a hive, exactly the type to merit the attention of his fine Italian hand. Isacco chuckled dryly. He planned so carefully and worked with such consummate cunning that he had never been apprehended. A detail amply attested to by the fact that he still drew breath. In his profession, you were caught only once.

But then, Baldo was an artist in his chosen field. A specialist. His specialty was shops, and these were selected with an eye to business. A careful man, Isacco Baldo. As unregenerate a son of Satan as could be found throughout the length and breadth of the Italian peninsula.

Calmly he crossed the street and stopped before the door, his close set little eyes gleaming brighter than the gold and silver being worked within. Pointing his head up so that his short beard jutted, he entered, giving the door a searching sidewise glance. It would not prove troublesome. The window, however, seemed easier. He walked around the shop's front with just the right touch of bored interest, while every detail of the interior etched itself in his memory. His eyes ranged farther back, to the stair leading up—owner's apartment, likely. No problem there. He took careful note of the door at the back leading to the workmen's quarters. That door he would have to watch. He turned to the young man who walked over to him.

"I bid you good day, friend," he spoke cheerfully. "I am a goldsmith from Naples, seeking employment. Can I be of service here?"

Felice Guadagni looked him over. He was a young man who had finished his term as apprentice in the shop Cellini operated before the sack. Now a journeyman, he functioned as a sort of supervisor. It was his dream to purchase an interest in the business and become the Florentine's partner.

"Sorry," he answered, "we have all the journeymen we require. Try the Del Moro shop, up the street."

"Look you, friend," the stranger countered, "I am newly come to Rome and am anxious to view the manner and kind of work done here. Do you object to my looking around a bit?"

Felice again looked the man over. The fellow was tolerably clean,

204

well enough dressed, and had very muscular hands—the mark of a journeyman goldsmith. He seemed just what he said he was, a practicing artificer.

"Go ahead," he nodded. "So you don't disturb the men and their work, understand?"

Isacco stopped here and there, staring. His mouth watered. Two stout, iron-banded chests stood against the rear wall. That would be where the work was locked during the night. When he came to the table where Cellini labored, completely absorbed in the morse, his eyes bulged out. Holy Christ! What a haul! Those gems alone would bring in a fortune. He was rich! Tonight!... He must take no chance on those jewels being returned to their owner. It had to be tonight.

A light drizzle was falling when he returned long after dark. He waited stolidly, silent and patient, for the period between midnight and dawn. A short cudgel with a knotty knob at one end was stuck in his belt and he fingered this whenever a footfall echoed along the wet street. He noted that the window was solidly shuttered and that the door was probably easiest after all. Isacco selected tools from various pockets and went to work on the hinges. He worked quietly and with speed.

Nasone came awake and lifted his head, listening intently. That scratching rasp that mingled with the snores and breathing of the men —it wasn't like any of the usual night noises. He yawned and stretched. No point in setting up a howl. Probably just another rat under the floor planks. He let his shaggy head sink back on his paws, and dozed off. A sharp grating noise brought his head back up with a snap. That was no rat!... at least no ordinary one. A low growl rumbled in his throat as he felt a breeze waft into the room. The front door was open! He sniffed. A new smell reached him, a scent that belonged to no one in the house. He bounded up and padded silently into the shop.

Isacco had stopped to empty a drawer which had been left slightly open, preparatory to closing and bolting that rear door, when he was startled by a low snarl. A dog! He had not seen the beast during the day, hadn't expected one, and consequently had not prepared against it. He flung out his cape just in time. Nasone leaped, tearing a long rent in it. The intruder swung his club in the dark, knocking Nasone off balance in mid-air. The dog gave a startled "Yi-i-i" as the cudgel splatted against his ribs. His lips curled back. Snarling, he hurled himself at the man, snapping his jaws on a forearm, shaking, ripping and tearing. The club slammed down on his head and sent him reeling

205

along the floor with streaks of vivid lightning flashing in his eyes. Nasone needed help. He raced into the workmen's room, barking furiously, pulling off bed covering. Some of the men woke up and began throwing shoes at him. His fault! He did bark like that sometimes, when a rat squeaked and he couldn't get at him.

Pawing at the floor boards in a spitting rage, he bounded back into the shop. The man was frantically trying to open the chest where the master kept his work. Something snapped—the lock. Snarling savagely, Nasone sprang anew, biting and ripping away cloth. The intruder clubbed him again and sent him rolling along the floor. Barking, biting, clawing as well as he could, he went on harassing. A voice yelled from the workmen's quarters.

"Nasone! Quiet! . . . or I'll come out and beat the devil out of you! Catch that rat tomorrow. *Silenzio!*"

The intruder was badly frightened. Nasone could sense it. He gave up the chest, grabbed up a bundle he had made of the workmen's clothing and ran out the door. Growling and snarling, Nasone fought him every step of the way.

Out in the street Isacco sped swiftly in the dark. Nasone raced after him and leaped, clamping his teeth on trunks and thigh. Isacco dropped the club, drew a dagger and slashed out with it. Nasone whimpered and twisted in the air, knocking the blade out of the thief's hand. The burning pain crazed him. He let go and leaped blindly, tearing off a portion of the man's doublet.

Windows were being flung back. Doors opened. Isacco called for help against the mad dog attacking him. Men ran out in their night clothes and blows began to rain down on the bleeding Nasone. He had to give it up. Still snarling savagely, he turned away and loped homeward, stopping only to let his soothing tongue lick at the ugly gash in his flank.

Cellini heard nothing of the commotion. Normally he was a light sleeper. But Angela had remained all night; and in their hunger for each other, sleep, when it came, was the deep heavy slumber of exhaustion. Neither heard a sound till well after sunrise, when the angry howls of the men below aroused them.

Flinging on some clothing, the startled goldsmith ran to the head of the stair.

"What's all the noise for? What has happened?"

206

"We have been robbed! Someone has broken into the shop and carried off every blessed thing—even our clothing!"

"Here's Nasone lying in a corner, badly hurt! He has a deep cut in his flank!"

"All that barking and growling during the night! ... The poor beast was calling to us for aid!"

Every particle of strength drained out of the goldsmith's body. His face, to the lips, became as white as his shirt—whiter! His eyes wrenched around the room to the chest where the Papal jewels were stored. *Santa Maria Vergine!* the lock on it dangled! His jaw went slack, letting his mouth gape foolishly. This! after the affair with his brother's murderer, was the end of everything. It meant the gallows—disgrace—dishonor! The Pope would never swallow a wild tale about a robbery. And were he given a century of time, he could never make good the value of those gems. All was lost.

His legs buckled. Flashing lights danced in front of him. He sank limply to a seat on the stair step, croaking out an appeal in a hoarse whisper.

"The ... P-pope's ... jewels ... Oh, my good God! ..."

Felice was already flinging back the lid. His hands clutched madly. He shouted:

"*Iddio sia laudato!* They're all here, Benvenuto! The gold and the stones ... all safe!"

"G-God above! Thanks!"

The next thing Cellini became aware of was Angela bathing his face with a sopping cold towel. He pushed it away. Still wobbly, but with restored spirit, he rose to his feet.

"Go and get yourselves some clothing," he told his shopmen. "I will pay for it. More at leisure I will hear how the thing happened and what was taken. Has anyone gone to advise the authorities?"

"*Sì.* Hermano has run to summon them. He's the only one of us who has pants."

The goldsmith nodded. That meant Clement would soon hear of the robbery. "Then I must take the gems to the Vatican as soon as possible."

His enemies at court, he knew, would lose no time in using the incident to their own advantage and to discredit him in the eyes of the Pope. The direction which their insinuations would take also was obvious. He, a young man, entrusted with a fortune in gems, had engineered a plot whereby his shop was robbed for his own gain. Simple. Such treachery had to be squelched quickly.

Leaving Felice to handle the matter with the Bargello, Cellini dressed and sat to a hurried breakfast, then took up the morse and jewels and hurried off.

He had reckoned correctly. Pompeo and his entire court clique were hard at work: Francesco del Nero, Zana dei Biliotti, Girolamo Schio, Traiano, the others, all were wielding the daggers of spite and envy. The Pope was in an ugly mood. Those jewels were costly.

The goldsmith was announced and ushered in. He took care to appear unruffled as he swaggered into the room and knelt before the Pope.

Scowling darkly, Clement rasped at him: "Well! ... Well! ... What is it? What are you come to do here?"

Cellini answered nothing, only arranged the gold and gems on the table.

"Here, Holy Father, are all your gems. Not one is missing."

The Pope's thunder-hued visage cleared as by magic.

"Ahhhh! In verità sei benvenuto!" he chortled. "You are indeed the welcome one!" He lounged back. *"Ma prego,* tell us what happened. We have heard many evil rumors ..."

Cellini gave a lengthy and elaborate report, while Clement cast dirty looks at the calumnious scoundrels around him who had so berated this young man's quality of mind.

"Go, my Benvenuto, for no doubt you must see to setting your shop in order. And know that you have proved yourself an honest man, which, indeed, we have always known you to be."

Nasone was preened, pampered, petted and fed with a slavishness that pleased him mightily. His master even had a leech in to look over and dress his wounded flank. That last, however, was an awful mistake. For when he next went to lick at the wound with his healing tongue, the taste of it had him spitting for an hour.

XXIX

For ALL THE GOOD WILL OF THE POPE, THE goldsmith's packet of trouble was far from empty. The Mint-Master of Rome involved him in a fresh supply of it by bringing a distressing piece of news to Clement's attention. A quantity of false coins were making an appearance in the city, he told the Pontiff. Coins made of worthless metal, but admirably stamped. In fact they were so well stamped that this was possible only with dies such as those made by the Mint's own Stamp-Master—Benvenuto Cellini.

Clement listened and examined the spurious coins. But when the Mint-Master began hurling charges, he curtly shook his head.

"No, Master Giacopo," he flatly responded. "You must look elsewhere. Benvenuto has more than proved himself an honest fellow. What say you, my lords?" Clement looked around to the gentlemen who were in attendance.

Most agreed with him.

Giacopo Balducci remained openly skeptical.

"God grant the matter turns out as Your Holiness infers. Know that we have doubts about this man, and also some small proofs against him."

"Proofs?"

"The dies, Most Blessed Father."

"Bosh! Could you truthfully swear that no one but our Benvenuto has access to the dies? Many other people have the use and the handling of them. Some could have been stolen. Are you certain you have not become lax with the precautions used at the Mint? Could you say, further, that these coins were actually made from such dies?"

"I cannot, Your Holiness. Yet it is clear that he can make as many dies as he pleases."

Clement shook his head and turned to the Governor of Rome.

"Messer Gregorio, this is a serious and intolerable affair. It must not be permitted to continue. You must use the utmost exertion to discover the malefactor responsible for it. Our Mint-Master will give you all possible assistance. See to placing yourself at the orders of my lord Governor, Master Giacopo."

"In the meantime, Blessed Father, it were wise and desirable to see that Cellini does not attempt to fly from Rome."

The Pope made a face. He didn't like to go that far on the strength of evidence so flimsy it was nothing more than conjecture. Still, he had to make a show of complete co-operation.

"Very well. See to it. Have him watched—but carefully! Take care to be circumspect. He must not learn of it."

Cellini learned of it two hours later, from friends at court. Two days later the Pope sent for him and the morse. Adroitly and cautiously Clement led the conversation around to the topic of coinage.

"Tell us, Benvenuto," he asked casually, as one man making small talk with another, "should you have the heart to coin false money?"

The goldsmith was prepared for that one.

"It is not so much a question of heart as of wit, Holy Father."

"How so?"

"Surely Your Sanctity will agree that did I choose to enter such a dishonorable field, I would do better at it than the rascals who set their hands to this vile work. They are not men of ability or talent. These are wretches who are incapable of earning money honestly. While I, with such poor wits and skill as I possess, can always earn sufficient to keep me in comfort. Let us examine the case: every morning, before dinner, three crowns find their way into my purse; the customary payment for the dies made under my supervision at the Mint. In this activity alone I earn, by God's grace and Your Holiness' favor, a greater sum than I could steal through false coinage. Hence my remark that it is a question of wit rather than heart. Does not Your Sanctity agree?"

Clement was not a fool. He ordered the Governor to continue to press a diligent search, but to pay no further attention to Cellini.

"It is not him we seek," he said, "and we are not disposed to anger and insult him with such attentions. We should then run the risk of losing him for our service."

The Mint of Rome, alive with agents and spies, soon turned up the counterfeiter—a stamper named Cesare Macherone. A bird-brained metal founder also was arrested as an accomplice.

On that same day Cellini and Nasone were strolling along the

Piazza Navona; the dog nosing curiously, cocking a leg where fancy willed, or stopping to bark at the cats and pigeons. They had come up opposite the gate of the Bargello, when Nasone suddenly drew in his lolling tongue and stiffened into alertness. The Florentine loitered at the gate, idly listening to a dispute between a goldsmith with whom he had a nodding acquaintance, and the Corporal of a squad of blacklegs. Ser Donnino had caused a man to be detained on the charge that he had entered his shop and robbed it; and having done so was finding it difficult to sustain the charge.

Nasone growled nastily. His ears snapped straight in the air and turned slightly. Clicking his jaws shut, he thrust his muzzle forward, sniffing delicately. Nasone's nose never failed him. That scent was unmistakable. Here was the cudgeler of dogs! Him who had ripped into his flank! His lips curled wolfishly. A forepaw clawed back at the cobbles underfoot.

Cellini, giving attention to the dispute, heard a savage snarl and saw a blur of motion explode past him headed in the general direction of the suspect's throat.

Isacco Baldo fought back as best he could, having neither a club nor knife to aid him. His clothing was in shreds, his right calf badly chewed, and both hands and forearms bleeding profusely, before the startled catchpolls recovered from the surprise and came to his assistance. That mattered little to Nasone. The memory of the blows and knife thrust rankled.

"Look you!" called the Corporal to Cellini, who had run into the *cortile*. "Call off this murderous hell-hound or we will be forced to kill him!"

The goldsmith grabbed at the dog, holding him back despite outraged snarls. He was as surprised as anyone there. Nasone was known throughout the neighborhood for his friendly disposition.

The vanquished Isacco cowered and tried to readjust what was left of his cape. In doing so some small packages dropped from a concealed pocket in its hood, to the ground. Ser Donnino started and sent up a loud yell, pointing excitedly.

"There you are!" he shouted to the blackleg Corporal. "The very proofs you seek, *per Dio!* Here is the property I have just described to you!"

Cellini was staring wide-eyed at the suspect's hand.

"And that ring," he rapped out sharply, "is *my* property!" The blinding light of reason burst over him. *"Ala fede del giusto Cristo!* This is the knave who broke into my shop! Wherefore, my dog recognizes him!"

He released Nasone, who instantly flew at Isacco's throat.

Baldo was finished. The dog was too powerful to hold off indefinitely. He screamed for aid.

"Misericordia! Pietà! I swear to return all that is yours. For the love of Christ, call off this murdering beast. Mercy!"

Once more Cellini took hold of the slavering Nasone. Isacco limped behind two constables and emptied his pockets, returning the small quantity of metal and jewelry he had stolen from the Florentine's shop, and not yet disposed of. He added a purse of twenty-five crowns to pay for the clothing and anything else, whining for pity the while.

"Ask pity of God," Cellini snapped at him coldly, thinking of the fright he had received on the morning after the robbery, "I intend to do nothing either for or against you."

For a fact, justice was speedily served. In a few days the metal founder began his journey to the galleys. Cesare Macherone was hanged in the Banchi, directly opposite the doors of the Mint, so that the other employees could see the price of folly. Isacco Baldo, for all his cunning, danced at the end of a rope reserved for his kind in the Campo di Fiore.

Cellini got on with the morse.

And then, during a spell of mild sunny weather—it was the more inexplicable and extraordinary in that no rain had fallen for some time —the Tiber swelled into raging flood. It happened suddenly, violently, without warning. Bridges were torn away by the pounding stream. Buildings toppled. Fearful, inundated Rome was overcome with awe by the spectacle of mighty power unleashed and unrestrained. The churches on high ground were packed with penitents fervently chanting the *Miserere.*

The Florentine had no time to be awestruck. His house and shop were in the Banchi, alongside the Tiber, where the danger was greatest. There was that morse!

"There's an evil spell on this piece," he muttered to Felice. The water in the shop was waist high and rising. "It has a curse on it. I don't believe I'll ever get to finish it."

Petulantly he examined it. All that remained to be done was to set in the diamond and touch up the gold work here and there.

Scowling and mumbling he methodically removed the jewels from their settings and turned the gold over to Felice. The jewels he placed in his pocket.

"I'm going to try to reach Giovanni Gaddi at Monte Cavallo," he told him, "and turn these over to him for safekeeping."

"That will not be easy, Benvenuto." Outside the flood waters were roaring.

"I know!" cried the exasperated goldsmith. "What else can I do? If anything were to happen to these stones ... If I were to lose them—" He did not need to finish.

Descending from a window he began fording the turbulent, debris-littered streets. It took six back-breaking hours to reach high and dry Monte Cavallo, where the lord Giovanni was staying. As Clerk of the *Camera* he took over the keeping of the gems, and poured out a goblet of wine for the dripping goldsmith.

"I wonder what's to occur next," Cellini complained bitterly, while Messer Giovanni wrote out an official receipt. "That morse may be the sort of commission a goldsmith would sell his soul for, yet I've had nothing but trouble since I started on it. By God!" he gulped down some wine, "it's turning my hair gray!"

In two days the waters receded and the city again became habitable. Clement sent over the diamond and Cellini pushed on industriously, fighting what he had come to regard a grim race with Fate. Angela let drop the hint that she was in dire need of clothes to replace those ruined in the flood. He immediately saw her satisfied, over and above her dire needs. Unfortunately, her mother took note of the splurge and followed with demands of her own: clothing, new furniture, new bedding, new ...

"*Ala croce del Santo Cristo!*" howled the Florentine, waving wildly, "I've taken all I can from that drudge! You've got to make her understand that I am not the Mint! I do not coin money at convenience! I must earn what little I possess. I know!—I know!—" he yowled, stopping to kiss Angela's eyes "—it's not your fault." He paced frantically, finally sinking on a settle.

"Listen to me, *mia cara,* some time ago our friend Piloto offered to let me have the use of a little house he owns near Ostia, by the sea. I'm coming apart with all this tension. Let's take a holiday. That morse will be finished in a few days—if the good God will permit it! After that, ten days by ourselves, with not a care in the world. What say you?"

Angela hugged him furiously.

213

"Bene! But be careful not to tell your mother a word of this until we are ready to start off."

A week later, breathing a happy sigh of relief and vowing a score of vigil lights to Our Lady of the Traspontina, Cellini called on the Pope and presented the finished morse.

The beaming Clement was at his most voluble.

"Absolutely the finest masterpiece of the goldsmith's art ever seen in Rome!" he sang out. "The finest ... absolutely!"

The court concurred with loud applause.

"Were I a wealthy emperor," Clement continued with his declamation, "I would bestow upon you, my Benvenuto, as much landed estate as your eye could survey. But being nowadays only a poor and bankrupt sovereign, I can, at best, only see to it that you are supplied with such crusts of bread as will satisfy your modest needs."

The Pope flowed on with a spate of words, holding the finished morse fondly. Cellini waited patiently until he finished.

"Since Your Holiness thus makes known your mind," he murmured sagely, "I make bold to beg for your condescension. Know, Blessed Father, that there is now vacant a post of Bedel in the College of the Mazzieri."

The Papal Bedels were mace bearers, their office that of beadles or State Sergeants, who, in all official functions, walked before the Pope with the Apostolic arms, carrying rods which resembled the fasces borne by the lictors of ancient Rome. The position drew a salary of a little under two hundred crowns a year.

"Not good enough, *maestro mio,*" returned the Pope grandly, changing from a personal to a formal mode of address. "It is our desire that you receive a grant of greater consequence."

That the Bedelship was inadequate payment for a commission on which he had labored for nearly a year, Cellini knew. On the other hand, it would serve nicely for a start in that direction.

"Holy Father," he countered, looking to make the most of the opportunity, "I beg, then, that you will deign to confer this trifling post upon me, by way of earnest."

The court was amused.

"So be it," laughed Clement. "However, we do not wish to see you waste your time in the service of this office. We will grant your petition on the condition that you make some arrangement with your fellow-Bedels, so that you will be exempted from performing the duties."

"I bow to Your Holiness' request."

Cellini uncovered and bowed, backing away to the door. Annibale Caro withdrew with him, to offer congratulations.

"You handled that superbly, Neutino," he enthused. "Indeed, you handled the Pope with greater ease than could his own kinsman, my lord Ippolito. He left shortly before you arrived, in a tearing rage."

"Why so, Annibale? He is usually so calm."

"Haven't you heard? Clement made him a cardinal! Ippolito has been fighting the move for weeks. The Pope forced him to accept the office. Told him to stop balking and being so contrary and independent, that he owed it to the family and all that. Behold, another Cardinal de' Medici!"

IN MAY IPPOLITO WAS MADE A PAPAL LEGATE and sent off to Hungary on a lengthy political mission. Barely a month later Alessandro started for Florence to replace Baccio Valori as Head of Government. Clement was up to his ears manipulating the much desired alliance between his House and royal France. Things were shaping up well, beautifully in fact. King Francis promised that his second eldest son would wed Catherine, leaving Clement hopeful that the gloomy young Henry of Orleans might outlive the ailing Dauphin and thus make his little Catherine Queen of France.

With the details of these cabals behind him Clement looked for some recreation, so he called in the Florentine and ordered a chalice. The Papal specifications called for a grail of exceeding mastery of design. Cellini promptly set to work on a model. He designed a gold cup with an intricately sculptured stem. Three scenes suggested by Clement —the Nativity, the Resurrection, and the crucifixion of St. Peter—were to be engraved on bosses set in the base. The knop was to be fashioned in the form of three sculptured figures representing Faith, Hope, and Charity.

Clement gloated over it and ordered five hundred gold crowns to be given over so that work on the piece could get under way.

Taking note of this favorable reaction, the goldsmith decided not to let any grass grow under his feet. A nice little post had recently fallen vacant, and, after all, the Pope had promised!

"Your Holiness is aware," he began, "that there is now vacant the Office of the Privy Seal?"

Clement arched an eyebrow. "Indeed?"

"Since Your Holiness has in the past promised me some such benefice, I beg that you will see fit to give me the preference in this post."

That promise had been made in the exuberance of a yesterday long flown into the Limbo of time. Today was something else again.

"*L'Uffizio del Piombo,*" Clement answered, with not a hint of the florid panegyrics of that forgotten yesterday, "is a post that has annexed to it a salary of well over eight hundred crowns a year. Did we let you have it, you would give over all your time to scratching your paunch and would entirely neglect the practice of your magnificent art. And we should then have to bear the blame for this grave sin."

The goldsmith blinked in amazement. Was this the promised reward for all that labor? He was aware that the memory of princes and rulers was notoriously short. But this—from a Medici Pope! He was amazed, but not to such an extent that it kept him from whipping back a resentful answer.

"Holy Father, a cat of good breed hunts the better on a full stomach. It then has less to think about and all its faculties are directed to one end. Such, also, is true of any man of talent, be he honest and able in his art. Your Holiness has only to look about you to see that those princes who provide such with the means to live comfortably are always better served. They but water the roots of genius and of talent, which are ever inclined to enter the world in low station. I perceive that, for myself, I did but dream in expecting any such favor. Happy am I to have received my poor Bedelship. Without a doubt Your Sanctity would do best to bestow this present post on some courtier who would not immediately give over all his time to scratching his belly! Your Sanctity should not follow the example of Pope Julius, of illustrious memory, who did not scruple to bestow this same post on the venerable Bramante, and who was repaid by the many noble works which that genius left behind to the eternal glory of that great Pontiff."

He waited for no more, not even for permission to withdraw. In a towering fury he bowed and left, choking over the thought that he had been cheated of a year's labor—and by a Pope!

Red-faced with embarrassment, Clement frowned irritably. "That

216

devil of a Benvenuto," he muttered peevishly, "will not bear a word of rebuke. We were half disposed to give thought to his request; but it is not right to be so haughty with a Pope. Therefore we do not know what we shall do in the matter."

Since this was an ideal moment for burying a knife in the Florentine's back, Girolamo Schio, patron and well-wisher of the venomous Pompeo, offered advice.

"Most Blessed Father, this Cellini is young and better suited to wear a sword than the robe of a friar. Let Your Holiness see fit to bestow this present post on our wondrous Bastiano, who has long awaited a mark of Your Sanctity's favor. Some time or other you can bestow on Benvenuto a benefice better suited to his temperament than this present one."

The provoked Clement was inclined to agree. He turned to Baccio Valori, recently returned to the court from Florence.

"When next you see Benvenuto, let him know that it was he himself who presented the Office of the Privy Seal to Bastiano. Let him know also that he may reckon on receiving the next of the better posts that fall vacant. Meanwhile let him look to his manners and to finishing my commissions."

Cellini reached the shop fully intending to pack and run off to Florence.

"To be used in such manner," he boiled at Felice, "and by a Pope who is a fellow-Florentine! By God, I'll never again set foot in Rome while he reigns!"

"You're in a blind rage, Benvenuto," cautioned Felice, frowning. "Don't do anything until you have cooled a bit and can think more reasonably."

"Why should I not be in a blind rage?" choked the Florentine bitterly. "I've been gulled of a year's effort! Good Christ!"

"Well . . . that's not exactly true, although you have been ill-used," Felice told him. "But you can't go to Florence now. You shouldn't, in any case. You know very well how things are there these days. Your friends Varchi and Piero Landi both have written telling you how unsettled the city is since Alessandro made himself Duke."

The young Alessandro had assumed control with all the subtlety of a sledge-hammer. He had abolished the Signoria and the Republic and made Florence a duchy, with himself as the sole and absolute ruler.

He had even renamed the Palace of the Signoria. It was now *il Palazzo Vecchio*—the Old Palace.

"What will you do when you arrive there?" pressed Felice, noticing that his words were taking effect. "Twiddle your thumbs? There will be few patrons in your native city right now. You yourself have told me that the only masters who are doing anything at all are those engaged in erecting tombs and monuments to the victims of Alessandro's tyranny. Think a bit before you make this rash move."

Glumly Cellini nodded and went up to his rooms. Felice was right. For the present he would do best to remain where he was.

The next evening he encountered Baccio Valori, who was en route to the Vatican behind two torch bearers.

"Ah, Benvenuto, well met," he called to him. "I have a message for you from His Holiness."

In a friendly manner the courtly politician repeated Clement's words.

Cellini shrugged despondently. "Messer Baccio, I shall press on with my work with the greatest application, but with no hope of receiving any reward for it."

"How now, master!" Valori professed to be amazed. "Come. Is this the way to reply to the overtures of a Pope?"

"My lord, everything considered, it would be madness for me to think otherwise. Who but a madman would pin any hopes on these empty promises? I shall do this work, knowing that I will receive nothing for it beyond the wage due any journeyman. *Arrivederci.*"

At home—more fuss and feathers. Cellini had learned to answer a curt "No" to the demands of Madama Beatrice. He reached his apartment to find Angela fretting.

"What is it, little kitten?"

"Mama! She's been storming all afternoon. Complaining that I'm neglecting her and that I am seeking to leave her and that she doesn't have the means to live on—"

"She and I both," the goldsmith interrupted sourly.

"—and that we would be better off elsewhere. Has she been after you again?"

"Again? Still!"

Angela began wailing.

Frantically Cellini dug into his purse and quieted the screams of the voracious Beatrice. He stayed away from the Vatican, and worked

218

on the figures for the knop of the chalice. Valori, he suspected, must have repeated his words to the Pope, for it was two months before Clement grew sufficiently impatient to order Roberto Pucci to take a little notice of what Cellini was doing.

Pucci called the next day and began to chat politely on this and that.

"And how is that chalice coming along, Master Benvenuto?"

Cellini had been waiting for that question. He'd had the answer ready for weeks.

"*Messere,* I have been laboring on this piece," he held up the nearly completed gold figures of the sculptured knop, "for several months. The gold given me for the purpose has been used up—for the piece itself and for labor costs. I beg you make request of the Holy Father, in my name, for a similar amount, to be used partly for finishing the chalice and partly to pay for the labor of doing so."

Messer Pucci offered the opinion that this did not seem to him the most tactful method in the world for dealing with such a personage as Pope Clement. It was hardly the usual custom to request a Supreme Pontiff to pay for a commission before it had been finished. He promised faithfully, however, to report the request.

Thereafter he called every day. Nothing more was said of additional gold; and Pucci never brought any.

In the midst of this febrile calm the shrewish Beatrice, dormant for some weeks, started up anew. The old girl called and calmly asked for enough money to move herself and family into larger and better living quarters.

"Madama Beatrice," patiently explained the goldsmith, "you must somehow realize once and for all that, unlike yourself, I am compelled to earn what little I have. I cannot continue to satisfy these unending needs of yours. What is it I am expected to use for money? I am a goldsmith, not an alchemist! You have two sturdy sons. Assure them that honest labor does not cause a fracture of the spine, and get what you need from them. Leave me in peace!"

"Ah, sad destiny that is mine!" bewailed Angela's mother. "How can you expect that I live under conditions that would shame a pig? To dare use me so! I, whom you deprive of the comfort of my daughter!" A shrill acerbity crept into her already disagreeable voice, making it grate like a rasp. "She is always here with you! Never at home with me, as she should be. Alas! Poor forsaken creature that I am—reduced to the condition of a common drudge!"

"What new nonsense is this? I've been paying the wages of your servant for so long, I've come to regard her as a member of your family!"

"By Christ his cross! Must this too be flung in my face? Must I fall into the muck of a cesspool to prove my need?" Her voice rose to a shriek. "I will have you know that I must have better quarters! Either that or Angela remains at home!"

"So be it, damn you!" yelled the aroused Cellini. "I have not the means to install you in a new house! And in any case, I have decided to quit Rome. You shall have to find another golden stream, *madama!* This one has been drained dry! Further—"

A shopboy pounded on the door.

"Master," he bawled loudly, when the yelling within subsided, "the noble Messer Pucci waits below."

Waving a disgusted farewell to Beatrice, whose face had taken on a look of cunning concentration, Cellini flung out of the door and went down to the shop.

Pucci looked over the sculptured figures of the knop before he spoke.

"His Holiness," he said, when he finished the examination, "is making preparations for a journey to Bologna, where he is to engage in discussions of State with His Imperial Majesty. He is impatient to see how the chalice is coming on and bids you bring it to the Vatican tomorrow morning, Benvenuto."

That evening Angela wondered aloud at the subdued mood her mother was in.

"It's not like her at all. At first I thought she might be ill, but she isn't. I don't understand it."

"She was here this morning," Cellini told her. "I gave her to understand a few things. Listen to me, my angel. I've made up my mind. Tomorrow I go to the Vatican to show that chalice. If the Pope treats me fairly, I'll make arrangements with him to finish it in Florence. If not, then I have resolved to leave Rome as soon as possible. Are you ready to come with me?"

"Whenever you wish and wherever you like, my poor distracted love," Angela sighed and sent her lips fluttering over his face.

The next day the Pope was too fully occupied to see the goldsmith.

"Some unexpected business," Sanga told Cellini, "requiring immediate attention. I am aware you were expected, Benvenuto. There is nothing that can be done. His Holiness will not be able to receive you today. Attend him tomorrow morning."

Cellini spent the day and night fretting. Angela did not come. In the morning he returned to the Vatican.

Pope Clement did not have much to say. He looked at the figures and nodded solemnly, as if pleased.

"As Your Sanctity can see," began Cellini, a trifle more softly than usual since the soil underfoot was slippery, "the most important and difficult portion of the piece is almost finished. I beg that Your Holiness will advance some gold, as I explained to Messer Roberto."

The Medici continued to examine the gold sculpture. There were times when this goldsmith of his was inclined to be amusing. If he wished to occupy his time in butting his head against a stone wall— well, let him. Clement slowly raised his eyes and let them flicker carelessly over Cellini's face.

"Attend—" he drawled, with a thin edge of impatience in his tone "—attend to the work and see to completing it."

Cellini flushed. This was no haughty Salamanca, to be used as a stepping stone. This was Clement—supreme ruler of Church and State —who, did he wish to, could crush him like a cockroach, and with far less trouble. The goldsmith bowed, determined on the course he would take. Let the Medici crush if he chose.

"I shall finish the work," he stated flatly as he withdrew, "when Your Holiness pays over some gold."

Clement had already turned away.

On his way home the embittered Cellini thought over his stand. It was stupid to bicker with a Pope. He knew that. But to allow any man—even a Pope—to defraud him of his due was a matter reflecting on his honor as an artist and a man. It was an affront not to be borne. In the present case he could do little. Certainly, he could take no personal action against the Pope. So then, the shop he would place in the charge of Felice, with whom he would leave instructions to return five hundred crowns to the Pope. Since he was resolved not to finish the chalice, he must return the gold given him for that purpose. Then he and Angela would run off to Florence ... If not Florence, then somewhere else. It mattered little where they went. They could leave tonight. Why wait?

He stomped angrily up the stair, calling to Angela.

She wasn't there.

"That's strange." Cellini was vaguely disturbed. She had never before been absent for so long. Perhaps she was ill? She had been troubled with a slight rheum. Nothing serious, but it might have taken a bad turn.

"Nuncio!" he called down to his house servant. "Nuncio, run to Lady Angela and find out if she has been taken ill. If she has not, tell her I must speak with her. Say that it is of the greatest importance."

He was packing when Nuncio returned. The youthful lackey came in softly.

"Did you find her well?" the goldsmith demanded. "Is she coming?"

Nuncio swallowed. "There's no one there, master. Not a soul. The house is empty."

Cellini stared blankly.

"I asked the people next door," continued the lackey. "A woman told me the entire family went away last evening, every last one, to Naples. She said—"

"What!"

"—that the Lady Angela was weeping very loud."

Cellini took hold of himself. "Which road did they take?" he snapped. "Did you remember to ask?"

"*Sì.* This neighbor said she heard Madama Beatrice call out to the carter to leave the city by the Porta San Pancrazio and that they intended to take ship at Civita Vecchia."

That bitch! Somehow she had caught on to their plan to run off and had acted in the nick of time.

"Run, Nuncio! Saddle my horse! Quickly! Fly!"

He might still be able to overtake them before they took ship. The pace of a cart loaded with the belongings of a family could not be very rapid. He would reach Angela in time. He must.

The frantic Cellini pounded into the seacoast city of Civita Vecchia shortly after nightfall. All along the route he questioned innkeepers, wayfarers and peasants. None could give any information.

In the streets of the squalid old port he babbled his query in every public place, to every port guard and sailor he met. Not one had seen the party he was seeking. In the inn at the sign of the Two Feluccas, he was more or less set to rights by the ruddy old boniface who operated that hostelry.

"Not many travelers from Rome to Naples go by way of this port, young man. This city is used largely by travelers from the north. To take ship for Naples, from the capital, one goes by way of Ostia. It's quicker that way, and cheaper."

Cellini fell rather than sat on a bench when he heard that. A haunted agony came into his eyes. He understood, then, what he would have instantly realized if his mind had been functioning normally.

"That old bitch did this purposely, of course. Gave out that she was traveling by this route to throw me off, knowing that I would be certain to follow. Meanwhile she's on her way, undisturbed, by way of Ostia. I've been a stupid fool! And it's too late now..."

Bleared eyes looked up at the sympathetic boniface.

"Brandy!"

That marked the beginning.

For five days thereafter the little port city was flung into such tremors, and by a single youth so thoroughly and completely drunk, that no one there could recall ever having seen the like of either. He stumbled in and out of taverns, leaving the shambles of disaster and the imprecations of bewildered proprietors behind. The girls of the town were in ecstasies. Here was a man! He bedded every wench that crossed his path, bar none. He fought anyone who dared look into his blazing, brandy-filmed eyes for longer than a passing glance. And when the black-legs tried to take him—woe and alas! The Bargello was badly worried. This roaring wildcat was far and away beyond his provincial ken. Four of his most sturdy catchpolls lay flat on their backs: one with a sword thrust through him, another slashed with his own dagger, and the other two in a severely mauled condition. One of the latter had been pounded into the floor of a tavern, a heavy table bench used as a hammer for this purpose. Just what did it take to subdue one Tuscan madman? He was assembling a troop of blacklegs for this purpose, determined to do or die, when the word came that the maniacal Florentine who had been wrecking the Port section of the city had galloped madly out of the south gate, headed in the direction of Rome.

"*Iddio sia benedetto*," fervently whispered the Bargello to himself. And then, more loudly, "Good riddance!"

XXXI

BEFORE LEAVING FOR BOLOGNA CLEMENT AP-
pointed Cardinal Salviati Legate of Rome and gave over to him the
charge of the city. There were other instructions as well, among them
the order to push Cellini along with the Papal commission.

"Our Benvenuto," Clement told the Legate, "is a fellow who
esteems his great talents but slightly, and us even less. See to it that he
is kept moving along, so that we may find the chalice finished when we
return."

Salviati, one of the five Medici cardinals elevated to that office by
Leo X, was a grandson of Lorenzo the Magnificent. He was a nobleman
who did not believe in indulging the humors and caprices of artists.
Princes of a stature like himself were not obliged to put up with such
nonsense. A week after Clement had started off he sent word to the
goldsmith, bidding him bring along the chalice.

Dejected and forlorn, to say nothing of the after effects of his
rampaging in Civita Vecchia, Cellini was clearly in a miserable condition. He hadn't done a lick of work on the chalice. What the Legate's
reaction to this state of affairs would be he did not know—and cared
less. He did, however, take himself to the Vatican.

Salviati gave the baggy-eyed goldsmith a haughty look. "Where is
that fantastic onion stew of yours?" he demanded. "You've dawdled
over it long enough! Have you finished it? Well?"

If nothing else, the Legate shook the Florentine out of his torpor.

"Monsignore!" he yowled back, aroused by the barbarous reference
to his work, "know that I have not finished my fanstastic onion stew!
Nor do I intend to do so until you give me the onions to finish it with!"

The Legate all but fell off his chair.

"Hah! Do you dare make games with me, *birbante?* Perhaps if I
sent you to the galleys and let you limber up those lazy muscles a bit,
you would acquire sufficient grace to go on with your labor and correct
a portion of your manners as well!"

Cellini's hackles were standing straight in the air.

"Reverend Sir! When I am found guilty of crimes which merit the galleys, you may send me there! Until such time, I have no fear of them. As for this... this onion stew of mine—not another stroke of work will I do on it; nor will I again answer any summons to come into your presence, unless I am dragged here by your police!"

The Cardinal went a bit glum at this outburst. He would have liked nothing better than to have this presumptuous malapert flogged till the blood ran; but the Pope wanted a chalice, not a goldsmith with a lacerated back or chained to a galley oar. He brought his voice down to a lower register and temporized.

Cellini would have none of it, cardinal or no cardinal. He stormed out of the Vatican and every time the Legate sent a messenger, he gave the man the same answer: "Tell my lord Cardinal to give me the onions and I will finish my onion stew."

And while he bickered, the goldsmith brooded over the bitter loneliness that had become his lot. He involved himself in quarrels, in other love affairs. He hired a luscious servant girl who was willing and eager. Nothing helped. Lonely, weary weeks went by before a letter came—a letter from Angela. All it told him was that she was in Sicily, extremely unhappy.

Whenever he went up to his rooms there were reminders of her. He decided to move away. Felice was made a partner and the apartment above the shop turned over to him. Cellini rented a house behind the Banks, just off the Strada Giulia, and stayed away from the shop as much as possible. He did his work in the studio of his new home and let Felice handle the work at the shop. But he couldn't move away from himself. The sadness remained. There was no escaping it. Even that healer of all hurts and wounds, time, refused to come to his rescue.

Cardinal Ippolito returned to Rome just as the goldsmith came down with an inflammation of the eyes. In spite of it he went to pay his respects to the young Medici prelate. For that matter, there was pain in Ippolito's eyes too, though it was not of any physical variety. His was the type that corrodes the soul, a deep intense hurt, mixed with a smoldering hate. He never made reference to the tactics used to supplant him in the rule of Florence, but if anyone wished to know his true feelings, they were visible in his eyes—particularly when Alessandro's name cropped up.

Cellini's eye ailment worsened until he began to despair of his

225

sight. A nagging suspicion of what had caused the malady began to gnaw at him, increasing his disturbance of mind.

Clement returned from Bologna.

Salviati gave an account of his dealings with the goldsmith that had the Pope boiling. It wasn't long before the Florentine received a curt summons to report to the Palazzo Papale. He doddered off to the interview, in anything but a relaxed condition. Nuncio was leading him by the arm.

As was to be expected, the Pope wasted no time on preliminary courtesies.

"Come forward and give me here that work. Is it finished?"

Cellini displayed the figures of the knop. Nothing else. There was nothing else to show.

Astounded at such unbelievable insolence, the Medici worked himself into a frenzy.

"As there is truth in God!" he blazed, "I tell you—you who make a boast of fearing no man—that were it not for my honor before the world, I would have you, together with your work, flung out of yonder window!"

"No one in the world," cut in the goldsmith defensively, "would expect a blind man to execute such a work as this!"

The shouting Pope heard only a reference to a "blind man."

"Come closer here," he bellowed. "What was that you said?"

In self-defense, Cellini shouted back: "And if I am blinded by a sickness, how can I go on working?"

"Bah!" Clement waved a whole arm. "Don't try to gull me! You had sight enough to find your way hither! I don't believe a word of it!"

"Your Holiness can ask your doctor who is tending me, and learn the truth from him!"

The Pope cooled. He sank back.

"Very well!" he answered tartly but with greater calm. "More at leisure we will learn if what you say is true."

The relative quiet which followed this utterance provided an opening. Cellini used it to give his version of the altercation with Salviati.

"...Referring to my work as an onion stew!" he yelped. "Threatening me with the galleys! What right does His Eminence have to use me thus? Shortly thereafter," he lied shrewdly, "a fever attacked me and I lost my sight. I have been unable to work since."

226

Clement screwed up his lips, looked around to his gentlemen and flipped a hand. *"E bene,"* he conceded, "one can give instructions to people, but not the discretion with which to carry them out. In truth, I did not tell my lord Cardinal to pursue the thing with such ferocity. If what this laggard tells us of his illness is true, which I shall presently learn from my physician, he deserves some compassion."

The Papal medico did full justice to Cellini's claim. The more so since he could hit on no remedy which would relieve the ailment. Instead of showing improvement the perverse malady grew steadily worse. The whole of the goldsmith's body broke out in little red blisters.

"It's the French disease," Cellini groaned miserably to the coterie of doctors he called in to examine and lambaste him with cure-alls. "I'm certain of it. I caught it from the young servant wench I kept in my house."

The leeches collectively shook their heads. "This is not *il mal francese,*" they averred. "It is a disorder of some other kind. Something rare—a malady we are unable to recognize."

The inability to give it a name did not stop them from pasting him with poultices and salves, dosing him with purges, and bathing his eyes with a distillate of corn flowers. There was no improvement. The goldsmith decided to take the matter into his own hands and try the "holy wood."

The leeches were horror-struck. "Why!...in your present weakened state, the extreme abstinence that is required for such a cure will be the death of you! Utter nonsense! This is nothing more than foolhardy idiocy!"

"None the less," countered Cellini obstinately, "I am resolved to try it. And why not, pray?" he peevishly inquired. "Are your remedies and treatments of any use?"

They had no answer for that.

Being careful to scrupulously adhere to the stringent rules attendant on this quasi-medical, quasi-religious fetish, the goldsmith began drinking the decoction boiled down from the holy wood: a greenish-yellow, horrible looking, vile tasting, resinous liquid...Guaiacum...the *lignum vitæ* of the ancients...*legno santo* to the superstitious of medieval Italy.

Contrary to the sanguine expectations of the learned men of medicine who waited for death to knock on the door, a few days of the cure

227

brought on a vast improvement. Thumbing his nose at the astonished leeches, Cellini continued the ritual for fifty days—and emerged as sound as a nut.

By then it was late fall. Perfect shooting weather. After all the trials and tribulations he had undergone, the goldsmith felt a need for a little recreation. He and Nasone took to the fields.

What the doctors and the *legno santo* had been unable to bring about, the wind, rain, and marshy bogs of the Campagna accomplished with ease. All of the Florentine's previous ills put together were as nothing to what came now. He was at death's door—and this time it was not just a figure of speech.

The spirit, however, remained uncowed. Weak in body, but strong and firm in his faith, the goldsmith again decided to take The Wood. The medicos howled louder than ever at this second display of madness.

Four days after having recommenced the ritual, the fever was gone. So much for doctors! In two weeks he was up and about, weak but pushing along with his work.

XXXII

A GOLDSMITH FROM PARMA, YOU SAY? *UN PAR-migiano!* What happened then?" Annibale Caro lent an attentive ear to the details of Cardinal Salviati's latest attempt at toppling Cellini from his perch.

Battista Sanga turned from the columned belvedere where the two were standing and grinned. "You know His Holiness, Annibale. He cannot resist the testing of a new talent. The fellow is not a Parmesan. He is a Milanese named Tobbia."

Salviati had been made Legate of Parma and was now residing in that city. He had come across a goldsmith there with whom he was much taken and had promptly written to Clement, thereby succeeding in venting his spleen at Cellini from a considerable distance.

...If your Holiness desires, I shall be pleased to send this able artist to Rome. Your Sanctity will then have at hand a means of bringing down the overbearing arrogance of this favorite of yours. Certain

I am, Most Blessed Father, that my Tobbia's efforts will please you far more than Benvenuto's ...

"His ability as a master remains to be seen," offered Caro with a shrug. "Parma is not Rome, my dear Sanga. Able artists are available here in any number. This Tobbia may be a daisy in the weed patches of the north, who would go unnoticed in the rose gardens of this city."

"We will soon be able to see for ourselves, old fellow," laughed the Papal secretary.

"You mean the man's coming here?"

"He will arrive in a few days. And let me tell you, in spite of the press of affairs surrounding the coming marriage of Catherine to Prince Henry, His Holiness is thinking only of the competition he wishes to set up for the two artists."

Tobbia arrived in Rome and was presented to the Pope. In appearance he was ordinary, a big-nosed man of medium height, with blunt unprepossessing features and a straggly, meek little beard that gave his face an apostolic cast.

Clement requested him and Cellini to appear at the Vatican.

"Our reason for summoning both of you lies in our desire to have you furnish us with a design for mounting a unicorn's horn, the finest which has ever been seen, and of which we have made a most fortunate purchase. It is our intention to present this rare object to His Christian Majesty, King Francesco, on the occasion of our Catherine's marriage to his son. Let it then suffice for us to say that the presentation must needs be suitable to the splendor and magnificence of this great prince, as well as of the high esteem in which we hold him. The mount must be imaginatively designed and superbly wrought in gold. Do you, therefore, make up sketches for this purpose, so that the best of these may be put in hand."

Cellini worked out a design which seemed to him suitable for so rare and valuable an object. When the cartoons were finished, the two goldsmiths were called to the Papal palace.

Tobbia's design, like the man himself, proved to be commonplace. He fashioned a mount in the form of a candlestick, with four little unicorn heads at the base. The horn was stuck into it like a tallow candle. To Cellini's eye it was utterly devoid of imagination, exactly the sort of performance to be expected from such a dullard as Tobbia looked to be.

229

Messer Traiano edged over to him, anxious to uphold the honor of a fellow-countryman and do a little digging under the Florentine's feet at the same time.

"This is a marvelous conception," he told Cellini. "Don't you agree, master?"

Tactless as ever, Cellini spilled over. *"Una maraviglia!"* he told him, with sarcastic emphasis. "A real marvel of marvels! By God! now I've seen everything in the world there is to see, and can die a happy death!"

Clement looked up, frowning and displeased.

"Show me your cartoon!" he ordered.

It was a drawing of a fanciful unicorn's head, part horse, part stag, with a flowing mane, rich in ornamental goldwork. The horn projected gracefully out of its forehead. Directly the sketch was seen by the courtiers crowding around the Pope they gave it the palm, applauding loudly.

"It is excellent," agreed Clement. "A masterful and richly imaginative work. Well done."

Traiano looked pointedly around at the Milanese faction of the court, and offered an opinion.

"Blessed Father, such a work as that cannot possibly be finished in time."

Frustrated, Clement was compelled to agree. The work had to be finished by the time he left for the coming wedding. He was at the point of asking Cellini how long it would take to complete, when the Milanese attacked.

"Holy Father," said one, "to send anything as magnificent as this object into France is a grave error."

"Pray inform us how so, *signore?"*

"Please to reflect, Your Holiness. These French are people of no culture. They will not be able to discern or understand the excellence of Cellini's piece, even if this able master could somehow succeed in completing it in time for your needs. Grotesques such as this one of Tobbia's, which can be finished quickly, are better suited to their tastes and will please them as well."

Clement sat thinking and nodding.

"Consider also, Blessed Father," maintained another, "that if the affair is thus disposed of, Benvenuto will be able to devote himself entirely to finishing the chalice you desire. You will then see two separate works completed at once, and this poor man who has come to Rome at your bidding will find some employment."

"That is most wisely thought on, my lords," concurred Clement. "We must think a little on this matter before deciding." He looked at the two artists. Cellini seemed bored. "We will advise you of whatever decision we come to in a day or so."

The Master of the Wardrobe, Giovanni Aleotti, came to inform the Florentine of the Pope's decision. Pompeo's clique had won the scuffle.

"Know you, Benvenuto, that His Holiness has commissioned Tobbia to mount the alicorn. Our Holy Father bids you finish the chalice."

"My lord, I desire nothing more than to complete this beautiful work. Yet I beg you understand that the material of which it is fashioned is gold. His Holiness must give me some if he desires me to finish the thing."

"Oh! Oh! *Oimè!* Don't ask for gold of the Pope or his fury will be the ruin of you!"

"Oh! Oh!" mimicked Cellini. "In that case, *signor mio,* I pray you teach me a little of how one can make bread without flour!"

Being a bishop, Messer Aleotti disliked being joked by a low craftsman. He hurried back to the Pope and made a well garnished report.

Clement flew into a passion. "We shall see," he fumed. "We shall wait and see if he is so mad as not to finish it."

The brooding Florentine no longer seemed to care what happened. Angela was gone, nothing else mattered. In his heart and mind he knew that his ridiculous stand would accomplish nothing to his advantage. It only provided his enemies with all the ammunition they needed. He was making it easy for them. Pompeo, full of hate and envy over the morse and the continual preference Cellini received, never let the smallest opportunity pass.

"If Your Sanctity were to deprive him of his post at the Mint," he suggested to the Pope, "he would perhaps take it into his head to finish the chalice."

Cellini not only hadn't completed it, he had not reported to the Vatican for almost ten weeks.

"No," answered Clement. "Benvenuto is an ass to behave in this fashion, granted. Yet were we to do as you suggest, two evils would occur. We would then be ill served in the Mint, which concerns us greatly; and we should most certainly never obtain the chalice."

Abetted by his uncle Traiano, who had developed a vehement dislike for Cellini, the two eventually prevailed on Clement to remove the Florentine from his post as Stamp-Master. The position was given to the Perugian goldsmith, Girolamo Fagiuolo.

To Pompeo fell the charge of informing Cellini of this move. He relished the office. It warmed the cockles of his spiteful soul. He dawdled over the words, savoring each as he voiced them to the angered master.

"... and His Beatitude bids me say to you," he ended maliciously, "that if you do not quickly finish the chalice he will deprive you of other things as well."

"Tell His Holiness," snapped back Cellini, "that he has deprived himself, not me, of the Mint; and that he will be doing the same with regard to those other things. Tell him also that if he should ever wish to confer the post on me again, nothing and no one on earth will induce me to accept it."

Glaring at the ungainly jeweler as he spoke, Cellini searched in vain for the reason behind all his underhanded meddling. There wasn't any. It would be a simple thing to understand Pompeo's actions, even to excuse them, if his own interests were involved. They weren't! There were a dozen instances, the alicorn and the present case among them, which had nothing whatever to do with him. He was in no way involved in the work and stood to gain nothing. Then why all the venom he was spitting?

Pompeo had sped off like an arrow, to repeat the goldsmith's angry words to the Pope.

A week went by and Pompeo called again. This time his fat wattle was stiff for anticipating the angry howl his words would wring from the Florentine. He let his heavy lips set in a half-smirk, half-sneer.

"The Pope no longer desires you to finish the chalice and wishes it returned in exactly the present state. You are to hand it over to me. I have instructions to deliver it to Tobbia, who will finish the work on it." He leered.

"Stinking offal!" Cellini's furious look wiped the leer off Pompeo's face in short order. "That's better," the goldsmith nodded. "Give yourself pretentious airs with me, you drone, and I'll undertake to show you how little it pays. See to carrying out what the Pope has ordered of you—but with care! lest you be made to pay for your vulgarity."

Pompeo's toadlike, beady eyes, lost in the expanse of his face,

232

gleamed wickedly. He swallowed and licked his lips. "About the Pope's request? ..." he asked sullenly.

Cellini curled a lip at him.

"This is not a thing like the Mint, which can be taken away from me at pleasure. I have received five hundred crowns from His Holiness. These are his property and I will immediately give them up to him, but nothing more. The work itself is mine and I shall do with it whatever I think or please. And now get out of my sight and smell, you pig! You bring the stench of the gutter with you."

It wasn't Pompeo who called again, three days later. It was two chamberlains, Pucci and Aleotti. The Parmesan goldsmith, Tobbia, was with them.

"Benvenuto, since you have chosen not to comply with Our Holy Father's requests on easy terms, he has sent us here with a charge. He commands now that you give over his chalice or accompany us to prison."

The unprepossessing Tobbia stepped forward loutishly. "I will take the work with me to my new shop. Give me also," he added presumptuously, of a mind that no man would dare defy the commands of a Pope, "the model and design for the work."

Cellini sneered him into a corner before replying to the two courtiers.

"My lords, were I to give up this work I would be yielding my own property, which I have every right to defend. More than this, I have no intention of allowing my labor to fall into the hands of some crude ignorant beast," he eyed the fidgeting Tobbia significantly, "who will promptly destroy its beauty, caring nothing that he does so."

"Follow your own mind in the matter, master. Only resolve what you mean to do and hasten to do it."

The Florentine picked up his cloak and cap.

"I am ready, *signori.*" Throwing a final glance around the studio, he closed and locked the door. "It is well that you have come for me," he told the noble blacklegs. "A man of my parts deserves catchpolls of no meaner quality than Your Lordships. Take me where you will."

Laughing and chatting, the two chamberlains leisurely strolled to the palace of the Governor. Their prisoner walked between them.

The Governor was primed and waiting. With him was the Procurator-Fiscal, Benedetto Valenti. They waited sternly, impressively.

The weighty atmosphere made Pucci laugh. "We give this prisoner

233

up to Your Excellencies, and charge you take good care of him," he grinned. He and Aleotti withdrew.

Cellini nonchalantly removed his cloak, not in the least dismayed by the lowering looks of Governor Gregorio Magalotti. He looked at the two questioningly, waiting for either to speak.

Messer Gregorio began a long harangue, bullying, exhorting, expostulating, and giving fatherly advice.

The goldsmith cut the piece in two for him and held up the ends for inspection.

"Excellency, this procedure is an act of bald injustice, far beneath the honor and dignity of a Pope. The Vicar of Christ cannot act after the fashion of some despotic and petty lordling who can be as willful as he pleases. He cannot with impunity commit such a dishonest act of tyranny and violence as to take from any man that which is that man's own!"

The Governor reverted to being a policeman and snapped: "Benvenuto! you are seeking that I shall treat you as you deserve?"

"*Messere!* you will treat me with honor and courtesy, if you wish to act as I deserve!"

"Send for that work at once!—and see that you do not wait for a second command!"

The goldsmith smiled impudently. "My lords, have you the patience to listen to four or five words spoken in my own defense?"

"If God will undertake to bestow it upon us!"

"Then look you, *monsignori.* If a man has ordered a palace, he could with justice tell the man building it: 'I do not wish you to go any further with my palace,' and after paying him his due, he has every right to dismiss him. In like manner, if a nobleman commissions the setting for a jewel and sees that the jeweler is not serving him as he desires, he could say: 'Give me back my gem for I do not like your manner of work.' Now in my case none of these arguments apply. Nothing can be commanded of me beyond the return of five hundred crowns. You will get nothing from me other than this sum. Go and tell this to His Holiness. Your threats cause me no alarm. I have no fear of my own faults."

The Governor and the Fiscal went to consult with the Pope.

Cellini, under guard, paced the floor of a long hall until the two officials returned and ordered him back to the Governor's chamber.

Il Magalotto glowered. "Benvenuto, I have been commanded by

234

the Pope to order you thus: Either produce the chalice instantly or look to arranging your affairs."

Cellini shrugged impassively. "I do not believe that the Holy Vicar can act with such injustice. Do what you wish."

"Very well. Just two additional words from His Holiness, before I execute his commands. It is his will that you have the work brought here, and after I see it packed and sealed, I am to take it to him. He promises not to break the seal and will immediately restore it to you. This he wills in order to preserve his own honor in this mad affair. Well, then?"

Clement quite naturally could not allow himself to be bested by a mere goldsmith. All of Rome would laugh. Cellini grinned.

"Most willingly will I comply with such a request, my lords."

The chalice was sent for, the gold work set on the wood and wax model, and the whole of it packed and sealed. The two noblemen returned to the Vatican, taking the box with them.

Clement turned the package over several times, not knowing whether to laugh aloud or give himself over to furious anger. The affair was so utterly and completely stupid that the Medici wondered how in the world it had ever cropped up.

"Have you seen the work?" he asked Magalotti.

"Yes, I have, Holy Father. It was packed and sealed in my presence. It seemed to me a truly admirable thing."

Considerably annoyed, Clement kept turning the box, finally breaking the seals and tearing off the string.

"Messer Gregorio," he told the Governor as he did so, "tell Benvenuto that Popes have the power of loosing or binding things of far greater consequence than this."

He examined the chalice with the utmost care. "Exquisite," he mused to himself, beckoning to Tobbia. "Give us your opinion of this work," he requested.

The Parmesan answered candidly. "Your Holiness, this is one of the finest things I have ever laid eyes on."

"Do you feel equal to producing a piece of like excellence, and in this exact same style?"

"I do, Blessed Father."

Clement turned to Magalotti. "Discover for us whether Benvenuto will give it up as it is. If so he shall be paid the value fixed upon it by men of knowledge in this art. If he will undertake to finish it himself,

235

let him name a certain time; and if you are convinced that he means to do the work, you have our leave to grant him any reasonable accommodation he asks for. If you get nowhere—which we fear will be the case with this too headstrong young man—give him orders to return the five hundred crowns to our jeweler, Pompeo."

Cellini was somewhat abashed when he saw the broken seals, but not overmuch. For all he was an artist, he was also enough of a realist to understand that the Pope, like any other man, was human. He would, however, neither part with the unfinished piece nor go on with it. Obstinately blind to his own best interests because of what he still regarded a barefaced swindle, he brought the chalice back to his studio and straightaway carried five hundred crowns to Pompeo, demanding a signed and witnessed receipt.

Smiling hugely, the jeweler took the money to Clement, which upset the Pope considerably. Clement had presumed that it would be some time before Cellini raised so much cash, and hoped in that time to pick up the thread of their association. Now here was this smirking ass with the money in hand, thinking he had done himself proud.

Disgusted by such low stupidity, Clement belabored the Milanese with a withering scorn that left the jeweler cowering.

"Go and find Benvenuto," the Pope ordered, "and show him what little civility your ignorant nature is capable of showing. Tell him for me that if he is willing to finish that piece in the form of a reliquary to hold the Holy Host, I will allow him all the accommodations he desires, provided only that he work on it. Go!"

Pompeo cringed out and ran off to find the Florentine.

Cellini listened silently while the jeweler ate his crow. His mouth wrinkled as Pompeo drooled sugary compliments. He waved him silent.

"Have done!" he erupted scornfully. "Pah! *Scimiotto!* Your manners, like your methods, are as repulsive as those of an ape. Say to His Holiness that I kiss his feet and that I desire nothing more than to faithfully serve so great a prince; and that day and night I shall never fail to give thought to how I may do so." He paused briefly to let his face grow suitably ugly. "So much for His Holiness. Now as concerns you. The Pope has all the servants he requires, therefore see to it that he doesn't send you around here again. Give thought to your safety and keep that long nose in your own affairs and out of mine... For if, after having delivered my message to the Pope, you ever again meddle in any of my affairs—I care not how trivial the meddling—I swear it on the Cross, you will answer for it with your blood! Get out of my house!"

XXXIII

COMFORTABLY SPRAWLED AT ONE OF THE tables in the stone-flagged yard of the Colombo Bianco, Agnolo Gaddi stretched out his legs and meditated on an answer for the question put to him. While he mused he indolently watched the flocks of white doves, which gave the tavern its name, strut and flutter around the spraying fountain of the piazza.

"Still and all, my erudite Fra Elia," he answered, turning to the Sicilian priest seated opposite him, "I incline to the opinion of Annibale Caro here. The Black Art is the Black Art, and there's the end of it. I can see no difference in the distinctions you make between your so-called 'good' or 'bad' sorcery. It's all of a piece to me—intercourse with the Devil!"

"By no means, my dear Agnolo," answered Fra Elia in a deep voice startlingly at variance with his lean and shrunken frame. "Surely you will own that a man like myself can undertake such a study in order to make use of the art as an instrument of knowledge, rather than as an instrument for promoting evil intent?"

"*Coglioni!*" Caro leaned over the table for the pitcher of wine and refilled his cup. "I fail to see the point of it, Your Reverence. Granting what you say, there remains the fact that in such unholy work one is dealing with the fiend, as Agnolo has pointed out. Do that and the pit yawns before you. What say you, Cencio?"

Vincenzio Romoli shuddered. He was a lively enough youth, but he had no liking for the topic under discussion.

"I agree," he nodded, wishing in any case to take part in the conversation. "These are impious practices. Conjuring up the Devil from Hell!" He gulped some wine. "Selling your soul and accepting damnation as your lot!"

"If the exhortation is properly managed," Fra Elia interposed, "no danger results either to the body or the soul."

"Va bene." The nephew of Giovanni Gaddi carved slices of cheese and sausage, eating as he spoke. "Since you are a priest it may be supposed you know whereof you speak. Still—" he straightened, looking out into the square. "There's Neutino. *Olà,* Benvenuto!" He stood up and waved, signaling the goldsmith to come and join them.

"You have met Don Elia, Neutino?" he asked when Cellini reached the table. "No." He presented him.

Cellini bowed to the priest's greeting, looking him over as he did so. The man wore motley, the parti-colored dress effected by seers, astrologers, and some doctors. He was round shouldered and stooped, thinly fleshed and frail looking, with dark dry skin drawn tight over the bones giving him a skeletal look. His deep sunk eyes were intensely active over a beaklike nose and thin, bloodless lips. A sparse beard clung to his chin, like blades of grass to a rock crevice. Fra Elia looked like no priest Cellini had ever seen.

"Sit you down and join us, Neutino. We were just discussing the Black Art. Here, moisten your tongue."

"Gràzie," the goldsmith nodded and seated himself. "The Black Art?"

"Sì. Don Elia here is a man of elevated genius, very learned in Latin, Greek, and Hebrew. More, he is highly skilled in necromancy."

"Ah! Un stregone?"

"Ma che!" Fra Elia came to his own defense. "I am no common warlock, casting spells or dealing in five-*soldi* charms and philters, my dear Master Benvenuto." He seemed much taken with the bold directness of the Florentine. "I interest myself only in the higher learning and applications of this art. Tell me, have you ever seen anything of this marvelous pursuit? Do you know anything of it?"

"By my faith, Your Reverence, be it said frankly I am a man of lively curiosity; and although I have long had a desire to see and learn something of this wondrous art, an opportunity has never presented itself."

"So?" replied the Sicilian affably. "Have you understood that the man who sets himself in the way of such a bold emprise must be of stout heart, of redoubtable and inflexible courage, of steadfast will?"

"Jesus," breathed Vincenzio Romoli.

"As regards courage, of heart or mind or soul," Cellini pointed out to the shrunken featured Fray, "I could provide all that might be needed and perhaps have some to spare."

238

"Neutino," Annibale interrupted, "suppose during such an adventure the Horned One himself were to appear. What would you do?"

"Tell him to go to Hell, I suppose," Cellini answered with a grin.

Fra Elia waited for the gale of laughter to subside.

"Indeed?" he nodded, looking keenly at the Florentine. "Do you know, I have no doubt but that you would say exactly that. Perhaps I can put myself in the way of being of service to you. If you are serious in wishing to see something of the art of necromancy, and have the heart to dare it, I will undertake to satisfy your curiosity."

The goldsmith was perfectly willing. "Agreed, *per Bacco!* You have only to tell me when this is to be."

"Before I can give you that answer I shall have to consult the stars, and search for other signs as well. It is necessary to resolve the most auspicious time for such an undertaking. It will require much effort and considerable preparation."

"How long will it take?"

"It is not possible to say with certainty. If I start on it this evening and all goes well I can perhaps have the answer by tomorrow morning. Will that suit your convenience?"

"Entirely."

"Very well. In the meantime you can see to finding a comrade or two to take along. Also, you must find an innocent youth of fifteen or sixteen years. This last is important. I shall bring along a student of the occult arts who will be of good service for such a project as we will engage in."

"I'll go along." Agnolo Gaddi offered himself. "I would like, once and for all, to see just what there is to this Black Art, even if I do chance placing my soul in the hands of the fiend. How about you, Annibale?"

"I cannot join you. I leave tomorrow for Florence—on the affairs of your illustrious uncle, my lord Giovanni. You are going, Cencio?"

"Who? Me?"

"Of course." Agnolo refilled the wine cups all around. "Surely you won't allow such an opportunity to pass?"

The youth was trapped. He could not extricate himself without betraying his fears, and he would rather have died than do that.

"Oh, sure. Yes... Yes, of course..."

"*Eccellente!*" Cellini slapped the table top, delighted with the promise of an intriguing adventure. "I'll have my little Nuncio along.

239

He's just fifteen. However," he added, with a sidelong glance at Fra Elia, "I cannot vouch for his innocence."

"He will do, I think," the Fray told him.

"Good. Then all that remains is for you to let us know when it is to be."

"Quite so, Benvenuto. Also, we shall have to repair to some secluded spot where we can proceed unobserved. As you know," he sent a meaningful look around the table, "in matters such as these a certain amount of discretion is necessary. There are many who might misunderstand the simple intent of our experiment and report us to the authorities, perhaps even to the Holy Office. You know what happens to witches and warlocks?" Again the meaningful eyes swept the company. *"Bene!"* Fra Elia sat thinking a while, the others watching quietly. "We will go," he said, looking up, "to the Colosseum."

"Good Christ," whispered Romoli.

That evening the weird looking Fra Elia busied himself with his instruments and charts, preparing for the ritual by which he hoped to wrench the information he sought from the skies above and the nether lands below. He was in the study and laboratory of his house, a chamber which occupied the whole of the upper floor under the roof. It was a large room with a sloping, raftered ceiling, high on one end of the room and low on the other. Scattered around was an amazing assortment of paraphernalia and instruments. There was a furnace along one side. There were shelves laden with retorts, phials, alembics, mortars, crucibles and panniers of all sizes and shapes. These were used for refining and compounding the secret formulas necessary to success in the necromancer's art. Locked cupboards held the precious substances used for this purpose. Cabalistic charts lined the walls. Books lay about in heaps; ancient weighty tomes written in various languages.

A long table held an assortment of globes and astrolabes. There were rolled-up scrolls; some useful merely for casting a horoscope; others with more selective and refined uses. A small trivet alongside the table gave off a wispy plume of fragrant smoke.

In a corner a black hen with a red comb, feet tied, clucked resentfully.

A lamp shaped like a hydra hung from a chain attached to a rafter and cast a fitful reddish glow. Its light was enlivened but little by the yellowish gleam of a sputtering candle.

The necromancer was gowned in a costume fitting to the work at hand. A long robe of black wool, with a deep cowl, covered him from his head to the soles of his pointed poulaines. Mystical symbols and devices were embroidered on its somber surface, bespeaking the intent of the wearer to commune with the denizens of the world below. Around his waist there was clasped a belt held by a curiously worked buckle. It was a wide cincture made from the brilliantly beaded hide of a serpent beheaded in the full of the moon at the stroke of midnight. This was a talisman of great power. Wearing it, the sorcerer could practice the Black Art in all its most potent ramifications, with relative impunity. None but the most powerful and mighty of evil spirits—only the Princes of Hell—would dare offer molestation to the wearer of it.

Seating himself at the table, Fra Elia drew forward a carefully prepared parchment scroll covered with spaced mystic symbols. For a long time he studied, making copious notes and calculations, frequently consulting several globes on which the zodiacal signs were engraved on movable bands which permitted them to be juxtaposed with various other celestial bodies. Several other instruments of palpably eastern origin and manufacture were manipulated and consulted, the while careful notation was made in the interstices of the prepared chart's geometric patterns.

At length Fra Elia arose and paced quickly to the end of the room where the roof sloped down. It had a large window set in it. The weak light made him seem more sepulchral than ever as he worked an astrolabe and determined the positions of certain stars and planets, carefully checking his calculations against astronomical charts before entering the positions on the parchment.

A long period of study in several heavy volumes, rich with the lore of the astrological and cabalistic arts yielded additional material. Finally all was ready, and the terminal ritual preparatory to the final calculation got under way.

Seizing the black hen, he slit its gullet with a little curved knife, and while he mumbled an esoteric invocation, held the pullet's body so that a single drop of bright-red blood splattered on five talismanic signs of the chart. More quickly now he inscribed symbols on the paper, continuing his muttered pronouncements.

There was a brief interval of silence before the final calculations. Muttering, computing, Fra Elia worried the chart, turning and looking at it this way and that, until an answer had been deduced. It was done!

He smiled—as one who has succeeded against heavy odds. All was lucid. The answer could not be clearer. The edicts from on high—and below—had combined to make known their secrets to him. They unequivocally declared that the period following the midnight of two days hence would be most propitious for a convocation of the fiends of Hell.

XXXIV

At fra elia's house cellini and his companions met the collaborator who was to aid their attempt at intercourse with the Devil. He was a pallid, vacant-looking native of Pistoia, named Frania. The goldsmith, Agnolo and Cencio peered at this specimen askance. He was, or at least he looked to be, an individual on whom Satan had left an indelible stamp.

"Are we ready?" asked Cellini, feeling a little uncasy but interested in seeing what would come of the night's work. "Shall we start out?"

While the others emptied the mugs Fra Elia passed around, he took up a torch and lighted it at a wall cresset. At the door he passed this to his young lackey Nuncio.

Agnolo Gaddi paused to look up at the lowering sky. It was a dark night, heavy with rain clouds scudding swiftly in the wind. In the distance a faint rumbling and occasional flash made the threat of storm seem acute.

"I hope it doesn't rain," he said loudly, secretly hoping otherwise. "That would ruin everything, would it not?"

Fra Elia snorted scornfully. "It will not rain, my friends. This night is auspicious. It is so written in the stars."

Nuncio's knees were knocking together. He looked around helplessly. Cencio Romoli and Gaddi seemed listless and apathetic, as full of misgivings as himself. His master, Benvenuto, actually seemed cheerful! And those two sorcerers! ... they weren't men at all! These were devils incarnate! An unholy duet who exuded the fumes of the pit! Why? ... Why had he allowed himself to get mixed up in this devilry?

"Oh good Christ! what am I doing here?" he blabbered.

"Eh? What's that, young Nuncio?" Amused at the lad's obvious fears, Fra Elia frowned and looked at him sharply.

To the youth it seemed that a demoniac gleam had come into the warlock's eyes. He crossed himself furtively.

"N-n-nothing," he stammered.

Fra Elia smiled balefully.

The Evil Eye! Nuncio blanched and looked away. Too late! No two ways about it, he was being readied for Hell. In an ague of fear there flashed across his mind all the stories of witches and devils, incantations and spells, with which his mother had regaled him through the years. Without making the least effort he could picture her by the hearthside, recounting those fearful tales of evil; of the blood of newborn babes, mould scraped from the faces and scalps of corpses in the dead of night; all used to bring on horrors that defied description. Of *il folletta,* a demon who for untold years had roamed the countryside. An imp of Hell who could not be seen, but whose wicked handiwork was visible to all eyes.

Shivering with dread, he curled the two shaking middle fingers of his right hand, clasping them with the thumb. The small and index fingers remained stiff and extended. Jabbing this horn-like talisman at Fra Elia, he fumbled through a stuttered invocation calculated to ward off the spell of the Evil Eye.

Agnolo Gaddi was in much the same straits. Indoors he had not minded so much; but outdoors in the dark was something else again. He was in a fearful dilemma. Being a fairly devout Catholic he naturally looked on a priest as a man of God. How look on this one who was also a practitioner of the Black Art? A consort of Satan! Gripped in credulous dread, rooted in superstitious fears, he did not know how to turn.

Shuddering he stole another glance at the two handymen of Satan. Frania, with his vapid, carelessly arranged face blank as a bed sheet, was bad enough. Fra Elia, clad all in black, with the pomponed peaks of a conical cap dangling down his ears, looked enough like a hideous gargoyle to make any decent Christian scream. The emaciated frame, pale drawn lips, unwinking eyes, dank hair, the ghastly skin which in the dim torchlight took on a greenish tinge...

"God's wounds!" he gasped. "He looks like a corpse freshly dug up. A true devil's advocate, this! Holy Saints preserve me!" Here was no mortal being. Here, walking along with them, was a specter—a wraith—a dismal shade loosed from some foul corner of Hell, for their undoing! "Jesus Christ!" he prayed.

Cencio Romoli was stupefied. He stumbled along, his mind a blank void.

While half the company was occupied with this self-inflicted corrosion of the mind and abuse of the soul, the whole of it made its way through streets black as pitch, to the Piscaria. They circled the Teatro Marcelli and trudged silently to the deserted section of Rome which extended southeast of the Capitol square. Before them the ancient Roman forum hulked blackly in the night.

"We had best put out the torch," vouched Fra Elia. "From here on the less attention we attract, the better for our purpose."

Nuncio extinguished the torch, marooning himself in a darkness that was as thick and heavy as a pile of blankets and much more oppressive. Four vague moving forms were faintly discernible to his fear-dimmed eyes. Fra Elia seemed to have vanished, melting from the corporeal into thin air.

"Holy Christ," choked the lad, "have mercy!"

Hunching up his shoulders, he groped his way along until a rat, foraging in the roadway, squeaked underfoot and scampered off, freezing him in overwhelming terror. Cellini had to walk back and take hold of his arm. Even so, at the slightest noise reaching his hypersensitive ears Nuncio shrank into himself like a wounded snake.

As if in answer to his prayer the clouds thinned and broke, allowing moonlight to flood through the breach and bathe the ruins all about them in silvery magnificence. Fra Elia instantly reappeared, a dangling disembodiment of face and hands suspended in air. It was some time before Nuncio recalled the priest's black clothing, which would not be visible in such weak light.

There was not a soul in sight, unless it was some lost soul—invisible to mortal eyes.

Made uncomfortable by the long, sustained silence, Cellini started a conversation, choosing a light but pertinent topic for discourse. Almost immediately the sound of human voices began to dispel the gloom.

"Tell me, Fra Elia," he began, "is all one hears concerning these charms and philters true?"

"My boy, the answer to that depends largely on what you hear," came the sage reply.

"Well, as an example, I know a lord who claims to have pur-

244

chased a potent charm—costing him many gold ducats—which he used
to win over the scruples of a fair and noble mistress. Until then she
would have nothing to do with him. Now she's worn him down thin
as a sheet. Can't get enough of him!"

Both the Fray and his collaborator unctuously agreed that such
could indeed be true.

"Oh yes, my Benvenuto. Such results are readily got by any who
have gained a fair knowledge and skill in charms and philters. Usually,
it is the woman who engages in play of this sort; a female seeking to
win over some particular male, rather than the other way around. There
are exceptions, naturally."

"Women," added Frania disdainfully, "have since the beginning
of time made it a point to seek out some disinterested male from a
multitude of more than willing ones. They always desire one who is a
bit more difficult to obtain. Hence the widespread use of love philters
and love charms." He shrugged uncomprehendingly. "Women!..."

Nuncio brightened perceptibly. The subject was to his taste.

"I know of one such wench, Master Benvenuto," he chattered.
"The servant maid of our next door neighbor, Ser Tommaso. She purchased three charms and a philter from that old crone of a Mona Mari-
anna who lives down near the ruins of the old Ponte Sublico, and used
them on Master Tommaso. They worked fine. He gets into bed with her
all the time now—or so I hear."

Even Cencio laughed.

"Can you compound such wondrous things as that, Your Reverence?" continued the naïve lackey.

"Oh, I could do this easily enough, young man."

But, pressed the youth, these runes were all of lasting effect were
they not? Results were...well, permanent?

"Yes," nodded the conjurer. "That is quite true."

"Well...is it possible for you to make up something that isn't...
well, that won't last so long?"

"Ah?" Fra Elia seemed deeply interested. "Let me see if I understand you correctly? You want no truck with these usual charms and
potions. What you are interested in is a philter that will charm some
pretty little wench— cast a spell over her—but for a short period only?
You have no desire for any lasting endearments? Merely a decoction
that will...warm her up a bit, so to speak?"

"Exactly, Your Erudition."

245

"For the space of, say, an evening . . ."

"Uh-uh."

". . . the affair of an hour or two . . ."

"*Ma sì!*" Nuncio nodded vehemently.

". . . in short, a matter of touch and go?"

"Just so!" Taken all in all, this evil looking lazar was not a tenth so bad as he seemed.

"Bah! Utter nonsense! For such dabbling as that a young blade like yourself needs no charms or philters other than those you already possess."

"Heh?"

"My dear boy!"

"Eh . . . Oh? . . . Oh! . . . I see!"

"*Ecco!* Firm and upright. Nothing more than this is needed."

Disappointed, Nuncio looked glumly about. They were treading the timeless dust and rubble of the Via Sacra. Ragged pillars stood like forgotten sentinels along the way, mute remnants of cloistered archways eroded by the winds of centuries, succumbing to the slow decay of time's inexorable march. They passed a succession of theaters and colonnades, emerging in the Campo Vaccino where the Arch of Titus reared up, phantom-like, before them. Down the rutted road, the stark outlines of the massive Flavian amphitheater could be discerned.

Fra Elia, meanwhile, had warmed to Nuncio's simple thoughts on the opposite sex. He picked up the thread.

"To continue our discourse on play of the sort you have in mind, young man," he pointed out solemnly, "I pray you take care whom you select. It is most needful to avoid doing with the wrong wenches. You must abhor the wicked and the perverse. And above all!" he raised a finger skyward by way of emphasis, "above all! beware of a Succubus!"

God above! All of Nuncio's previous fears, and some new ones, came back with such a rush he stumbled. A Succubus!

Nuncio did not know what a Succubus was; moreover, he did not wish to know. He could well imagine some unfettered fiend or other, some new horror that would send him shrieking in terror every time he thought of it. He was far better off not knowing. Ignorance, very often, is so beautifully blissful a state.

But Cellini too was interested. The horrified lackey could see the question forming on his master's lips. There it came! "D-d-damn," he yapped.

246

"And just what would a Succubus be, Your Worship?"
Nuncio gulped in dismay.

"The Succubus, my dear Benvenuto," Fra Elia replied with a calm that curdled the blood, "is a demon that has within itself an insatiable fire and lust, which it refreshes and sustains by sucking out souls. It is a devil that has assumed the form of a woman wondrous to behold, in the full bloom of beauty, irresistible, capable of imparting joys comparable to nothing on earth. And while she thrills the body," the sorcerer's voice was vibrant, "she consumes and destroys the spirit of those unfortunates she has ensnared!"

"God's blood and bones!" whimpered Nuncio.

"Oh, Christ!" groaned Agnolo.

"*Oimè!*" Cencio could only whisper.

"Beware of such as these," thundered the Fray, eyeing the quailing lackey. "I say beware! Her kisses devour. Her laugh is as the sound of celestial music. Merely to gaze upon her incites a man to yield up his spirit. Her look is so warm, it thrills the belly. Her voice fills the brain, debauching the mind. She engenders a diabolical heat. When she is aroused her eyes flame up so brightly, there can be seen therein the blazing fires of the pit. When embraced she will rage like a tempest—biting, squeezing and writhing in voluptuous abandon. A poor sinner emerges from such a bout bruised, torn, and crushed, ready for the flames of Hell because of the love that churns within him until his soul is drawn from his body and possessed by Satan ... Because, during this time, this she-devil is draining out his vital seed and spark, as through a spigot!"

Nuncio was fascinated. For all his fear and dread, to his youthful imagination this was completely enthralling ... such a charming way to die!

"I can see some slight difficulty here," vouchsafed his more realistic master.

"How is that, Benvenuto?"

"Discerning a Succubus? This must be quite a problem?"

"How so, my dear fellow?"

"I have never yet come across a female who didn't have something of the devil in her."

"True," mused Fra Elia, nodding fairly. "True enough. Some more than others, but to speak the truth, in all world it would be next to impossible to find one lacking in this quality. Yet it is said that in hav-

247

ing to do with the Succubi, a man may more or less recognize them by reason of the irresistible allure, the diabolical charms they are capable of exerting, thus making slaves of those whom they embrace. Slaves who can do naught but return again and again to the couches of these sirens from Hell."

"In that case, good Fray," the goldsmith admitted, "I am dead and damned!"

"More to the point," Fra Elia went on, "Frania here can tell of a specific case. He was in Bari when the authorities there succeeded in apprehending just such a she-devil. Tell them of her doings, Frania," he invited.

The collaborator swelled to the task. "I recall the incident well," he said importantly. "At the time I was studying the conjurer's art with a learned master who settled in that city after a long journey in the East, where he acquired all the great occult secrets of the ancients.

"This *demonia* had been under suspicion for some time, in that two of her lovers had already been placed beneath the sod—victims of their extravagant amours. When a third followed, the authorities broke into her house where they found her already engaged with another victim, a little minor lordling who was there with her, imperiling his soul. It was said that he had been shut up in her house for a full two weeks, during which time she denuded him of love, morning, noon, and night, taking all of it and leaving none in his heart or elsewhere, for others to enjoy. He had been reduced to a sorry state when they burst in upon them—emaciated, pale as wax, his bones disjointed, his bowels crushed, withered and useless as a dried-up worm. So much under the spell of this *demonia* was he that despite the pleas of his confessor he would have returned to her had he not been forcibly restrained; so much did he still yearn for those supernatural embraces that bring on eternal death rather than bring forth new life."

Nuncio was licking his chops.

"What became of her?" asked Agnolo timorously.

"Oh, she was brought to trial; but on maintaining that her only reason for having to do with men was due to her great taste and desire for enjoying the delights of love, she was ordered put to the question. A little of that and she quickly made open confession of her guilt and heinous sins."

"And then?"

"Already more than half dead from the torture, she was ordered to undergo the ordeal of fire. You see, the authorities wished to determine exactly if she was or was not a demon. If, on the flaming pyre, she burned, then she was human. On the other hand, if she was not consumed by the flames, it could only be due to the fact that she was a demon. And so, to the edification of a multitude who had come from leagues around to witness this spectacle, she burned—in truth, much like any other creature!"

XXXV

By THEN THEY HAD PASSED THE COLOSSUS NEronis and were approaching one of the vomitoriums of *Il Colosseo*. The goldsmith relit the torch just as the clouds closed in again, shutting out the moon. The shadows it cast flicked and pranced across the stone ruins like the dancing at a witches' sabbath. The wind moaned through the open vaultings of the giant arena. In the distance a bell chimed faintly. It was midnight.

Inside the crumbling oval walls the group picked their way between tumbled fragments of stone. Fra Elia led them to a mound of rubble near the center of the arena, open on all sides. There was a raised stone platform set between two jagged columns, which bore a rough resemblance to an altar—but not a godly one.

In a disquieting silence the four neophytes dumbly watched Fra Elia and his acolyte open packs and set out equipment, robes, and the precious substances to be used during the invocation. A brazier of charcoal was lighted and while the fire burned bright the two sorcerers enrobed themselves in the habiliments of their craft.

Cellini was grimly still. Agnolo stared with his mouth open. Nuncio chewed and gulped like a cow with her cud. Cencio's scalp prickled. He could feel the hair on the back of his head go stiff while he watched the two wraith-like figures draw on those awesome robes. When the firelight flickered on the serpent-skin belts, his eyes bulged so they threatened to leave their sockets. Using his fist in place of a mere finger he crossed himself repeatedly, commending his soul to its Maker. When he began mumbling Ave Marias, Frania turned sharply.

"Have done with that cackling!" he hissed savagely, while Fra

Elia scowled approval. "Do you wish to be the ruin of us all? Think what we have come here to do!"

For answer thunder rumbled threateningly and a brief flash forked across the distant reaches of the sky.

"*Santa Maria!*" gasped Cencio, near to collapse, "one cannot even call on Heaven for aid! We are lost!"

With the precise movements born of long practice the two magicians were describing two circles, one within the other, around the stone platform. Methodically they inscribed mystical symbols and talismanic signs between the circumferences, mumbling incantations as they worked.

These preliminaries over, Fra Elia turned to the ashen quartet.

"We are about to begin," he informed them in a cold distant tone that seemed the voice of doom. "Look you do quickly what we tell you to do. Stand firm in your resolve or untold harm will result. And when we introduce you into this mystic circle, make certain you do not tread on or otherwise mar the cabalistic symbols between the lines."

"*O Dio adesso aiutami,*" groaned the paper-white Nuncio.

To the chanting of a litany so horrible it had even Cellini quaking, the two warlocks made their entrance into prescribed sectors of the circle. Continuing the chant they signalled separately to the four laymen and as each approached the outer line, took hold of his hands and introduced him to the relative haven of safety inside the band of occult markings.

Fra Elia again looked on them with his unwinking eyes.

"Vincenzio and Agnolo, you two will see to aiding Frania in the ordering of the essences and drugs for the fire. Benvenuto, take you in hand this pentacle." He handed over a standard in the form of a six-pointed star. "When I bid you do so, turn quickly with it toward the points I shall indicate to you. Nuncio, you will remain under the pentacle, close by your master. Now then, is all understood?"

Uncertain glances and a licking of dry lips were the only answers he received.

Appearing satisfied, he nodded gravely to Frania who began heaping perfumes and rank smelling drugs, gums and resins on the glowing pannier. A swirl of dense smoke arose immediately. It too had the smell of evil.

While the smoke steadily increased in volume and enveloped them in its rank density, the necromancer began the awful invocation of the

250

Devil, signaling to the goldsmith to turn this way and that with the pentacle. Reciting from various demonic hymnals, scrolls and missals, chanting in an eerie voice that sent icy shivers chasing each other down the backs of the four novices, Fra Elia called upon the Legions of the Damned by virtue of the power of God the Uncreate, the Living and Eternal. He shrilled out portions of the oration in Latin, Greek and Hebrew, and they lost nothing of their evil flavor for not being understood.

Loudly he ordered Frania to cast into the flames the marvelous and potent formula of the famous magician of the East, Ibn es Sehr. Unknown to anyone there, this magical substance was, in reality, a quantity of mirage-inducing hasheesh mixed with fragrant musk and frankincense.

Proceeding onward, he conjured the seven principal Devils, demanding their aid in temporarily releasing some few of their myriad cohorts. He had a special exhortation for that prince of all demons—Satan himself.

During this collective self-abuse of the nervous system, the four listened in a revulsion of horror, rooted to where they were standing. If they had entertained the slightest doubt of Fra Elia's ability for commerce with the Devil, here was proof in abundance of his unholy power in the Black Art. With their own ears they could hear him conjure up the Prince of Hell himself. Already, through the swirls of the heavy blue and brownish clouds of pungent vapor, they fancied forms were taking shape. They could distinguish them now! Horrible, unearthly, gruesome apparitions with swollen, bloated features, blazing mouths, talon-like claws, and lashing tails!

The whole of the Colosseum was filled with legions of fiends and demons!

In abject agony Cencio and Agnolo mechanically heaped on the drugs and perfumes calculated to keep the demons at bay. Frania looked pleased. Fra Elia was beaming.

"Benvenuto, ask something of them."

Drowsy, possibly from fear, more likely from the smoke, Cellini unlocked his teeth. In a quavering voice he bawled out the thought ever uppermost in his mind.

"I demand to be reunited with my Angela!"

Thunder rumbled in reply. The viscid, evil smelling smoke—and all the fiends—writhed in unison.

The sorcerer was listening intently. He looked at Cellini.

"Heard you that which they have answered, Benvenuto? Within the space of one month she will be together with you!"

The goldsmith had heard nothing; but from what he was seeing with his own eyes, plus the terror that was upon him, he sincerely believed what the old warlock told him.

"I pray you stand firm, *maestro,*" implored the priest. "By the Eternal! there are legions here, a thousandfold more than I have summoned—the most dangerous of all the denizens of Hell. It behooves us to be most civil and dismiss them gently, lest we anger them."

"Cristo in cielo," Cencio quaked like a leaf.

Nuncio was so overcome he was belching. Slobbering in alarm he rounded his back, shrilling out that four huge giants among the millions of fiends swarming all around were bent on forcing their way inside the circle. Long pointed ears they had; bright red horns—sharp as tines— sprouting from their foreheads; and cloven hoofs in place of feet. Their barbed tails were twisting in an angered frenzy!

The necromancers themselves, not being immune to the drugged smoke, began to tremble. Fra Elia made pathetic use of mild and gentle persuasions, cooing and urging the demons back to the flaming pits from whence they had sprung.

Cellini was as badly frightened as any, but somehow managed to show it least. Not so his lackey. Nuncio momentarily expected one of those four fiends to swoop in, impale him on fire-red horns, and fly off to the pit. His legs gave way and he sank to the ground where he huddled against his master, forcing his head between the goldsmith's knees.

"Fulmini!" he jibbered, his voice a high-pitched whine. "They come! *Ahi-i-i-i-i!* Oh, Christ! Oh, Mother! What an end!"

His teeth chattering like castanets, Cellini loudly offered reassurances he was far from feeling. "Courage! These creatures are inferior to us! What we look upon is nothing more than smoke and shadow! Courage!"

Nuncio raised his head. "Holy Saint Andrew! The place is in flames and the fire is coming toward us!" He covered his face with his hands. "God's wounds! We are all doomed! *Ma-aaah-ahhhhhh!*"

"Stand truly firm by me, Benvenuto," babbled the sweating necromancer, "and we will yet surmount this grave danger. See to having a quantity of *assafetida* flung upon the coals!"

252

A look in the direction of the quaking and gasping Frania showed him choking on fumes and fully occupied with duties prescribed by the emergency. Cellini turned to Cencio.

"Make you the fumigation, Cencio!" he yelled at him.

The youth was rooted in terror. Immovable. Beyond all help and helping.

Agnolo Gaddi was little better off. His eyes bulged and were starting from his head for the fear that was upon him.

With a heartiness as false as a beggar's prayer, the goldsmith reached over and clapped him on the shoulder. "Agnolo, at a time like this a man should bear up, not yield himself to terror and fright. Show some of your usual boldness and spirit. Come, bestir yourself and throw a handful of that *assafetida* on the fire."

Making an effort of herculean proportions, Agnolo moved—and his bowels, before and behind, let go with a mighty blast. The volley was more effective by far than any *assafetida* would have been, for this mundane demonstration released the Florentine from the grip of terror. He roared with laughter.

Hearing him, Nuncio looked up.

"Corpo di San Stefano!" he blabbered. "That did it! The stench is driving them off! They flee in haste!"

None the less, Fra Elia continued his diplomatic overtures to the fiends for another hour. Not till the distant church bells were tolling the first of the canonical hours did he leave off; and he ended then only because Nuncio—whose youth and supposed innocence were presumed to give him special sight in this deviltry—told him that only a few demons remained in the amphitheater, and these were keeping at a distance.

"It's time, by God," breathed Cellini, wiping his face and watching the two conjurers disrobe and repack their gear. Matinsong had just rung. They had been in the circle for three hours.

Agnolo collapsed in a disinterested heap on a chunk of stone and listlessly began tugging off his trunks and drawers. Cencio stood looking up at the sky and wiping sweat from his brow. The heavens continued to grumble threateningly, but as the sorcerer had foretold, it did not rain.

"Sacred Mother," he gibbered. "What a night!"

Silently, by torchlight, huddled close together, the group stumbled homeward. Only Agnolo changed position. Bare from the waist and covered only by his cape, he moved from right to left as they changed direction, in order to keep to the windward side of the party.

Nuncio huddled in the center, one desperate hand clutching the necromancer's robe, the other his master's cloak. Ordinarily, touching any portion of the sorcerer would have been regarded as the heinous equivalent of a baleful glare from an Evil Eye; but this was no time to be finicky or hypercritical. He was still seeing devils!

"God's teeth!" he rattled, "there's two of the bastards gamboling and skipping along the rooftops!"

Fra Elia nodded gravely. "In all the years I have been engaged in this art," he told them seriously, "I have never before met with anything so extraordinary as this night's affair."

With that he sank into deep thought and did not speak again till they were on the Strada Giulia. There he turned to the Florentine.

"Benvenuto, I have a project to propose. You must join with me in consecrating a book. With such a fabulous codex at hand, we shall be enabled to acquire immense wealth. With it we can call up certain powerful fiends and demand that they disclose to us some few of the hidden treasures with which our earth abounds. Think of it! Opulence and power will be ours! We can become the richest of men!

"Tonight," he continued, his voice tinged with scorn, "you saw fit to demand the fulfillment of a love affair. Bah! This is trumpery! Nothing more than a display of the vanity and folly of youth—a matter of no consequence whatever. You must turn to more serious and useful projects."

"Were I a Latin scholar, Fra Elia, I would be more than willing to engage with you in such a venture. But I am a goldsmith, not a Latinist."

"My dear fellow," the Fray argued, "this is of less than no importance. Did I require such, there are Latinists in any quantity available to me. No. What I require and have great need of is a man who is as firm and resolute as you have shown yourself to be. There lies your advantage! Heed my counsel, young man. Think upon this matter."

He argued all the way to Cellini's door, where the four left the priest and his unholy companion, stumbled onto beds and dreamed of nothing but devils all the night through.

XXXVI

WELDED TOGETHER BY SO INTIMATELY TER-
rifying an experience, the initiates of that Black Circle got to meeting
almost every day in some tavern or inn, to while away a congenial hour
in recalling and discussing the lurid details of that phenomenon. To the
goldsmith Fra Elia's importuning was unending. He wanted Cellini
to knuckle down to the business of consecrating that book to the Devil.

"How much time would such an affair require, Fra Elia?" Cellini
asked one evening. The two happened to meet earlier than usual in a
trattoria near the Banchi.

"My boy, a month, less than a month, would see the matter completed to our great benefit."

"And where would we have to go? From all you have said I imagine a suitable locality must be found for such an undertaking?"

"That too has received my careful consideration, Master Benvenuto.
We will take ourselves to the mountains of Norcia."

Norcia was a region in the central Apennines. A craggy, sparsely
populated district which had for centuries been a spawning ground for
witches and warlocks, poisoners, and craftsmen of like ilk.

"A master with whom I studied my art," continued the cadaverous
Fra, "performed an enchantment such as I have in mind in a place
close by Rome. He selected a village in the Sabina, some seven leagues
from here, a place called Badia di Farfa; but he met with very great
difficulties, which we can avoid in the country of Norcia. Also, the
peasants there are sympathetic and can be trusted in matters such as
these. And since they themselves have had great practice and skill in
the art, valuable assistance will be available to us."

Cellini thoughtfully tapped his wine cup on the table top. The
thing would use up a great deal of time, and there was another matter
on his mind. There had recently come to Rome a Bolognese artist of the

255

highest reputation, an engraver believed to be without peer in his field. He had met this master, Giovanni Bernardi, and had seen some of his work. It left him speechless with admiration and an envious yearning to compete with the man and prove himself Bernardi's equal. The engraver was in Rome to make a commemorative medal for the Pope. Immediately after having learned this, and with the greatest secrecy, Cellini had set his hand to cutting Clement's portrait on a medal of his own design.

"I don't know what to do," he demurred, thinking of that medal. "I am currently engaged on a work with which I intend to crush my enemies at court. With a display of genius rather than with personal courage or skill at arms. I just don't know..."

"Benvenuto, I did not intend to break this news to you so crudely, but now I must. Last evening I cast your horoscope in an effort to determine if you would accompany me or if I would proceed alone. Unfortunately I was unable to divine an answer to this question from what the stars foretold. Yet there was one thing the inexorable celestial cosmos did make entirely clear. You are menaced with a peril. A danger which is imminent. The stars foretell an encounter of some kind which you should shun."

"Is that so?" Cellini brightened considerably. A sparkle came to his eye. Since the loss of Angela life had been so dull. A little brisk excitement would not be unwelcome. Angela! He repeated the question he had asked every day since the experience in the Flavian arena.

"Which reminds me," he requested of the somber priest, "we are now into September. Do you still believe that I shall be reunited with my Angela within the time given out by those fiends? The twenty-fifth of August that was. Two weeks ago!"

Fra Elia snorted in derision. "My dear fellow, devils, when they have made a promise, never break it! As sure as you draw breath, this Angela of yours will be with you by the twenty-fourth of this month. But how much more fortunate would be your case if you joined with me and departed on this venture. You would then escape this disaster I see impending over your head like some giant sword. Heed my words, Benvenuto. Come away with me."

In the end it was the artist in Cellini that won out over the promise of wealth. Not that he spurned the possibility of riches. It was simply that he could not bring himself to abandon the pursuit of the beautiful

256

and his ability to create it. So while Fra Elia chaffed and fretted, the goldsmith got on with the medal of Pope Clement. Completely absorbed in this, he gave no further thought to devils or their pledges, to books of enchantment, Fra Elia, not even to Angela.

About a week later Cellini made one of his rare visits to the shop. It was late afternoon, close to the hour of Vespers, when he started out. A teeming downpour had turned the streets into quagmires of sticky mud through which he made his way with difficulty, but the visit could not be put off any longer. There were commissions waiting which needed to be discussed, and work on them could not go forward until this was done. The details were all purely routine and an hour's talk with Felice covered everything. With that behind him, Cellini gave Nasone a final pat and rose to leave.

"You know that Alessandro del Bene wishes to talk to you about some work," Felice told him as he walked to the door.

"Yes, Felice. He sent me a note. In fact, I'm going to his house now. *Allora—*" he waved to his partner "*—arrivederlo.*"

Leaving the shop Cellini walked off in the direction of the Del Bene palace. As he was crossing over to the Via Giulia he saw a notary he knew approaching from the opposite direction, and paused to salute him.

"Good day to you, Ser Benedetto," he called cheerfully. "How fares the notary of the Chigi on this—"

"Get out of my way, you ill-mannered ass!" snarled Ser Benedetto by way of reply. "You are unfit to converse or mingle with Christian men!"

Ser Benedetto had blood in his eye—in both eyes. The goldsmith did not, of course, know that shortly before he arrived at the shop this same notary had strolled by in the company of his employers, some merchants of the Chigi family. As he walked past Felice had called out loudly and rather rudely, demanding the long overdue payment for some rings Benedetto had purchased weeks before. Hearing of the default the Chigi scolded their employee roundly. One word led to another until, thoroughly aroused by his flip retorts, they dismissed him from their service on the spot. The enraged notary was returning to the Cellini shop, intent on revenge.

Cellini's face underwent several changes of color and began to go stiff.

257

"Why this insulting speech," he snapped back harshly. "Are you suddenly become insane?"

"Are you suddenly become insane!" mimicked the notary in a snarling whine. *"Palle!* You and that whoreson partner of yours cause me to lose my place and you have the barefaced gall to salute me as if nothing had happened!"

"What are you talking about?"

"As if you didn't know!" Ser Benedetto growled out the gist of the matter. "I have you and your partner to thank for it! Base scoundrels, both of you!"

Fra Elia's warning flashed a brilliant track across Cellini's mind. This was the quarrel the sorcerer had foreseen and spoken of! He must restrain himself. Hold himself in check. But—good God above!—how?

"My dear Benedetto," he remonstrated, squeezing his teeth together in an effort to keep under control. "I know nothing at all of this affair. Absolutely nothing. Go and finish it with Felice. Since you started it with him, he will know what answer to give you. Why fly into a rage and hurl insults at me? The more so since you well know me to be a man who does not bear such abuse."

"Merda! Not only do you know all about it, you are implicated in it! As for your bearing abuse! *Porca miseria!—"* Benedetto's snort of contempt stung like a lash. "I am a man who can make you two sneaking skulks bear far heavier loads than this!"

How bear that?

The crowd that had gathered silently watched the goldsmith explode. Even then he sought only to relieve his feelings a little, without greatly endangering himself or the notary. Scooping up a handful of mud and refuse he hurled it into his adversary's face.

Benedetto charged at the same time, lowering his head like a bull in such a manner that the streaking mud took him on the crown of the skull. It should have done nothing more than dirty him up a bit. It would have done no more than this, had there not been a jagged stone the size of a plum mixed in with the noisome slime garnered from the gutter ditch. Benedetto fell in the street, blood spurting from a gash in his head.

Cellini looked on dumbly. He shrugged. This was Fate. Destiny. Suddenly he realized ... "Jesus! I've killed him!" He took to his heels.

As he sprinted nimbly away, Pompeo, en route to the Vatican for a conference with Clement, turned the corner. The notary lying in the street, wallowing in his blood, excited the jeweler's interest. He stopped to ask what had happened.

"Who struck him so mighty a blow?" he inquired after hearing a broad outline.

"The goldsmith, Benvenuto of Florence. I don't blame him a bit. This jackass asked for what he got."

"*Cellini!*" The flash of pure rapturous delight was so intense it caused a pang of exquisite anguish. Properly managed, this episode could be made to serve a long-looked-for end. Now he could not only get rid of this Florentine, but more than adequately repay him for everything.

"*Porco cane!*" the Milanese jeweler gloated, "I must get me to the Pope at once!"

He went so far as to interrupt a conversation the Pontiff was engaged in.

"Most Blessed Father," he cut in, "Benvenuto has just now murdered Tobbia! I have seen the thing with these eyes!"

Clement's face contorted into instant fury. Imperiously, he beckoned to the Governor.

"My lord Magalotti," he choked, "you will press an immediate search for this murderous madman. And after you have taken him you will hang him within the hour, on exactly the same spot where the homicide was committed! We charge you further not to come again into our presence until you have fully carried out our commands!"

Pompeo turned exultantly to his chamberlain uncle.

Traiano leered approval.

The goldsmith, meanwhile, had taken refuge in the house of Giovanni Gaddi, with the intention of getting out of Rome as quickly as possible. There was no coping with his malignant destiny. How could one contend with what was written in the stars?

Messer Giovanni advised less hurry. "This evil may not be as great as you imagine it, Benvenuto. Let us find out if it has caused any stir. Annibale—" he gestured to the poet who functioned as his private secretary, "go to the Vatican and see what you can learn of this. We will wait for you here."

Caro was on his way out of the room when one of Ippolito de' Medici's gentlemen was announced. He had, said the major-domo, requested immediate audience and had openly admitted he was seeking Cellini.

259

"Bid him enter," Gaddi ordered his chamberlain. "Annibale, wait a moment."

The Medici courtier quickly outlined Pompeo's distortions and Clement's action.

"Tobbia?" asked the confused Cellini, "I don't understand, *messere*. My dispute was with one Ser Benedetto, a notary."

"That's as may be, *maestro,*" the courtier replied. "My Lord Cardinal has sent me to make this report and to warn you that at the moment nothing can be done in the way of aiding your case. The Pope refuses to listen to a word. His Eminence suggests that you leave quickly and so avoid the storm. You are not safe in any house in Rome."

"Alas, my Benvenuto," Gaddi was genuinely moved, "there is nothing I can do to aid you!"

"Think no more of that, my lord Giovanni," Cellini promptly rejoined. "With the help of God I intend to look out for myself. All I require is that you give me the loan of a horse."

"Massimo!" Giovanni turned, shouting, "see to having that newly purchased stallion saddled! *Subito!* Let a loaded arquebus be made ready! Run, I beg!"

"Messer Giovanni," the goldsmith's tone turned grim, "there is yet another request I would burden you with."

"Anything, my boy, anything. You have but to say it."

"I beg you will have a message carried to Pompeo, on my behalf."

"It is done, Benvenuto. What is the message?"

"Tell him that I shall keep the promise I made him. Tell him there will come a time when he will be unable to hide behind the mantle of the Pope and will have to rely on himself alone. Tell him, my lord, to be ready—as I shall be!"

PART III

PART III

XXXVII

Mounted on a spirited Turkish black, a wheel arquebus wound up and ready across the saddlebow, Cellini trotted to the Ponte Sisto, arriving there as a mixed squadron of the Bargello's guards converged on the bridge from the opposite direction. To turn back was out of the question. All of the Gates on the western side of Rome would have been warned by now. The east Gates were his only remaining slim hope of safety. And even there the goldsmith was assuming that the Governor would believe it unlikely that a wanted man would chance capture by crossing the city, and so take his time in sending word to those more distant portals.

Pulling his *berretta* down around his ears, the goldsmith sidled over to a cart traveling in the same direction and passed over the bridge without being challenged. At a spanking trot he traversed the city, leaving it by the Porta Pia. No one paid him any attention. Only a madman would have tried to escape in that fashion.

Cellini galloped hard along the Via Nomentana for about a league. At a point near a group of eroded sepulchers he transferred to a little used side road which branched off into a tangle of mountains. It led to Palombara, a little Sabine village north of Tivoli, the fief of a friend and patron—the Papal *condottiere,* Giovanbatista Savelli. He would be safe there, and, he hoped, welcome.

The hope was not misplaced. Savelli entertained him lavishly for two days, after which the soldier advised against continuing northward, especially to Florence.

"To go on to Florence, my dear fellow," warned the Papal Captain, "is madness. You will only enter another wasp's nest. They will send you back in chains; or worse, hang you there and send back your head. No, no. Follow my advice. I'm older than you and more experienced in these things. I've been contending with them all my life. Take yourself

263

out of any region where the long arm of the Pope can reach out for you. Naples is your refuge. Nice city too. I'll provide you with another horse and a traveling companion. That black devil you were riding will be returned to Messer Giovanni. I'll advise him of your change of plan as well."

Cellini turned south, circled a wide arc around Rome, and took the overland route to Naples, roundly cursing the perverse ill fortune which, together with his untamable temper, so persistently plagued his every move. He halted for the night at an inn just outside the south gate of Velletri.

The next morning, after breakfasting and settling accounts, he was leaving the place when he heard himself being greeted loudly. Startled, he froze in his tracks.

"Cellini! By the rood! *Buon giorno*. What brings you south? Going on a journey?"

The goldsmith turned—and began to breathe again. It was the sculptor, Antonio Solosmeo. Cellini grinned up at him as he descended the stair.

"Hello, Antonio. I'm for Naples. And yourself?"

"Naples? Excellent! I will have good company. I'm going there myself, after I stop off at San Germano and inspect the progress of a commission I've been set to by Pope Clement—the tomb of his cousin Piero. I have been given the task of finishing the statuary and erecting the tomb at Monte Cassino. What takes you to Naples, Neutino? Business?"

Cellini sighed. "When did you leave Rome, Antonio?"

"Yesterday afternoon."

"And you don't know that Pope Clement is intent on hanging me?"

"Oh, that!" grunted Solosmeo, rounding his eyes. "What's this, *per Dio*? Do I understand you aright? You haven't heard how that affair has come off?"

The goldsmith stared and shook his head.

Solosmeo waved a hand. "All cleared up. I thought you already knew. You are in no danger from the Pope."

"For the love of Christ! Tell me about it."

"Of course. Exactly as it occurred. It happened that I was on the spot. That same evening when Tobbia was reported slain by that ass of a Pompeo..."

Clement was concerned over what, if anything, was being done about the remains of the slain Tobbia. He felt a certain responsibility since it had been by his order that the Milanese goldsmith had come to Rome—to meet his end. He sent a servant over to the Tobbia household to learn if assistance of any kind was needed to provide a suitable funeral, a seemly interment in consecrated ground, anything.

The unsuspecting servant entered Tobbia's home and aged ten years by the fright he took on seeing the "dead" goldsmith hard at work. Not only was the artist very much alive and completely unharmed, he knew nothing at all of any trouble and hadn't seen Cellini for at least a week. As for today, he told the Papal servant, he had been so pressed with orders waiting to be completed he had not set foot outside the door.

The servant returned and made his report.

"What! ..." Clement sputtered resentfully, "what manner of gulling and cozening is this?" He glared around at his courtiers. "Do any of you know of this—this monstrous thing?"

Ippolito stepped forward and explained.

"Of course," Clement nodded. "Up to a point I am at fault. I refused to hear a word." Glaring angrily, he addressed Messer Traiano. "Get that incredible imbecile in here instantly! You know whom I mean!"

Pompeo faltered into the presence babbling out an excuse of mistaken identity and sobbing for pardon. He was so badly frightened his flaccid face looked like mouldering bread dough.

Clement extended a finger under his nose. "Don't think for a moment that you could ever succeed in talking your way clear of this. You are a vile scoundrel! A complete rascal, good for naught but to lie and cheat! You very nearly made me an unknowing accomplice to a homicide. I am well aware that I have but to nod my head and there would be visited upon you the full and just punishment your infamy deserves. I do not intend to nod. I shall leave that for another. For harken well to what I tell you: You have stirred up a serpent whose bite is mortal and who will give you your just deserts. Get out of my sight!"

"... and there you have it as it happened, Neutino," Solosmeo concluded. "Clement later ordered Cardinal Ippolito to take some little care of you. In any case, you may certainly return to Rome whenever you please. Clement has left for Marseilles, to perform the wedding ceremony between Catherine and Henry of France."

"That bastard of a Pompeo," muttered Cellini.

Sighing with relief he shrugged off the mood. "The devil! As long as I'm on the way I will continue to Naples. Heaven knows I have earned a holiday. Come, Antonio, I'll tell the soldier accompanying me to return to Palombara and then bear you company south."

Laughing and singing they continued the journey which took them through the sun-drenched hills of southern Italy. At Monte Cassino Cellini joined in the inspection of Solosmeo's project, the tomb of the exiled Medici who had drowned near Gaeta thirty years before. It was an edifice of heroic proportions and had been in work for nearly two years. Some first-rate talent had been engaged on it. Antonio da San Gallo was the architect who designed it; Francesco da San Gallo and the Neapolitan master, Matteo de' Quaranta, had executed the larger figures. Solosmeo was completing the sculpture and the decorations before erecting it. Piero de' Medici was to sleep the slumber of eternity beneath a mausoleum suitable to his name and station.

From San Germano and Cassino the two made their leisurely way to Capua and Aversa and came within sight of the capital city of the kingdom which then sprawled over all of southern Italy and Sicily.

A half-league or so from the city gates they were accosted by a corpulent individual, mounted on a shuffling, lop-eared nag so badly spavined its hocks were the largest part of its legs.

The obese one bowed as deeply as his paunch would allow and began to orate in a mellifluous singsong.

"*Signori,* I have journeyed out to meet Your Worships in order to extend an invitation from the most excellent inn in all of Napoli. Do but allow me to be your humble host and I guarantee the cleanest rooms, the most comfortable beds, and the finest fare in south Italy. *Ah-h-h-h-h-!* We have a *cuoco* so adept in his art, the mere smell of his unsurpassingly succulent dishes will make you swoon with pleasure and delight!"

"We have already made other plans," Cellini told him shortly.

That meant less than nothing to the boniface.

"*Ah, il signore* is a Tuscan! Know that I have resided in Florence for many years. A great Gonfalonier of that Republic, the illustrious Carlo Ginori, was my frequent guest. I am most partial to gentlemen

266

from the north such as yourselves. Why, we are, Your Lordships and myself, in a sense—*paesani!*"

"Even so, my good man, we have other plans."

Again mine host completely ignored the remark. In honeyed, dulcet tones he got right along with his not yet finished sales message.

"At the Porcetto Grasso—that's the name of my inn, gentlemen. And a proper name it is! Indicative of my fare. I say, at my hostelry, gentlemen like yourselves can count on hospitality and service the like of which has never been seen. More, I maintain a cellar that is without equal in the world! The finest muscadines; the oldest *alicante;* table vintages so dry and limpid the tongue and palate can never leave off the savoring of them. And specialities! ... Hah! *Vino di Borgogna, di Bordo, Lacrima Cristi, Oporto, Madeira* ...anything at all! Ask for it— we have it. And reasonable, gentlemen!" The innkeeper clasped his hands in amazement. "It is astonishing that I can offer these rare delicacies at such ridiculous prices!"

Solosmeo ignored him and gave over his attention to eyeing a flight of kestrels, high in the air, hovering almost motionless against the wind.

The boniface kept on chattering, trotting sometimes before, sometimes behind the two travelers. He was beginning to make a pest of himself.

"Tell me something," requested Cellini. "Since you operate the best inn in Naples, it follows that it is favored by anyone of consequence coming to the city. Can you tell me anything of two Sicilian women who resided there at one time. One of them is an old whore called Beatrice. Beatrice Catelli. She has a daughter, a beautiful daughter who is a dancer. A dream from heaven walking upon this our earth, bearing the name of Angela. Her's too is a proper name!"

Whores and hotels. Ever an inseparable combination. Mine host shrugged ample shoulders and gave up. He was beaten.

"Pah! God grant an ill year to all courtesans and those who favor them!" he answered scornfully, spurring his nag down the road. Another prospect had come into view.

"*E bene,*" Solosmeo said brightly, "at least you got rid of him. That's something. My thanks for doing so."

Cellini brought up a deep sigh. The deep, heart-rending sigh of a languishing and forlorn lover.

267

"I don't know that I deserve them," he replied. "I lost more than I gained in that exchange. That poltroon has brought Angela back to my mind. Ah, Angela... Angela! There was a girl, Antonio. The only one in the world. Unsurpassed!" Cellini sighed again.

"Women," countered the philosophic Solosmeo, flipping a hand, "are like those hills over there, my friend. All of them different, yet all of them exactly the same. They differ in size, in contour, but other than that they are identical—all alike."

"Not my lovely Angela," chirped the goldsmith dreamily. "She was always winsome and gay. A little expensive, frankly, but every moment with her was a frolic and a joy."

"And that's the way for a wench to be, *per Bacco!*" agreed his companion. "I like them that way myself—lusty and gamesome. Some of the dreary, sorrowful bags you run into nowadays are enough to make a man retch!"

"What a figure," reminisced the yearning Cellini. "What structure. And what a covering for it! A tawny skin that defies the mind and tongue to describe it adequately. It was like—like cream splashed with the pink of rose petals and touched with the tint of a ripe olive. Smooth as velvet and sweet as honey. Eatable, my dear Antonio. Positively eatable!"

"Juicy, hah?"

"*Ah, sì!* Believe me, old fellow, you never in all your life saw her equal. Tender... warm ...soft ... She had a pair of—"

"Look, Neutino!" interrupted the sculptor, pointing down the road, "here comes that whoreson of a boniface back again."

The innkeeper had actually succeeded in bringing his nag to a sort of canter. He drew rein alongside.

"I have just now remembered," he puffed, "...two, perhaps three days ago, an elderly woman and a girl moved into a house next door to my inn. I know not if they are Sicilians or anything else, but they bear the names you mentioned."

Solosmeo snorted. Cellini was just as skeptical but unwilling to overlook any chance where Angela was concerned.

"The name of Angela," he told the innkeeper, "has so great a power over me that I am even willing to put up at your inn. My friend here must go elsewhere, since he is come to this city on matters of business. Ride ahead. We will be in Naples before sunset and I mean to have a bath as soon as I dismount."

268

The minutes used up in making himself presentable were as years —centuries. Ready at last Cellini ran to the house pointed out by the boniface. He was perspiring as he approached the wicket and knocked.

A servant girl opened the door. No, the *madama* was not at home. Yes, she was a Sicilian...A daughter? But yes! A dancer, *sì*. Her name? Why, it was Angela. Where?...She was upstairs...

"*Angela!*"

She was so completely stunned, she paled. "Neu...Neutino..."

He was crushing her to him, kissing her greedily, pulling his lips away only for an occasional muttered endearment or a gasp of air.

The servant girl had rushed headlong up the stair, taking after the maniac who had flung past her. She looked and smiled and quietly closed the door.

"*Ah-h! l'amore,*" she whispered with a small sigh. "*L'amore...*"

It wasn't until dawn that either spoke rationally again. By that time the flame had cooled to a gentle caressing warmth and Angela nestled in the cradle of the goldsmith's arm, pensive and dreamy-eyed in the after-languor of exhausted emotions.

"Do you know," she whispered, her lips against his ear, "I intend to mark off yesterday's date and make a feast day of it, and celebrate it as an anniversary. The day on which I was reunited with my beloved. It's a miracle. September the twenty-fourth...*Ninnetto!* what is the matter?"

Cellini had stiffened into muscular rigidity. He gaped at Angela, open-mouthed.

September the twenty-fourth!

"God's teeth," he whispered. "Oh Holy Saints! One month—exactly!"

XXXVIII

Leaning back in his chair cellini pushed his plate aside and watched Angela sip her chilled *Lacrima Cristi*. He sighed with contentment and the thought came to him that here in Naples Nature and Man seemed at last to have coalesced and created an atmosphere satisfying in the extreme. Here, on the balcony opening out from his spacious room, Venus and Lucullus had only to reach across a table to join hands. And more, one had only to look up and out and gaze upon a vista that held all the dreamlike texture of a fairy land slowly succumbing to the enchantment of the Neapolitan night.

Directly on the right were the rocky bastions of ancient Ischia, washed by a sea whose vitreous blue resembled a fragile porcelain Clement once showed him; a bit of fired sand, created, according to the Venetians, in a fabulous and far distant land called Cathay.

Farther south, unsurpassed Capri rose out of the Tyrrhenian Sea in a refulgence of milk-blue mists sparkling against the setting sun. To the left of the isle Sorrento speared heavenward, merging in a now less soft sky tone that was more the deep purple-like azure of the amethyst. And dominating the whole with the splendor of its inherent might was the thin pale gray wisp of Mount Vesuvius' smoky plume.

Closer by and lower down the slope of the hill on which the inn stood, the beehive that was Naples offered a never ending kaleidoscopic stream that was more detailed, vivid, and intense, if not nearly so vast, breathtaking, or delicate.

The dinner finished, Cellini rose from the table and sank on the couch near the railing. Angela followed silently with their goblets and squeezed down beside him.

"It's all so beautiful," she whispered, the touch of lisp slurring her words ever so slightly. "It's like a dream. You, this balcony, the isles out there, the sea, lovely Naples below and all around—everything. It makes one want to stay here on this spot for all eternity . . . let it go on forever and ever and ever, and never end."

"It's almost as beautiful as you, my adorable star." The Florentine slipped an arm around her possessively. She nestled closer. "If anything on earth could ever approach such beauty."

Holding her, feeling a serene contentment, he watched the day fade; first losing itself in the deep purple of twilight, and then slowly and imperceptibly stealing off into velvet darkness. The heavens blossomed with a radiance of stars. Lanterns began to wink here and there, touching the darkening city with specks and motes of gold. And then, quietly, with a silent grandeur, the moon slipped from behind the sliver of cloud where she had dipped to preen like a coquette before showing herself to the night.

The moonlight streamed down, permeating everything it touched, leaving a cold glowing edge of limpid silver. The night air was so clear it seemed brittle. The stir of a crystal-like breeze, laden with the tang of the sea and sweeping along with it a scent from the gardens below, seemed lost in the deep still immensity of the night. Its lilting murmur was like the whispered echo of a love song.

Cellini closed his eyes. Here, beside him, was Angela. Angela, whose mere presence excited, whose kisses inflamed, whose touch was ecstasy. He opened his eyes and looked at her sheening in the moonlight. There was a silent invitation in her eyes, in her parted lips, in the tremor of anticipation that trembled through her as he drew her close and kissed her and waited for the night to grow older.

As was expected of a visiting celebrity, the goldsmith went to pay his respects to the Viceroy, Don Pedro Alvarez de Toledo, a crusty old soldier and Marquis who ruled a vast Italian realm in the name of an Austrian who was king of Spain. Cellini was agreeably surprised to discover that his name was well known to Don Pedro and the nobles of the viceregal court. Only his chance remark that he had come to Naples for a holiday kept the Viceroy from voicing a desire to acquire an example of the Florentine's artistic skill. The Spaniard's eye, however, took instant notice of a diamond ring Cellini wore on his finger— as Cellini had meant that it should.

"What is that marvelous stone you wear, *maestro experto?*" Don Pedro's Italian had burrs in it and was still heavy with the idioms of his native Spain. "An example of your mastery in the jeweler's art? May I look at it?"

The Florentine removed the ring and presented it to the Spanish nobleman.

"Marvelous," mused the Viceroy, handing it back. "If you are of a mind to offer it for sale, I pray you give me the refusal of it."

The ring had been worn for just that purpose. Cellini promptly offered it again to Don Pedro. *"Al suo servizio, Eccellenza,"* he bowed.

"It pleases me." His Excellency turned and shifted the ring, delighted with the fire glinting off its facets. "Tell me in a single word the price you have set upon it."

"Its value, noble lord, is exactly two hundred crowns."

"A fair price," nodded the Viceroy. "Although its beauty results largely from the masterful manner in which you have set the gem."

"Not so, Excellency. It is the gem itself that makes for such a dazzling effect. Here—" Using a thumb nail the goldsmith pried open the setting and removed the stone, handing it to the Viceroy. Its sparkle was almost as brilliant as before.

"*Vaya!* We must not let such an opportunity pass," smiled the *hidalgo*. He nodded to a secretary who wrote out an order for the money, which the Don signed with a flourish.

Cellini bowed his thanks, well pleased with the morning's work, and took himself off. Angela was waiting for a tour of the thriving port city.

The Neapolitan shops were treasure-troves of the arts and crafts spanning all the lands that bordered the Mediterranean and far beyond. The wares of Barbary, Egypt, Greece, Turkey, the Levant, the Canaries, all tempted the eye of the passer-by. There was jewelry in which had been worked the swirling arabesques and ciphers of the Mohammedans, the stylized and highly colorful patterns of the Egyptians, the mawkish and fetish-like horrors of the African, and all the phallic significance of the inscrutable East. Angela amassed a collection of expensive trinkets.

The antiquities in the city and its environs were equally worthy of careful study, and Cellini lost no time in sketching and modeling outstanding bits and fragments of Greek and Roman art. He spent whole days on sections of buildings still rich with the beauty cut into the eroded stone by the long dead and forgotten artisans of the Caesars.

One sunny day they spent at a beach hidden behind a little cove about a league west of the city. With not a soul in sight, Angela quickly stripped off her clothing and dashed out into the surf. Her more prosaic companion set four bottles of wine to chill in a nearby brook before joining her.

The distant harbor was alive with the bustle of shipping. Feluccas, tartanes, barques and coasting vessels were taking on or discharging cargo on the quays, or cruising in and out of the placid, dappled waters of the bay. Fishing boats darted around a squadron of three war galleons standing haughtily apart, pitching idly against their anchor chains. Aloof and proud and silently powerful, each with the unfurled ensign of royal Spain waving from a masthead.

Lolling on the sand, waiting for the dinner hour, Cellini began a sketch of Angela, posing her as a Venus in the act of rising out of the sea. He did not depict her with the calm aloofness of Botticelli's already immortal painting; nor yet in the robust, strapping proportions favored by Titian. His Venus, formed by the foam of the sea, had all the rounded curving charms of Angela—drawn realistically, from life.

"This is wasted, left like this—a simple little sketch," he told her later, re-examining the drawing after they had slowly worked their way through a basketful of food and the wine. Spread out under the branches of a large oak, it had made a tasty dinner. "It's much too well conceived a treatment of you. If you will continue to pose, *dolcetta,* I'll do it over in colored chalk. I have some here."

"Whatever you wish, *tesoro mio,*" Angela replied drowsily. The food and wine had made her sleepy.

"You're certain you don't wish to put on some clothing? This sun is strong."

"No clothes, my love. If I must sunburn it has to be all over. Otherwise, when next I dance I will exhibit red ankles and white calves, red face and white shoulders, red hands and white arms. No. That will not make for a nice effect."

Cellini looked at her. There was nothing wrong with the effect she produced as she lay there, eyes closed sleepily, her slender, honey colored body stretched out on the grassy slope of the rise. The pad slid unnoticed to the ground. One never tired of looking at Angela. Everything about her was so well arranged. Even such a little thing as the nipples which crowned her breasts varied from the norm. Cellini studied the curves of her bosom, a structural type fairly common among the women of southern Europe, and differing from the globular symmetry that was classically Grecian. Full underneath, slightly concave along the upper curve, and distinctive for the nipple being set above the center. In most women the nipple was brownish in color. Not Angela's! Hers were pink—an exquisite coral.

"When shall I pose, Neutino?" Angela yawned.

"When you like. Now, if you're not too lazy . . . and stand here in the shade where you will be more comfortable."

Angela struck a pose and Cellini began the color sketch, imparting to it as close an approximation of the vibrant pigmentation of the original as all his skill would permit. He worked slowly, feeling blissfully at ease.

273

"By the way, little fawn, I meant to ask you. How went your dancing engagement yesterday?"

"Oh-ho! Beautifully. One such each month and I could live like a princess, and my mother like a queen—which is what she would like. The entertainment proved to be an important affair. In fact, the Viceroy was one of the guests. He applauded louder than anyone. Crowded with nobles. That Neapolitan must be as rich as Croesus. He is very free with his bounty when pleased, and I expect he was pleased with my dancing. He showed it in the payment for it, at any rate. Do you know, I believe he would have liked to show me something more, except that his lady hovered about like an eagle. Ha, ha! You should have seen him. He was as angry as a cockerel tied to a post. All he could do was hand over a nice little purse, squeeze my hand, and tell me how gracefully I danced, simpering and eyeing *madonna* crosswise the while." Angela threw her head back and laughed roguishly.

"You teased him?"

"No. On my honor. I think it was only that I made him a little hungry. Poor old thing. You should have seen her! ... No wonder he was generous! Mama gloated over the money all evening."

Cellini made a sour face. Madama Beatrice had been relatively quiet and subdued here in Naples, although her demands remained as exorbitant as ever. He looked up at the sky. The sun was well along in its downward slope. Time to start back.

When he reached the inn after seeing Angela to her door, the obese boniface held out a letter. It had arrived by post, he said, not an hour before.

Cellini turned it over. The waxen seal bore the arms of Cardinal de' Medici. He tore it open and read hurriedly.

The Pope, wrote the Cardinal, had returned from Marseilles and was somewhat concerned over the fact that the goldsmith had not yet come back to Rome. Cellini was to ride posthaste, without delay of any kind, for such would be to his great advantage, and dismount at the palace of the Cardinal ...

He immediately ran to Angela, drew her off to a corner, out of earshot of her mother, and read the letter to her. Beatrice watched with covert expectancy from the corridor.

Angela dissolved into tears. "Stay here in Naples," she sobbed, "where we have been so content."

"I can't do that, lovely blossom. Think! I owe my life to Cardinal

274

Ippolito's assistance. Surely you can see that I cannot disregard his request, or worse, ignore the Pope. I've done far too much of that as it is."

Angela continued to sob on his shoulder.

"Come with me to Rome," he requested. "If you do, I'll give you the two hundreds crowns I received from Don Pedro."

The tears stopped as if a spigot had been turned off. Angela grinned up at him. "I'll come," she whispered. "I'll leave with you at any time you say."

Beatrice had been eyeing all this whispering from the hall and had surmised its purpose. She stalked into the room, a frown folded in a heavy crease along her forehead.

"It is clear that you two are plotting something." Beatrice's beady eyes sharpened with a greedy glint. "If you are planning to run off to Rome with my Angela, Benvenuto, leave me fifteen ducats so that I can travel there after you."

Cellini looked her over with dull eyes. "I will leave you thirty ducats; just so you leave us in peace."

"I nearly forgot," Angela broke in. "I'll need a traveling gown. I saw one only the other day, in a shop. A beauty. Black velvet. And not very expensive—"

The goldsmith nodded. Apparently two hundred crowns were not enough to cover the purchase of a gown. "Very well, I'll buy it for you. Send a servant for it."

Beatrice smiled avariciously. This youth was so obviously taken with her daughter ...

"I too will require clothing, Benvenuto."

Cellini's mouth wrinkled. "So be it," he waved. "You can have that as well."

"And there will be a sum needed to cover expenses for my sons—"

An evil smile quirked the corners of Cellini's lips. "Do I seem to you more cooked than raw, my dear Beatrice? Just what the devil do you want of me? Angela will have two hundred crowns. Enough to keep you and those two lazy bastards of yours in all comfort for at least a year! You are not satisfied?"

"No! We are not!"

Cellini looked from one to the other in frowning surprise. This must be some sort of game? He turned to Angela.

"I don't understand this at all," he told her. "It seems to me that

275

two hundred crowns is a great deal of money. Certainly it is more than you have need of. What can you possibly do with all of it? In the time I have known you I have been giving you money, jewelry, clothing, over and above your every need. Besides this you earn tidy sums with your dancing. Much more than the average man earns. Over and above all this, your mother has been squeezing me dry. What do you do with all this money?"

"We buy land in Sicily," Beatrice snapped wrathfully. "Do you imagine that my daughter can go on dancing forever? Or that she will always be young and beautiful? She has her future—and her mother's—to think of."

Angela lowered her eyes before the goldsmith's wrathful stare. The appalling thought came to him that all he had ever been to this girl was someone who paid the way for her and helped secure the independence she desired. What she had given in return was not love, but a sort of payment for value received...Like an item of merchandise exchanged in barter. His face hardened and the vein that meandered across his temple began to throb.

"Is that how the matter stands?" he rasped out bitterly. "This love you bear me—it has a value which may be reckoned in ducats? Is that all I have been to you? A means of support?"

"That's not so," wailed Angela, dissolving into tears once more, "and you know it! I love you. Adore you. I always have."

The goldsmith laughed coldly, feeling all the rankling frustration of outraged male pride. Here again was another ironical jest from the Fate that plagued him.

"The hell with you," he snapped. "The hell with both of you!"

Beatrice's face fell, as her daughter's wails rose. She was aghast at the thought of losing what had already been promised. "You're not going to leave Angela...who loves you so? Perhaps...perhaps we have been a little too forward and unreasonable in our requests, but that—"

Cellini had reached the door. He turned angrily. "You greedy gutter bitch," he spat at her. "You are lower in the living scale than any animal! A pimp, who sells her own daughter as if she was a common whore! May a canker rot you for it!"

He flung out of the house, slamming the door with such a hurtling crash it brought every neighbor in the vicinity to his windows.

XXXIX

MUCH TOO AROUSED TO PUT OFF HIS DEPARture Cellini left Naples that same night. He would have left at night in any case, because of the money he was carrying. There were too many bandits in Naples who took note of the direction taken by lone travelers. He returned to his lodgings and hired a young husky vouched for by the innkeeper, and purchased horses for the journey. Well mounted and armed, wearing steel corselets and hats, the two set out as soon as the goldsmith had packed his belongings.

As for Angela, tomorrow, next day, or next week, he knew he would begin to miss her again. He knew she had bitten into him too deeply ever to be completely removed. But today, tonight, right now, he was too full of the bitter anger and frustration that comes upon any male who has been gulled by a pretty maid, to do anything but curse his gullibility. The taste of gall ran in his mouth. To have been used in this manner! God above! In the future he would damned well know better! The servant, Aldino, had a bad time of it for the first few hours of the journey back to Rome.

Nor was the goldsmith far wrong in his estimate of the dangers of the road. At Ponte a Selice, a little hamlet between Aversa and Capua, they had a stiff brush with two hooded horsemen. The tussle was a brief one, for the bandits had no desire to engage victims who were so well armed and capable of defending themselves. They turned tail and galloped off.

From Capua they traveled by easy stages along the main road, enjoying the laden olive groves and vineyards, heavy with fruit, that crept up and down the sides of every hill, and the ruins of former Roman glory that were everywhere to be seen in this region so rich in the history of civilization. Cellini stopped frequently to sketch and did a little hunting in the thickets and coppices that stretched out from both sides of the road. They teemed with game and ruins. Near

277

Anagni, only a short ride from Rome, they came on a grassy tract alive with nesting grouse. An hour's hunt brought in a half-dozen choice birds. The goldsmith was preparing his gun to add another to his bag when, fumbling with the musket lock, he ripped the skin of his hand. It was only a scratch but it bled a great deal.

"There's an inn down the road," Aldino pointed, "through that copse. You can wash off the blood there."

"Good." Cellini looked up at the sun. It was late afternoon. "It's still early, but we will put up there for the night and ride off fresh in the morning."

They walked to the place, leading their horses. A sign swinging over the tavern door pictured a squawking parrot with vivid blue plumage and proclaimed to the world that this haven for the weary traveler was Il Pappagallo Azzurro.

The inn room was redolent with the odors of garlic, hot olive oil, roasting meat, and the heavier musty smell of wine. Mine host, all smiles and forelock touching for any guest as formidable looking as this one, advanced with chuckles and low bows of welcome. A party of Neapolitans, including a lady, were seating themselves at table when the blood-smeared Cellini, all corseted and helmed and with gun in hand, entered, followed closely by his equally steel-clad servant who flourished a long halberd. The men promptly came to their feet, muttering to God for assistance and furtively fingering their swords. The place was known to be a hangout for murderers, road-agents, and similar merry-andrews with misplaced senses of humor.

One of them, more forward, or more concerned, than the others, walked over, mouthing solicitude over the goldsmith's wounded hand.

"*Per Dio, amico!*" he cried, shaking his head in what obviously was meant to pass for pity, "you seem to have had a time of it! Met with an accident, have you? A fight, perhaps? Tsk-tsk-tsk...Is the wound serious? Who might you be?"

Cellini laughed. "Rest easy, *messere*. I, like yourself and your companions, am a traveler to Rome. I cut my hand while shooting some birds." He turned to the host. "*Massaio,* have you something I can use to bind up this scratch?"

"Perhaps I can be of service, *messere*," a silvery voice pealed boldly from the direction of the table.

The goldsmith looked over, instantly enlivened. The voice belonged to the woman seated with the Neapolitans. She beckoned him with a

278

pink finger. Bowing graciously he started over, inspecting as he walked. A beauty! And a lady of quality! Her flashing sloe eyes, under carefully plucked brows, were full of meaning and had a way of lingering. Small straight nose. Lush red lips that invited—implored. The deep oval of her traveling gown exposed the superbly rounded tops of twin temptations.

"*Caspita!*" he muttered, smiling over at her, "this is interesting. Here's choice material!" The well-born mistress of some noble, like as not.

Whoever and whatever she was, she sent a surge through him when, having led him to a corner basin, her fingers tickled over his hand as she cleaned the scratch and bound it with her own embroidered handkerchief.

"There you are," she smiled brightly as they walked back to the table. "Now you are again equal to new."

"Far better than that, *madonna*," he simpered. "The touch of you is an inspiration." He turned to her companions who continued to look askance, and bowed. "My name, *messeres*, is Benvenuto Cellini. I am journeying from Naples to Rome."

"Cellini? The Florentine master in the service of His Holiness?"

"The same, sir."

"Well!" Much of the suspicion fell away. The men introduced themselves, but the goldsmith wasn't listening. He was ogling the young lady in a completely frank manner which betrayed an unmistakable intent.

"And I am the Lady Nicoletta degli Octavi," she cooed. "Will you sit with us while you sup, master?"

Cellini bowed again and ordered the host to fetch in his thickest soup, tastiest roast, and oldest wine.

"...and see that my servant is taken care of," he commanded grandly.

While the innkeeper was off seeing to these requests the goldsmith looked over the public room of the *osteria*. It was far cleaner and better stocked than most hospices located at a distance from city walls. Hams, flitches of bacon and fat sausages hung in disordered array from sooty ceiling beams. Peppers, garlic, cloves, spices and herbs, were festooned all around, for decorative as much as utilitarian effect. A fire crackled in a fireplace which could have accommodated half an ox. Its sooty cupola led upward to a gigantic flue. The log fire released a

279

pungent smell of burning resin that mingled with that of the game and poultry turning on the spits above, acquiring a juicy golden patina. A comfortable, cheering place, the inn room of the Blue Parrot.

All through supper and into the evening Cellini chatted, smirked and flirted with the brown tressed Nicoletta. She was no Angela, but she was frisky and thoroughly charming and had no objections whatever to the Florentine's attentions. Nor did her traveling companions interfere or seem in any way affronted. In fact, they too favored the hearty interest he displayed, earthy and physical though it obviously was. If he was what he said, the Florentine master, Benvenuto Cellini, it did no harm. If he wasn't—then better to keep his mind occupied on Milady Nicoletta.

The boniface did considerable furtive watching of his own before turning away with a contemptuous shrug of weary shoulders, muttering to himself. What the devil! That was inkeeping for you. Never a day passed but in walked some trollop; and always there was some lazar around waiting to try her out. He resolved to make this truculent looking bravo pay well for that bedding privilege. He would pay too! Mine host recognized the signs, could tell from the way the goldsmith was mewing and chortling and drooling that the wench had him over a barrel with his tongue hanging out, and no mistake. What the devil! Innkeeping!

The entire company set off together the next morning. And if Nicoletta's sloe eyes kept turning on the goldsmith with looks so full of intimate understanding that none felt the need for explanations, all displayed the good sense and breeding to seem totally unaware of them. The Neapolitans were not entirely at ease, so the traveling arrangements were cunningly contrived. Cellini rode well forward, side by side with the laughing Nicoletta. His servant rode at a suitable distance behind. The others drew up the rear. It was an arrangement which, for Cellini at least, made the short ride to Rome a thoroughly enjoyable one.

The party entered the city by the San Sebastian Gate, where the goldsmith separated himself amid what was now great cordiality from the Neapolitans. There was a lingering farewell with Nicoletta, after which he rode on to the Medici palace. Cardinal Ippolito had him in as soon as he dismounted at the door.

"Welcome, *maestro!* I am happy to see you once again. How went things on your holiday?"

"Most tolerably, Eminence." Cellini decided to keep his personal afflictions to himself. "Let me offer my humble thanks for the assistance and favor Your Lordship has displayed toward me."

The Cardinal flipped a hand and smiled.

"Reverend lord," continued the goldsmith, "now that I am once again in Rome, I beg you make me secure from imprisonment."

"Do not disturb yourself over such trifles, Benvenuto. All will be taken care of. Messer Pecci..." Ippolito eyed one of his gentlemen "...pray inform the Bargello in my name that he is not to lay a finger on Benvenuto. By the way, how fares the fellow who was the cause of all this tumult?"

Piero Pecci made a face and waved eloquently. "Your Eminence, he is doing badly and will do yet worse when he learns that Master Cellini is returned to Rome. That poltroon is willing to die if in doing so he could inconvenience our Benvenuto here."

The Medici laughed. "Come, the fellow is only proving he is a Sienese. Vindictive devils, all of them. Benvenuto, for your own credit as well as ours, stay indoors for a few days while we issue our instructions. After that go where you wish and let fools die as they please. I will inform His Holiness of your return."

Cellini went home and back to work on the medal of Pope Clement. The engraver, Giovanni Bernardi, was no longer in Rome, which upset the original plan. However, that master had left some of his work behind which the Pope could use for a comparison if he saw fit to do so.

Working steadily he finished the portrait and blocked in the reverse. The design he evolved for the latter commemorated the peace which had prevailed throughout most of Italy since the fall of Florence in 1530. It showed a slender feminine figure—copied from a sketch of Angela—clad in a diaphanous tunic girded at the waist. She held a torch in one hand and was in the act of setting fire to a bundle of arms and weapons. A Fury struggled vainly against the fetters that held him chained to the columns of a temple in the background.

All of which took time. Pope Clement kept asking Ippolito why Cellini did not make an appearance, and the Cardinal could only answer that the goldsmith seemed all taken up with some work about which he would say nothing. Clement was pettish and cranky. He was in bad health and the Marseilles excursion had told on him. Peevishly, he ordered a favorite of his to keep the goldsmith in mind and look in on him now and then.

Pietro Carnesecchi made the usual call and placed a commission of his own while he tactfully gave the goldsmith to understand that Clement desired his services.

"Most Excellent lord," replied Cellini, "I beg you inform His Holiness that in a few days I will call and offer abundant proof that I have never abandoned his service."

As soon as he completed the reverse to his satisfaction he stamped samples of the medal in gold, silver, and copper, and carried these to the Papal palace. He showed them first to Messer Pietro.

The Florentine courtier-prelate whistled.

"Corpo di Bacco, maestro! The Pope will want to see these at once. Come...I will escort you. Our Holy Father has just now finished dining and is taking the air in the belvedere. He is not feeling too well."

Cellini had a shock when he saw Clement. The Pope seemed to be gravely ill. He was pallid and worn, his hands shook, his eyes were glassy looking. He seemed stooped and shrunken—more like an old man in his dotage than the keen-eyed Clement of yesterday.

He may not have been feeling well, but Clement was as gracious as ever.

"Welcome, welcome," he smiled, paraphrasing the goldsmith's name. "It has been some time since we have seen you and we feared you had forgotten us. Know that we have missed both yourself and the fruits of your splendid talents."

The impetuous and irrepressible Cellini let fly. "Your Sanctity may recall," he returned dryly, "that but for chance, the fruits of your servant's admirable talents would have been missed forevermore. Through no fault or yours or mine, perhaps; rather because of the traducing malice of lying tongues. Wherefore, Holy Father, I implore and beseech that in the future you stay the wrath of your descending arm until all the facts are known to you."

Clement colored a bit, more than a little embarrassed by the goldsmith's sermon. He changed the subject easily.

"What have you brought us in that packet, master? Our Cardinal Ippolito has informed us that you were occupied on a commission of moment."

282

"This is the work of which he spoke, Your Holiness. A commission of importance, which is to be presented to the greatest prince in the world. I have secretly undertaken to cut a portrait of Your Sanctity and have brought this so you may judge of any merit it may possess."

Clement beamed. He was charmed. He let the examination of the medal draw out. He was enjoying himself. Such mastery in art was always a joy to look upon. He called for Bernardi's medal, all the medals there were, and when they were brought in he and Messer Pietro and the horde of other courtiers made a careful comparison while they argued, commented, or exchanged views.

"By the eternal, my lord Pietro!" Clement exclaimed to his favorite, "the ancients themselves have never seen medals the like of these!"

"An astonishing piece of work, Blessed Father. I have never before seen such superb detail."

"Just so!" agreed Clement. "Well, then, Benvenuto, have you devised some new method for stamping medals? These are marvels!"

"It's all in the dies and the manner in which these have been made, Your Holiness. You are pleased?"

"Immensely! So well pleased that we here and now commission an additional reverse for it. We have a certain project in mind. Do you make one which shows Moses in the act of striking the rock and water issuing from it. Use with it an inscription... something, such as... *Ut Bibat Populus.* Yes, that will do. We desire this reverse to serve in commemorating the well we have given the good people of our Orvieto, the which is all but completed."

And that well, mused Clement as he admired his portrait, was worth commemorating. Work on it had begun when he returned to the war ravaged capital from which he had escaped after the sack. In Orvieto he had taken note of the scarcity of water in that city, built as it was upon rock. The springs which supplied this most precious of all fluids were all at a distance. It was not only an inconvenience, but a threat which would keep the city from growing any larger and richer. On his return to Rome he ordered Antonio da San Gallo, the architect and director of the Works of St. Peter, to draw up a design for a large well inside the city. Master Antonio's effort was a masterpiece. A shaft ninety-two feet wide was cut through solid rock to a depth of two hundred and sixty feet. It had two flights of hanging steps, one above the other, which were so contrived that beasts of burden could enter and, descending by means of low steps, arrive at a bridge placed over

283

the bubbling spring. Without turning, the beasts then continued onward, ascending the other flight of steps and out through a separate passageway. Clement nodded. Such a worthy enterprise needed a medal to commemorate it.

"Go, my Benvenuto, and work on this new design; and before you return with it we will have given thought to your prospects. Leave these medals. We wish to enjoy the study of them a little more."

XL

THE DESIGN FOR THE NEW REVERSE, NORMALLY a trivial and very simple matter, became troublesome. Try as hard or as often as he would, Cellini found that it refused to come to him. He couldn't visualize it, couldn't nail it down. There was another image in his mind's eye, the image of Angela. She had broken through the thin mist of memory he had erected as an ineffectual barrier to shut her out of his brain. It did not work out the way he planned. The nagging insistent thought of her persisted, hounding him and pushing every other thought out of the way. "I love you. Adore you. I always have," she had told him. He had found, and lost her again—this time because of his own intemperate angry blundering.

Grimly he pushed on with the Moses design. What should, for him, have been the work of a few hours, lengthened out into three weeks of frustrated, nervous scribbling, before he succeeded in working out what seemed like an acceptable composition.

He took the cartoon and called at the Vatican.

The Pontiff was resting in his bedchamber, with two physicians in attendance. Clement was despondent, looked very tired, and in worse condition than on Cellini's previous visit. Even his conversation was dull and listless—an unusual thing with him. He brightened somewhat while he looked over the new design, but not much. He made some minor suggestions and smiling weakly, waved the goldsmith off.

Cellini returned to his studio and started on the die for the reverse immediately. He buried himself in shop commissions. The days and weeks dragged along in what became a torment of anguished remembering. A part of him was missing. Angela was not there.

When the die was well enough advanced he made a rough stamping and brought it to the Pope. But in the passing weeks Clement's condition had become grave. So ill he was, that Cellini was not permitted to enter the Papal suite. Thinking it wise to try to glean some details of the Pope's actual condition, he lingered in the antechamber. At the Vatican one could learn many things simply by being present.

A half-hour later one of the Papal doctors, Francesco Fusconi da Norcia, came out. The goldsmith knew him well and so did not hesitate to exchange greetings and walk off down the hall with him.

"I am told His Holiness is very ill, Messer Franco?"

The doctor nodded somberly. "I fear that is true, Benvenuto. He needs rest, complete rest, which he cannot obtain. As you know, the press of duties constantly lying on the shoulders of the Pontiff is such it would weary the soundest and strongest of men. Over and above which our Holy Father is tormented by this recent defection of the English, who have now separated themselves from our Holy Mother Church and set up a religion suited to their own fancies. Tsk! What heresy!"

"Do you believe he will recover, in time?"

The doctor looked carefully about. "Between ourselves and the sleeve of our doublets, Benvenuto, I would not count on it. I have seen this malady slowly coming upon him during the past months. His condition is now dangerous. All the physicians in attendance are agreed on this. It is not necessarily desperate, understand, but I for one regard it as unlikely that he will ever cast it off. His strength has slowly been sapped from him since the time of the sack." The leech clapped the goldsmith on the shoulder. "Keep these words of mine in confidence, Benvenuto. I go to see to certain medications. *Addio.*"

Cellini walked glumly homeward, much disturbed, and not merely for professional reasons. He had a deep and genuine respect for the Medici Pope and regarded him, as indeed he was, a man of high learning and gifted intelligence. True, he had had differences with him. But the goldsmith was not so blind or wrapped up in himself as not to fully realize that it had been Clement, as much as his own talent and skill, who had constantly aided him to his present high reputation as an artist and master of the first rank.

Engrossed in these thoughts as he walked along the Via Giulia he slowly became aware of a feeling of discomfort. What caused it he was at a loss to explain. It was vague. A premonition. Not the usual thought of Angela, but rather a presentiment of some kind; as if the feeble minatory finger of some sixth sense was striving to penetrate his consciousness and point something out. Time and again the uncomfortable feeling stole over him, making him pause and look around. It was bewildering. Each time he did so he wondered why. Yet it persisted all the way home.

In the studio he removed his light cape and sword belt, dropped them on a bench in a corner and began climbing the stair to his rooms, stripping off his doublet. He was midway up, the doublet slipped over one shoulder, when he heard the studio door creak open. He turned to see who it was—and although he had never before laid eyes on the trio he knew the purpose of their call. Here was the answer to that feeling of discomfort. He had been followed home!

They were gaudily dressed, all three. Soldiers. Neapolitans by the look of them, with mocking eyes and faces hard and blank as pieces of slate and about as nervous looking. The last one in appeared to be in charge. He hung back and let the other two stroll toward the stair and grin evilly up at the goldsmith. Cellini waited, lips set in an uncompromising line, a brow arched inquisitively. He needed no details to fill in this picture. This was a welcome arranged by one or more of his "friends." Pompeo, most likely. Or perhaps Traiano or Micheletto, or all three together. With the Pope dangerously ill they were being a little beforehand. It was an easy arrangement. There were plenty of these hired hands available, all of them eager to pick up a few ducats for a little spare time work.

As casual in his motions as were those of the trio, Cellini finished removing his doublet and waited. He was caught there on the stair, like a roach on a bare wall. Whatever else he did he must get to his sword.

One soldier reached the stair. The other had stopped to look around blankly. The man in charge reclosed the door softly and was leaning against it, one hand on his hip, the little finger of the other engaged in picking his nose.

The first bravo set a foot on the first step, and paused. He was squat and solid, a tough and mean looking butcher's lackey. He chuckled deep in his throat, as if amused at playing the role of cat in this cat-and-mouse routine.

286

Cellini's face went as stiff and bleak as an early March wind. The vein at his temple swelled and began to pulse rhythmically, but he made no move—not yet.

The chuckler looked up. "Don't freeze there on the stair, master," he gloated. This was so easy. "Come on down and greet your guests. We have a certain project in mind." His hand toyed with the hilt of a dagger almost as long as a sword. There was no hurry. Plenty of time. "Eh, there's a little carving that needs to be done." He chuckled again.

The goldsmith waited silently. His eyes looked carefully around. He wasn't in any hurry either. What he was going to do, he was going to do.

The leader at the door sneered softly, and the man at the foot of the stair began to climb, drawing the dagger. It was starting out of its sheath when Cellini's doublet slapped him a stinging blow across the face, wrapping itself around his head.

Vaulting the stair rail the goldsmith leaped toward his sword belt. The other soldier cut across the room between him and it, drawing a poniard. The bravo at the door stopped picking his nose and straightened.

Cellini did not stop. Along the way he picked up a heavy work stool and swung it down across the face and shoulder of the ruffler in his path. The man's arm cracked like a nut between the jaws of a nutcracker and the poniard fell out of his hand. A tinkling, pattering sound, like hail striking gently against a roof, served notice that some teeth had been dislodged by the encounter. He went sprawling, yowling in pain.

Jumping lightly over him Cellini reached his sword as the first would-be assassin charged in with his long dagger. The leader too was moving forward, drawing a sword. The affair was no longer as easy as it had appeared.

Grasping the hilt of his sword Cellini swung the entire belt in a sweeping arc. The sheath flew from the blade with not a split second to spare. He brought the naked blade into position just as the dagger hacked at him.

This was no time in which to engage in fancy flourishes. The goldsmith parried the cut, forcing his opponent's weapon to a side. In the same motion he disengaged his sword from the dagger and slashed downward, slamming the flat of the blade across the man's upper arm. The ruffler lurched back, stumbling against the third bravo. That pro-

287

vided a brief space of time. All the time the Florentine needed. His blade snaked in under the soldier's dagger and pierced him through the heart.

Before the man fell, before he stopped twitching, Cellini had leaped aside to face the remaining ruffler as that worthy lunged in with a thrust in *quarte* that would have skewered him like a hare had he not leaped blindly backward to avoid it. He went crashing against a cupboard, sending its contents all over the room.

Seeing the speed of that move and the even quicker recovery and counterthrust, the now solitary bravo's face went pasty. The former assurance washed off it like sea water draining off sand. From the hunter lurking to strike at an unsuspecting victim, he had become the hunted fighting for his life, retreating before a barrage of thrusts, cuts and slashes, each of which jarred him to the ankles as he parried desperately.

The goldsmith kept edging in, thrusting and lunging so viciously that the soldier was forced to back away constantly, crashing against everything behind him. The studio was a shambles of overturned furniture, broken bric-a-brac, and scattered tools. The leering smile was on Cellini's face now.

The ruffler was sweating, his arm growing insupportably heavy. He took to hewing at the Florentine in the manner of a man chopping wood. Cellini promptly came in over the descent of the hacking sword and thrust at the bravo's chest. The blade bent like a bow. Had he not pulled back instantly, it would have snapped. The man was wearing steel underclothing.

"Very droll," breathed Cellini, answering the ruffler's sickly sneer. "A pity you didn't think to encase your throat as well."

The Neapolitan's answer was a desperate lunge. Cellini parried it and retorted with a thrust of his own, then wheeled and slashed in a savage cut, sending the bravo stumbling again, his breath wheezing like an overworked bellows. The goldsmith followed relentlessly, balancing nimbly. He flicked his blade in a feint that sent a gleaming streak of blue light dancing along its surface. As he expected, his opponent lunged in under it. Stepping lightly aside Cellini swung his sword in a circle, putting all the strength of his arm behind the slash. His sword slammed down on the soldier's near its hilt, and tore it from his hand. It struck the floor with a resounding clang and bounced nearly to the ceiling before bounding away.

A dazed, bewildered look spread over the panting bravo's face as he stared down at his empty hand. He gasped and jerked his head quickly as the point of Cellini's sword came in under his chin. He gaped stupidly, eyes rolling. One confederate lay crumbled on the floor, still and lifeless. The other was moaning, alternately clutching his shoulder and feeling gingerly at a badly gashed mouth.

"How now, little dove!" sang the goldsmith, flicking the tip of his blade at his assailant's chin. A pearl of blood began to swell out. "All through with your cooing?"

The man gasped again, speechless with dread.

"*Ah, sì*, whoreson! I have a strong arm. It is a mark of my calling. You will also find, and that shortly, that my steel too is well whetted—that's the mark of another calling." Cellini spat in the man's face. The bravo, aghast at his impending death, was too distraught to wipe off the spittle.

"No! . . ." he wheezed. His hands moved in vague supplicating gestures. "No! . . ."

"Oh, yes!" chortled the Florentine. The blade flicked again. A round red pearl appeared on the soldier's throat. "Son of a disease! Make your peace with God. I will wait for the space of a single paternoster, after which I mean to slit your dirty gullet from ear to ear—and then listen while you try to suck in air through the opening!"

"No!" wailed the ruffler, in mortal anguish. "You wouldn't do that, master? Oh . . . oh, no! . . . *Ahhhhhhhhhh! . . .*" The blade had flicked again. "*O Dio santo, aiutami!*" He sank to his knees, clasping his hands at the goldsmith.

Snorting in disgust, Cellini gave him a kick that sent him sprawling on his back. The blade came over to rest against his throat.

"Pray!" snapped the goldsmith.

"D-d-don't, master! I'll . . . I'll tell you everything. I promise. Who employed me . . . how much . . . you don't know that, do you?" The man was sobbing, frantic with fear, unable to take his eyes from the gleaming point of steel that hovered so implacably. They crossed myopically in a converging squint.

"Well—?" asked Cellini.

The Neapolitan's breath quickened. "See," he whined, "I knew you were too good a man to butcher me in cold blood. I'll tell you everything, master. Everything!" He raised his head. The prodding blade tip made him knock it back against the floor.

289

Cellini felt like spitting again.

"Out with it," he rasped impatiently.

"It was a fat man, *maestro*. He sent us word to meet him at the Taverna del Leone, over near the Via di Ripetta. A big, tall man, growing fat around the belly, with a large fat face and small eyes. He pointed you out when you left the Vatican . . . Gave us fifty crowns, and the promise of fifty more when—" the man gulped and continued in a whisper "—when the—the affair was concluded."

"The man? Bearded? Old or young?"

"About in his middle years, master. No beard. His hair is black, graying."

Cellini pursed his lips. That let Micheletto out of the thing. He wouldn't have gone this far in any case. With him it was a purely professional squabble. It was Pompeo who had made the arrangements. Pompeo, no doubt backed by his conniving uncle, Traiano. About what he suspected. He would have to settle with that lout.

"His name?"

"I . . . I d-d-don't know that, master," came the stammered reply.

"Hah! *Bastardo vigliacco!* You dare try to gull me? The truth, scum!" Again the blade flicked. Another pin point of blood appeared.

"I don't know the man's name!" screamed the bravo. "I swear it!"

This craven swine was probably telling the truth, thought the goldsmith. It was unlikely that the gentleman who panted so for his blood would give his name to hired assassins.

"The money that was paid you? . . ."

"I-I- . . . I have it here, master."

Cellini held out his free hand.

With a feeble groan the ruffler unlaced the purse from his belt and handed it up.

"This," the goldsmith informed him scarcastically, "will pay for the damage to the room." He brought the flat of the blade down across the Neapolitan's stomach. The man gave a startled scream.

"Get up. Get up!"

Cellini's cook and housekeeper, who all through the fracas had huddled in the kitchen in a palsy of terror, gingerly stuck her head into the room.

"Do not be alarmed, Assunta," called the goldsmith a little belatedly, seeing her head blinking in the door. Her eyes were wide with fear and uncertainty. "Go back to your work—but wait! First, bring in a broom, a pail of water and some rags."

"You," he ordered the ashen soldier, "gather up all arms, including the poniard you are wearing, and throw them into the room atop the stair."

While that was being done under the watchful eye of the goldsmith, the wide-eyed Assunta brought in the supplies and vanished back into the sacred and far safer precincts of her kitchen.

"Now," said Cellini, leaning on his sword, "start cleaning up this room."

Disconsolately the ruffler began housecleaning.

The Florentine unlocked a side door which opened into an alleyway beside the house. He dragged the dead assassin out and threw him into the alley. Returning, he clutched the wounded bravo by the hair and began to drag him out. The man thought it was the end and screamed, imploring mercy.

Cellini gave him a backhanded belt across the swollen mouth which quickly brought the screams down. He whimpered all the way across the room and out into the slime of the passageway. The goldsmith waited until the third ruffler finished with the room and then pointed to the same door.

"And drag those invincible compeers of yours away with you," he sneered at the crestfallen soldier. "Where, I care not. Also, it would be wise if you took yourselves out of the city. If ever I again set eyes on either of you, I will not be so merciful. You understand me?"

"I-I can't move them alone, master," wailed the woebegone Neapolitan.

"Now that is a pity! Get that screaming whoreson out there to help you. He still has one serviceable arm. Out!"

XLI

THE FIRST PRECAUTION CELLINI TOOK WAS TO bring Nasone in from the shop and give him the run of the house. If one attempt had been made, there could easily be others; and Nasone could be relied on not only to give warning but to help out as well.

Whenever he left the house, one might have thought the goldsmith was off to war. He was armed to the teeth. Under his doublet he wore a shirt of fine link, extremely pliable chain mail. He never walked close by the walls of a street; a knife wielder could pounce with too much ease. He kept to the center, and turned all corners wide.

The new reverse was well along. The shop was busy and he went there more often than usual. Of Pompeo he saw nothing. He made discreet inquiries, only to learn that no one had seen him recently. It was thought that the jeweler had gone off somewhere. The Pope continued ill and the Milanese was keeping out of his way. It was logical enough.

All through the summer Cellini stewed in a ferment of his own devising. The attempt on his life had kept his mind occupied for a time, but as the thrill of combat, and the expectancy of more, wore off, the torment of Angela's loss returned. There were lots of other girls about —very pretty girls. But where, in all the world, was there another with Angela's irresistible allure? Another who was capable of imparting the thrill of that soft delighted sigh she breathed against his lips when he kissed her? Wallowing in this self-inflicted despair he had a flash of happy inspiration. Why not write to her? Of course! That was the solution! He would write, explaining the unbearable pain of their separation, beg her forgiveness, and ask her to return and be loved forevermore. Aghast at his monumental stupidity in not having thought of it sooner, he quickly made an arrangement with a post courier to Naples. He gave the man a gold ducat, and minute directions.

"What's more," he promised, "I will pay down another ducat when the letter is delivered. Two ducats, if you bring back her answer!"

The courier returned in three days—with the undelivered letter in his hand. The house to which the Master had directed him, he told the troubled goldsmith, now was empty. The family who lived there had long ago moved away, no one knew where. It was believed they had quit the city. The man was very sorry over his inability to carry out the assignment, but he had done all he could.

Cellini took the news sadly. It was hopeless. Too late. Like an utter fool he had waited too long. Angela was completely, irretrievably lost. All his life he would have to pay the price of his idiocy. The angry words which had parted them returned to mock him. Into his mind there leaped the images of a hundred, a thousand, endearing things—and all of them were Angela. She was the budding blossom of a beautiful springtime; the warmth of a summer day; the trill of a nesting bird; the ripple of moonlight that gleamed on a darkened sea. Full of hopelessness, he went feverishly on with his work, plagued by the knowledge that he would never see her again.

Toward the middle of September he managed to complete the reverse; and shortly thereafter word came that the Pope's condition was improved and that he would receive him. The goldsmith carried the new dies and stampings to the Vatican immediately.

Clement was in bed, very pale, very weak, very ill. His greeting was kindly and graceful, but it came in a weak whisper. And when Cellini voiced the hope that His Holiness soon would be up and about, Clement smiled wanly and wearily shook his head.

"I doubt it much, my Benvenuto," he replied in the thin-voiced rasp of the gravely ill. "I am of the mind that soon I shall be passing before the throne of Him who is the greatest of all princes and kings. But tell me, have you brought the new reverse?"

"I have everything here, Blessed Father."

"Good. I will divert myself with an inspection of them."

He sent for spectacles and additional lights. Ippolito, who was in constant attendance, helped to raise him; but it was evident that Clement could no longer see clearly. Cellini's eyes filled as he watched his princely Medici patron fumble and feel at the dies and medals with his fingers.

Clement sighed.

"I am concerned about you, Benvenuto. If it please God to give me back my health, I will make things right with you. So then, I must rest. Go, and return again soon."

Three days later Pope Clement died.

Sorrowfully, Cellini put aside the newly finished medals. All the labor on them was lost. They would no longer serve their intended purpose. The next Pope's interest would lie in his own pontificate, not in that of his predecessor. It meant, also, an entirely new regime. New courtiers replacing present favorites; different artists replacing those who had been high in the favor of the deceased Pontiff; new intrigues, new friends, and new enemies—for the envy would remain. That was an everpresent fixture. The Florentine knew he could count on consideration from the next Pope, but he knew also that it would never be the same sort of patronage he had enjoyed under Clement.

The next day the goldsmith dressed for a last call on his noble patron. He wore his finest clothes, a beautifully chased sword and an ivory and gold hilted poniard. A medallion of San Lorenzo hung from a heavy gold chain over his black doublet. His *berretta* was of black velvet and had a white plume.

He walked to the San Angelo bridge, crossed it, and made his way to St. Peter's.

Clement was clad in white robes, reposing on a catafalque covered with a drapery of white brocade. The snowy pall was an iridescent gleam of embroidered silver, gold, and precious stones, winking in the light of the tall candles set all around it. The Swiss guards, with grounded halberds and two-handed swords, were as motionless as statues. The movement around the nave and the transept was hushed. The bell in the campanile of the Capitol—which knelled only on the death of the Pope—tolled slowly, sorrowfully, endlessly. A choir of Benedictines intoned the *Miserere*.

Straight and erect, eyes fixed before him, Cellini strode to the foot of the slanted couch of death and knelt to kiss the feet of the dead Pope, weeping as he did so. He clasped his hands, and with bowed head recited the Psalm which was being chanted.

Ippolito de' Medici approached as the goldsmith rose. The Cardinal seemed to sense the artist's feelings for he said nothing as they withdrew to a side arch, where Cellini offered condolences.

Ippolito smiled his sad smile and shrugged lamely.

"My dear Benvenuto, death is so very final. What can one say when it strikes?"

The clamor outside the church filtered in. There was tumult in the city. The temper of the Romans was ugly. The deceased Clement was being lampooned and blamed for all the disasters the Christian world had suffered during his pontificate; especially for the sack of the city, the ravages of which were still in evidence. There were angry rumblings and the openly avowed threat to desecrate the body of the dead Medici by dragging it through the streets on a hook. Only the protection provided by one man restrained the mob. And that man had no cause to bear any loving feelings for Clement. He had been lied to, cheated and robbed. It was not Alessandro, snugly settled in the newly created Duchy of Florence, who shielded the remains of his father. It was Ippolito de' Medici.

Cellini glumly returned to the Banchi, looking on the commotion in the streets. The civil arm of the law died with the Pope. The Cardinal-Chamberlain of the Holy Roman Church was nominally in command of the Papal forces, but that meant little or nothing. Anarchy reigned and would continue to reign until the next Pope was elected. Until then safety lay only in armed strength. From the Ponte San Angelo to the Tavern of the White Dove, the goldsmith circled around the numerous street brawls, conscientiously keeping clear of them.

At the tavern he found Agnolo Gaddi, Caro, and Alberto del Bene, brother of Alessandro, watching the confusion in the piazza with a detached interest. Rufflers, thieves, road-agents, come to the city for easy spoils, strutted arrogantly, studiously looking for unarmed or poorly armed victims. Only when the patrols of one of the District Leaders of Rome filed through the street did the leers come off their faces. The sight of the guards sent them slinking into doorways and provided a momentary lull which was shattered the instant the armed men turned a corner.

"I wonder how long it will be before we have a new Pope?" Gaddi mused aloud. "For myself I've no objection to all this brawling, but it's dangerous for too many innocent people."

"Who can say?" shrugged Caro. "It may be next week. It may be months. We waited nearly ten weeks when Adrian died. Here, Neutino —you are far too glum and downcast. Drink up."

"You will have noticed, *ragazzi,*" Agnolo went on, "that there has been none of the usual chatter and accusations that Clement was poisoned. Not yet, at any rate."

Alberto del Bene waved a hand. "The people have other things on their minds."

Gaddi's eyes were sweeping around the Piazza with lively curiosity. He started abruptly when he looked in the direction of the Castle bridge, and the wine cup he was lifting to his lips halted in the air as he whistled silently. His foot nudged Alberto and when the Del Bene turned to him he swung his eyes meaningfully toward the street leading to Sant' Angelo. The youth looked, rapped the table lightly with his knuckles, and immediately arose and went to a nearby table where he began whispering to three gallants seated there. Gaddi turned to Cellini.

"Neutino, look over to the north of the Piazza. Slowly."

Cellini casually turned his head.

Pompeo!

His face stiffened like a board.

Alberto returned and sat down. Behind him an unobtrusive move-

295

ment began. The three gallants sauntered over, apparently hungering for the view on this side of the Square. They lounged, fingers idling on dagger and sword hilts.

"He is among a group of nine...ten armed men, Neutino," chortled Agnolo. "We are not ten, but we will give an account of ourselves. What we lack in number," he chuckled gleefully, "we make up in fire!"

Cellini stared while Pompeo strolled leisurely opposite to where he sat. To draw a weapon now would endanger the lives of friends who were in no way involved in the quarrel. His wrangle with the jeweler was entirely personal. Whatever risks were entailed must be met by himself alone. He clenched his teeth and sat motionless, his eyes blazing on the Milanese who stopped to fling a laugh of derision in his direction. In the middle of ten armed men Pompeo was not afraid.

"Who are those men?" rasped Cellini. "Do any of you know?"

One of the gallants standing nearby turned his head. "Catchpolls! Those miserable bastards are blacklegs, every last one."

"Draw!" hissed Alberto. "We're ready and waiting! For the love of Christ, draw!"

Pompeo stood and sneered.

Cellini remained seated, motionless and sullenly silent.

Pompeo guffawed loudly and went off toward the Chiavica. His escort, sneering at the craven group sitting in the yard of the tavern, followed, tossing their heads insolently.

"Why the hell didn't you draw?" Agnolo was red with embarrassment and anger.

The goldsmith twisted in his chair, so aroused he was sweating.

"I like you boys," he told them, "and it is more than mere fondness. It is a real affection. I do not intend to let you risk your lives in any personal quarrel of mine. I can take care of that by myself!"

Alberto del Bene scowled furiously. "We understand, Neutino. But to remain seated there—and let those beasts insult us so!"

Cellini smiled thinly. "My dear Alberto, you live near here?"

"Of course," Alberto nodded. "You know that."

"Go home."

"What!"

"Please. I will have need of you—and soon."

The Del Bene did not argue. He left.

"You others, lose yourselves...quickly! And don't mix into this thing!"

296

They melted away quietly.

Cellini finished his wine and strolled off toward the Chiavica, a place so named for the huge drain it contained. The street there forked out in different directions, one leading to the Campo di Fiori, past Pompeo's house.

The jeweler was not in sight, but Cellini caught a glimpse of his blackleg escort loitering at a corner. Pompeo had entered an apothecary shop. The goldsmith sneaked up nearby and hid in a doorway. With quiet, deliberate calm he waited until the jeweler came out; waited until the group separated to make room for him in their midst. Then he flew at him.

Rushing at the group he pushed the two closest men violently into the others, sending them stumbling against still others of their comrades. Before any could recover to make a defensive move, Cellini had grasped the screeching Pompeo by the front of his jerkin and pulled him out into the street. The gold and ivory hilted dagger was drawn and in his other hand.

"Go on, you bastard!" he snarled into the bloated gray-white face of the Milanese, "let me hear you laugh again!"

"*Pietà!*" Pompeo screamed in terror.

"Here—all the pity you deserve!"

The dagger flashed as he spoke. In abject fear the jeweler wrenched aside his head. The blow caught him beneath the ear. The scream choked and became a gurgle. A second thrust followed in a blur of motion. The gurgle dropped to a whisper and the fat man went limp.

"Now," panted Cellini, "our score is evened out!"

XLII

STOOPING DOWN, CELLINI PULLED THE DAGGER out of what had been Pompeo with his left hand. The right was drawing his sword. The clash had been so sudden and swift that none of the stumbling catchpolls was able to prevent it. It was over and done before they recovered their balance or wits.

Drawing back, dagger in one hand, sword in the other, the goldsmith waited for an attack that did not come. All ten of the blackleg heroes circled around the corpse, muttering among themselves, and paid no attention to the killer.

Cellini walked off. The bloody dagger in his hand sent pedestrians scampering out of his path. Near the street intersection Piloto the goldsmith came running up, sword drawn and ready.

"Gossip, now that the mischief is done, let us see to your safety. Where are you bound?"

"To the house of Alberto del Bene," replied Cellini. "Only a few minutes ago I told him I would soon have need of him."

"Well then— *avanti!*"

Together, naked blades ready, they trudged along the avenue. It was not the Bargello they feared. That official functioned under the law—and at present there was no law. The two were wary of an ambush. Their eyes scanned the streets before, behind, and above. No one molested them. Every person on the street stayed well out of the way.

At Alberto's house Gaddi and the others were waiting. Word had already been sent out. Within minutes, gallants from all over the Banchi began to crowd in. By the time the sun had set the Del Bene house was an armed camp and the Florentine could have been got at only by means of a sustained assault.

Cardinal Cornaro heard of the affair and promptly sent thirty soldiers commanded by a Venetian captain. They had been sent, the Captain said, to escort the master to the Cardinal's palace, where he would be even better protected than at present.

"What do you think?" Cellini asked Alberto.

"I would go. Pompeo and Traiano have the Milanese faction on their side, and that is a powerful group. Don't overlook Traiano, Neutino. And don't underestimate him either. He is a dangerous man. I say go to Cornaro's palace with the Captain here. It would be unwise and impolitic of you to refuse this mark of his favor. Besides, you will be safer there."

Traiano wasted no time. When word of his nephew's fate reached him he sent a Milanese of high rank to Cardinal de' Medici.

"Such a dastardly crime as this, Eminence," the nobleman cried to the Cardinal, after he had related the details of the killing, "cannot, must not, be permitted to go unpunished. Particularly since our beloved Pompeo was so staunch and zealous a servitor of our exalted Holy Father, of blessed memory—God rest his soul!"

Cardinal de' Medici waited, unimpressed.

298

"Messer Traiano," continued the Milanese, "respectfully requests that you will not only see to it that this knave is punished, but rather that you yourself will undertake to mete out a proper chastisement."

Ippolito smiled knowingly.

"This Cellini—this knave you speak of—would indeed have been guilty of a dastardly crime had he not undertaken to commit this lesser one. My lord, convey my thanks to Messer Traiano for sending me this information and advise him that his nephew has been repaid in his own coin. Possibly you are ignorant of the fact that this staunch and zealous Pompeo, a short time ago, hired assassins to do to Benvenuto what Benvenuto has now done to him." Ippolito beckoned to an attendant, a distantly related Medici. *"Messere,"* he ordered, "I charge you to search diligently for Benvenuto and bring him here to me, for I wish to aid and protect him."

The Milanese, turning beet-red, bowed and withdrew.

Bernardo de' Medici knew where to look and had no trouble locating the goldsmith. He called on Cornaro the next day, bowed before the Venetian Cardinal, and suavely outlined his kinsman's desire to be Cellini's protector.

Touchy as an old bear with a new cub, his mountainous pride sensitive as an open wound, Cornaro looked down the length of his patrician nose at this overweening courtier. The presumption of these Medici was beyond expression! They were ever of the opinion that in all the world only they counted for anything—as witness the bald insolence of the request casually voiced by this dullard . . . another of the Medici, of course! The whole of their House badly needed to be set to rights.

"Pray inform my lord Cardinal," he replied in a voice heavy with imperious sarcasm, "that I am quite as well fitted to protect Benvenuto as is His Eminence. What does His Lordship imagine he can do, that I cannot do as well—or perhaps, to speak candidly, a little better?"

Using all the diplomatic tact at his command, Bernardo deprecated the imputation. No such thought had ever entered the mind of the lord Ippolito, he simpered. Who was there that would deny the mighty power, the courage, intelligence, high nobility of mind, the *virtù* of so great a lord as the magnificent Cardinal Cornaro? He managed to soothe a few of the nobleman's ruffled tail feathers. The Venetian was nodding in full agreement as this panegyric unfolded.

Seeing this, Bernardo begged for the privilege of a few words with

299

the goldsmith on certain matters ... matters, he hastily interjected, noting that Cornaro's face was again acquiring a wine-like tinge, having nothing whatever to do with the present affair.

But the Venetian's pride was smarting. The merest implication of inequality had been more than enough to cause an inner writhing.

"For today," he fumed, "Your Lordship must reckon on having already talked with Benvenuto. Pray convey my most profound respects to my lord Cardinal. And for the rest, I bid you a pleasant day, *messere!*"

Ippolito's anger easily matched Cornaro's. To dare insinuate that the goldsmith belonged anywhere than under the protective wing of the House of Medici, when it was known that Cellini had been in the Medici service for years! Cornaro was behaving like an old dotard. Attempting, in this underhanded way, to enhance his reputation and prestige as a patron of the arts by making a virtual prisoner of a master who had risen to the stature of best in his field.

When he heard of the squabble the goldsmith acted shrewdly. Taking great care that Cornaro should not hear of it, he called on Ippolito and thanked him for the offer of assistance. That done, he adroitly requested that the Cardinal grant him the additional favor of allowing him to remain where he was.

"Eminence, my lord Cornaro has shown me great courtesy. Do you allow me to remain there with him, I shall have gained a friend the more in my hour of need. Other than that Your Lordship may dispose of me as you will."

Soothed by the knowledge that the master knew where he belonged, Ippolito flicked a hand and nodded graciously.

"Very well, Benvenuto. Do whatever seems best to you."

"I humbly thank Your Eminence."

Within a week the College of Cardinals assembled in a conclave which lasted barely an hour. Virtually by acclamation, Alessandro Cardinal Farnese realized his lifelong dream and was elected Pope. He took the name of Paul—Pope Paul III.

A whole new era was being ushered in with him.

The former Parmesan prelate and new Pope was as worldly and as luxurious as the dozen and more of his immediate predecessors. He came from the same ruling class and social stratum. He was as gifted and cultured, as impeccable in the social graces. His high intelligence and capacity for affairs had won him the favor of every Pontiff he served. His ambitions followed close behind the trail of his instincts. He was as able, as crafty, as dangerous and as ruthless as any of the former Pontiffs. But he had to be careful. He had to be much more careful than a Medici, a Della Rovere, or a Borgia ... Much more! An era of reform was under way. The clamor of public opinion was beginning to make itself felt all over Europe. The pressure it exerted forced him, from the very beginning of his pontificate, into a role for which he personally had little sympathy—that of patron of counter-reform. One of his first official acts was to appoint a commission whose duty it became to weed out the existing evils within the hierarchy of the Church.

The first days of Paul's succession were given over to that and to taking firm hold of the reins of government. Important offices were filled, commands of moment issued. The wheels of Roman justice and of Papal authority began to revolve again.

With the affairs of Church and State under control, the Pope turned his attention to the most pressing of his current personal needs. Now that he had at last gained the Papacy, the fact must needs be made known to all men. Coinage served this purpose—little pieces of metal, each stamped with his portrait, or, for the time being, his arms—little pieces of metal that ranged far and wide and proclaimed to the world that a new Sovereign Pontiff reigned in Rome. Pope Paul was very interested and very much concerned about the artistic quality of his new coins.

"We have been Pope for some few days now," he complained to the fawning, favor-hungry courtiers unctuously hanging on his every breath, "and we have not yet received a visit from the first goldsmith in Rome. One would suppose Benvenuto to have the grace to pay homage to his new Pontiff. The more so since we are disposed to give over to him the task of striking our coins. Where is he? Why has he not come?"

The present Papal favorite, Latino Juvenale, stepped up and made answer.

"Supreme Holiness, know that Master Cellini is in hiding."

"Hiding? Him! ... From what?"

"The matter of a homicide committed on the person of one Pompeo, a Milanese jeweler."

"Ah, so. Well, at least we understand why he failed to call on us. We did not know of Pompeo's death, though we are well acquainted

with the arguments of the quarrel. These are all on Benvenuto's side."
Like most of his contemporaries, Paul regarded homicide as a triviality
—a venial sin. "Since these facts are so well known" mused the new
Pope, giving thought to his own needs, "let a safe-conduct be made out
for him at once, so that he may be most secure against molestation. We
have need of his talents."

The Papal secretary was a Milanese, a friend and former patron of
the defunct Pompeo. He rallied to the cause.

"Blessed Father, in these first days of your Papacy it is not wise to
grant pardons of this kind."

Pope Paul frowned. He had been Pontiff for no more than a few
days and already these apes were presuming to advise him in his personal needs. Had they not yet learned that it would cause less stir were
he to hang a saint rather than an artist? The saint would instantly be
welcomed into Heaven. No one could say where the artist would go.
And wherever he went, his talent went with him. It would no longer
enrich the world. In any case, he did not want a hanged goldsmith.
He wanted coins. Artistic, beautifully designed coins.

"You do not understand the case as well as ourself, Messer Ambrogio," he replied irritably. "Know that men like Benvenuto, unique
in their art, should not be bound by the law. They stand above it. And
how much more true is all this in the present case, since he has received so much provocation. See to the safe-conduct, for such is our
desire."

XLIII

SO YOU CAN SEE, BENVENUTO," THE ELEGANT
Latino allowed a pained expression to cross his face, "that these foes of
yours have no intention of allowing you to work unhindered."

The courtly scholar and antiquarian sat back and let his eyes roam
around the studio. The safe-conduct had been delivered two days before
and he had called to commission the goldsmith to begin work on one
of the new coins.

Cellini airily waved a hand. "I never object to competitive trials
where my work is concerned, *signor mio*. At the same time, I am curious. Who started all this?"

"A group rather than any one individual," Juvenale answered. "The Milanese faction at court. Messer Traiano had his share in the thing, and one supposes it was he who egged the others on. It happened thus: the Pope gave orders that you were to design his coins. They pointed out that you were unsuited to the task. His Holiness, perceiving their drift, scolded them roundly. Whereupon Ambrogio Recalcati suggested a competition to determine who could best carry out this important assignment. As a result you are to compete with several worthy men, Fagiuolo and Micheletto among them."

"So be it, *messere*. I shall begin work on a design immediately."

In a few days the dies for a crown began to take form. The coin Cellini designed depicted a half-figure of St. Paul, encircled by the inscription: *Vas Electionis*. The latter was meant to tickle the Pope's vanity by implying that his election resulted from a rare and almost unanimous voice vote of the College.

Pope Paul felt nothing but satisfaction when he saw the result. Most of the court agreed, although the Milanese faction did its utmost to malign every part of it. They raised all sorts of objections.

The Pope listened quietly, his austere, thinly fleshed face set in placid lines, his sharp eyes fixed intently on each speaker. He drew a finger along the prow of his jutting nose, let it play in his long white beard, and toy with the *mantelletta* of crimson-edged velvet around his chest and shoulders. Paul had long slender hands, with long slim fingers. He took pride in them. At length, the finger came to rest on the table, caressing one of the newly stamped crowns. He had heard enough.

"We have listened patiently and as long as seems to us necessary," he broke in. "This has now become idle chatter and serves no purpose. It is clearly to be seen that Benvenuto's talents are more than equal to our needs, and far surpass those of the others in the test. Wherefore we do not desire to hear more of who will strike our coins. Only Benvenuto will have to do with that."

The Florentine flushed with pride and moved on to the next square in the chess game for Papal favor. He had it much at heart to regain his former post at the Mint.

"I thank Your Supreme Holiness with all my heart for this mark of favor and patronage. Your Sanctity may be aware that I once held the post of Stamp-Master and that this was taken from me at the instigation of certain evil-spoken individuals. I beg that Your Holiness will see fit to confer this office upon me and so insure that only the finest dies are used to stamp the coins which are to glorify your reign."

"Blessed Father!" the Papal secretary almost shrieked, "this cannot be! If it becomes known that Your Holiness has set an unpardoned criminal in such a post it will cause great harm."

Paul pursed his lips, pondered, and decided to take the advice.

"In this thing, Benvenuto, our Messer Ambrogio is entirely correct. It is necessary that you first obtain pardon for the homicide. Yes," he nodded, "a full and complete pardon ... which you can secure through the Caporioni of Rome, during the Holy Marys festival next August. It is the practice, during this feast, for our District Wardens to pardon and free twelve outlaws. We shall see to reserving a place for you. In the meantime we will have another safe-conduct made out, which will keep you secure until then."

It was soon clear that the combined weight of the entire Milanese party would be unable to push Cellini out of court. So the versatile Traiano set in motion a long range plan he had devised. If the immediate future would not supply the opportunity to avenge his nephew, then this in time would bring it about. It had in it the elements of the dripping water technique he and his late kinsman had successfully used on Pope Clement.

Some time before he was slain Pompeo had set aside three thousand ducats to be used as the dowry for an illegitimate daughter of his, to assure her a favorable connection. Three thousand ducats could easily buy a minor lordling husband. The girl herself was implacable in her hatred for the slayer of her father and wanted nothing so much as to see him hanged, or at the very least, suitably punished. With both these salient facts in mind, Traiano called on the girl and had a long talk with her. When he finished he made a call on yet another bastard. This one the son of the Farnese Pope—the openly acknowledged son. Pier Luigi Farnese.

Pier Luigi suffered from a money disease, and Traiano was well aware of that too. The youth had been appointed Captain-General of the Church and Gonfalonier of Rome. He was indulged in every whim by his doting parent, who regarded no act of nepotism too bald where this beloved son was concerned. In spite of all this, the slender, almost effeminately graceful Pier Luigi still had a perpetual need of money. He leaned back and looked at Traiano through half-closed eyes. Outwardly he was gracious and noncommittal, seemingly listening only out of politeness. Inwardly, he was interested, but of this he gave no sign.

"My lord could contrive that your present favorite, Pietro dei Stefani, will ask for her in marriage," patiently explained the Milanese, "through the medium of Your Lordship. The dower thus would be placed in your hands for safekeeping..." Traiano shrugged expressively. Pietro was a country lad, of excellent family, but not overbright. For the girl, in point of position, the match would be an extremely good one.

Pier Luigi fondled the short stubble of beard that circled his mouth and covered his chin. He looked a great deal like his father. Slender, thin-faced and thin-lipped, brown-eyed, big-nosed, he had fine hands and was infinitely graceful. He was interested. Pietro was an ass. And three thousand ducats were always useful. But why was Traiano putting a relative's dowry in his way?

"You make an interesting point, Messer Traiano." His eyes were dreamy. His fingers left the beard and began to stroke a cheek. "Yes, interesting. And yet... why do you make it? Pray, enlighten us."

"It is simple enough, Magnifico. It is our desire—my cousin's and mine—that the murderer of her father, my late nephew, be made to pay the penalty for his heinous crime."

"Cellini?"

"The same, Your Grandeur."

"My father's favorite master? You are mad!"

"A favorite today, Your Sublimity, and perhaps tomorrow and the next day. But in time—" Traiano flicked a hand.

"Ah! I begin to understand you, messere. Not today or tomorrow, necessarily; but someday..." Pier Luigi smiled derisively. "Bene, we shall see."

As Traiano expected, the match was quickly arranged. As he further expected, the groom saw nothing of the dowry. All he acquired was a bride obsessed with a single nagging propensity that speedily drove him to his lordly master.

"My lord, you must have this Cellini taken up or I shall go mad! This woman I have taken to wife does naught but plague me regarding this and the matter of her dower."

Pier Luigi dismissed all with a toss of his curly head. "Rest easy, my dear Pietro, and inform your lady on my behalf that Cellini will be

305

apprehended as soon as the first flush of his favor with the Pope has passed away."

About the dowry he said nothing. Pietro asked again and was fobbed off with a pretext.

Two months of that and the Farnese began to run short of pretexts. Pietro was making deplorable demands for his money. His bride was more intent than ever on revenge. She meant to have it or her dower. And worst of all, in his present high position, Pier Luigi had to tread carefully lest he show himself to the world as a clumsy, avaricious fool. He sighed deeply and sent for Zima the Corsican. He also summoned Traiano and Pietro to his apartments at the Vatican.

Zima listened carefully while his lord and master sketched out the affair. Through the years he had served with Pier Luigi in various military campaigns for and against the Holy See. Together they had taken part in the sack of Rome. The Corsican soldier entertained a lively regard for the Farnese prince. It bordered on respect. Zima had seen Pier Luigi in action, stripped of all gloss and pretense. He knew the man's capacity, his real self.

"And what is Your Lordship's will in the matter?" he asked when Pier Luigi finished.

"Simply this. Do away with this troublesome insect of a goldsmith, but without openly involving yourself. It is known that you are in my service and I must not be implicated in any way. The thing must be handled with caution. Be circumspect. This fellow is a favorite at court and is highly regarded as a master of the first rank. Handle it with the utmost discretion or not at all. Do I make myself clear?"

"Completely, *Grandezza.*"

"*Va bene.* We'll have the others in then." The Captain-General rang a bell. "Bid Traiano and Dei Stefani enter," he ordered the page who answered the signal.

Traiano eyed the slim, short Corsican with interest. A single glance sufficed to fix the fellow's calling. He examined him with an appraising eye. Zima was well proportioned and set up, muscular and wiry. His dress was up to the minute in cut and gaudy decoration. His fingers glittered with rings. A gold chain was slung around his shoulders. A large ornate pendant hung from his left ear. These were all attestations of successful enterprise. Only a successful bravo could afford such trinkets. When he acknowledged the introductions, Zima's manners were elegant. His Tuscan was fluent and tainted with the mere trace of an accent. The raw inner steel was plated with burnished gold. He was a perfumed assassin.

While Pier Luigi explained the part he was to play, Zima fingered his ear pendant and lounged.

"You are certain you can make an easy task of this, friend?" Traiano was skeptical. "It is most important that it come off without our being implicated in any way."

Zima waved with raffish grace. *"Messere,* do not trouble yourself further with this matter. I have a talent for these things."

Traiano nodded. The man seemed confident enough. "We shall see. Do you handle it as well as you make out and I promise to add a hundred crowns to your purse."

Again the raffish wave of the hand. "Then Your Excellency must count on paying down the money. The thing will be as easy as sucking a fresh egg."

But the Vatican had a thousand eyes—and Cellini, many friends. No sooner was this secret pact ratified than its intent had been divined. Zima was seen entering the Gonfalonier's quarters; and quite everyone knew that this little devil of a Corsican soldier doubled as a bravo for his master. The other two following him in. The smug smiles of pleasant anticipation when they departed ... Inferences were deduced, implications analyzed.

Cellini was quickly advised that a ruffler of Pier Luigi's had probably been assigned to attend to him. A vivid description of the little man was forwarded at the same time. The hint was enough.

Cellini again donned chain-mail underclothing and kept arms at hand day and night. He stayed indoors as much as possible and never ventured out after dark. When business affairs called him out he was attended by hirelings of his own. Taking him by surprise would not be easy; as a matter of fact, it would be impossible.

About a week later a page called at the studio, summoning the goldsmith to the Farnese palace, where Pier Luigi wished to speak with him. Cellini went off at once. Some time ago the Gonfalonier had voiced a desire to commission several large vases. It was possible that he had made up his mind in the matter.

With his escort trailing behind him, Cellini strode rapidly down the Via Giulia toward the Palazzo Farnese, which faced on the Campo di Fiori. It was early afternoon, the siesta hour, and the streets were nearly deserted. He came to a corner and following his usual custom turned it wide. As he did so he noticed a man rising from his seat in a nearby tavern, a short man who walked slowly to the center of the street. The goldsmith had no trouble recognizing him. The fellow's description had been precise. It was Zima the Corsican.

Whistling the tune which served as a signal for his escort Cellini slackened his pace and drew nearer the wall, giving the soldier a wide berth with plenty of passage space.

Zima sauntered nearer along the same wall. He was feeling pleased with himself. This dolt of an artist had fallen into the trap with a nicety that bade fair to make for a quick and satisfactory bit of work.

Drawing nearer, the goldsmith stopped and gave the ruffler a bleak once over. A dangerous little bastard, he looked to be.

"My little warrior," he droned out at him, "if it were night one could suppose you had mistaken me for someone else. But with all this beautiful daylight there is no doubt of your knowing whom you seek, eh?"

Zima made no move to step out of the way. He smiled a serene, cheerful, sympathetic smile which conveyed the thought that there was nothing personal in what he meant to do. It was all a matter of business —a detail. You were in somebody's way, and he was being employed to remove you. *Ecco.* That was all there was to it and there was no need to harbor any ill feelings.

"My dear fellow," he spouted loftily, mincing forward with a foot, "I don't understand what you are saying."

Cellini let his hand curl lovingly around the hilt of his sword. "You don't? How droll! Perhaps not. On the other hand I perfectly understand what you are saying and also what you would like to do. The little task you have taken in hand—it is much more difficult than you imagine. It may turn out on the wrong end for you. In fact, I am certain it will."

The Florentine's escort strolled up dispassionately and posted themselves on either side of the Corsican. They too smiled, but not at all cheerfully. Their grins were flat and had no joy in them whatever, only expectancy. They were working men, not artists.

Other people walking by paused to see if the argument would develop into a brawl.

Zima turned slowly right and left. If the two huskies frightened him, it did not show. He changed color a little and his intentions evaporated. He tried a loud laugh, but his heart wasn't in the effort.

The sound that came out was flat and unreal and nothing to his credit. The business had got out of hand. Even if Pier Luigi hadn't advised the greatest discretion he would have withdrawn. At the same time it was irritating to be bested in this fashion at one's own game.

"Another time, perhaps, we will meet again," he told the smirking Cellini in brittle tones.

"Any time, little soldier," answered the goldsmith, still caressing his sword. "I'm always ready—and you know where and how to reach me."

He stepped casually around him and went on to the Farnese palace, where Pier Luigi expressed surprise at seeing him. The Farnese immediately surmised that the stratagem was Zima's, and that it had failed. No, he said, chewing his lip in vexation, he had not sent for him. In fact he himself was leaving for the Vatican, to attend to some business affairs.

Cellini returned home but there was no time for self-congratulations. Not two hours later Annibale Caro galloped to the door and burst into the studio.

Cellini stared apprehensively. Only a grave emergency would make the courtly Annibale act in this abrupt manner.

"*Che è?*" He asked, frowning. "What's wrong, old friend? You look as if—"

"Neutino," Caro interrupted, "I must speak to you at once!" He motioned to the housekeeper who was busy cleaning the room.

"Assunta, please leave off and continue later. I wish to talk with Messer Caro . . ."

Annibale waited until she had closed the door behind her. "I have raced here from the Vatican. Pier Luigi is there. He came to confer with Crespino, the Bargello, together with Traiano and Pietro dei Stefani. My lord Giovanni heard of it and drew Crespino into conversation when he came out. All Messer Giovanni could glean from him was that he is to take someone into custody. One hour after sunset was mentioned as the time. No doubt, that is when it will be done. The streets are quiet and free at that time. You know what this means?"

Cellini nodded brightly. "Of course. I am the game they seek to trap. Pier Luigi has discovered that his little Corsican is not up to the task and so is taking other means. At one of the clock, you say?"

He looked at the clock set in a corner of the studio. It was twenty-two. Caro followed the look.

"Three hours. Time enough if you set off at once. Can you?"

"Yes. Everything is in readiness. I've been expecting something like this. I never did put much faith in that last safe-conduct. It was signed by the Governor, not the Pope."

"Florence, Neutino?"

"*Sì.* I'll travel by post ... the same way I came here. I must pack some clothing." Cellini embraced his friend. "To offer you thanks is to offer nothing. You know my heart? Voice it for me, to yourself and to my lord Giovanni—and leave here, my friend. You must not be found in or near this house."

"*Va con Dio!*" Caro flung back at him. He was already out the door.

XLIV

THE FIRST DAYS IN HIS NATIVE FLORENCE CELlini spent quietly with Liperata, who was busy rearing a family of her own. She was a self-effacing, soft-spoken young woman, five years younger than her brother, and much concerned over what she regarded an awful aptitude for acquiring enemies.

On the third morning after his arrival he went to pay his respects to the Duke. But Alessandro was not at the Medici Palace. He chased around Florence for nearly two hours before he located the nobleman, at the palace of the Pazzi—visiting the wife of Lorenzo Cibo. The "visit" had lasted all night, and it brought a smile to the goldsmith's lips. Varchi had written him of this affair, and the account of it had been entertaining.

Cibo, Marquis of Massa, was known to be considerably irked by these lengthy and too frequent visits with which the Duke honored his well-favored Marchioness. Openly he could do nothing, since if he so much as breathed a word the orgiastic Alessandro would have his head rolling in short order. But there were other ways.

Keeping himself entirely out of the picture, an arrangement was entered into between Ippolito de' Medici, Gianbatista Cibo, and an unnamed close relative of the lady, whereby the Marquis would be rid of the antlers that so disfigured the mental image he had of himself. Simultaneously, Florence would be rid of her raging tyrant. With great secrecy, unknown even to the lady who most certainly would not have favored the plan, a barrel of gunpowder was conveyed into her boudoir and positioned under the bed where the Duke usually made sport. Everyone entertained high hopes. But through some inexplicable mischance the powder failed to ignite. The Duke's undesirable attentions continued, as did the growth of the Marquis' phantasmic horns.

Cellini stated the reason for his call and asked that word be sent in to His Excellency.

A youth of about sixteen years came out with the Duke's answer, a young noble with the beautiful eyes of the Medici and the quiet poise and bearing of one far older in years. Cellini had never seen him before. He was the son of Giovanni delle Bande Nere, the youthful lord Cosimo de' Medici.

"His Excellency bids me say that he will be occupied for the next three or four days, Master," the youth said in a soft voice. "He requests that you attend him then, at which time he will be most pleased to receive you. Also, because of this inconvenience, he bids you seek out Niccolò da Monte Aguto, who will give you fifty gold crowns. Our Duke presents these to you as a token of his favor and his good will." He handed over a signed authorization.

Having known Niccolò since early childhood, it did not take Cellini long to find him, receive the gold, and return to his sister's house with a delightfully weighty purse dangling from his belt.

A host of old friends called. His closest cronies, Varchi, Piero Landi, and several others, came every evening to sit around a roaring fire and talk over old times while eating roasted chestnuts and consuming flasks of *alicante*.

He waited a week, and then made his second call on the Florentine ruler.

When he arrived at the ducal palace he found Alessandro at dinner, attended by Lorenzino de' Medici, a distant cousin who had become the Duke's close companion and confidant. The youth was a slightly built lad of twenty years, slender as a willow wand, with a pink-cheeked, almost beardless face, deceptively frail and delicate looking. His appearance and manner masked the lithe, supple-muscled body of a panther, with mental and moral qualities to suit. Cellini had known him in Rome, before Pope Clement banished him from that city. There he had for no apparent reason knocked the heads off a row of fine antique statues of the Emperor Hadrian. The vandalism had so enraged the

311

Pontiff he was of a mind to have him hanged, but had ended by banishing him from Rome instead. Clement thought him mad, and indeed if anyone cared to study him closely they might have noticed a strangeness in his eyes. They were the beautiful eyes of the Medici, but there was something about them. They were depthless. Remote. Deep black pools, still as death and free of any human emotion, with a smoldering hidden away within which might well have indicated an incipient madness. Lorenzino was not insane—but he was not normal either.

Alessandro de' Medici had a very cordial greeting for the goldsmith. He had seen that medal made for Clement and the new coins for Pope Paul, and he wished to be similarly honored.

"You must remain here in Florence in our service, Benvenuto," he demanded.

"The opportunity to serve Your Highness will be a privilege and a pleasure," Cellini replied suavely.

"Good! Good!" beamed the Duke, while Lorenzino nibbled at a chop and looked on indifferently. "We are much pleased! Tell us, Benvenuto, are you of the mind to get to work quickly?"

The goldsmith had called for just that reason. There was no telling how long he would have to remain in Florence and he wanted to stop wasting time.

"I place myself at Your Grace's orders," he answered.

"Excellent! It is our desire that you get to work on our coins immediately. For your first effort, Benvenuto, design for us the forty-soldi piece. On the face of this we wish to see our portrait head; and on the reverse, those of our special patrons, San Cosimo and San Damiano. Let us see something fine. Something on the order of those excellent coins you have executed for Pope Paul."

Cellini made an arrangement with a goldsmith friend for the use of a shop, and started on the design and dies for the first coin. He was so anxious to show his native Florence what he could accomplish in this art that in a comparatively short time he brought stampings of the new coin to the Duke for approval.

Alessandro was delighted with it. Here at last was a portrait that did him full justice, that showed his profile in the full majesty which was its due. He was tired of looking at the deformed, lumpy lout pictured on his old coins. He was so pleased he caressed the samples, mewing like a cat.

312

"Sangue di Dio! This is the finest example of coinage that has ever been seen! We shall order coins struck from these dies immediately, Benvenuto. Well done!"

The courtiers surrounding the Duke pressed around to examine the coins and approved loudly. But Alessandro asked for no opinions. The only one he was interested in was his own.

"Since my lord is pleased," ventured Cellini, "I make bold to request that you make a provision for me, so that I may better serve you. Excellency, I ask that you grant me the lodgings of the Mint."

The Mint appointment he requested was identical with that of Stamp-Master in Rome, with the notable addition that a splendid studio and apartment went with the office.

"Do you remain in our service, Benvenuto," answered the Duke, "and we will grant all you request and more. Meanwhile, we have given orders to our Mint-Master to pay out the moneys due you for your labor. Go to him for this—and get forward with our other coins."

Dies for the *giulio* followed. The obverse depicting a seated San Giovanni, with Alessandro's armorial bearings on the reverse. Next came the half-*giulio*. On this coin Cellini engraved a head of San Giovanni in full face, an extremely difficult feat since the modeling of the head had to be properly brought out on a very thin and small piece of silver. It was a tour de force which brought resounding plaudits from the Goldsmiths' Guild.

The next coin was a gold crown bearing a cross surrounded by cherubs, and the arms of the Duke. The goldsmith brought samples of it to the palace.

Alessandro was in his wardrobe, examining an arquebus, when Cellini was ushered in. The only courtier in attendance was the Master of the Wardrobe. Cellini had many times noted the fact that Alessandro frequently was alone, or attended by only one or two of his courtiers, and had wondered about this. It was laxness of an order which betrayed either supreme overconfidence or rank stupidity. But perhaps this was the Duke's way of showing contempt for his very numerous enemies.

Alessandro set the gun aside and looked over the coins.

"My lord," began Cellini, as he had done twenty times before, "if you are content with my service, I again beg that you will make out my appointment and assign me the lodgings I have asked for."

The Duke was forever promising, and forever putting this off.

313

"I am entirely satisfied with your service, Benvenuto, and am well-disposed to grant your request. *Caspita!* This crown is even more handsome than the other coins ... Ah! Interested in this gun, are you?"

The goldsmith was eyeing the remarkable little weapon on the table. It was a wheel arquebus, a marvel of precision gunsmithing. Its exterior was superbly engraved and ornamented.

"Here—examine it." The Duke handed it over. "I know how much pleasure you take in these things. It has been sent to me from Germany. What do you think of it?"

Cellini whistled and looked it over reverently.

Alessandro went on: "As a token of my satisfaction and an earnest of my promises, I give you leave to choose any arquebus in my armory, excepting only this one which is a gift. There are many others here no less excellent and of even greater beauty." Laughing at the look of pleased surprise on the goldsmith's face, he walked out, leaving Cellini behind to make his selection.

But in spite of the lordly and expensive gift, the Mint appointment remained unsettled. Cellini was performing all the duties of Stamp-Master. Only ducal confirmation was required. A sheet of paper bearing the Duke's hand and seal was all that stood between him and a handsome salary and the luxurious apartment. The next time he called he again requested that the matter be settled, but Alessandro had something else in mind.

"That can wait a bit, Benvenuto. First we would like you to execute a fine portrait medal of ourself, in the excellent style of that which you made for Pope Clement."

Salary and luxurious apartment instantly shrank to less than nothing. Charmed and delighted to learn that the unused medal of the deceased Pontiff had created so much interest, Cellini offered to start immediately.

"If Your Excellency will permit it, I would like to begin on a wax model right away. This afternoon."

"Start whenever you please, master. The sooner the better. We will give orders that you be admitted into our presence whenever you call to work on it."

Three sittings for the wax model and it was clear to the goldsmith that unless he eased the pressure of his other duties, the medal would prove a lengthy affair. He rushed word to Felice in Rome and had him send out Pietro Galleotti, a young journeyman whom he had trained in his methods of coinage, and when the youth arrived put him to work at the Mint. That solved the problem—for about two weeks. Then other troubles cropped up. Pietro did not get along well with Ottaviano de' Medici.

Ottaviano was another of the distantly related Medici in the ducal court, a sly, insufferable martinet who was forever sticking his nose into everything. He had never liked tne too forward Cellini and the dislike extended to the new journeyman. The petty tampering which Cellini had been too busy to bother with increased until Pietro was having a bad time of it.

"Look at these," he told his master one day, holding out a fistful of coins. "They were struck from the dies I made last week."

Cellini examined the coins. There were scratches on each of them.

"What happened here?" he asked, frowning up at Pietro. "Let me see the dies from which these were struck."

Gallcotti handed over three sets of new dies. All six faces had scratches on them and these naturally were transferred to any coins minted from them.

"What the devil happened?" Cellini asked again, his face beginning to tighten. "I know you too well to think this your doing."

The young journeyman waved angrily. "The eminent Ottaviano! This is his latest triumph! He has ordered that these new dies be mixed with the old ones. Look at them! Three sets ruined! Why? What does he or anyone gain by this?"

Cellini raged into Ottaviano's quarters.

"Am I to understand that my new dies were handled as they were at the order of Your Lordship?" he choked, flinging several of the marred coins on the table in front of the nobleman.

Ottaviano deigned to lift his eyes to the goldsmith and nod haughtily.

"By the cross of the just Christ! Why? Surely it is plain that such stupid and needless interference is causing damage to the dies and to the coins struck from them?"

The lordly Medici looked down his nose. "It pleases us to have it so," he loftily informed the blazing goldsmith.

The Cellini dander climbed higher still. "I've no doubt of that. The point of the matter is that it does not please me!"

The nobleman's eyes widened. "And if it should please the Duke to have it so?"

"It still would not please me!" snapped Cellini. "The Duke is not an ass! And this thing falls below the intelligence of one. It is neither just nor reasonable."

Ottaviano struck a pose and disdainfully flicked a hand. "Take yourself off," he sniffed. "You will swallow the thing thus if you burst for doing so. Remove yourself from our presence. Away with you."

Spouting vehement curses all the way to the Medici palace, the goldsmith related the conversation, with embroidery, to the Duke, while the latter sat for his portrait.

"...Three sets of dies ruined!" he complained bitterly. "I entreat Your Excellency not to allow my fine coins to be harmed in this idiotic fashion. Also," he continued, deciding to voice a desire which he'd had in mind for some weeks, "I wish to make request that you grant me permission to leave your service."

The Duke was in a stew of his own that day. A week before he had received the unwelcome news that a delegation arranged by the numerous Florentine exiles had left Rome for Tunis, where the Emperor Charles was busily waging a war with the infidels of Barbary. The delegation was headed by Ippolito de' Medici, and a petition was to be presented to the Emperor requesting that he remove the infamous Alessandro from his place as Duke of Florence. He was worried. In the hands of a man as capable as Ippolito, that petition and that mission could be dangerous. He had countered the move by despatching a special emissary of his own, and it was anxiety over the effectiveness of this special ambassador that had him stewing. He'd received no word from him.

"Eh? ... What's that you say?" he scowled at Cellini. "Leave my service? Coins? Nonsense, Benvenuto." The scowl became an irritated frown, an easy transition for him. "I shall see to it that your coins are not harmed in any way. The matter is as important to me as it is to you. This Ottaviano of ours is growing too presumptuous. Leave him to me."

Somewhat mollified, Cellini finished the sitting and left. But when later that day the letter arrived from the Vatican advising him to return to Rome as quickly as possible if he wished to secure his pardon, he felt greatly heartened. There was a full and ample safe-conduct enclosed, this one signed by the Pope, which guaranteed his safety, and he was glad to make use of it as an excuse to get away. Florence under the rule of Duke Alessandro was a Florence different from the city he remembered and loved. Life there had become strained and tense. The Duke's

316

portrait needed only another sitting or two. It was still in wax, but having finished that, he could cut it in steel anywhere, in Rome as easily as here in Florence.

Shortly after noon on the following day he called on the Duke.

A peevish Alessandro lounged in bed, suffering from the after-effects of his debauch the night before. He propped himself up on pillows and posed, bleary-eyed, for two hours while Cellini finished the model.

He was not at all pleased when the goldsmith exhibited the Papal safe-conduct and spoke of his recall to Rome.

"Heed my wishes in this thing, Benvenuto." The Medici Duke was vexed and half-angry. He had a nasty headache. "Stay here in your Florence. I will provide for your appointment, give you the lodgings in the Mint, and much more besides. Were you to leave my service, who will be able to strike off the beautiful coins you have designed for me? To say nothing of this fine medal? Stay here!"

"My lord, everything has been thought out in your interests. My leaving will not prevent me from completing this medal; while in the matter of the coins, the young Roman I have caused to come here to our Florence will serve Your Excellency well until my return. Know that in Rome I have a shop with many journeymen, and a pretty business afoot. Also I must secure my pardon in that city. These matters are important to me. When I have attended to them and set them in order, I shall instantly fly back to Your Lordship."

Lorenzino was in the ducal bedchamber, looking on with bored disinterest. Alessandro signaled to him to join in pressing the goldsmith to stay on.

The youth sighed faintly. "Benvenuto," he said mechanically in a voice which plainly indicated he did not care whether Cellini remained in the city or went straight to Hell, "you will do best for yourself by staying here in Florence, as my lord Alessandro wishes."

"I cannot, Messer Lorenzo. I must first secure my pardon in Rome, else I will remain a criminal and a fugitive in the eyes of the law there."

Lorenzino turned his eyes on Alessandro and let it go at that.

"*Signor mio,*" pressed Cellini, "I pray you let me have your good will. I promise you the satisfaction of a finer medal than ever I made for Pope Clement. Messer Lorenzo here will give me a subject, and I will make a fine reverse for it."

Lorenzino arched a brow. "Yes," he replied, pleased with the idea.

317

"Yes, of course. I will give thought to this. The reverse for that medal must be such as will be fully worthy of His Excellency, our Duke."

Alessandro laughed sarcastically. "Then give him the reverse quickly, Lorenzino, so that he can make it here, without leaving us."

The ducal favorite smiled blandly. "I shall give thought to the matter and give him a subject as quickly as I am able. It will have to be such a one as will cause the world to marvel."

Alessandro laughed again and rolled over on his side.

Cellini withdrew without further ceremony and began making arrangements for returning to Rome.

XLV

It IS GOOD TO SEE YOU AGAIN, BENVENUTO." Felice and his partner smiled at each other as they rode down the darkened Corso. He had waited for Cellini at the city gate and was accompanying him home. "How did things go in Florence?"

"Not too well, Felice. I was busy and did a great deal of work, but the city is much changed. To speak the truth I was not at ease there. I'm glad to be back in Rome." He sighed. "Well, here I am. I'd best put up at an inn until my house is set in order."

"That will not be necessary," Felice told him, "I have already seen to that. Everything is arranged and ready. Nuncio is there waiting for you to dismount. A laundress who rented two of the downstairs rooms while you were away is your new cook and housekeeper, and I have engaged Cencio Romoli to act as your house steward. There will be a fire blazing in your room and an excellent supper waiting on the table. Are you hungry?"

The goldsmith made a wry face. "Not much. I don't know what the devil is wrong with me. For several days now I have been unwell." He eructed loudly. "There, you hear? It has been this way since last week."

"You've had a tiring journey, nothing more. Some good food and a sound sleep will take care of everything."

Cellini ate little of the tasty supper that had been prepared for him. He greeted Cencio Romoli and Nuncio, and sat to nibble at the food while he talked with Felice. When his partner left, shortly afterwards,

318

he saw to it that the doors were carefully locked and bolted and went up to bed, intending to rise early and call on the Pope. He must thank Paul for the favor he had shown.

It was still dark when he was awakened by a furious pounding on the street door. He rubbed his eyes open and leaned back on his elbows, listening. The pounding increased rather than diminished. He got out of bed and taking up a lamp which he kept burning all night, pattered to the head of the stairs.

Cencio was in the hall below, holding a sputtering candle. He looked up at Cellini with a worried frown on his face.

"Go and see what madman it is who raises such a row at this early hour," the goldsmith called down to him.

While Cencio went to open the wicket he returned to his room and slipped his undercoat of fine-link chain mail over his shirt. He lighted another lamp and was picking up clothing at random when Cencio ran in.

"*Al corpo di Cristo,* it's the Bargello's men. Catchpolls! The captain in charge says if you do not open the door at once he will break it in."

"They are all armed?"

"Everyone!"

Cellini paused and looked at Cencio, his face set in grim lines.

"Go and tell the whoresons I am putting on some clothes and that I will come down in a minute." The pounding started up again. "Go on down there, before they break in the door."

That this was another trap he did not doubt. Very likely he was about to be slain while attempting to escape from the civil authorities. Chewing over this unpleasantry he selected a long dagger and unsheathed it. The Bargello and his catchpolls had no quarrel with him; but with Pier Luigi pulling the strings to which these officials danced, there was no telling to what lengths they could be forced. He picked up the safe-conduct and glanced through it. It was all in order; a full and ample warrant of safety, signed by the Pope himself. He walked to the window in the back of the hall which looked down on a garden, and peered cautiously below. That exit was sealed off. A group of blacklegs waited there with their weapons drawn and ready.

He turned back and walked downstairs, watching Nuncio and Cencio exchange vacillating glances between the street door and each other, and took up a position facing the door. Behind him was a bare wall. The long dagger was outthrust and ready in his right hand, the safe-conduct in his left.

"Now—don't be afraid. Open the door, and then stand back . . ."

The guard captain, Vittorio, and two of the catchpolls sprang in as the door swung, thinking to take the victim by surprise. One of them nearly skewered himself on the dagger. They drew back hurriedly, while other blacklegs crowded into the doorway.

"Eh," Vittorio growled resentfully, "something more than words will be needed here."

Cellini flung the safe-conduct at him. It fluttered to the floor near his feet.

"Read that, blackleg! And since I am safe against seizure I mean to see to it that neither you nor any of your mongrels lay a finger on me!"

Vittorio looked around to his men. "Seize this fellow and place him under arrest," he snapped, making no move himself. "Later on, at leisure, we will examine the paper and see if it is all he says of it."

Cellini shifted lightly, making certain of his stance.

"So be it!" he snarled. "Come ahead. Which of you will be the first to die?"

The space around the door was jammed with blacklegs, but none made a move. Each waited for someone other than himself to take the goldsmith into custody.

Vittorio was thinking, and from the pained expression on his face it could be seen that the process came hard with him. Nothing, positively nothing, had been said about that piece of paper on the floor . . .

"Send in the clerk," he bawled back over his shoulder. Being entirely illiterate, Captain Vittorio could not himself decipher the marks on the paper.

"Read that aloud," he snorted contemptuously at the scribe who shuffled into the room, pointing at the floor.

All through the reading Cellini never wavered from his crouched stand.

When it was finished Vittorio disgustedly jerked the warrant from the hands of the clerk and threw it back on the floor. Words! Slamming out of the house he stalked off into the night, leaving his men to follow.

Too disturbed to find sleep, the goldsmith sweated and tossed for the remainder of the night. Morning found him limp and ill, his

320

stomach disorder greatly increased. As soon as it was daylight he sent word to Giovanni Gaddi, asking his advice. The kindly Florentine lord came over with his own leech, one Bernardo da Todi, who promptly attached a half-dozen of his namesakes to the goldsmith's buttocks and let them feast while he examined, felt and probed with dirty fingers.

Ser Bernardo was a disciple of Galen who had a fair knowledge of routine symptoms. In fact, if these were sufficiently acute he could sometimes distinguish between maladies. In the present case, however, he fell back on his usual dodge when faced with any of the innumerable ills to which the digestive area of the human body was liable, and which he could not recognize. All such physiological phenomena he classified under a single broad heading: Cellini was suffering from a colic. A slight attack, nothing serious, abetted perhaps by the fright he had taken. No more than this.

"Drink a glass of good Greek wine and keep your spirits up," he prated, scraping the leeches off the goldsmith's rump so that he might sit up and clothe himself. "The disturbance is slight. It will pass off quickly and all will be well with you."

Gaddi looked on happily. "This goes more pleasantly than I imagined. I had even ordered my servants to bring food." He pointed below, where the rattling of crockery could be heard. "I thought it might be necessary for me to remain here with you. Caro and the others will be here shortly. I left word for them before I came here. Thus we will dine and talk in a most agreeable fashion, as good comrades should. I have received an important piece of news, which you will all want to hear."

The food and the company quickly revived the goldsmith's spirits, and he enjoyed both.

"What is this news you spoke of, Messer Giovanni?"

Gaddi looked around intently. "Ippolito de' Medici is dead! . . . Murdered!"

Everyone gaped at him.

"Most of you know by now that Ippolito was en route to Tunis, where he was to confer with the Emperor on the affairs of Florence. *Bene,* late last night I received news by special courier. Benvenuto, it was your friend Benedetto Varchi who supplied most of my information. It is strange that this news should reach Rome from Florence rather than from the south. Ippolito had been poisoned."

"But how? . . . Who? . . ."

"The assassin is said to have been a certain Giovanni Andrea, a native of Borgo San Sepolcro." Gaddi shrugged and grimaced. "What will you? He was a hired assassin. The real murderer is that man who paid for the service rather than he who performed it ... Alessandro, of course."

"Start at the beginning, Messer Giovanni, and give us all the details."

"Very well. Although there is not much to tell. I repeat, most of you knew that Ippolito had been selected as Ambassador by the *fuorusciti,* who have increased to such large numbers since Alessandro became Duke. He was to journey to Tunis, where Charles is engaged in war with the Turks and Saracens. There he was to present the petition of the exiles, requesting that the bestial Alessandro be removed from his position as ruler of our Florence. I recall how delighted Ippolito was with the assignment as he set off. He was to take ship at Gaeta, but he paused at Itri, a nearby village, to await the caravel on which he was to embark for Africa. At dinner he drank a cup of poisoned wine and died in a convulsion. The assassin eluded Ippolito's gentlemen and servants and made his escape. Varchi swears he is in Florence, hiding in the Medici palace. There you have it, my friends. The entire plan gone up in thin air—or I should say, in a cup of bad wine."

All through dinner they discussed the happening at great length, but by the time the meal was ended the shock of surprise had passed and they forgot the homicide. Ippolito was dead. Amen!

Cellini spent the afternoon and evening overseeing the cut of the clothing he and Cencio were to wear in the coming festival of the Holy Marys. In Viterbo he had purchased blue sarcenet, a soft silken fabric which made a fine show when cut into jerkins and gowns. The two were to be identically dressed; Cencio going before him, carrying the lighted taper of a *penitente* for his master.

The next morning he called on the Pope and expressed suitable thanks for the favor shown him in the matter of the safe-conduct. He said nothing about the incident with the Bargello. It would have served no purpose had he done so.

Paul acknowledged the grateful words with a nod.

The goldsmith made ready to counter the next move.

"Holy Father," he requested, "In this matter of my pardon, I beg that you grant me the dispensation of remaining out of prison." It was

322

customary that the twelve outlaws who were to receive pardons remain in prison for the day and night preceding the feast, and Cellini had no illusions over what would happen if he let prison doors clang shut behind him.

"Not so, Benvenuto," responded Paul. "No. Such is the custom, as you well know. You must conform to it, like the others. It would not look well otherwise."

The Florentine bowed to the will of the Pope.

"In that event, I again thank Your Holiness with all my heart for the safe-conduct you have given me. I shall make use of it to return to Florence, where Duke Alessandro awaits my return."

Paul frowned. He did not wish to lose his prize goldsmith. Particularly, he did not wish to lose him to a Medici Duke. The Farnese Pope did not like the Medici. He turned to one of his confidential servants.

"Let Benvenuto's pardon be granted without the usual term of imprisonment. Draw up his *motu-proprio* here, that all may be right with it; and as soon as we have signed it, see to its being properly registered at the Capitol. Well then, Benvenuto, have we pleased you in the matter?"

Cellini's thanks were unctuous. Not even a Pier Luigi would dare quibble with that order.

And so on the following Thursday, belching most of the way because of the stomach disorder that was still upon him, the Florentine walked in the solemn procession that filed a tortuous way along the crowded streets to Santa Maria sopra Minerva, and from there to Santa Maria Maggiore. It was a colorful cortege. First came the golden statue of the Virgin, borne aloft on the shoulders of ten nobles clothed in gowns of crimson damask. The Pope followed, riding on his white mule, and surrounded by his principal dignitaries. Behind him were the highest ranking officers of the Papal armies, in full panoply. Behind them, in magnificent disorder, rode the cardinals, archbishops, bishops, and other important prelates of the Holy See. A company of Swiss guards carrying pennons and banners, dazzled the eye with a continuous blaze of color. Then came the District Leaders of Rome, the *Caporioni,* gowned in blue and purple. The twelve outlaws came next, each flanked by two sponsors and sometimes preceded by an attendant who carried a lighted white torch or large wax candle. A horde of monks and friars belonging to various orders, ended the long train.

Thus, mingling with eleven thieves and felons of varying degree

323

and guilty of miscellaneous offenses, while a chorus of massed voices resounded the *Te Deum,* the procession wound its triumphant path to the basilica, and Cellini was shriven of his crime.

XLVI

THE FEVER STRUCK FOUR DAYS LATER, AN AGUE that alternately boiled and chilled the blood, burned and froze the flesh. Bernardo da Todi again came to probe and feel, chuckle and prescribe; but even Gaddi admitted that his medico was less than useless.

The best of the available doctors in Rome were called in to belabor and dose. The fever worsened. Cellini became delirious. The leeches muttered darkly, collectively shook their heads, and despaired of his life.

Not even Francesco da Norcia could find a ray of hope in the darkness of the cavern he explored. Like his colleagues he could make use only of what little knowledge was available.

"I am unable to determine the root of the malady," he complained to Gaddi and the ever-present Felice, with mounting irritation over his inability to do so. "This makes doubly difficult the possibility of purging it from his body. It is a certainty that this raging fever results from an ailment centered in the belly. You have noted he cannot retain any food other than thin liquids? And for two weeks he has complained of a stomach disorder. I fear for him. We will continue to make use of the remedies indicated by our art; but at the same time, Felice, indulge him. Give him whatever he asks for. Make him as comfortable as possible for whatever time remains. And mark you, as long as there is breath in him, do not hesitate to send for me, no matter what the hour. One thing more. Let a priest be summoned to administer the last rites of the Church."

A gray-robed Franciscan responded to the sick call, but the goldsmith could neither make Confession nor take Communion. The holy oil of Extreme Unction was administered while he raved and ranted at Felice, screaming at him to drive away the old scoundrel who was dragging him into a large boat.

"His raving increases," Gaddi whispered to the weeping Felice. "He has read Dante and in his present weakness imagines that Charon

324

of the *Inferno* comes to drag him into the barge and transport him across the river to Hell. Alas, this goes badly."

There were a few lucid hours during which Cellini talked reasonably with the friends thronged around his bedside. But old Charon remained even during these periods of calm. The specter became an obsession. Ludovico da Fano asked him to describe the phantasy.

"He is old and gnarled and unbelievably evil," gasped Cellini. "He wears a long black gown that covers him from neck to feet. There! Beside you! He is coming around the bed! Cannot you see for yourself? Bent and ugly, small and horrible, with the empty shrunken face of the damned! His eyes flame with the fire of the pit, and his hands are but skin and bone. Their touch as cold as... He clutches at me again! Felice! Drive him off! You hear me, Felice? Angela! Angela, help me! ...He is dragging me..."

Cellini relapsed into wild delirium.

After a long time the raving broke off abruptly and he went suddenly limp. The shuddering, labored breathing weakened, seemed to stop for minutes at a time, then altogether. Annibale Caro laid an ear against his friend's chest. He could hear no heartbeat. They waited for another hour. There was no change. Somewhere far off in the night a cock crowed. Da Fano felt the goldsmith's hands.

"He grows cold, *amici,*" he told them sadly. "He has expired. Let us go below and recite the prayers for the dead."

They pulled a sheet over the body and left it.

Felice ran all the way to Francesco da Norcia's house and pounded on the door until the doctor himself came down. Tearfully he begged the sleepy-eyed medico to come and see what he could do.

"What then has happened?" requested Francesco peevishly. "Has he become worse? How is he?"

"He is dead, Messer Franco," blurted Felice.

"Dead!"

Messer Francesco, after all, had his pride. He had served several Popes and, not for nothing, was regarded as one of the first physicians and surgeons of Rome. He had his dignity to uphold. Over and above this, in common with the old, he was cranky and did not relish being rudely awakened from a sound sleep at such an hour, to be informed of a patient's death.

"Dead! Then what the devil do you want of me?" he squalled. "I feel quite as sorrowful as you, for your partner was dear to me. But

325

I am not God! Of what use can I be to a dead man? What would you have me do—blow breath up through his rump and bring him back to life for you?"

Felice walked off, distraught and weeping.

"Come back here!" called the repentant Messer Francesco.

Felice ran back to the door.

The doctor brought out a small vial filled with an oily essence.

"There are times when men appear to be dead and are not. Take this oil and anoint Benvenuto's pulses and heart. Pinch his little fingers and toes sharply at frequent intervals; and if perchance he should revive, which is doubtful, send for me at once."

Most of the men had gone when Felice returned from his errand. Caro was still there and helped carry out the medico's instructions.

"Mattio is going to write to Benedetto Varchi in Florence and advise him of our friend's death, Felice. So you need not send advices there. All this," he added with a shake of his head, "is useless. There is nothing more to be done for our Benvenuto."

The faithful Felice would not leave off.

They rubbed and kneaded and pinched for three hours. The new day dawned. The sun rose. The goldsmith underwent no change. There was no sign of life . . . no pulse . . . no breath . . . no movement. Felice abandoned hope. He gave instructions to send for the corpse washers and for the preparation of a shroud.

And as he did so Cellini regained consciousness and began screaming at him to help Angela drive away the old terror who was dragging him into the boat.

Annibale Caro nearly fainted from shock.

Felice ran to the bedside, swinging frantically at the air around the bed, and yelling to Nuncio to fly for Messer Francesco.

The doctor arrived in record time. "Amazing!" he exclaimed. "We must do everything in our power to save him. Positively amazing! He has been brought back from the grave!" He sat and began writing out treatments, and made up a list of drugs, unguents, plasters, oils, lotions, perfumes, nostrums, spices, pastes, fomentations and fumigations . . . nothing was to be overlooked. He intended to try everything. "And now," he stated proudly, smacking his lips with the delight he felt— that essence had done this thing! "Let us bleed him."

Some twoscore leeches were attached to the goldsmith's buttocks and allowed to bore, suck and chew them to a pulp. He revived! The

326

fever subsided a little and the delirium passed. His friends and neighbors crowded into the room to see with their own eyes this miracle of a dead man restored to life.

Instead of sharing their joy, Cellini made out his will. His money, gold, silver, and jewels, were to be given to his sister Liperata. The remainder of his property, and fifty gold ducats, to his partner and friend, Felice.

Felice clapped him around the shoulders and told him he wanted only to see him well again.

"If you wish that," panted the Florentine, "hold tightly to me and drive away that old bastard who waits at the foot of the bed. He fears just two people, Angela and you!"

Annibale Caro gulped and looked anxious.

"That phantasy is still upon him," he mumbled nervously to Messer Francesco. "Has this severe fever unhinged his reason, do you think?"

"Who can say, my son," replied the medico gravely. "All we can do is hope otherwise. Meanwhile let him rest as much as possible. Felice, I charge you hold closely to the treatments I have written out. I will return later."

The illness dragged on with little or no improvement. The fever and the inability to hold food reduced the goldsmith to a wasted, shaking and quivering framework of skin drawn over bones; a meager skeleton with fever-bright eyes peering out of sunken sockets, and parched yellow skin drawn over a face that grimaced like a death's head.

Liperata and her husband arrived from Florence, thinking Cellini dead. They brought with them a sonnet Benedetto Varchi had composed to the memory of his lifelong friend. It was addressed to Mattio, the poet who had written him the news of Benvenuto's passing; but Liperata gave it to her brother, knowing that he would treasure it.

> *Who, Mattio, shall ease our pain and grief?*
> *Who now shall bid our flowing tears to cease?*
> *Alas! 'tis true—our friend hath found release*
> *And now is flown, leaving us here to grieve.*
>
> *He hath to Heaven flown; him who in Art's*
> *Immortal spheres was ever without peer.*
> *Yet midst the mighty dead he hath no peer!*
> *Nor in this world his like shall more be seen.*

O tender soul, if from thy place above
Thou can'st look down on him who lovèd thee,
View tears which mourn thy loss and not thy works.

Now thou on thy Creator's face dost gaze,
Him who this world created; and can'st see
The Form thy skill hath here so oft' expressed.

Francesco da Norcia stopped in two or three times each day, always bringing in some new remedy, hoping to come upon the means of restoring and strengthening that wracked and pinched body. He was at his wits' end, despairing of what to try next. Nothing seemed to help. Cellini was tormented by a raging thirst, and not even this could be assuaged. For it was agreed that he should be limited to small quantities of liquids, lest the fever be given additional fuel and so rise again.

One morning Felice was called out to attend to a shop matter, and while he was gone Cellini half-wakened and called out. The servant woman came in and softly asked what he wished.

He looked uncomprehendingly up at her through fevered eyes. "Angela?...Is it really you?" He gazed intently and sadly shook his head. "No...No, you are not Angela..."

"What do you wish, Master Benvenuto?" the woman asked again. "Can I get something for you?"

"Bid Angela come to me," rattled the goldsmith. "My Angela... and have her bring some water. Water! That crystal water cooler over there, filled to the brim with clear fresh water!"

The maid worried her lips for a moment, nodded to herself, and ran to fill and bring it.

Nuncio looked on, shook his head, but said nothing.

"Put it to my lips and let me drink..." He gulped down a good flask-full of the liquid. *"Domineddio!"* he quavered, "though it kills me, it was worth it. Never have I tasted anything sweeter than that."

He sank back and fell into a deep, coma-like sleep. The woman covered him. He began to sweat. Perspiration oozed out of his pores and drooled down his skin like rain.

Felice returned and asked how the master was getting on.

"I don't know," answered the lackey. "He awoke while you were gone and asked for water. The servant wench brought him that cooler full of it and he drank nearly all of it. He has been sleeping heavily since."

"Good Christ in Heaven! And you allowed her to do it?" He hit Nuncio a cuff on the side of the head. "This means his death!" Pale with anger and concern, Felice grabbed up a wood stave from a pile near the fireplace and began beating the servant girl. "You traitorous bitch!" he screamed while he laid on, "you knew he was not to have water! You have killed him!" The whacks beat an accompaniment to the maid's screams.

Cellini was dreaming. A soothing, marvelous dream. He was lying on a lush grassy bank, near a murmuring river, and Angela was there beside him, drawing soft, cool fingers over his brow and breathing her sweet cool breath against his cheek. Then, suddenly and inexplicably, the scene darkened and changed. He was in a deep, ugly cavern, standing helpless by the shore of that awful River. Old Charon was stepping out of his boat, coming toward him with stout ropes in his hands. This time the specter intended to bind him tight before transporting him on that dread river journey. A taste of salt was strong in his mouth. The touch of those dank bony fingers, so different from Angela's soft caress, made him writhe in revulsion. His throat was so constricted he could not utter a sound. Just at that moment Felice came dashing up, pulled Angela out of the way, and struck the horrible Ferryman a blow with an ax. Charon went reeling back, screaming in terror: "Let me go! Let me go! and I promise not to return!"

He awoke. The servant girl was running around the room, screaming at the top of her lungs. His brain was strangely clear and lucid. The haze which had been cast over it was gone.

"Do not harm her, Felice!" he cried as loudly as he could. "Leave her alone, I pray you. She has saved my life. I feel much improved. Only lend a hand that I may change my bed clothing." He was soaked with sweat.

In the middle of the commotion Francesco da Norcia walked in, followed by his colleague, Ser Bernardo. Felice hastily explained.

"Oh power of Nature!" exulted Messer Francesco. "She indeed knows her needs, and we who are doctors know nothing at all!"

"Ha-ha," gabbled Bernardo. "It's a great pity he didn't drink all that water. It would have cured him on the spot. All along I have had it in mind to try water purges for this disorder of his."

329

"Bah!" The old doctor gave his colleague a baleful look. He had never thought very highly of Ser Bernardo. "You bray like an ass!"

"Messer Franco!"

"*Minchione!*" snorted the old fellow. "I repeat, you bray like an ass! Here, I will prove my words ... Benvenuto—" he turned to the wide-awake goldsmith who looked better than he had in weeks "—could you have drunk more water?"

"No. That which I drank satisfied my needs and quenched my thirst completely."

"Note well that fact," Francesco scowled at his brother-medico. "Nature has seen to her precise needs, taking neither more nor less than she required. Further, if you were of the mind that Benvenuto's recovery would have been aided by water purges, why did you not say so? If you had, you could now take credit for a very difficult cure."

Ser Bernardo stuck his beard in the air and stalked indignantly out of the room.

When Cardinal Cornaro heard of the goldsmith's improvement, he offered to send him to a villa of his at Monte Cavallo. The hospitality was quickly accepted by Messer Franco, who ordered his patient transported there at once. Cellini made the journey in a chair, wrapped in blankets against the cold.

The final stages of the ailment erupted minutes after the goldsmith arrived at the place. He began to vomit, spewing endlessly. A part of this regurgitation was saved to show to the doctor. No one could say what it was that had come up. It looked like a large worm, about a quarter of an arm's length in size, speckled green and black and red, and covered with long hairs.

When he saw it, Francesco shook his head in wonder. It was beyond him. But he knew, instinctively, that this meant the end of the malady.

"Now that you are cured of your disease, Neutino, beware of irregularities until you are stronger. You have been knocking on death's door these many weeks. You can die, you know? What is more, one day you will. Now that God has spared you so that you may execute more of your fine works, give thought to yourself. Let immortality wait, and attend to your recovery."

XLVII

W HEN ANOTHER WEEK PASSED WITHOUT IM-
provement, Cellini resolved that if die he must, he would do so in his
native land. The fever was gone. There was no pain. He was eating—a
little. But his weakness made life a burden. He and Felice set out for
Florence, the goldsmith traveling in a basket lined with straw.

He arrived home in time to learn that Duke Alessandro wanted to
hang him. His sister laughed and wept in the same breath. Niccolò da
Monte Aguto rushed to him with the news.

"I've heard the Duke say it would have been better if you died in
Rome, Neutino. You have come here only to put your head in a noose."

"Hang me for what, Niccolò?"

"For being a traitor to the State!"

"And who accused me of being that?"

"That bastard of a Giorgio Vasari!" exclaimed Niccolò. Having
seen Alessandro in action, he was concerned for his goldsmith friend.
"He was egged on to the thing by Ottaviano de' Medici—and damn
him to hell too! They have inflamed the Duke against you. You know
of the Ippolito affair? The petition he was carrying when he...he
died? Well, Giorgio told the Duke he heard you boast, in Rome, that
when the time came you would be among the first to leap the walls of
Florence and turn the tyrant over to his enemies, the exiles."

"Nonsense! I have been very ill and have not so much as set eyes
on Vasari in Rome. Also, I never take part or sides in these political
squabbles. This is known."

"I know," Niccolò answered bitterly. "But what does my knowing
it amount to if the Duke believes otherwise? As I say, the words were
put into Giorgio's offensive mouth by Ottaviano. What displeasure have
you given to that evil man?"

"Ottaviano? None! It was the other way around. He caused several
of my dies to be ruined and we bickered over the matter. I complained

to the Duke who promised to look into the thing. I suppose he put him in his place. He's behind this, hey?"

"Of course. While you are here in Florence be careful what you do, and above all, what you say. I hope the Duke doesn't send to take you."

"Why should he? I am unable to get about and can go nowhere. Niccolò, when will you see the Duke?"

"Today, I am going to the palace from here."

"Then please remind him that Pope Clement also wished to hang me, and just as wrongfully. Ask him to give me time to recover a little, and I will show him the error of this absurd plot against me."

Felice returned to Rome to look after the shop. Cellini remained in Florence in the care of Liperata, and after several weeks' rest felt up to the ordeal of facing the Duke of Florence. He had himself carried to the Palazzo Medici. Alessandro was not there. He was attending a Council meeting and was not expected to return for some time.

"Put me down on the terrace near the entrance," requested Cellini. "I will wait for him."

An hour later Alessandro strolled up surrounded by courtiers. He paused in front of the goldsmith, staring down with interest.

"My lord." The withered and shrunken Cellini may have been ill but there was no whine in his voice as he spoke. "I have come here to demand justice! The charges made against me are false. They must be tried and put to a test. I will not allow myself to be traduced in this manner by a worthless ass. I must be cleared!"

Alessandro shrugged indifferently. He hadn't really put much credence in the chatter about Benvenuto. One and one did not equal three. Cellini was an artist, and like most recognized masters kept strictly apart from politics and political factions.

"Take heed to regaining your health, Benvenuto," he told him shortly. "Forget the rest. It means nothing and has deceived no one." He passed inside.

His attendants followed at his heels, smiling down at the goldsmith. Lorenzino still looked bored. As he strolled by he smiled the weakest, most fragile smile that could be smiled, waved a hand languidly, and walked into the palace after the Duke.

Niccolò was flabbergasted.

"How you managed it I'll never understand!" he told his friend that night. "You escaped a dreadful peril, believe me. Varchi has no doubt told you that here in Florence a day rarely goes by without someone being executed or exiled at Alessandro's order. I thought your fate to be indelibly inscribed. Take my advice, Neutino. As soon as ever you can, get away from here. Ottaviano is not going to take this upset calmly."

Cellini stayed in Florence until he was able to ride. When he was strong enough to do that he started back to Rome, saying nothing to Duke Alessandro or to anyone else. He no longer looked like something one might set out in a field to frighten off the crows. He was eating like a famished mule and filling out to his old self. On the road south he took his pleasure, traveling by easy stages and stopping off frequently. By the time he reached the capital he was ready to get back to work.

He began to cut Alessandro's medal in steel. He wrote to Lorenzino and asked him to send the promised subject for the reverse so that he could complete the commission. That eternally bored courtier responded that, night and day, he gave thought to nothing else and would send the thing along as soon as he was able to. Meanwhile, the goldsmith worked on the portrait die.

He worked slowly and carefully, intending to make of it an outstanding and exceptional performance. And such indeed it proved to be. The head was so well done that he took to showing it off a bit to the frequent visitors that dropped in every day to pass the time in the Cellini studio.

One of these callers was Francesco Soderini, an elderly nobleman and inveterate foe of the House of Medici, and one of the too numerous Florentine exiles. The old fellow nearly strangled when the goldsmith, inadvertently perhaps, showed him the portrait of Alessandro.

"Pah! Cruel wretch that you are!" he exploded. "To think that you, a Florentine, would strive to immortalize that tyrant! That raging beast! A single look at this medal proves that it is your finest effort in that art, and amply demonstrates that you are our enemy and their friend. *Sciocco! Imbecille!*" Messer Soderini was frothing. "Both Clement and Alessandro had it in mind to hang you without cause. That was the Father and the Son! ... Beware now of the Holy Ghost!"

"My dear Messer Franco," soothed the goldsmith, "pray, compose yourself. This, for me, is merely another commission, nothing more."

"*Che palle!*" retorted the angry exile. "I swear it by all the saints in heaven, at the very first opportunity I will rob you of those dies and destroy them!"

"My thanks for telling me so, Messer Franco," Cellini calmly answered, knowing only too well that the fiery old codger's hatred for Alessandro was such, he would do just that. "I shall take good care that you never see them again."

The half-finished medal was put aside to await the reverse from Lorenzino. The shop was busy, but on run-of-the-mill work. As a result, when Pope Paul sent an excited summons ordering the goldsmith to drop everything and repair instantly to the Papal palace, Cellini rushed to the Pontiff, hoping and praying that some worthwhile commission was in the offing. He was informed that a matter had come up, of the greatest importance and most extreme urgency.

"We have just received advices," Paul told him excitedly, "that the Emperor Charles is to pay us a visit. He is now resting in Naples from the rigors of his victorious campaign in Tunis and will shortly leave for here. His Catholic Majesty graciously means to pay his respects. Wherefore we would hear your ideas concerning a suitable gift of honor which we shall make him on his arrival. Bear in mind, Benvenuto, that this must needs be fitting to his high station as well as our own. Think on this, and give us some marvelous conception— one that will be fitting and which might possibly be finished by the time he arrives here."

The goldsmith went through all the motions of a man engaged in deep thought.

"It seems to me, Holy Father, that a crucifix—a golden crucifix, richly worked—would not be amiss of the occasion when one considers that you are the Vicar of Christ on earth. I have already on hand a finished group of three figures which will serve admirably as a part of the base for such a work. This in itself would cut the time necessary to complete the whole by half. Such a worthy gift would confer high honor on Your Holiness as the donor, as well as on myself for creating it."

Pope Paul screwed up his mouth and nodded wisely. "Your idea appears to us a good one," he ventured. "Yet all must necessarily depend on the piece itself. On the design of it. Run, Benvenuto, and make it in wax so that we may see how it will appear."

Cellini ran. To the three figures of Faith, Hope, and Charity, made for the never finished chalice of Pope Clement, he added a base and a cross of yellow wax. While he worked on it a thought struck him which made him smile. Ever since his recovery he had been waiting for

334

his enemies at court to begin anew with their malicious troublemaking. And now, for the next few months at any rate, he would be safe. Not Pier Luigi, not Traiano or anyone else, would dare make a move so long as he was engaged on this present emergency for the Pontiff.

In two days he finished the wax model and rushed to the Pope with it.

Paul was completely satisfied and quickly came to full agreement on all points, including the price for the work.

"Do you wait a bit and we will have the gold brought in," the Pope told him.

"Not so, Blessed Father. It is too late at night." It was close to midnight, no time to be carrying gold around the streets of Rome. "Please to have this made ready and I will return early in the morning. It will be safer thus."

The Pope nodded and ordered Latino Juvenale to see to it.

But when Cellini called on that courtier the next morning, Juvenale was insolent and very arrogant.

"It is for us nobles to invent, and for you artificers to execute according to our desires," he informed the goldsmith by way of salutation. "After you left here last night we thought of something far superior to your conception, and it is this we mean to have you execute."

Cellini countered with a black look. Disparage his work or nail him to a cross—it amounted to the same thing.

"What new stupidity is this?" he snapped out. "Superior work? Let me make it clear that neither you nor the Pope can think of anything superior to a work in which the figure of Christ plays a part! Now get on with your courtier's nonsense and tell me what you have to!"

Without another word Juvenale rose and stalked haughtily out of the room. He went in to the Pope and tried in every way he knew to have the work given over to another goldsmith. Paul flatly refused and ordered that Cellini be summoned at once.

"Your answer to the presumptuous words spoken to you was proper and entirely correct, Benvenuto," he told the goldsmith, while his favorite flushed a bright red. "However, we have changed our mind and wish to make use of a handsomely illuminated Book of Hours which has come to us from the estate of the Cardinal de' Medici. This will admirably serve our purpose. Afterwards, we can return to your idea in connection with another gift we have in mind. Now to get to

335

the missal, we wish to have the book enclosed between covers of massive gold, richly ornamented and adorned with jewels. We shall turn all the materials over to you here and now so that you may begin work immediately."

Cellini did not argue. He accepted the commission and left the Vatican with gold, jewels, and illuminated manuscript, to a value of well over eight thousand crowns. He went briskly to work and had the cover well advanced when the Emperor arrived in Rome.

Triumphal arches had been erected. The mood of the city was gay. The entry of such a personage as a victorious emperor was certain to be a sumptuous and an entertaining event. All along the route the streets were jammed with madly cheering thousands who had forgotten or were willing to overlook the fact that the man they cheered was the man responsible for having their city sacked.

The Emperor's entry had all the pomp and splendor that was expected, and more. Princely courtiers and dignitaries, resplendent in robes lavishly garnished with gold and gems, rode horses caparisoned in brocade trappings, gold and silver stirrups, and jeweled bridles. Any horse and rider there could have ransomed a city.

Charles himself was rather somber by comparison. He rode a white horse and wore black, with few jewels. A splendid cape, trimmed with ermine, drooped from his round shoulders. A black hat sat rakishly on his head, with a ring of silky white plumes around the brim.

Behind him came a personal bodyguard of two hundred knights, clad in damascened parade armor. The ladies of the retinue traveled in litters curtained with gold brocade. The multitudes of servants, down to the meanest kitchen slave, were dressed in silks and velvets—trumpeters, musicians, acrobats, jesters and dwarfs, hundreds of them. Huntsmen in sturdy wool held the leashes of three hundred couple of hounds. Falconers marched with the bird assigned to each perched on leather-covered wrists. There were companies of musketeers, halberdiers, pikemen and crossbowmen. Gaudily dressed pages sprayed handfuls of coins into the multitudes that packed the streets. Constables and city guards armed with long wood staves thumped and whacked at such of the populace who pushed out of line or were forced out by the wild scramble for the silver coins. Cries of *"larghezza! ... larghezza!"* mingled with screams and groans as the clubs slammed down against heads and shoulders. A few skulls may have been cracked, but this in no wise detracted from the high lustre and glamor of the occasion.

336

In all, some fifteen thousand souls made up the retinue of this one king—His Imperial Catholic Majesty, the Holy Roman Emperor, Charles V.

After the parade there was feasting in the streets. Oxen stuffed with smaller animals were roasted whole, hacked apart, and passed out to all comers. Bread and cakes of every description were distributed from all sides. Wine barrels were broached on every street corner from the Ponte San Angelo to the Ghetto degli Abrei. One of the triumphal arches erected in the center of the line of march was crowned with two Imperial eagles perched between couchant lions. From their gilded beaks, into cup-shaped troughs, there spewed continuous streams of wine—one white, the other red. By nightfall the populace was in a stupor of drunken frolic.

Directly on his arrival at the Vatican, Charles presented the Pope with a diamond valued at twelve thousand ducats.

Paul sent for Cellini, bidding him bring the missal in its present unfinished state.

"This diamond," the Pope told him, "we desire to be made into a ring to the measure of our finger; but first Benvenuto—" Paul was distressed by the unfinished appearance of his gift to the Emperor "—let us hear your advice. What apology can we make to His Majesty for the uncompleted condition of this our gift to him?"

"It can be pointed out that my illness prevented this, Your Holiness. His Majesty will certainly notice my present thin and somewhat wasted condition and will readily believe this to be true."

"Excellently thought on!" Paul slapped the arm of his chair. "The suggestion is good, and it pleases us. But look you, Benvenuto, when you present the book to the Emperor you must add that, in our name, you are being presented along with the work."

"Let Your Holiness trust me implicitly. I shall carry out your wishes to your complete credit and satisfaction."

Paul's nod was a little dubious. "*Va bene!* We may say that you would acquit yourself nobly if you have the courage to address the Emperor with the same spirit in which you address us."

Cellini let his brows arch. "Holy Father, be assured that I shall be at far greater ease. The Emperor is but a man like myself. While in the person of Your Sacred Holiness I look upon a far superior human, a near divinity, adorned as you are in the ecclesiastical robes

337

of your high and holy office, to say nothing of the dignity of bearing which results from Your Sanctity's venerable age."

Paul beamed with pleasure. "Go, then, Benvenuto," he smiled, "it can be seen that you are a man of parts. Do us honor, for it will be to your advantage."

The Pope ordered out two Turkish horses which had belonged to Clement—a stallion and a mare—which were to be presented to the Emperor by Messer Durante, a Papal chamberlain and the Prefect of the *Camera*.

Together with that nobleman Cellini walked down the long hall to the chamber where the Emperor was resting. The horses, each led by a groom, entered first. They were so spirited and handsome that everyone in the room, including Charles, looked on with interest.

Cellini and Durante advanced with all eyes upon them, the courtier stumbling along in a splay-footed walk that resembled the waddling of a duck. It was Durante's misfortune to be awkward and ungainly. He lacked grace of person, and the effect was heightened by the awe he felt. He fumbled a great deal and panted as if from fatigue.

The goldsmith, on the other hand, advanced lightly and surely. He was not over-impressed. To him, emperors, kings, princes and nobles, were simply men favored by fortune and the accident of birth. He strode confidently forward to the dais at the far end of the room, studying the Emperor with lively curiosity the while. So this was the mighty Charles of Austria? They were both of an age, having been born in the same year. Yet Charles looked twice his years.

He was of middle height, bent and stooped, wan looking and a little lumpy. He had keen eyes and a nose that beaked out a bit at the center. His chin was so large and long it gave the lower half of his face a misshapen look, not entirely hidden by his beard. He was again wearing black—a taffeta gown, with a loose jerkin over it. A furred hat of Flemish origin had a heavy seam across its crown, making it look like a giant codpiece. There was a thin gold chain around his neck, holding a diamond encrusted pendant.

Three paces from the dais Cellini halted, the covered missal under an arm. Durante stumbled up to Charles and made a floundering obeisance. Even the Emperor smiled. He began to deliver the speech Pope Paul had taught him.

Cellini peered more closely at Charles.

The monarch had a jaded look, pale lips. His breath was short

338

and wheezy with asthma. His mouth hung open; the misshapen chin would not allow his teeth to close properly. He suffered from gout. One foot was swollen. A gold-headed cane rested against his chair. His legs were reedy and looked very weak.

The table was laden with food: stewed beef, roast mutton, baked hare, and a capon. There was a heavy gold goblet and several pitchers and flagons. Charles was something of a glutton. He favored Rhenish wine and put away flasks of it at every meal.

Durante was near the end of his speech. Cellini uncovered his work.

The Emperor's eyes swung toward him.

The goldsmith advanced as Durante shuffled back, swept off his cap and bowed, sinking slowly to one knee. Unlike the unfortunate Durante, the gesture showed poise, elegance and charm—as it was intended it should.

"Sacred Majesty, our Holy Father, Pope Paul, sends this illuminated Book of Hours with this cover of wrought gold as a gift to Your Supreme Highness. And since the cover is not yet finished by reason of my severe illness, His Holiness makes a gift of myself, together with the book, in order that I may complete it to the full satisfaction and pleasure of Your Majesty, and to do your will in any other work."

Charles nodded affably. "This superb work is most acceptable to me, and so, also, are you. However, it is my desire that you complete it for me here in Rome. When it is finished, and you are restored to health, you will bring it to me, Master Benvenuto."

Cellini's eyes widened. He had no idea that the Emperor knew him by name.

Charles cleared that up with his next remark.

"Some time ago, I saw that morse you made for Pope Clement. We discussed it at length. Admirable!"

The delighted goldsmith chatted easily with the monarch on various topics relating to the arts. When a lull occurred, he bowed and retired.

As he did so Charles summoned a chamberlain. "Let five hundred gold crowns be given over to Master Benvenuto immediately."

The gold was brought to the Papal suite and the assembled courtiers were asked which of them was the Pope's man who had spoken with the Emperor.

Messer Durante quickly stepped forward—and took the five hundred crowns.

The not-yet-fully-recovered Cellini almost came down with another fever. He complained bitterly to the Pope.

Paul told him not to be uneasy. "We know how the thing happened. We know, further, that you have conducted yourself well and ably and with high honor; and of that money, we shall certainly see to it that you obtain your just share."

XLVIII

THE POPE WAS ANXIOUS TO HAVE HIS NEW DIAmond set in a ring. The missal, he pointed out to Cellini, could now wait a bit. It had been presented to the Emperor and the whole business had come off very well. Charles would soon be leaving to visit his future son-in-law in Florence, and from there he was going north to engage with the French with whom he was again at war. His mind would be fully occupied for months. Thus there was no longer any need to hurry the book along.

The Florentine set to work on it. It was a difficult stone to set, and even more difficult to tint properly. The present tint and setting were the work of the ablest jeweler in Venice, the great Miliano Targhetta. To Cellini fell the task of competing with the excellence of this renowned master, and, if possible, of surpassing it. Pope Paul did all he could to help. He sent four of the best jewelers in Rome to the goldsmith's studio to act as consultants. Cellini got along fine with three of them. The fourth, one Gaio of Milan, was naturally hostile, being a Milanese.

The group discussed the stone and deliberated. The diamond was somewhat thin, and unless it was tinted and foiled in exactly the right manner and with exactly the right coloring, its brilliancy would not be enhanced and the whole effect of its beauty spoiled. It was a trying test of knowledge and skill.

"You must positively keep Miliano's tint, Benvenuto," prated Gaio. "You yourself know that tinting a diamond is the most delicate and difficult process in the jeweler's art, and Miliano is easily the greatest of living jewelers."

There, the jeweler-goldsmith from Florence had ideas of his own. "I glory in competing with so able a master," he answered sharply. Then, ignoring Gaio, he turned to the others, "Observe, gentlemen, I am preserving Miliano's coloring material. I will try to equal or better this. If I cannot improve upon it, we will recolor the gem as it was."

"Eh," sniffed Gaio. "Do but equal that superb tint and I will doff my cap to you!"

"And if I should surpass it, what then? This will merit two liftings of your cap?"

"*Certo*," agreed the pompous Milanese, smiling around to his colleagues. "But permit me to remind you that you have not yet equalled it, much less surpassed it. Talk is one thing, performance another."

The goldsmith began compounding the pigmented gum-mastic tints. He was frequently up before dawn and as frequently continued his experiments into the night, galled into feverish activity by the sneering Gaio, who called every day to inquire sarcastically how he was coming on. The Emperor left Rome for Florence and treated the populace to another parade. Cellini did not bother with it. A journeyman and a shopboy were brought in from the shop to help out with the work in the studio. He prepared hundreds of tints, tested them, discarded, improved, selected ...

When he was ready to show results he summoned the four consultants.

"First of all," he told them, "I will tint the stone with Miliano's coloring."

He did so and showed it around.

There were grave nods of approval. A beautiful thing, Miliano's coloring.

"Now, I will tint it again with a coloring of my own ..."

Cleaning off the stone, Cellini retinted and passed it around again.

"*Corpo di sangue!*" One of the four, his old friend Raffaello del Moro, shouted gleefully. "He has done it! Benvenuto has surpassed Miliano's tint!"

Gaio could not believe what he saw. He took the gem and examined it scrupulously. "Christ! It's worth two thousand ducats more!"

"And now," crowed the Florentine cockerel in his grandest manner, "let us see if I can surpass myself ... Wait here a bit." He cleaned the stone again and went off to a little cabinet.

He returned with the stone tinted anew.

Gaio's eyes enlarged to the size of saucers.

"I can't believe it. By God, this is witchcraft! I would now value this gem at eighteen thousand ducats, whereas we ourselves valued it at twelve. I'm going to tell the Pope of this. I shall ask that Benvenuto receive a thousand crowns reward for the tinting and setting of it." Gaio had the ear of the Pontiff at his disposal. He held a position similar to that of the late Pompeo.

True to his word he hurried to the Pope and told him what he had witnessed. "A miracle!" he exclaimed. Paul sent messengers three times that day, to ask if the ring was finished.

It was locked in its setting at twenty-three o'clock, and hurriedly carrried to the Palazzo Papale. Cellini approached the door of Paul's study and drew aside the drapery.

The Pope was in private audience with the Marquis del Vasto, Viceroy of Milan, who had come south to try to sway Paul from his neutral stand in the war between Spain and France. He was not succeeding.

"We tell you, no!" the Pope was insisting as the goldsmith raised the drapery. "In this matter we intend to remain neutral and nothing else!"

He saw the movement at the door. "Who is there?" he called.

Cellini stepped into the room and presented the ring. Paul drew aside to examine it, while the Marquis retired to one end of the room, openly irritated by the intrusion.

"Benvenuto," whispered the Pontiff, turning the ring to various angles, "begin a conversation of some sort and do not leave off speaking so long as that man remains in the room."

Selecting the tinting of diamonds as his subject, Cellini discoursed for an hour and a half before the fuming Alfonson d'Avalos' knees began to wobble and forced him to leave. The goldsmith hardly blamed him for the anger visible on his face.

The Pope was amused and highly pleased.

"Go, now, Benvenuto, and in a little while I will give you an even better reward for your service than the thousand crowns Gaio tells me your work deserves."

As the Florentine withdrew, the courtiers in attendance crowded around the Pope to examine the ring. There was high praise. The Pope beamed.

"We are much pleased with the diligent manner in which this worthy master is serving us. We mean to find a suitable reward and repay him for such high merit and devotion to our needs."

It was the opening Latino Juvenale had long waited for. He pursed his lips thoughtfully and looked with serious eyes at the seated Pope Paul.

"There is no doubt that Benvenuto is a master of unquestioned genius," he averred. "It is also true that everyone naturally feels more good will for his own countrymen than for others. Still and all, one ought to consider well the manner in which one may properly speak of a Pope!"

The touchy Paul frowned slightly. His fingers began to comb his beard. "What do you mean, Messer Latino? We do not entirely understand."

The courtier lied with easy grace. He was wise in the ways of courts, and he knew the Farnese Pope.

"Blessed Father, this Benvenuto has had the audacity to state that Pope Clement was the finest, the most talented and distinguished Pontiff ever to attain the Papacy, and that history would so record his reign but for the fact that he was cursed with ill fortune for the greater part of it. He has said further that Your Holiness is—is exactly the opposite ..." the courtier faltered very effectively. "I ... I do not care to say more ..." Latino affected to be embarrassed. Messer Ambrogio and Traiano nodded to the Pontiff, supporting the allegations.

Paul's face had become a dark cloud. "Get on with it," he rumbled. "What did he say of *me?*"

"*E bene*," Latino sighed and drew a handkerchief across his lips. "Your Sanctity must hold me excused for words I only repeat. He said that on your head the tiara weeps; that you seem a trussed-up bundle of straw, clothed in finery; that in statecraft you are next door to a dolt! And that you wallow in perpetual good fortune."

Juvenale had chosen the right kind of ammunition. Each barbed shaft struck the target squarely. Paul writhed inwardly. If there was one man he thoroughly hated it was Clement VII. He hated even the memory of the late Pope, whose internecine maneuvering had robbed him of years of the Papacy—the one all-absorbing passion and ambition of his life. But for the Medici he would have attained the

343

Chair years before. He despised the man, his House, anything and everything connected with the name.

Paul shrugged off the words as the prattling of a low craftsman—a donkey, beneath contempt. But from that moment on the Florentine goldsmith's favor began to decline.

Cellini perceived it at once. No longer was there the free and easy access to the Papal apartments he had long enjoyed. It became difficult to see the Pope; and when he did see him Paul was coldly formal and distant. Cellini had frequented courts for too long a time not to see that something was amiss. For a time he thought it was the doing of Pier Luigi. He made inquiries. Gaddi finally weakened to the point where he told him what happened, but he would not name the calumniator. The goldsmith never could discover the man's name. Every friend he had at court flatly refused to name him—and for good reason. They knew Cellini would kill him. They also knew that if the goldsmith killed the Papal favorite, his own life would be forfeit.

The cover for the Book of Hours was taken up again. Enough work remained to be done on it to keep the goldsmith and the young journeyman from the shop fully occupied.

A commission came in for a large shield, to complete a panoply of parade armor. Cellini brought in another journeyman from the shop, an expert Perugian, to help out with the work on hand, so that he could start on the new commission, and began to design an oval buckler, well over the length of a man's arm in size. But the work came hard. He was fretting and stewing over the trouble with the Pope. He had to keep one eye on Pier Luigi and half the other on Traiano and the Milanese. What small portion of sight and mind remained he divided between the gold book cover and the new shield. The gold cover fulfilled his every requirement for such a work. But the design for the shield began to worry him.

Up until now, the squalling, the bickering and the brawling he had engaged in had never interfered with the ideal he had set for himself—his constant striving to achieve creative perfection. But, as he worked on this new design, he was beginning to take note that the harassment in which he was constantly involved was making inroads in the artistic quality of his work. The mere suspicion of such a possibility was enough to create agony. He threw away the design he was working on and started another, one which contained nine allegorical scenes, each

344

to be carved in low-relief. He worked with the utmost care and when this was finished he examined the cartoon with a severely critical eye. It was good, but at the same time there was the nagging thought in his head that he should have been able to do better—much better. Fretfully, he began to model the figures for the scenes, carving these on soft wax plaques. Three of these were feminine figures, and this brought in a new model—the lovely Joanna. She was a ravishing brunette. Sultry. Black-haired. Almond-eyed. Full-lipped and full-breasted. Beautifully formed... And what she did most was remind him of Angela. The which, added to all his other woes, served to make him the most completely miserable male in all of Italy.

Benedetto Varchi sent word that Duke Alessandro had married Charles' fifteen-year-old bastard daughter, as had been planned for so long. The ceremony had been very colorful, performed amid great pomp in the church of San Lorenzo. While reading the letter Cellini recalled the Duke's unfinished medal and resolved to complete it as soon as the two commissions in the studio were out of the way.

The book cover was finished first; and when he carried it to the Pontiff, Paul could not refrain from praising it. His coldness quickly returned, however, and he again became distant and aloof.

"Your Holiness will remember," Cellini reminded him hopefully, "that the Emperor voiced the desire that I accompany this work." It was too much to hope for, but if he could transfer to the patronage of the royal Charles...

"We shall do as we think fit in the matter," the Pope rejoined frigidly. "For yourself, you have performed your part of the affair very well." He beckoned to his secretary. "Messer Ambrogio, we charge you see to it that Master Benvenuto shall be well paid for the work he has done." He waved the goldsmith out.

A note telling him that the money was ready came the next day, and Cellini made an expectant call for it. He received five hundred crowns, and an itemized account. One hundred and fifty crowns in payment for the diamond ring, three hundred and fifty for the gold book cover—the last a time-consuming work, richly ornamented with figures, swirling arabesques, jewel settings and enamel work, which by itself should have brought a thousand crowns. He was a recognized master of the first rank. He had given months of labor, masterful artistry and skill to the work. He maintained an expensive shop and studio, employed the most highly skilled journeymen he could find. All this in order to assure the highest order of craftsmanship and finish for the creations of his hand and mind. And it was being paid for with the figurative equivalent of a sack of chestnuts.

Cellini the business man said not a word, but glumly took up the money and turned homeward. The insufficient returns he had just received, though bothersome, were not what concerned him most. The fear that was growing in him, gnawing at him, was the realization of what was happening to Cellini the artist; for the artist in him would not and could not be gulled. This part of him had seen that the handwriting on the wall was plainly to be read, and that he would be a fool to disregard it. He must act, and act quickly, before it was too late! The situation here in Rome had reached the point where it was interfering with the artistic merit of his work—and this must never be permitted to occur! Money, and the success its possession implied, were one thing. He wanted them, of course. Any man wanted these things. They were normal desires. Brawling and bickering, which satisfied his ego and spirit, he loved for their own sake. But first, last, and always, he was an artist! The Almighty had created him for this end, and it was to this end that he had dedicated his life.

It was clear that he could no longer hope to attain the perfection he strove for, here in Rome. He must leave this city and start off anew somewhere else, where did not matter so long as his mind and imagination could return to the path from which they were straying. Yet where could he go? It was quite a question, that. Should he return to Florence? No, he would not go back to Florence. He had as many envious enemies in Florence as in Rome. Well—almost as many; and these would prove an obstacle for what he had to do. Naples? There were too many memories in Naples. Angela! Spain, perhaps? No, it was pointless even to attempt to storm the busy Charles. He was forever chasing here and there to fight another war. Where, then? Some of the men he had known in Florence, exiles now, had entered the service of France and were writing glowing accounts of King Francis. His valor in war. His passion for the arts, of which he was a great patron, and of his desire to bring the culture and learning of Italy into his country. He was said to be very partial to Italian masters. Why not go there? Why not go to France and seek the patronage of Francis?

Scowling over his thoughts he walked unseeingly to his house door, nearly running into a little cart drawn up close by the entrance. The two donkeys hitched to it looked at him with their usual drooping

346

docility. The carter dozed peacefully on his perch, unmindful of the fact that the boxes and bundles in his conveyance thus stood exposed and unguarded behind him.

Still scowling Cellini pushed into his downstairs studio. The two journeymen, Ascanio and Girolamo, were whistling and busy at their work, the shopboy running to and fro, watchful and alert to be of service. All three glanced expectantly up as the master entered; but seeing the thunder and lightning in his eyes, said nothing as he stomped upstairs, muttering and angry, to put away the coin. He flung back his apartment door, stepped inside—and halted with an incredulous stare. The bag of crowns fell with a thump as he stood motionless, his mouth hanging foolishly agape.

Angela was standing near the center of the room, looking timidly and anxiously at him, leaning slightly against the long heavy table.

XLIX

SHE WAS STANDING TENSELY, BREATHING deeply, as if frightened, and now and then weaving a little, even while she half-leaned a hip against the table. Her fists were tightly clenched as she looked at the startled goldsmith, and her eyes had that wet gleam which is but a hair's breath removed from tears. There was a small, a very small, smile trying hard to appear cheerful as it played around her lips. It was wan and tentative. Undecided. Hopeful.

She expelled a long breath and shook her head wearily.

"I ... I had to ... come ..."

The tears came as Cellini ran to hold her close. Nothing mattered now. Not anything! Angela had returned to him. She was here—his again! All the pent-up yearning, the tormented longing for her, made him tremble as he strained to press her closer to him, his mouth crushing hungrily over hers, making her gasp for air as he kissed her furiously, on her lips, her eyes and cheeks, her nose and chin, her neck and throat, her shoulders. Angela had returned! Without her, life had been an empty gesture. Like the words of a song for which there is no tune. Living was the futility of extending one's hand to pluck the moon from the sky. The arm reached out, but there had been no Angela to see, to touch, to hold. And now!—

"My love," he whispered, kissing her eyes again and tasting the salt of her tears. "Without you, the whole world had become dark. There was no joy, no happiness. Now," he kissed her lips and caressed her back, making her lift herself closer to him. "Now the light shines bright again. The sun, the moon and the stars, all have returned with you. The yearning emptiness that was in my heart, the longing for the nearness of you, is no more. You are here, close to me again."

Angela sobbed, hugging him and burying her face on his shoulder. "Hold me tight, Neutino. Don't ever leave me again."

"Leave you, my angel? You will never know what torture I suffered for those angry words in Naples. The torment of longing and wanting you—who are more than my life—my dream of paradise. You are all that is lovely, all that is desire. You are—you are my Angela."

Holding her around the waist he drew her over to a settle. "Come, sit here and dry your eyes. They are much too beautiful for tears. I wish to hear all that you have done, every thought, every action, every word, since last I looked upon your loveliness. But first—" Cellini rose to fill and offer that token of Italian hospitality borne through centuries of time, a glass of wine. "You know," he continued, sitting close to her, "I wrote a letter to you, imploring your forgiveness and begging you to come to me; but you could not be found. I was told you were no longer in Naples."

"We moved from the house we occupied when you were there," Angela murmured, her eyes shining. "Shortly after you left, Mama decided to take a house on the other side of the city. I wanted to write, but after you had gone away she became so angry she would never allow it. I wanted, many times, to come to you here in Rome. To run away. She stopped that too." Angela sighed, her breath catching in her throat from her recent tears. "Once I succeeded in secretly packing some of my things and very nearly got away; but she discovered my arrangements, locked up all my clothing, and took the money I had saved for that purpose. From then on, excepting just once, every time I was engaged to dance, she made one of my brothers accompany me. I was never allowed out alone. She even threatened to denounce me to the Bargello and have me brought back by force if I dared to leave her. She would have done it too. You see, my love, I did not then know that she had made plans of her own—which concerned me as well as herself."

"How did you manage to get away from her, then?"

"I didn't, really. As it turned out, it was the other way around. She left me. Actually, the *sbirri* in Naples managed the thing; for in the end it was the police who made it possible." Angela shuddered and remained silent for a moment. "It was horrible. Horrible!"

"She got into trouble with the police?"

"Bad trouble. Very bad! And I was involved in her scheme, although I knew nothing about it. That's what saved me. But for the fact that this was proved, it would have gone badly with me."

"Tell me about it, my dream."

"Even now, Neutino, all I know is what the authorities told me. And that was after Mama and my brothers had run off—to Sicily, I think. I did not tell the police that, but she would go there, I'm certain. In the mountains of Sicily she would be safe. They will never find her."

Cellini chortled at the thought of a fugitive Beatrice, unable ever again to show her face on the Italian mainland.

"What happened?" he asked, gloating.

"It came about this way: Some time ago, Mama was approached by a certain Calandrino Garo, a fairly wealthy old bone-bag who lived just outside Naples, and who did very well for himself. He owned large land holdings—vineyards, olive groves, fruit orchards, big farms, and such. Much of his land he rented out for husbandry, and lived very handsomely on the proceeds.

"This scabrous old goat had seen me dance at some affair or other, and finding himself taken with me, made inquiries as to who I was and where I resided, and then, secretly, unknown to me, he quietly approached my mother and began making overtures. He wished, he told her, honorably to marry me—why, I cannot know! Just about all he would have been able to do is crawl into my bed and lie there, warming himself like the gnarled and crooked old rat he was! He had more than sufficient years to pass as my father. I tell you honestly, Neutino, if it had come to the point where I would be forced to wed him, I would have killed myself!"

Cellini scowled. "What was it he proposed to Beatrice?"

"You know Mama? It was she who, in the end, did most of the proposing. When it came to striking a bargain that served her advantage, Mama was more than a match for Calandrino. He had to make free with his ducats. She demanded title to a suitable house, two servants, several tracts of land which she was to have the rental of, a vineyard, and a pension payable every month. All this was to be hers for the remainder of her life—in return for my hand." Angela made a face. "There was a great deal of haggling, but Calandrino finally agreed and wrote out a testament. Mama called in a notary to attest the document, and so it was."

The goldsmith's eyes grew smoky. That Beatrice! "What of all the land you had been buying in Sicily?" he asked. "Surely that brought in a nice revenue?"

"Apparently it wasn't enough for her," Angela answered shrugging. "Or perhaps it was that, even though she had the use of the money it earned, the land itself was all in my name. I just don't know the answer to that, Neutino."

Cellini snorted indignantly. "What happened then?"

"There was one little obstacle which prevented the fulfillment of their bargain, and my sale. That old goat already had a wife!"

"Ah! I begin to see the reason for the catchpolls!"

"Sì. Late one night I was returning home from an engagement. I don't know why, but on that one occasion neither of my brothers accompanied me. When I reached our house I found it turned upside down and inside out. Everything and everyone was gone. Early the next morning, just after dawn, the blacklegs came and searched the place. They found nothing, so they took me to the Podestà. Fortunately, he was a nice old gentleman. He had seen me perform often and was disposed to be kindly. He told me not to worry and to have no fear since the truth was already known and I was in no personal danger, and that I was brought in because the Bargello was very much interested in learning the whereabouts of my mother, Madama Beatrice Catelli.

"I told him of the condition in which I found the house and that I knew nothing of my mother's whereabouts. I was very frightened, not knowing what to say, or do, or even think. I imagined all sorts of awful things. It was then that the Podestà told me of the arrangement that had been entered into, and which was to take effect as soon as Calandrino's present wife had been properly disposed of. I'll never forget what that judge told me. Never! It was terrible!"

"Take a sip of wine, my love," Cellini told her, caressing her shoulder. "If the matter is painful to you, speak no more of it."

"No, I wish you to hear everything. Besides it's all over and done with now. What makes me shudder is what might have happened. The

Podestà said that Calandrino was a truly incredible imbecile. But for his crude stupidity, a murder might have been committed with impunity. As it happened he had been apprehended on the previous day, and was being held for trial on the charge of the attempted murder of his wife. The authorities seemed to have no doubts as to the outcome of it. This fool, the Podestà told me, had been so maladroit in the handling of the attempt, it had resulted in his immediate arrest. He had been so inept as to fling the poor woman headlong down a well—this in broad daylight—no doubt in a silly effort to have the death appear accidental. Not only had there been two eye witnesses to this ill-advised action, the woman's fearful screams aroused the whole of the vicinity. It had been easily possible to remove her from the well-pit in time to save her life. In fact, except for the shock of fright, she suffered only a few bruises. And there you have it, Neutino."

"What happened to the old drone, Angela? Do you know?"

"Yes. He was hung on the Cord and questioned. He speedily made full confession to everything, and admitted that I knew nothing of the scheme which he and Mama had connived at. The authorities believed this because, as they said, he was questioned till both his arms were practically wrenched from their sockets, and he never changed a word of his confession. Also, a brief further investigation abundantly proved to their satisfaction that I was possessed of a malicious person for a mother. After a long time they allowed me to return home, but warned me to remain in Naples for a few days, in case I should be required to give testimony during the trial."

"Was it necessary? Did you have to appear?"

"No, thank God. The confession was more than enough. Calandrino was found guilty on one day, and hanged like a dog the next." Angela shivered. "I heard about the hanging. The people gibed and jeered at him all the way to the scaffold. They roared with laughter as he danced in the air, yelling that he was stepping right merrily, like the young buck he thought he was. The worst one present was his wife. She laughed and cursed all through the spectacle."

Angela shook her head sadly. "A few days later the Bargello came and told me I was free to go or do what I wished. I asked about my mother and he told me frankly that if she is ever apprehended she will suffer a similar fate. Poor Mama. I don't think she deserves that."

Cellini beamed, pulling her over to him. "What then? You came here to me?"

351

"No, my own, I couldn't. I had too little money on hand. Traveling is expensive—and Mama took away every blessed thing but my clothing and some jewelry. So I had to remain in Naples until I saved enough. It was a month before I could come to you."

"Where you belong, *per Dio!* But enough of this unpleasantness. It grows late and you must be hungry." The goldsmith pursed his lips. "This reunion calls for a celebration. I know a *trattoria* close by where the food is excellent and the wine superb. We will drink *Lacrima Cristi,* just as we did on that balcony in Naples. Do you remember, my pigeon?" Angela nodded and cuddled against him. The goldsmith kissed her ear. *"E bene,* when we have supped we can come back, and I will show you how very much I've missed you."

When, much later, they returned, Cellini carried an additional pair of bottles of the *Lacrima Cristi.* That sparkling wine always served to revive wonderful memories of days and nights in Naples. Memories which, indeed, became infinitely more real in the somber lamplit gloaming of his rooms. The flickering yellow rays sheening off the midnight of Angela's hair, touching her tawny satin-smooth skin with an edge of shimmering liquid gold, sent a tingle stealing over him as he watched her.

Angela was searching through a bundle and pulled out a set of miniature brass cymbals, which she fitted on the thumbs and middle fingers of both hands. Kicking off her slippers, she shook her hair free and looked at him saucily.

"I am going to show you a new dance I learned in Naples, from an infidel girl who was taken on a Moorish galley. It is called the Dance of the Desert Wind and it is very daring. Watch!"

She raised her arms and started beating a slow metallic cadence. Her arms, and then her body, began the slow undulating movements of a dance that was part oriental, part Arabic, part African, and voluptuously sensuous. It brought to mind the waving rustle of palm fronds stirred by a desert wind. Slowly the cadences increased, then diminished, the sinuous movements expertly following the tempo into the climactic sequences. Angela twisted and whirled until the gulping Cellini grabbed her about the waist and drew her close, kissing the hollow between her breasts.

Her arms around his neck, Angela flung back her head and chuckled musically.

352

"What it most needs is a proper costume," she told him impishly, eyeing him sideways. "This one is too . . . complete."

"I agree," nodded the goldsmith, squeezing her. "There's far too much of it." He looked into her eyes. "My own," he asked gently, "are you very tired?"

Angela rubbed her cheek against his and breathed a softly whispered assurance in his ear.

It was a month before Cellini again gave thought to the routine matters of life and to professional affairs. The two journeymen were busy on the shield and several other small commissions which were being handled in the studio rather than the shop. Since a watchful eye was all that was needed to keep them going in the right direction, he went back to the medal of Duke Alessandro.

Lorenzino de' Medici still had not sent a subject for the reverse, and he was far too important a courtier and nobleman to be ignored. The goldsmith wrote to Florence again, this time to his friend Niccolò da Monte Aguto, asking him to speak to the young lord and let him know that the completion of the medal waited on him alone.

Niccolò replied promptly.

. . . I have, as you requested, spoken to that bizarre and quite mad little lordling of a Lorenzino regarding the medal. By way of reply he made me a little face and said he gave thought to nothing else in the world but that reverse, and that he had not yet worked one out which satisfied him as being worthy of Duke Alessandro. I am of the mind that he is merely chattering when he speaks of working on it. All his time is taken up in cavorting and whoring with the Duke. Were I in your place, my Neutino, I would invent some suitable fancy out of my own head, cut it into the die; and when it is properly finished after the manner of that so marvelous art of yours, bring it without hesitation to the Duke. For the rest, things here are much the same as when you left us. Our Florence remains a sullen, angry thing, which I for one find very frightening. God alone knows where this pass will lead us, or when all this will end . . .

Cellini began to sketch out a design of his own for the reverse as a new year began. Things were pleasant and peaceful. The intriguing of his enemies at court was not bothersome. Angela was here beside him.

Life was full, almost complete. It had purpose. The weather was snappy and brisk, ideal for hunting. It was never truly cold in Rome and in the surrounding Campagna. And there were geese, ducks, and hare in abundance in the marshlands north of the city.

"Let's go on a hunt tomorrow, Neutino," Felice, who had called at the studio to discuss some shop work, looked inquiringly at his partner. "This weather is too fine to waste indoors. What do you say? Are you engaged on anything of importance here?"

"Nothing that can't wait, Felice. Both Nasone and myself will be the better for some outdoor activity, and a good bag will provide the game for a pleasant supper. Let's start out early."

That fifth of January was a clear, sparkling day, one of the finest in weeks. They spent it hunting in the hilly marshes near La Magliana. The sport was good; toward evening they had full bags of game. Felice had long since strapped his gun to his saddlebags; and with night coming on, Cellini decided to call it a day. They turned their horses back to the city and Cellini whistled the shrill signal that called Nasone to him. The dog did not appear.

"Look down there," laughed Felice, nodding toward a clump of rushes down in a ditch. "When it comes to hunting, I'm afraid you two are pretty much alike."

Nasone had established a point and was frozen into immobility, waiting patiently for his master to flush and fire.

Cellini dismounted and smilingly loaded his light fowling piece. It was dusk by then, too dark for accurate shooting. None the less he did not wish to disappoint Nasone, who delighted in retrieving game. He aimed as best he could, and fired.

The single ball brought down two geese. Nasone bounded off after one. The other, badly wounded, was flapping about in the ditch. The goldsmith jumped down the decline, catching it at the expense of a boot full of muddy water. Climbing back up, he upended his leg to drain out the water and stuffed the wet boot with the warm feathers of his last kill, to keep out the cold. By the time he remounted it was dark.

They rode along a hilly rise of land, open on all sides. Ahead and below them down the road a wooded area stretched out almost to the city gate.

Behind them, off to the north and a little east of the road, the sky began to flicker. Pale, sparkling shafts of dull light took shape, danced about queerly for a brief luminescent moment, and died out. They grew

354

in intensity—and suddenly there was a bright flash which made the two horsemen draw rein.

"Is it going to rain, do you think?" asked Felice.

"Rain?" replied Cellini, looking up. "There's not a cloud to be seen anywhere."

They twisted in their saddles as another bright flash lighted up the north sky. It hung there for the briefest instant and then lost itself into nothingness. There was no noise. No thunder.

"What was that, I wonder?" Felice's voice was hushed.

Cellini silently shook his head, watching intently.

Then it came. Quietly. Quickly. Spectacularly. A striking if unusual display of the aurora borealis, rarely seen in these southern latitudes.

A huge, brilliant flash lighted the north sky. Wide vertical streamers and beams of light formed, rose and fell with a streaking motion, swelling and pulsing like a thing alive. They danced and sparkled, one lustrous portion a varicolored glow of vibrating light particles, while another portion changed from red to orange to yellow, green and blue, fading quickly and recurring instantly in some other part of itself. It lasted for a short space, then folded into an inverted beam. It seemed to gather into itself and suddenly explode in one immense blue-white shaft of electric brilliance that died in a spraying shower of sparkling motes of light, leaving only a star-filled black sky. It was awesome. Felice was shaking, suddenly very cold. Cellini gulped audibly.

"God above!" he choked. "What great miracle is this we see over Florence! It is a sign! Without doubt we will hear of some vast happening there." He hurriedly crossed himself.

Feeling subdued and fearful they started off again toward Rome.

"*Cristo santo!*" gasped Felice. "What a portent! This is the pre-announcement of some great occurrence. You are right, Benvenuto. We shall most certainly receive news of some great event taking place there. An uprising, do you think?"

"By God, that could be," mused Cellini. "Only the other day I received a letter telling me that the city is in a very disturbed state."

"We shall wait and see. Certain it is that we shall hear something."

As it happened, there was something rather unusual going on in Florence that night, something well out of the ordinary. Lorenzino de' Medici was providing the reverse for Cellini's portrait medal.

One fully worthy of Duke Alessandro!

L

IN HIS *CAMERA DA TOELETTA* ON THE SECOND floor of the Medici palace, Alessandro stood before a pier glass, ogling the reflection of himself. Pleased with what he saw, he preened foppishly. This was to be a night of nights! He smiled to himself as he gently rubbed perfume on the palms of his hands and patted this into his stiff curly hair, adding dabs of it to his lean cheeks. He paused to adjust the neckband of an embroidered shirt of fine lawn, then stepped back to gauge the full effect. He was wearing black trunks worked with arabesques in gold thread. They had bright red silk in the slashes. The nether hose attached to these were a tightly fitting buff satin. His feet were encased in square-toed red leather shoes, padded and slashed and laced to his ankles. His eyes wandered lovingly up and down. He looked a fine and noble hero, he thought—lean, virile, handsome. He made some minor adjustments in the fit of the cod-piece.

Still smiling he drew aside to a window and looked out over the Piazza San Lorenzo. The street was quiet and dark. It was a fine cold night, late, and few people were abroad. Absently he held out an arm, permitting his valet to clasp a jeweled bracelet over the puffed shirt cuff. His smile broadened into a chuckle. He had waited and waited for tonight, waited for months. For an even longer period he had yearned to possess the lovely Laudomia. She was the most beautiful flower in Florence ... and that took in a great deal. How old was she now? Let us see ... eighteen? ... Yes, eighteen. A fine, youthful age, full of the warmth and passion and vigor of youth. For months he had importuned, and for the same length of time she had scorned him. More, she had had the impudence to tell him to his face, *him,* the most powerful man in all Tuscany, that his suit was odious to her and that she could do without his unwelcome attentions. And now—capitulation, sudden and complete. It left him a bit breathless.

He had Lorenzino to thank for it, of course. It was his close friend and boon-companion who had made the conquest possible. He it was who had so adroitly made the celebrated Laudomia see the wrong of her action in spurning the ardor of the valorous and handsome Alessandro. He had convinced her that a noble and beautiful lady like herself did wrong in thus denying her lordly Duke and ruler... And she had listened to Lorenzino. Why not? Alessandro chuckled again. Lorenzino was her brother!

And tonight there was to occur the consummation of their passion and their love. The adroit Lorenzino had made all the arrangements. Everything was to be quiet and discreet. The rendezvous was to take place in Lorenzino's little jewel of a house, next door to the Palazzo Medici.

The valet held out a jeweled belt. Alessandro turned and allowed the servant to clasp it around his slim waist. A page knocked and entered softly.

"*Altezza*, the noble lord Lorenzino waits below."

"Bid him come up, hurry."

Lorenzino sauntered in lazily. He bowed. He too was dressed in black, though not so grandly as the Duke. He wore high boots and a long, sleeved doublet lined with miniver. A jeweled dagger glittered across his flat stomach.

"Is my lord ready?" he asked in a dull voice. He seemed totally uninterested.

Alessandro did no more than glance in his direction and smile, while he slipped on a doublet of black velvet decorated with wide bands of crewel work.

"In one minute, my good friend, I will be ready to accompany you."

He did not see the smoldering red surge come to the surface of Lorenzino's eyes. The hot glow quickly receded deep within and simmered there.

"I shall never, no never, forget this mark of faithful service, my dear Lorenzo," he told his companion unctuously.

Lorenzino smiled—with his lips. The eyes didn't smile, nor did the mind behind them. The eyes smoldered again, momentarily. Alessandro did not notice. He was in heat. But he did expect an answer. He looked up.

Lorenzino's eyes wandered across to the valet.

The Duke flirted a hand imperiously. The man padded out of the room like a ghost.

"You are but doing me honor, Your Grace," Lorenzino replied smoothly. "That I should be possessed of a sister who merits the attention of Your Excellency is the height of flattery and attainment. My sister now regards it so. *Come di fato,* she is impatient to demonstrate and prove her ardor for Your Grandeur."

Alessandro swallowed. His mouth kept filling with saliva. He hurriedly drew a gem-encrusted cap over his carefully dressed and anointed hair and made impatient adjustments. The red plumes on it dropped back over his shoulder like a spray of blood.

Lorenzino leaned against a table, his arms folded, waiting. His eyes were half closed. He looked sleepy, bored.

"Come, my friend, let us be off then." The Duke chortled, taking him familiarly by the arm.

They descended to the main hall, the servants and pages bowing silently as they passed. Arm in arm they left by the door facing the Via dei Calderai. Two pages were waiting with lighted lanterns, to precede them as they walked around the corner to the Via Larga and up the street to Lorenzino's small house. The link-boys were dismissed before they reached Lorenzino's door. A domestic opened this and Alessandro entered, followed by his friend. The servant did not remain in the house. He threw a cape over his old back and left by the rear door.

The younger man led the way into a comfortably appointed room. A fire blazed in the fireplace. Decanters and flagons of liquors waited on a table. Alessandro poured himself a glass.

"If Your Grace will make yourself at ease," Lorenzino waved around the room, "I will go to fetch Laudomia."

"Promise me you will hurry, my dear Lorenzo," Alessandro gulped from the glass.

"I will not be long, my lord, never fear," Lorenzino promised, bowing.

He left the room, closing the door behind him.

Alessandro removed his doublet and cap, finished his drink, refilled the goblet and carried it to a couch where he sprawled to await the return of his friend and procurer. He was in a hot frenzy and he quivered slightly. He had waited for a long time for this, and Alessandro did not like to wait—for anything.

The house was still, deserted. Lorenzino had sent all his servants off. This was reasonable, considering that it was his own sister who was involved in the liaison. Alessandro nodded to himself, taking another pull at his glass. The affair naturally must be kept quiet.

Minutes later he heard the front door open. Footsteps padded in the hall...light footsteps, two persons. There would be the inevitable pause, while Laudomia primped before entering and presenting herself to her Duke and seducer. That too was natural and to be expected. Alessandro lay back on the couch in an attitude of nonchalant unconcern. He closed his eyes.

One of the room's two doors opened. He smiled ever so lightly, keeping his eyes closed.

The door shut softly, almost tenderly. Then, silence. Alessandro waited expectantly for a light touch from smooth fingers, rousing him from feigned sleep to much more tender delights. It did not come.

He opened his eyes.

Lorenzino stood just inside the door. He had removed his doublet and hat and was standing, straight and slender, in black trunks, black hose, black boots, and a close fitting black waistcoat. Standing there, with the blade of his jeweled dagger gleaming in his hand.

Alessandro looked up at his face. It was calm, empty, bored looking. For the first time he really saw Lorenzino's eyes. The lava in them was erupting. The deep, still pools were brimming over.

"Heh?" he frowned, and in a smooth effortless lunge, sprang to his feet. "What's this?"

Lorenzino's legs slid apart. His lithe body bent forward in an alert crouch. The dagger blade glinted blue in the fist that held it poised and ready.

"What would you say it is, my lord?" The words floated in the air softly, unemotionally.

The other door opened and closed quietly. Another man was standing in the room.

Alessandro's eyes flicked toward the newcomer. He recognized him. At one time he had had it in mind to take him into his own service. Scoronconcolo was his name. A master in the art of assassination. One of the best. A human butcher whose services were for hire in murdering anyone—even the Duke of Florence.

Their eyes locked. The desperado held a poniard in his hand. He looked, and then he smiled, without conscience, without pity, without remorse. His eyes did not waver. It was Alessandro who looked away, back to Lorenzino.

359

"A coup! You? ... Why?" he snarled at the calm youth. "Why this?"

He had been duped into a carefully prepared trap. He resented that. He knew he was about to be murdered, and there arose within him a dread of death, but he showed no fear. He felt none, only a rankling resentment. There was the dread, and there was hate—but no fear. A man who knew fear wouldn't have lasted out a day as the tyrant of Florence. Whatever else there was in Alessandro de' Medici, cowardice was not a part of it. He did not quail, nor did he beg for mercy. He knew better. His swarthy features flushed and a thin beading of perspiration broke out along his forehead.

"Why this?" he repeated.

"Why this?" answered Lorenzino through his teeth. "You attempt to shift me into the position of playing the pimp with my own sister, and you ask 'Why this?' " He smiled, with his lips. "You black filth!"

Alessandro was touchy on the subject of his origin on the distaff side. "We are cousins! I am a Medici like yourself!"

"Cousin!" Lorenzino spat out the word, aroused in spite of himself. "Your mother was a black whore! Your father? ..." the youth shrugged ".... I know not what species of beast it was that spawned you, but it was not Giulio de' Medici. The foul bitch who brought you into this world gulled him into believing it was he. How she did that," Lorenzino shrugged again, "I know not. But there's no Medici blood in you. Even your mirror will tell you that!"

Feeling himself treading on uncertain ground, Alessandro swung back to his reason for coming to the house he was in.

"To say your sister brought you to this pass is a lie! A black lie!" he snarled. The hired assassin waited, breathing lightly. "True, I wanted her; but you were not forced into arranging this meeting!"

"Had I not done so my family would begin to disappear into exile or worse, until she gave in and went to bed with you."

"Words!" flung out the Duke, waving a hand wildly. He was viciously angry, seemingly oblivious of the drawn and poised daggers.

Lorenzino shrugged. "Words, then. Examine my motives, dear kinsman, and tell me why I do this thing."

"*Con piacere!* You are next in line for the succession! You mean to become Duke of Florence yourself!"

Lorenzino smiled again. "That might be the case. However, even

360

you know otherwise. Whatever I might wish to be, it is not Duke of Florence. I have no faction behind me, no influence, no political friends; nor have I ever attempted to gain such and you know it. So then, if it is not my sister, and not my personal ambition, then there is only one other explanation. Perhaps I grew weary of the monstrous despotism you imposed here. Perhaps when I saw what you did to Ippolito, my eyes finally opened and I saw the endless procession of men flowing to the gallows, to the headsman, to the dungeons, and into exile. Perhaps I saw then that no one was safe from your tyranny. Perhaps it awakened me."

"Then my successor, whoever he will be, will avenge me," Alessandro hissed. "He will have to! He will never sit safely as long as you are alive. You are doomed, both of you!"

Lorenzino answered calmly. "Not our friend here. For myself, you speak true. It is only a matter of time. *E bene,* I have never looked forward to old age—"

Alessandro sprang at him with the sudden surge of a steel spring.

The wary Lorenzino jumped lightly aside and swung the dagger at the Duke's head. Scoronconcolo lunged in and stabbed downward. Alessandro whined in pain for a brief moment. His mulatto skin turned gray. Blood spurted over his shirt, sprayed over the floor and his assassins. Lorenzino's dagger flashed again and again at the Florentine ruler's face, neck and chest. A cheekbone was shattered; Alessandro's face was laid open with gaping wounds. One eye was pierced.

Scoronconcolo had to grab at Lorenzino's arms to stop him.

"It is enough, my lord," he growled, breathing hard. "It is done."

He released his employer and stepped back, drawing the back of his hand across his mouth. It left a trailing red smear across his lips and cheek.

Lorenzino looked down, panting. His hired hand calmly drew out a silken handkerchief, pinched the triangular blade of his poniard between its folds and drew the steel through clean. He returned the weapon to its sheath, then wiped his hands and face. Wordlessly he handed the cloth to the young nobleman, walked steadily to the table and poured himself a goblet of wine.

"The horses? ..." he asked, looking over at Lorenzino.

"All arranged," the Medici answered, absently wiping his hands. "I have post horses waiting." He looked down again at the inert body. For an instant his eyes smoldered as before. He kicked it viciously, shrugged, and walked out to the hall. Scoronconcolo followed. The two assassins dressed for the street with the casual motions of guests leaving a house after paying a social call.

They left by the front door, strolled around to the Via dei Ginori where the post horses waited, and galloped off to Bologna.

The next morning Alessandro's chamberlains found their lord missing, and immediately suspected the worst. With great secrecy they began a cautious search, fearing a bloody uprising if the news leaked out before they were prepared for it. It was evening before they stumbled on the body. They waited till night and carried the stiffened corpse to the little church of San Giovanni, which was close by the Medici palace. There they washed off a little of the blood and made preparations for a burial.

Late the following night, still secretly, they carried the corpse through the pitch black streets to the church of San Lorenzo. Torches flickered weakly in the Medici chapel. Silently, sweating over the exertion, the chamberlains opened the sarcophagus of Lorenzo, Duke of Urbino, who had officially passed as the murdered man's father. Alessandro's royal wife was not present. There were no relatives. He had no friends. Despite the fact that this was a church, there were no priests present and there was no religious service of any kind. Alessandro had died and was being interred in much the same fashion as he had lived— like a wild animal.

The stone tomb was open. Within it lay Lorenzo, mouldering in death. Alessandro, in his embroidered shirt, was hastily tumbled in beside him. The cover slab was laid back over the tomb and resealed.

Above the hushed and sweating servants, Michelangelo's colossal figure, *Il Pensieroso,* brooded in silence, chin in hand, his stone face looking down disdainfully on the episode taking place at his feet.

Lorenzino and Scoronconcolo separated at Bologna, the hired assassin intent on getting out of Italy to a place where he could enjoy the fruits of his labor. He was now a wealthy man. The young Medici halted for a few hours, to wash off the blood and discard his blood splashed clothing, before continuing on to Venice.

He burst into the palace of Filippo Strozzi, the leader of the exiled Florentines in the canal city, and startled everyone in the house. The aging banker, widower of Clarice de' Medici, quickly surmised that something of moment had occurred and drew the youth into his study. His face lighted with an almost holy light as he listened breathlessly to the youth's story.

"As God has made me!" he screamed, "you have redeemed us all! You are the deliverer of your country and its people!" He embraced him and kissed him on both cheeks. "You are the Florentine Brutus!"

LI

WHEN THE NEWS OF ALESSANDRO'S DEATH reached Rome the exiles in the city went wild. For them this was liberation! Freedom! Soon they would be able to return home and perhaps carry out a little campaign of retribution—a little tyranny of their own.

Old Soderini drunkenly paraded along the Banchi and the Via Giulia on a bouncing mule, screeching and laughing like a madman. He had special words for Cellini, when he reached his studio door.

"Hah! Benvenuto!" he bubbled, "here is the reverse which Lorenzino promised you! This is your recompense for wishing to immortalize this Duke! An unfinished medal!" He laughed until he cried.

Another exile of rank, Baccio Bettini, came up and joined in the raillery.

"We have tumbled them down from their high and mighty perch," he chortled exultantly. The exiles were already taking full credit for the murder. "We have done with all of them!... While you sought to glorify them before the world. Hah!"

People stopped to stare at the house. Cellini came out, snorting with disgust; Angela peering from behind his shoulder in wide-eyed alarm.

"Blockheads!" he yelled defiantly. "I am a poor goldsmith serving whoever pays me, and you mock and jeer as though I were the head of a faction! Have I not done work for both you dunces? I want no truck with your stupid politics. Not yours or anyone else's. If I were interested I could easily prove to you that your present condition is due as much to your own greed and stupid bungling, as to the actions of Duke Alessandro!" The goldsmith had turned politician without being aware of it. "Let me tell you further," he harangued, "for the thing is plain enough for any fool to see. Before two days have passed you will have another Duke in Florence, one who may well prove to be much worse than the one you have put away! I have seen these little cabals take place before, my merry gentlemen. Go about your business and leave me to attend to mine!"

The goldsmith's angry words were as from the lips of an oracle.

There was utter confusion in Florence. The Signoria had been abolished; the city was without a government. The soldiers of the Emperor Charles, quartered there since the city's fall, maintained a show of order and stopped any rioting. But underneath this surface scab there was chaos. The city had a Council known as the Forty-Eight, filled with powerless pawns. Moreover, there was no one left on whom the Dukedom might logically devolve. Ironically enough, all of Clement's chicanery had been in vain. For with Alessandro's death, Clement's grand scheme collapsed. The elder branch of the Medici was extinct, bereft of all male descendants. Only Catherine de' Medici remained—and she was wed to France. The succession, if it fell, would have to fall to the younger branch of the *Ca' Medici*. There, Lorenzino was first in line. But the man who had slain the despot remained in Venice and was making no attempt whatever to gain the Dukedom for himself. Strozzi rushed back and was made one of the Forty-Eight, but that was as far as that had gone.

Then Cosimo de' Medici made his bid for power.

He was a youth of seventeen years, and a very artful young man, although no one knew that yet. Little, indeed, was known of him. His life had been quiet. He had visited Florence from time to time, the year before as Alessandro's guest. He lived in the country, devoted himself to field sports and the chase, and had never expressed the slightest interest in politics. He rode into Florence from the Mugello accompanied by two attendants, a retinue of less importance than that of any country squire. His demeanor was humble. He gave the impression that he was unlikely to take any prominent part in State affairs. He readily promised that under his rule all power would be vested in the Forty-Eight.

It was pathetically simple.

The four principals of that body—Valori, Strozzi, Guicciardini, and Acciajuoli—accepted him and pushed his election through the Council. He seemed to be exactly what they were looking for ... a none-too-bright young dolt, more interested in sports than in politics. A nonentity who would seek amusement, and leave them alone to rule the country. Intent on personal ambition and power, they delivered Florence into an iron hand that was much more subtle than ever was Alessandro's. Cosimo was a lad with imagination! He was much more intelligent than his predecessor—and not one wit less deadly.

It was two days after the goldsmith had made his prophecy. Soderini was in Cellini's studio discussing some work, when Baccio Bettini came in.

Soderini looked up and smiled a greeting to his friend and fellow-exile.

Baccio was considerably perplexed. He eyed the Florentine artisan askance. "It is pointless to spend good money on couriers," he maintained, "when Benvenuto here can tell us things before they happen!" He looked at Cellini curiously. "Are you a warlock? *Un stregone?* What spirit is it who tells you things?"

Cellini elevated his brows inquiringly.

"What is it, my dear Baccio?" asked Francesco. "What has happened?"

"News from home." He waved a despatch at Soderini. "Cosimo de' Medici has been elected Duke of Florence, but with certain restrictions. These last have been designed to keep him in check and prevent him from cavorting about as he pleases. Who knows but that we shall be able to return home soon."

Cellini laughed loud and long.

"Here, now, is my opportunity to jeer," he snickered derisively. "Look you, *messeres,* I am no politician. But in this present instance I do not need to be. I have a mind and I make use of it to think with. Consider what has happened! These men of Florence have set a youth upon a very spirited horse. They have clamped golden spurs to his heels; they have put the bridle freely into his hands; they have set him out on a wondrous field, a vast meadow filled with fruits and flowers and all the delights of the world. And having done all this, they then bid him not to pass certain limits! Good God in heaven! *Ignoranti!* Tell me, you masters of the art of government, who can hold him back when the desire to cross these limits comes upon him? Dolts! Can you enforce the law on the man who is the master of that law?"

The events taking place in Florence served to strengthen Cellini's intention to seek better fortune in a foreign land. Now that Angela was back in his arms, there was absolutely nothing to deter him. To return to his home city and set up shop there, ever in the back of his mind, was now out of the question. In its present unsettled state, it would have been madness to make such a move. And here in Rome his position was sinking ever lower, the favor of the Pope diminishing from day to day. His adversaries had succeeded only too well in completely maligning and discrediting him, aided more than a little by his own highly volatile self. Since his illness no one had molested him. But then, he had been engaged on important commissions for the Pope. Now that these were finished he could expect his enemies to resume their tactics; and being out of favor as he was, it would be a small matter to trap him. He could not contend indefinitely against men who were aided and abetted by the all-powerful Pier Luigi. It was best to leave Rome. He would go to France, make every effort to establish himself there, and then Angela could follow with their personal belongings. They would settle in Paris, and spend the rest of their lives in the idyllic consummation of a perfect love. What better than this?

Quietly and cautiously he began cleaning up his affairs. The shield was completed, and the other trifling works on hand transferred to the shop. He paid off the Perugian workman, Girolamo Pascucci, but the fellow did not want to leave him.

"My dear Pascucci, how can you remain with me?" Cellini argued. "The shop, as you know, is very slow. I am off to France on a wild chase, not knowing what I shall do when I get there."

"Take me with you, Benvenuto," proposed Girolamo.

"Take you to France with me!" Cellini eyed the man wonderingly. "Just who do you think I am? Some wealthy lord with gold in abundance to scatter to the winds? Are you aware that it will require a great deal of money to travel to France?"

Girolamo nodded. "Take me with you, master," he repeated, "and I will travel at my own expense. You lay out the money and I'll pay it back out of the wages I earn. If you decide to remain in France it will certainly be to your advantage to have workmen on whom you can depend. Isn't that so?"

It was Cellini's turn to nod. His journeyman's remark was logical and true. "And if I do not remain in France, what then?" he asked, wishing to cover all points.

"In that event I will return with you and work off the obligation here in Rome. Well, master?"

366

Cellini thought about the idea, then nodded again. "Very well. I agree to the arrangement. We will have a notary in to draw up an agreement. However, to speak the truth, I think you are making a mistake. You would do best by remaining here in Rome. You work well and will have no trouble finding employment."

"Perhaps. On the other hand this is a chance to travel a bit and an opportunity to make something of myself."

The other journeyman, young Ascanio, listened to the conversation with a long, glum face.

"If you intend to take him along with you," he grumbled, "why must I be left behind? I've been with you much longer than he has."

It was true. Ascanio had grown up in Cellini's employ, starting as a shopboy, then moving on to apprentice, and graduating into journeyman rank. He had evolved into a first-rate craftsman.

"Don't you start off," snapped the goldsmith irritably. "You're going back to the shop."

"I am not!" Ascanio sulked. "I've been with you too long to be left behind. I'm going with you to France."

"I won't listen to another word. I intend to engage horses for two. Just two! You understand?"

"I'll walk!"

Cellini waved his hands in the air and went on with his arrangements. Everything in the studio was moved to the shop. The lower floor was rented, while the apartment above was to be reserved for Angela's use, until he sent for her.

"Now, is everything clear, my dove?" the goldsmith asked her on the night before his departure. "See that you understand our plans. I don't know how long a time will be required, but just as soon as I come to an arrangement, I will write—and then you come on as fast as ever you can, with our personal trappings. The shop is to be turned over to Felice, as his own. Keep Nasone until you are ready to leave, and then give him to Felice. You understand?"

Angela sighed. "Don't be too long in writing. Promise?"

"*Amoretta mia!* Be assured of that. And remember to tell Felice to take good care of that dog."

Young Ascanio packed his few belongings into a bundle and slept next to the door that night. His master was leaving early.

The goldsmith and Girolamo mounted post horses at dawn. The

sleepy Ascanio disconsolately shouldered his bundle and began to slouch off toward the Porta del Popolo.

"Maledetto!" blazed the Florentine. "Come back here and get in the house, instantly!"

"I'm going with you to France," Ascanio yelled back mulishly.

Cellini started pulling his hair, but Ascanio was adamant. He dropped his bundle on the street and squatted on his haunches, resting until his master's tirade ended.

"I'm going with you to France," he repeated obstinately.

The goldsmith looked up at the morning sky. "Why?" he snarled at it. "Why is it that I engage such imbeciles?" The youth obviously was serious in his resolve and fully meant to follow them. He couldn't very well let him walk to France. As the young buck had pointed out, he'd been with him too long. He cursed again, briefly, and looked over to Girolamo. "You see what you've started? Ride down to the post station and get another horse. Why I must be used in this manner by my own workmen I will never understand, but get another horse so that young fool can ride with us or we will have him dragging at our heels over all of north Italy!"

The youth squatting in the street looked up, his face wreathed in a smile of beatic proportions.

PART IV

LII

From ROME TO FLORENCE; FROM FLORENCE TO
Bologna and Ferrara and Venice; and from Venice to Padua. In Padua
Cellini paused at the palace of Pietro Bembo. The eminent man of
letters hinted that he would like a portrait medal of himself, cut in the
exquisite style of Clement's. The goldsmith obliged him by modeling
it in wax, and promised to take it in hand wherever he stopped to work.

From Padua the journey became difficult. Northern Italy was once
again the arena for a war between Charles and Francis. To avoid the
warring armies Cellini went northwest into Switzerland, choosing a
route through the Grisons. It was May but the snow was massed high
on the ridges of the Alps as the trio made their way through the passes
of the Bernina and Albula mountains.

In Switzerland the goldsmith led the way down into the valley
of the Rhine, coming to Wallenstadt. There they met a Florentine
courier traveling the same route to Lyons. He joined the three, making
their number stronger by one.

On a lake between Wallenstadt and Weesen the boat on which they
embarked foundered in a sudden storm and came near to ending the
journey by drowning all of them; and after escaping that peril, the pack
horse carrying the money and valuables nearly fell off a high cliff while
they were scaling a pass. By afternoon all were so dog-weary, wet and
famished, they put up at a farmhouse. It had been more than enough
for any one day.

From Weesen they continued north to Lachen, procured guides,
and made for the northernmost point of the roundabout journey,
Zurich.

They rested for a day in that bright, clean little city, and started
for Solothurn. The roads south were good, and very well traveled. The
journey became pleasant and enjoyable all the way to Lausanne, and

371

from there to Geneva, where they crossed into France and arrived at Lyons.

The short trip from Lyons to Paris proved equally delightful, except for a single mishap. At La Palice a band of adventurers swooped down on them; but the trio were cuirassed, steel-capped and gauntleted, armed to the teeth and ready. They fought free of the brigands and raced for the next town. From there to Paris there was no further trouble.

In the French capital Cellini made use of one of the Florentine exiles in the service of France to help in securing an audience with Francis. The man was one of the French king's treasurers. He took his fellow-countryman down to Fontainebleau and presented him.

The goldsmith was instantly taken with Francis. The monarch displayed a brilliant mind and highly cultivated tastes. He spoke Italian, had a contagious smile and the easy manner which pointed up a magnetic personality. He was a well-built, tall man, with a florid, jocund face covered all around with a short curly beard. His nose was long and straight, very prominent. His twinkling eyes were wanton, filled with exuberance and gusto. They were the eyes of a voluptuary. That Francis was superficial and a wastrel who frittered away his time on inanities was first overlooked and then forgotten in the force of his personal charm. There was splendor in his manner and in his dress; and these found an echo in the impeccable munificence of his court. He had a passion for war. He thrilled at hunting and gaming. He loved *all* women, and kept a stable of royal whores. He had one pet hate of truly regal proportions—the Emperor Charles.

Unfortunately for Cellini, Francis was then involved in another war with this hated enemy, and was on the point of setting out for Lyons to join his army when the goldsmith reached the palace.

"Messer Giuliano here will take you along with us," the jovial Francis said to him, "and on the way we will discuss some commissions we have in mind for you."

That was the last Cellini saw of the French king. He followed the court as it straggled out along the road to Lyons, but it was plain by then that Francis, with a war to play with, would have no time for him. This also was the opinion of a nobleman with whom the goldsmith became very friendly on the road south—Ippolito d'Este, Archbishop of Milan and prince of Ferrara. Like all the Estensi he was a passionate patron of the arts, and enjoyed the company of artists. They relaxed him and put him at ease. It became the practice, every evening, for him to dine with Cellini and have long conversations on the arts. He had also some sage advice.

"You will do best, Benvenuto, to stay at an abbey of mine in Lyons." Like most of his class the Este was richly endowed with benefices. "There you can abide at ease until His Majesty's mind again turns from war to the arts—the which is not likely to occur until he returns from the present campaign."

"I was under the impression that King Francis was to stay in Lyons, my lord?"

"Not so, *maestro*," Ippolito assured him. "The army is encamped near there. He goes to join it and then move south to Grenoble. Stay at my abbey, Benvenuto. You will enjoy every convenience. You can set to work there if you are of that mind."

"I thank Your Grandeur for this generosity."

When the court reached Lyons Cellini was ill with a fever and fearful of a recurrence of his last illness. On top of that Ascanio came down with a quartan fever of his own. There was nothing left to do but return to Italy. The journey to France had been a mistake; a dismal failure.

Hearing the goldsmith's intention, Ippolito commissioned a silver ewer and bason, paid for it in advance, assured the artist he would advise him of the King's mind regarding entry into His Majesty's service, and wished him Godspeed.

Cellini took the words literally and lost no time in turning toward Italy. With his two assistants he traveled homeward by a shorter route through central Switzerland, across the Lepontine Alps, the Simplon Pass, and then south and east across Italy to Ferrara, where he stopped only to pay his respects to Ippolito's brother, the Duke Ercole II. The fever left him between there and Florence. Ascanio had long since recovered.

Nor did he stay long in his home city. Unrest there was much in evidence. Duke Cosimo had taken over full power. The exiles were mustering larger than ever and were raising an army with the avowed intention of destroying the new despot by force of arms. Cellini went back to Rome.

The old shop was turned over to Felice. His former partner made him a gift of it, and opened another for himself. Angela was ever near.

Rome was peaceful and serene. Traiano and the rest of the Milanese seemed to be making nothing of his return. Pier Luigi appeared to be totally disinterested; he had just been faced with the Duchy of Castro.

Cellini started on the ewer and bason ordered by the Este, and the medal of Pietro Bembo. Commissions from several nobles came in. He took on another workman. That made three, not counting shopboys and house servants. Other orders came, making it necessary to employ more journeymen. Within two months of his return he was thriving. The new shop was crowded with work. When Angela was too busy with her dancing engagements to pose for him, he substituted Joanna—and noted with pleasure that her voluptuous beauty no longer evoked any unpleasant memories.

There was a fair share of travail along with all the good fortune. Girolamo began to balk at paying back what he owed. The Florentine had laid out nearly seventy crowns and had agreed to accept repayment at the rate of three crowns a month, so as to cause no hardship. The Perugian workman walked out of the shop one morning, vowing not to pay back another *soldo,* and leaving his cursing master swamped with unfinished work.

"I'll fix that bastard so that he'll never again cheat anyone!" he howled indignantly to Annibale Caro, who happened to be there at the time. "So help me Christ, I'll lop off his right arm!"

"Don't be a dullard, Neutino," reasoned his friend. "Use your wits. You are angry now. In the circumstances that is natural enough. No one likes to be cheated. Still, it is no reason for going completely mad. If you act rashly you will not only lose the money due you but Rome as well, and perhaps your life along with both. Think, my friend! The effect of an act of violence cannot be measured in advance. When will you learn to estimate the power of those who seek nothing so much as to ruin you? You have powerful enemies. Leave sleeping dogs alone."

"What would you have me do," squalled back the aroused goldsmith, "allow myself to be so used? *Quel mostro vigliacco!* I would sooner die!"

"Do neither of these things. You hold a signed agreement. Have the lout taken up and then sue him before the Auditor of the *Camera.*"

Cellini followed the advice. It was the first time in his life that he had allowed a civil agency to redress a personal wrong.

He won the suit easily enough and had Girolamo thrown into prison. It brought satisfaction, but only at the cost of a great deal of

374

time. The new shop was proving itself the most successful and lucrative enterprise he ever operated, even without Papal favor. It was overwhelmed with work. To the new shop came the commission to fashion all of the ornaments—gold, silver, and jewels—for the coming wedding of the Duke of Bracciano and Francesca Sforza, the most talked about event of the year. Eight workmen toiled hard and long, the master of the shop longer and harder than any—for glory and for gain.

A letter arrived from Ippolito d'Este.

Benvenuto, our dear friend— During these past days this Most Christian King has recalled you to mind and has voiced to me his desire to have you in his service. To this I quickly made answer that I have your solemn promise to return at once to France and serve His Majesty, whenever he may deign to send for you. Our Gracious Majesty then made answer to me that it was his will that there be sent to you the provision for your journey hither and he immediately commanded his Admiral to make over to me an order for one thousand gold crowns. Now, Cardinal dei Gaddi was present during this conversation and he told His Majesty it would not be necessary to make out any such order, seeing that he himself had already forwarded you sufficient moneys to travel here and that you were even then on the way. It is possible that this remark of Gaddi's was made solely to heighten his own prestige as a patron of the arts in the eyes of our great King. If, then, as I think likely, this matter is as I imagine it, and the opposite of what Gaddi has stated it to be, do you reply to me without delay so that I can gather up the thread of the thing and have the gold promised by this most magnanimous of Kings sent to you . . .

A thousand gold crowns!

"Now here, by God!" he howled indignantly, waving the letter at an astonished Angela, "is yet another example of my perverse fortunes! Of the malignant stars which guide my destiny! Well I recall that little ass of a Gaddi, and his behavior during the siege of Sant' Angelo. Why the devil should that fool make such a claim? Is it done out of pure whimsy, as my lord Este points out? Out of sheer ignorance? Spite? What?"

Angela shook her head perplexedly, not fully understanding the gist of the matter.

375

"One thousand gold crowns!" yelped Cellini, swallowing nervously. "For traveling expenses! *Santa Maria benedetta!* We will be able to travel to France together, my angel. And in princely fashion!"

He dropped everything else and set to writing a hurried letter to the Este prince, telling him he knew nothing in the world of Cardinal Gaddi, that he could offer no explanation for his words, and that he was more than willing to return to France and enter the service of His Majesty.

While the goldsmith was inditing this frenzied epistle, the chief guard of the Debtors prison was pocketing a gold ducat and obsequiously ushering the freehanded donor of it into the large common cell set apart for defaulters whose station and purses precluded better accommodations.

"Pascucci!" he yelled stridently. "Girolamo Pascucci!"

The Perugian looked up. A visitor? To see him?

The jailer waved in the direction of the caller and turned to leave. "The guard at the door will open when Your Worship is ready to go," he called back from the hall. The door was already closing on the stinking hole.

In what little light there was Traiano Alicorno subjected the journeyman to an eagle-eyed scrutiny. This new plan of his was devised to play again on the cupidity of the Pope's son, and its success depended entirely on this fellow's ability to play out a convincing part. It was a pity, really, a great pity, that the whole of his scheme, as he'd originally worked it out, couldn't be managed. That would have been choice! But even to approach the girl would have been far too chancy. This Angela, for all she was a lass who liked the feel of gold coins—he had made it his business to learn that—was too taken with Cellini to warrant the risk. The slightest slip, and her wary lover would be on his guard, acting to check the plan. A real pity, all the same. Using her would have made for perfection. Unctuously, as he eyed the silent Girolamo, he let his mind linger over the subtleties of the plot he had worked out. She might have been made to inform, to swear to charges that would corroborate what this Pascucci would have to say ... *Caspita!* It would have provided that added fillip! Would have made for a vengeance of really high order! Ah well, no point in moaning over milk spilt from the pail. The present arrangement, if it came off as planned,

376

should work out almost as well. This lout looked as if he could manage to carry it off without any great difficulty. His face did not have that dull blank look of utter stupidity so often to be seen among the lower classes. In fact, his eyes held a gleam which might even pass for intelligence.

Holding a perfumed handkerchief to his nose in a vain effort to smother at least a portion of the foul stench of the place, Traiano decided he had little to lose for trying. This man did not know him.

"Fellow," he drawled, drawing the Perugian off to a corner, "I have made it to my interest to examine your case. How would you like to be free of this prison, and find yourself with fifty crowns in pocket besides?"

Girolamo licked his lips and nodded furtively.

"And at the same time," murmured the former first chamberlain, "have the opportunity to avenge yourself on the man responsible for your being here?"

Pascucci's eyes gleamed bright. He would give a great deal for such satisfaction as that. To be able to nail Master Benvenuto to a cross—and live!

"What is it you would have me do?"

"Will you do it?"

"Until I hear what it is, how can I say? You must know my former master. If in doing this thing he retaliates by killing me, what do I gain? What safety is there in this for me?"

Traiano nodded his satisfaction. This man he was dealing with was not a fool. He was quite pleased.

"In a manner of speaking," he told him, "you will be changing places with him."

"You mean . . . you mean he would be taken up and jailed?"

The unknown in the shadows nodded.

"Then I agree. Tell me quickly what I must do!"

"Listen to me," Traiano prodded the man's hate. "Act as I tell you to and you will be completely and entirely safe. This is what you must do, and do carefully—with intelligence and thought to the manner in which you speak and act . . ."

About two hours later one of Pier Luigi's private secretaries received a brief note informing him that if he would do his lord an excellent service he must repair immediately to the Debtors prison.

377

There was a man there who could tell him things, interesting things, useful to His Lordship, about a certain goldsmith named Benvenuto Cellini.

The secretary was not much interested until he came to the Florentine's name. That struck a responsive chord, a clear bell-like note that vibrated. He recalled that this goldsmith had caused considerable inconvenience to his lordly master. He went to the prison and interviewed the verminous Girolamo.

He heard just enough to send him scurrying back to the palace and beg a private word with his lord.

"Well, then," Pier Luigi laid his head back on the pad of the chair and looked over indolently, "what is this matter which needs so much privacy?"

The secretary sketched out the preliminaries.

"... being devoted to Your Lordship's service," he went on, "and knowing of Your Valor's—er—interest in this goldsmith, I thought it best to hear what the fellow had to say. He would not tell me all, but he says with conviction that he knows of a case wherein his former master enriched himself vastly at the expense of the Church. I gathered he has knowledge of this Cellini having stolen a large sum of money, and I thought to bring this to Your Highness' attention."

"You have done well," the Farnese prince told him. He closed his eyes and sat thinking. Cellini thus far had skillfully and cleverly blocked and checked every move against him. It was humiliating. This present matter was probably nothing more than spite being vented by a lout of a laborer who was seeking to revenge himself on the man who had, rightfully enough, thrown him into prison. Still, it might be worth looking into. Cellini was a bold man, capable of many things.

"This man," he asked, "what does he want?"

"To be released from prison."

"And you think he has something worth while to barter for this?"

"Such was my impression, Your Grace."

Pier Luigi nodded. "Very well, send for the knave. Have him brought here and we will hear him out ... and send for Crespino, the Bargello," he added. "It might be wise to be prepared for anything that may develop."

Girolamo came into the sumptuous room cringing. The sight of

378

Pier Luigi, flanked by the grim-faced Bargello, sent him pitching forward on his knees, groveling before the table at which the Gonfalonier of Rome was seated. Crespino stood at one side of it. The secretary was on the other side.

"Well! Out with whatever it is you have to say!" rapped out Pier Luigi, his nose wrinkling at the stench being exuded by the kneeling jailbird. "And keep you in mind this fact, losel. Dare to make any games with me, and I will have the hide flogged off your stinking back! Now get on with it."

Girolamo shuddered and gulped. He had gone too far to turn back.

"Will my lord see to my release and pardon, after I have told what I know?" The lice on him bit voraciously. He scratched hopelessly.

"We shall see. If what you bring us merits such action, we will keep to this condition... and stop that scratching! Get on. Out with the thing."

"Your Lordship may not know that I was in the service of my former master for some years and I am well acquainted with all his affairs. Many times, when he thought no one was about, I have seen him in a little room of his, gloating over a pile of gems which he keeps hidden away from all eyes. These jewels were stolen, *Altezza!*"

"Stolen gems! Stolen from whom?"

"From the Church, Magnificence. And it is not right to steal from Holy Mother Chur—"

"Get to the soul of the matter! You say he stole the gems from our Church? How did he—or rather, how could he do that?"

"*Magnifico,*" whined Pascucci, "one night, while he was drunk, I heard him boast of how, during the time of the great sack, he was in Sant' Angelo and Pope Clement called on him to melt down all the Papal ornaments..."

Pier Luigi looked over to the Bargello.

Crespino nodded. True, so far.

"...He stole them while he removed the stones from the settings. Your Highness has only to catch him unawares, so that he will not have time or opportunity to hide them somewhere. He has boasted that they are of a value equal to eighty thousand crown—"

"*Eighty thousand crowns!*" Pier Luigi snapped forward. Good Christ! What a windfall! He looked again at the Bargello. "Well, Crespino?"

Carefully studying the face of the informer, Crespino screwed up his lips and brought his head up and down.

"It is possible, Your Grace. There was great confusion at the time. And the events described took place as stated. I was there."

"See to this man's immediate release," Pier Luigi ordered his secretary. "Here, fellow—" he threw a handful of coins on the floor. "Where does your former master hide these jewels?"

"That I know not, Magnificence," quavered the workman, clutching at the coins. "It must be somewhere in the house, since I have seen him examining them there."

The Farnese threw a curt nod to the Bargello. "Take him up, Messer Crespino. Do this secretly and quietly. Take him up, and let us know when you have done so."

Anxious to make up the time lost the day before, Cellini was up and working three hours before daybreak, finishing one of the pieces for the trousseau of the regal Orsini's bride-to-be. As the day dawned and the shopboys set about opening the shop and sweeping it out, he put on his cape meaning to take a breath of air. Nasone was asleep on his mat in a corner, so he did not disturb the dog. He left the house and walked leisurely along the Strada Giulia, enjoying the cool morning breeze. Turning into a side street he walked off in the direction of the Chiavica. There were several men on the street, all walking in the same direction as himself. He turned another corner and found himself confronted by an armed squad. The nearby "pedestrians" edged in, encircling him.

He looked around uncomprehendingly. Catchpolls? He was surrounded by blacklegs, led by the Bargello himself.

"You are the Pope's prisoner," that official told him evenly.

The bewildered Cellini looked around again. He had committed no offense of any kind...

"Crespino, you have mistaken your man."

"Not so," answered the Bargello. "You are the artist, Benvenuto Cellini of Florence. I know you well. My orders are to take you to the Castel Sant' Angelo, where go lords and men of accomplishment like yourself."

Four of the blacklegs rushed in and pinioned his arms to his side. The goldsmith was too flabbergasted to resist.

380

"Leave him alone," Crespino ordered sternly. "See to it that he does not escape, but do him no harm otherwise."

The men released the artist and silently drew back to the circle surrounding him.

"Give me your arms, Master Benvenuto."

As Cellini's fingers fumbled with the buckle of his sword belt, he looked around yet again. He was standing at a corner of the street, facing an apothecary's shop. The place looked familiar. It came to his mind that this was the spot, almost the exact spot, where he had slain Pompeo.

Silently and bitterly he handed over his arms.

Traiano had won.

LIII

THE BARGELLO AND HIS SQUAD LED THE PRIS-oner to the central tower of Sant' Angelo, into a bare little stone chamber in the circular keep. Its door screamed as it closed. The lock bolts rasped into place and the sound of receding footsteps echoed dully into a flat silence.

The goldsmith looked around his prison cell. All things considered, he was not too badly lodged. Fresh air entered through a small, heavily barred opening. A straw pallet was set in a corner. There was a table, a stool, a small fireplace, and very thick stone walls. The door was made up of a double thickness of wood planks, worn smooth and shiny. It hung on heavy hinges, red with rust, secured by wide, nail-studded iron bands. He prodded the straw mattress and was surprised to find it soft and dry. He sat on it and looked up at the small window. By way of ironic parallel he could contemplate on finding himself a prisoner in a room not too distant from the quarters he had occupied when he helped defend the castle.

He stretched out on the pallet and, not without apprehension, waited for some word of explanation.

He waited a long time.

Pier Luigi, meantime, was acquainting his father with what he had learned, and what he had done about the information he had gleaned.

"I beg that Your Holiness will favor me with the reversion of whatever sum we recover from this scoundrel."

"Most willingly will we make you a gift of this, my son," Paul assured his offspring. "And more, we will do all we can to assist in the recovery of it."

"I thank Your Sanctity," exulted the new Duke of Castro. "I go to make arrangements for a proper interrogation of the prisoner."

"Yet wait, my son!" Paul told him hastily. "Heed our words. Move more slowly. Let us give this miscreant some time in which to mull over his sins. It may well be that nothing more will be required to make him amenable and yield up all he has pilfered from us. In the event that this does not suffice—" Paul waved expressively. "In that case, my son, we can move on to methods better suited to his temperament. Have no fear, in the end he will sing us his little song. But until such time, let the mind itself do the work of the rack and the *strappato*. We have found from experience that this is no less effective."

The mental conditioning lasted for eight days, during which Cellini paced the cold stone floor of his cell. He could learn nothing of why he had been taken into custody, or what the charge against him was, or what proofs existed. Twice a day, morning and late afternoon, some bread, water, and a little meat, fish, or cheese, was passed in by a prison lackey who never spoke a word, and when the goldsmith asked for news did not seem to hear. On the evening of the eighth day the turnkey pulled back the screaming door, allowing three armed guards and an officer to enter. The guards carried torches.

"Come with us," the officer ordered, waving him out.

Saying not a word they trudged along the winding stone halls, down a flight of steps, and out on the lower, semicircular keep. It was quiet and still. The night sky was dark and clouded. A solitary guard paced monotonously around the embrasures of this lower parapet.

Cellini filled his lungs with air that to him seemed cleaner and fresher than that in his cell, and descended the stair that led to the lower levels of the Emperor Hadrian's fortress-like tomb. Preceded by two of the guards he paced along a wide hallway lighted at fixed intervals by smoking torches set in sconces attached to the walls. They came to the open door of a large vaulted stone chamber. It was clearly a judgment room. Even its bleakness was imposing.

It was lighted by hanging cressets which somehow succeeded in casting illumination only on its lower half. The vaulting of the ceiling was lost in shadow, giving the room the effect of immense height. A fire crackled in a fireplace and sent wisps and tendrils of smoke snaking up the wall. The bare stone walls sweated like some bloated smooth-skinned thing hung out to dry. Straight-backed, uncomfortable looking chairs were all around. A long wood bench was set in the center of the floor, and a squat stone dais ran along the wall facing the bench. A plain, low dock was set on it grimly. Behind its top, three chairs loomed emptily. Draped on the front of the dock before the center chair was a hanging bearing the Papal arms.

A writing desk was set between the dock and the bench. A sheath of writing paper, a large ink horn and several quills were lying on its slanted surface.

The guards withdrew to the hallway and closed the ponderous door. Cellini seated himself in one of the straight-backed chairs. It was fully as uncomfortable as it looked. He waited silently, his face calm and relaxed. He had no doubt he was being watched.

A guard opened the door and passed in a scribe. The man walked to the writing desk, shifted the paper around, tested the quill points on the ball of an ink-stained thumb, and sat down, trying hard to look important. His eyes slanted over to the calm-looking prisoner.

Cellini remained silent and still.

Five minutes of that was all the scrivener could stand.

"I wonder—" he began, then stopped abruptly, surprised at the sound of his voice. He gulped and went on. "I wonder how long your examination will take?"

The Florentine shrugged with a well-affected indifference he did not feel. So, at last, he was to be examined? At least he would discover why he was being held.

The clerk opened his mouth, but snapped it quickly shut and busied himself with the tools of his calling. The closed door at the opposite end was opening.

Three examiners walked solemnly into the room and around to the dock. Cellini knew them. The first was Paul's Governor of Rome, Benedetto Conversini. The next was Benedetto Valenti, who continued in the office he held under Clement, Procurator-Fiscal. Last came a criminal judge, Benedetto da Cagli.

The inquisition started off with questions that pried into a score of inconsequential matters. They gave no inkling of what the examiners were leading up to, in the forlorn hope that the prisoner would wander into a trap by making some significant disclosure.

Cellini tired of that routine.

"My lords, for half an hour you have pestered me with inane questions and prattling fables which make no sense at all. Tell me what it is you want of me."

The centrally seated Governor warmed up. He was not accustomed to being addressed in such cavalier fashion by a prisoner.

"You are very confident, I see," he growled, "and too arrogant by far. Very well, I shall undertake to bring that mountainous pride of yours down to the level of a spaniel's belly, and this without further prattling.

"We know for certain," he proceeded, giving a grim toss of the head, "that during the time of the sack to which this unhappy city was subjected, you were employed as a bombardier in this very castle. Since you are a goldsmith and a jeweler by trade, Pope Clement, of revered memory, called you into secret counsel and made you unset all the jewels of the tiaras, mitres, rings, and such; and having much misplaced confidence in you, he afterwards ordered you to sew the stones into his clothing. While you did these things you reserved a portion of the jewels for yourself. Gems to the value of eighty thousand crowns!"

The figure impressed everyone, including the goldsmith. The scribe's eyes bulged as he wrote it down.

"This," went on the Governor, "has been told to us by one of your trusted workmen, to whom, in your conceit, you disclosed the matter. We now mean to have back those jewels, or their value in money. So if you have any hope of being released, tell us quickly where these are to be found."

Messer Conversini stared haughtily down. His words had no doubt crushed any hope this suspect might have had. The feeling evaporated in a flush of anger as he watched the accused.

Cellini burst into a roar of sarcastic laughter.

"Cross of Christ!" he howled. "Eighty thousand crowns! Is there no end to the folly of man? If your words are true, and this is what I stand accused of, then I run no risk at all."

"Fob off the matter in any way you like, Benvenuto," broke in the angry Governor, "only see to returning the property we have lost to you, and quickly! . . . or we shall turn to measures other than words!"

"Eighty thousand crowns!" crowed the goldsmith. "It will take some little time to raise such a sum. Does my lord Governor imagine I carry it around with me to settle immediate expenses?"

The irate official pushed back his chair and began to rise. The other examiners followed his example.

Cellini slammed his hand down against the arm of the chair.

"Signori! my examination is not over! Bring that to an end—and then go where you please!"

Angrily the Governor sank back into the chair. Da Cagli too had flushed. Valenti was calm and self-possessed. He had once watched Cellini at work with another Governor, and he knew his mettle. There was even a hint of expectancy in his eyes.

"My lords must be aware," snapped the goldsmith, "that I am not a common criminal! Why should I permit myself to be treated as such?"

"You have killed enough men to be so classified," replied the Governor resentfully.

"It is you who says so and no one else!" rapped back Cellini with heat. "And yot, if someone came to kill you, priest though you are, you would defend yourself; and in killing your adversary the law of God and Man would hold you justified and guiltless! I demand to be allowed a proper defense ... and to be judged fairly!"

"Go to, then," snarled the Governor, slouching back.

"When you first heard this unspeakable accusation you charge against me," Cellini flung out in a hard brittle voice, "did you credit the bare word? Was it not your duty, before you took me up, to investigate the charge and discover what I have done with the eighty thousand crowns? Such a sum is not easily hidden. Do Your Lordships suppose I have stuffed this into a mattress or a pillow, to sleep on? A hard bed that! With such a sum at hand I would naturally prefer a softer couch, not so? What, then, have I done with this vast sum? Have you the answer?"

The three judges were quiet. The scribe's quill scratched as he wrote down the words.

"In all the time I have been hidden away here—eight days, by God! —was it not your duty, as intelligent officials, to immediately inspect the record of all jewels which has been most carefully kept by this Apostolic Camera for the past five centuries? If you then discovered something missing, why did you not seize my shopbooks, and ascertain if I had sold or otherwise disposed of these? Have you found anything missing? Have you taken the trouble to so much as look at this carefully kept record? I doubt it much! Instead...this! You subject me to this stupidity! These are the thanks of the Vicar of Christ for my long and faithful and honorable service to the Apostolic Chair! This is the payment for my efforts during that awful siege! To be accused of sacking the Church, as did the heretics at that time!"

Grown pale with anger, the vein at his temple swollen and throbbing as he spat out words, Cellini was not yet finished.

"It was I who slew Bourbon as he strove to climb the walls, my lords! It was I who worked the guns on that dreadful morning and kept the Lutherans and Spanish and Neapolitan troops that had overrun the Borgo, from storming Sant' Angelo. You have spoken true, *messere*, I committed many homicides on that occasion! It was I who wounded Gattinara, in payment for his revolting insolence toward the holy person of our Pope Clement. It was I who severely wounded the Prince of Orange. All these things I have done—and more! How many creations, objects of beauty—ornaments, models, coins, medals, reliquaries—so valued and so esteemed by all the men of the world, have I made for the honor and glory of this Holy Church! And this is your presumptuous priestly recompense for one who has labored and served you with such good will?" Cellini's white face flushed. He spat on the floor. "*That* for your payment! Go and report my words to Pope Paul. Tell him that all his jewels are where they should be, in his possession. Tell him that for all I have done in the service of the Holy See, I have received only wounds and stonings and promises—promises which were never kept! And above all, my worthy lords, give him my thanks! I now know what to think of His Holiness the Pope, and of you, the ministers of his justice!"

The three officials listened in undisguised astonishment. No such blunt facts as these had ever before been flung at them with such vigor, with such devastating logic. They exchanged glances and seeing that the goldsmith had reseated himself, they arose, nodded curtly, and filed silently out of the room. Valenti had a twinkle in his eye.

Cellini was taken back to his cell.

LIV

PAUL AND HIS SON LISTENED TO THE REPORT
of the three examiners with mounting agitation. Their consternation increased when a careful investigation of the records, ordered by the Pontiff, accounted for every gem belonging to the Apostolic See. No one, it seemed, had thought to look into this obvious record before this.

Pier Luigi howled the loudest. He had behaved like an utter fool—an incompetent idiot. His father fumed more silently, but he too was in a passion; as much for his son's arrant stupidity as for his own gullibility. It was hardly proper that a supreme sovereign such as he show himself to the world as one so easily gulled. Worst of all, it was not possible to hush the matter up. The entire affair had been handled in far too brash a manner. It was too late to practice discretion. The goldsmith had many friends. Too many! A wave of ridicule was tittering through the court, directed at him and his son. It galled the Pontiff. Resentment he would have condoned—but ridicule!

And truly, Cellini's many friends were not idle. They saw to it that King Francis was not only advised of the matter, but kept informed regarding its progress. When it was clear that no case at all existed against the artist, the monarch sent instructions to his Ambassador. There was injustice being done against a worthy man whom he had sought for his service. No one, not even a Pope, could do this to François de Valois, *Rex!*

In his official capacity, Monseigneur Jean de Montluc, Ambassador from France to the Holy See at Rome, made formal request for audience with the Pope.

"Supreme Sanctity," the Ambassador's words were diplomatically suave, but the Pontiff missed none of the implications. "I have the honor to convey a message from my lord master, His Most Christian Majesty, King Francis, with reference to one Benvenuto Cellini, a goldsmith who for some time past has been held in a prison here. My valor-

387

ous lord, His Majesty, makes bold to lay claim on this person as a man in his service, and requests that the Holiness of our Lord will see fit to release him for this purpose, if he is found to be unjustly charged."

Paul was greatly disturbed by the simple request. The affair had made far more noise than he had imagined.

"My lord De' Montluc should pay no further attention to this rascal," he suggested, with no hope at all that the suggestion would be taken. "This man is ever causing us grief by reason of his brawling and general troublesome nature. In truth, we should advise His Gracious Majesty to leave him where he is, imprisoned for various homicides and other devilries. It is not safe to release him. We should be gravely concerned at freeing such a nature into your beautiful France."

Monsieur de Montluc bowed with cold grace. "Permit me to remind Your Blessed Magnificence," he answered in precise tones, "that in the realm of my great king, justice is most excellently maintained and administered. My revered lord is ever wont to shower reward and favor on men of parts and virtue who merit such. Equally, he is no less backward in chastising the troublesome. May I presume to inquire of Your Holiness if this fellow has been duly tried and adjudged guilty of such crimes as are imputed to him?"

"Not yet, *monsignore*... Ah, we are engaged in... in certain preliminaries... And in any case we may yet decide to make further use of him in our service." Paul was clutching wildly.

The Frenchman inexorably continued to enmesh him in a web of words.

"In this last detail, I must humbly point out that Your Beatitude had already freed this said Benvenuto from your service, not caring any longer to make use of this master's genius. When His Supreme Majesty saw this man in his own domain, he most willingly adopted him. Wherefore, I am come in his name to request that the Blessedness of God on earth release him into my hands."

Eventually Paul was forced to fob off the Frenchman with a gracelessness that was very distressing to the worldly Farnese. Yet how could he do otherwise? To release Cellini now would be to inform the world of his own gullibility and of the stupidity and cupidity of his offspring, who was Gonfalonier and Captain-General of the Church. There would be no keeping that Florentine quiet. Heaven alone knew what the utterances of that embittered ruffler would be, or what they might lead to. Paul had no wish to be discredited before the whole of the French capital. No! Far better to keep him where he was, in prison; and the thing itself as quiet as possible till it was forgotten. The stigma of despotic injustice, infamous though it was, was easier to bear than the odium of stupidity. And the Farnese was sufficiently vain and tyrannous to indulge this humor. He suffered no qualms at letting the goldsmith rot in prison for a crime he had not committted—that had never been committed!

The Castellan of Sant' Angelo was one of the Ugolini family, a Knight named Giorgio. Being himself a Florentine, he was sympathetic to the case of a fellow-countryman and did what he could to help relieve the dolor of the forced detention. He asked for the goldsmith's parole and, receiving it, let him wander freely about the castle. The cell was no longer locked up. The prison lackeys even greased the hinges.

There were other conveniences. Arrangements were permitted whereby better food would be served. The cell was thoroughly cleaned out. Furniture was purchased and brought in. The cost for all this was a bit fantastic, but it was worth it. Messer Giorgio went so far as to grant the goldsmith permission to work at his profession.

What with his obvious innocence to the charge against him, plus the favor being shown by the French king, Cellini was of the mind that Pope Paul's wrath would soon come to an end. He kept his shop open and working. Ascanio and Felice made daily trips to the prison, the latter out of friendship, the former to bring shop news and material for work. Nearly all the guards, jailers and prison lackeys became congenial and friendly. It was readily demonstrated that for a few well placed crowns, even Angela could be passed into his cell for an evening's diversion.

But the weeks dragged on into months and the looked for change in the Pope's attitude did not take place. Instead the affair went from bad to worse. Cornaro sent word that the shop was ordered closed, and frankly advised the goldsmith that the Pope would not hear of setting him free. The favor being shown by King Francis did nothing but infuriate the Pontiff and arouse his jealousy. Monseigneur de Montluc had, in the King's name, made request that Paul hand the artist over to the ordinary judges of the court for trial, and the request so irritated the Farnese he let it be known that Cellini was in prison for life.

Faced with that turn of events, the goldsmith began to give thought to possibilities. "What," he mused to himself, "if this Castellan who is now so friendly is compelled to act otherwise? I would then be left without hope. I would be locked away and treated like some caged beast. If that happened, my parole would be revoked and I might wish to make use of my wits. Better to prepare now ..."

Like a thoughtful little squirrel, Cellini began to store up nuts against the coming of a hard winter. Ascanio and Felice were told to start bringing in new bed sheets of a strong, coarse fabric.

"When I have used these," the goldsmith casually told them, "I will not return them for laundering. Instead, I intend to pass them out to these poor soldiers here. Keep the matter quiet, for if it becomes known that these miserable wretches are accepting gifts from me, they will run the risk of the galleys."

As the new sheets came in, the Florentine emptied the straw stuffing of his mattress and burned it. The straw was replaced with the sheets, cut into long strips. Quite a few were needed. If ever they were put to use, they must scale the height of Sant' Angelo's central keep.

When a prison drudge came to repair a piece of furniture, broken for the purpose, Cellini appropriated a pair of pincers. Ascanio and Felice were always searched before they were passed in; but Angela, who came only after dark, and only as the result of bribery, was not. When next she came she had a poniard strapped to her thigh. He hated to involve her, but someone had to know of his plans, and there was no other way of securing a weapon which might be needed if an attempt to escape was made. A large needle and a quantity of stout twine with which to sew the strips together were added to the precious horde. That took weeks. The goldsmith labored on the bason ordered by D'Este, but the work went hard. The confinement and the continuous threat hanging over him were sapping him dry, eating into him.

And then, Ippolito d'Este, newly created Cardinal of Ferrara, arrived in Rome.

Angela did not wait for the Ferrarese prince to settle comfortably into the social routine of the Capital, or even till he had paid his respects to the Supreme Pontiff. She had Felice get in touch with Cornaro, who in turn got in touch with D'Este, and the morning after the new appointee reached the city, she was ushered into his presence.

Cardinal Ippolito looked her over with a half-smile on his lips. He well knew what was coming. Cornaro had filled in the details.

"Yes, *signorina?*" he inquired pleasantly.

"My lord knows the reason for my visit?"

390

"I believe so. We can dispense with unnecessary preliminaries. How do you imagine I can be of help to your Benvenuto?"

"Your Eminence is aware that King Francis desires Master Benvenuto for his service?"

"Oh, yes. And also that affecting his release would be most desirable. But these things take time, my dear girl. In the circumstances—"

"You must aid me in arranging for his escape!" Angela blurted. "Else, they will kill him!"

Ippolito frowned. "I have every intention to sue for his release. Perhaps it is better arranged so. It will take longer, but it is safer."

"No, my lord! Understand, they will kill him. They dare not allow him to be set free, now that everyone knows he is so unjustly held. They will kill him first."

The Este pursed his lips. He did not believe the situation was that critical. Still?

"We will see." He turned to one of his gentlemen. "Alamanni, I desire you to learn what you can of this Cellini matter. You remember, we discussed it? Go to the Vatican and see what you can glean."

"And it please Your Eminence," the courtier replied. "I was aware that my lord would most certainly wish all information on the affair. This has already been done. De Montluc has tried everything in his power, but it has availed nothing. The lord Pier Luigi blocks every move. I fear that Master Cellini is in a most unfortunate position. This young lady speaks the truth."

"So. Thank you, *messere.*" He turned back to Angela. "It seems your fears may be justified, my dear. But then ... Tell me, do you know if Master Benvenuto has any plan in mind?"

Angela outlined the goldsmith's careful preparations, and the reasons behind them.

"Good. Benvenuto never struck me as the kind of fellow who would stand idly by, and not prepare against just such a possibility. You have been able to go to him then?"

"*Sì,* my lord. Several times. I am passed in, secretly, after dark. I will see him again tonight."

"Excellent. Acquaint him with this little conversation of ours, and tell him this. I will make whatever arrangements are necessary. But I, and he, must proceed carefully. A failure—" he waved eloquently "—must not occur. Consequently, it is necessary to move with caution. And thus, also, more than a few days may be required, in order to preserve the greatest privacy in the matter. When my arrangments are completed, I will get in touch with you. Leave instructions with my secretary as to how you may be reached."

"We are most thankful to Your Eminence for the favor you display."

The Este brushed it away. "I have met your Benvenuto, and liked him. He is a man of spirit, and an excellent master. To allow such a talent to rot, unjustly, in that hole..." Cardinal Ippolito sniffed. "A disgraceful thing. But in the meantime, my dear, say nothing to no one. No one but Benvenuto. You comprehend?"

"Trust me, Your Eminence."

"Very well. You will hear from me. *Addio.*"

Angela repeated the conversation to Cellini that night.

"Good," he told her. "That was well done. There is much that the lord Ippolito can do. He is a powerful man. Now we must wait and see what develops. You understand, Angela, I can do nothing while my parole is in force? I have given my word, my promise."

"That's silly!" Angela exclaimed. "How is your honor involved, when you are imprisoned so wrongfully?"

"None the less, it must be so. My word is given to the Castellan, and must be kept."

Angela sighed deeply. "As you wish, Neutino. There is one more point. I have no faith in these people here, and in such a place as this one can never be certain of anything. If for any reason I should not be permitted to come to visit you, I will see to it that word is passed in. The turnkey—he has received his share of crowns for these visits of mine. I'll have him bring the letter, which will contain full instructions. If he dares to refuse, I will threaten to expose him. That means a rope's end, so he cannot say no."

"I don't like to see you running such risks." Cellini frowned bitterly. "But what choice is there? Very well," he sighed, "we will wait and see."

For the next few days the goldsmith dabbled at his work, getting nowhere with it. Late one afternoon, as he was roundly cursing the futility of his existence, one of Messer Giorgio's chamberlains stepped into the cell.

The goldsmith, he explained, was invited to take supper with his lord, the Castellan. Would he accept?

392

Cellini accepted with alacrity and set about cleaning himself for the occasion.

The Castellan, Messer Giorgio, was afflicted with a recurrent malady of the mind. An ill which his abashed family kept carefully hidden, or at least as carefully as was possible in the circumstances. These mental derangements came and went, each attack more serious than the former and lasting longer. During such spells the Ugolini was kept indoors, under the watchful eyes of trusted chamberlains and house servants. In the periods between, when he was approximately normal, he was permitted to go abroad and commune with his fellows. But even at such times his behavior was frequently such as caused men to look sideways at the worthy Knight of Jerusalem. He would chatter a great deal and was wont to dance and skip about joyously. His family made it a practice to palm off these antics, made before a wondering world, as the playful bizarrerie of an eccentric. Actually, the Castle Warden was completely addled, as rattle-brained as a gourd loosely filled with pebbles.

The attacks to which Giorgio's wits were subject took form in various caprices and humors. Each differed from those which preceded it. During the last delusion, for example—one of six months' duration—he fancied himself a jar of oil, and went about anointing everyone he encountered with his hands. The last but one, he was a frog; and so he leaped and hopped about on all fours. On another occasion he was dead; and his distracted servants were hard put to refrain from carrying out his repeated command that he be buried.

This season, Messer Giorgio was a bat. His chamberlains, ever watchful for early signs, noted that he began chattering and jabbering about flying off somewhere, and prepared for the worst. At night he would take to racing around the battlements of the castle, springing lightly into the air, flapping his arms, and uttering high-pitched *e-e-e-eeeeee's* in the thin, keening whine of the night-flying mammal. The old retainers sent for doctors, who came, examined, shook their heads, and suggested that the patient be humored in all things and diverted as much as possible.

This was the reason underlying the invitation of the goldsmith to supper. He was expected to furnish diversion.

Cellini's first intimation of his host's condition came when he sat

393

down opposite him at table and looked over at the man to offer greetings. Giorgio's face was flushed. His eyeballs rolled about in a frightful manner, one eye looking out in one direction, the other veering off elsewhere.

"*Caspita*," muttered the Florentine under his breath, "what's wrong with this capon, I wonder?"

With the arrival of the food the situation ceased to weigh on Cellini's mind. That the replies he made were as inane as the questions they answered did not press heavily on his conscience. This was the first decent meal he'd had in months!

"Tell me one thing, Benvenuto," yammered the Castellan, his eyes acquiring a sudden luster and both converging to a focus on the same object, his guest's face, "have you ever taken the fancy to fly?"

The innocent goldsmith paused and pursed his lips thoughtfully. This was the first coherent query he had heard. It deserved a considered reply.

"My lord, it has always been my ambition to surmount that which is difficult for men to accomplish. As regards flying, our good God has seen fit to give me a body well suited for running and leaping. This, together with such talent which He, in His goodness, has bestowed upon my hand and mind, are sufficient to make me wish to try to fly."

"Ha! So? Tell me quickly, what method would you adopt? Flying creatures, as you know, make use of differing means."

The goldsmith thought about that detail and answered calmly. He was a lamb being led to the butcher's knife.

"Well, Messer Giorgio, having observed the manner in which various animals fly, and did I wish to imitate by means of art what they derive from nature, I would select as my model the most apt of these flying creatures—the bat."

"*Hah!* Ha-ha! Ho! You hear!—" screeched the Castellan at the top of his voice. "He says true! He says true! Ho-ho-ho! Hah! That's it! That's it! The bat's the thing!"

Cellini looked around wonderingly.

The chamberlains and table servants eyed each other mournfully. Their looks were sad. Things were not going along as hoped.

Messer Giorgio, on the other hand, was doing exceedingly well. His eyes blazed as they squinted and bored into those of his table companion.

"Benvenuto," he purred like a tiger at sight of a doe, "if one gave you the opportunity, would you have the courage to fly?"

"Do you give me my liberty, *messere*," replied the uncomfortable Cellini, "and I will undertake to fly from here to the Prati."

The Castellan's squint deepened. A look of diabolical cunning chased itself around his face. "And what," he murmured softly, "would you fly with?"

"I would make a pair of wings from fine, strong linen, suitably waxed and attached to my arms—"

"Hah! You see! You must make your wings! But not I! I already have mine!" Messer Giorgio's eyes began to roll wildly again. "You are a clever devil! Not for nothing has the Pope bidden me to guard you as I would my own eyes. And what do you do? Seek to escape me by flying off! I shall now have you locked up with a hundred different keys and I shall see you do not slip through the keyholes either! These will be plugged!"

"Christ in heaven!" gasped the unoffending prisoner. "Cry your mercy, Messer Giorgio. For the love of God, I have done no wrong!"

"No wrong? *No wrong!* To seek to fly from me! Ho! You people there! Bind me up this man and lock him up in his prison, that he may not fly away from here. And if perchance he should escape, see you that I am instantly advised of it so I can fly off after him. Ha-ha! *F-e-e-eeeeeeeeeeeee!* We shall see who can fly best and fastest!"

With a half-dozen servants clutching at him, Cellini gaped blankly at the spectacle across the table.

"So be it," he told the Castle Warden calmly. "I tell you this in the presence of your servitors. Lock me up well, and guard me even better. I take back my parole! and promise you only one thing—that I will escape!"

LV

GIVING THANKS TO THE ALMIGHTY FOR HAVing been a little beforehand of events, the Florentine waited anxiously to hear from Angela. Especially was he thankful that she had wisely prepared against just such an eventuality as had occurred. He was now

395

locked away in the cell, and visitors were no longer permitted. While he waited, he deliberated on the manner and method of his escape attempt. The only possible egress from his cell, as he had previously ascertained, was through the heavy door. The other two outlets, chimney and window, were too small, and the walls were too thick to permit the openings to be enlarged. He must get through that stout door, reach the tower of the central keep and let himself down to the ground, circle around to the back of the *castello* and scale the rampart built there as a part of the city wall.

Working only at night Cellini sewed the strips of sheeting together, making two lengths. That finished, he brought out the pincers and turned to the door.

With great care he began to pry out one of the long spike-like nails which held the hinges fast. The spike was badly rusted and the clinching of its point was covered by the double planking. The operation used up most of the night; and when the nail was at last removed, it became necessary to disguise that fact and prevent its being noticed.

To a supreme craftsman this was no trouble. Some modeling wax left over from the shop work done in the cell, mixed with rust scraped from old iron to the same color of the extracted nail, modeled with the point of the poniard— and no one in the castle could have distinguished between the real and the false.

Night after night the work slowly progressed until the hinges were attached by means of nails which had been extracted, cut short, and carefully replaced.

There were interruptions, even though he worked only at night. The Castellan, from time to time as the fits seized him, sent men to the goldsmith's cell to make certain that the prisoner had not flown from his stone coop. In spite of this the work was finished, and when he examined the hinge bands closely, Cellini was pleased to see that it would be next to impossible for the eye to detect any mark showing that either had been tampered with. He settled down to await word from Angela.

It came the very next day. The turnkey furtively slipped a note into his hands and quickly shuffled off.

The goldsmith examined the seals carefully before breaking them— the jailer might have read the letter before passing it in. They were intact. The prison lackey had not been interested; to him this was simply a love note, slipped in to a pining prisoner, a service for which he had been amply paid.

The letter was in Angela's hand.

The Prince has tried but can do nothing inside. You must find a way of your own. But without, all is ready. Lookouts will keep watch every night. When you are free of the place, wait till one of them reaches you. He will lead you to where I am waiting. My love, be careful! I pray for your safety.

And now there was only the matter of a favorable opportunity.

On the following Saturday evening, the shrieking wail of the demented Giorgio filtered faintly into the cell from the battlements above.

"*E-e-c-e-e-eeeceeeeeee!*" The keening hiss was nearly lost in the evening air. "You are all lying to me! He is flown away, I tell you! Let me go! . . . Let me go, I say, that I may fly off and catch him up! Certain it is that I can fly better and faster than he. Benvenuto is but a counterfeit bat—a false bat! I am a real one! Unhand me, varlets! Knaves! Leave me to act! *E-e-e-eee—*"

The wail broke off. There was the distant sound of a scuffle. Shortly afterward the jailer brought in the goldsmith's supper. He was hollow-eyed and weary looking.

"What's wrong up there?" Cellini asked him.

"*Diàscolo!*" sighed the turnkey, shaking his head. "The master grows worse. He has passed several days and nights in a mad frenzy and has worn us out. He wants to fly off from the battlements up above. All of us in the central keep are fervently hoping they will let him fly, or that he will select some other part of the castle for these antics of his. They're going to lock him in his rooms for two days and nights. That is fortunate. If we don't get some rest soon, we will all go mad!"

For Cellini it meant the time was at hand. Tomorrow night, a Sunday, would be ideal; the prison personnel were tired and spent from their long vigil.

At four of the clock on the next night, well after the last visit from the jailer, the goldsmith began final operations. He emptied the mattress and rolled the two long strips of linen around two sticks. Then he took up the pincers and began pulling at the door hinges.

The shortened nails came out without trouble, but it required three bitter hours of patient labor to remove the hinges from their rusted posts; and after he had removed them the door still would not open. The double planking and the lock bolts offered too much resistance.

Sweating and muttering, Cellini cut into the wood along the edge of the door. If enough wood was hacked away, the side could be pulled back far enough to permit its being pushed sidewards, thus sliding the bolts from the clasps. Since the labor had to be done silently, it was slow and tedious. It lacked but two and a half hours till dawn when, with a grunt, he wrenched the door free and gently laid it against the wall. He was wet with perspiration. There was little time left. The jailer made his first appearance shortly after dawn.

Shouldering the two rolls of linen he trotted down the corridor and up the stair leading to the latrines atop the central keep. There were no soldiers on duty there. Guards were stationed only from the lower keep down. His stay in the *castello* during the siege now was serving him well. He was acquainted with every detail of this central tower.

The night was clear and cloudless. Fortunately for Cellini there was no moon. His costume was hardly suitable for breaking out of prison. He was clothed all in white—hose, trunks, a short sleeveless doublet, and light gray buskins. Into the right boot, he thrust the sheathed poniard.

Inside the noisome privy he made his way to one of the wall vents which opened on a slanting roof that led to the rear of the castle. Leaping on the ledge, he sprang lightly out on the roof, gained a foothold on two jutting tiles, and clambered up and over to the rear of the fort. Against the circular wall of the tower he reached up, feeling around for another piece of antique tiling he knew jutted out there. Finding it, he attached the end of the longer of the rolled strips to it as securely as he could and let the roll tumble to the ground. It seemed to reach, but he could not be certain.

Strapping the remaining roll to his back he carefully wiped his hands dry on his trunks and looked up at heaven.

"My Lord God, I beg Thee give aid to my case and deign to assist this most humble of all the creatures Thou hast created. Thou canst see that my cause is just. Send me therefore of Thy divine assistance, and, whatever betide, Thy will be done."

Grasping the strip of linen in both hands and circling it in a loop around his left leg, he swung himself out and gently slid down the sheer stone wall of Sant' Angelo.

The space of two lifetimes passed before his feet again felt the reassuring touch of mother earth beneath them. He looked up, awed at the height from which he had descended. His forehead was pearled with cold sweat. He wiped it off. In a little while now, he would be free.

The stench of manure, guano, feed and farm animals, assailed his nostrils. He idly wondered why as he made his way along the earth-packed ground leading to the northern rampart. Reaching the point where the passage gave out on it, he found a high wall confronting him. In dismay he raced alongside it till he came to a door. It was locked and barred from the outside. A soft clucking sound made him jump and whirl, his hand curling around the haft of the dagger in his boot.

A hen strutted proudly by.

The Castellan had walled up this section of the grounds, converting it into a stable and hen-yard. The goldsmith was trapped inside it—like an impotent rooster.

Pacing frantically back and forth, kicking out savagely at anything in his path, vainly searching for a way out, he tripped on a length of wood and stumbled headlong into a pile of straw. Cursing and spitting out grain stems, he kicked aside the loose straw underfoot and uncovered a long pole. If he could manage to move it, it would do. The piece of tree trunk, for such it was, was heavy. Dragging it across the yard to the wall used up most of his strength. Lifting and propping it against the wall all but exhausted him.

With what little strength remained he clawed a way to the top of the wall by pulling himself up bodily with his hands. It flayed the skin off both palms. The wall top had a sharp ridge on its slanted surface. He straddled it precariously. His skinned hands were torturing him, and made it impossible to pull the pole up and over. Wheezing and panting, he cut off a portion of the remaining strip and tied it to the end of the pole.

The short drop of the hen-yard wall proved harder and more fatiguing than all that had gone before. Cellini was forced to sit on the ground and rest. The burning pain of his flayed hands was such a torment he tried to relieve it by bathing them in his own urine.

When his panting breath and pounding heart had fallen to near normal, he trotted silently around to the rampart along the west wall. He reached the battlements of this final hurdle and was fastening the last of the strip around one of them, when another sound made him whirl again.

It was no hen this time.

A sentinel making his rounds had spotted him and was watching in startled surprise.

Knowing that capture now meant removal to a cell from which there would be no escaping, the goldsmith yanked the poniard from his boot and walked grimly toward the guard.

The soldier apparently did not feel that his rate of pay warranted such risks as facing grimly determined escapees who came at him with drawn dagger and deadly intent. He gave no alarm, but quickening his pace he went off on his rounds, giving that section of the rampart a wide berth.

Seeing the action, Cellini wasted no time on speculation. He turned back to the battlement only to find another sentinel looking straight at him. The dagger was still drawn. But this lad too was seeing nothing, and walked quickly away from there.

The goldsmith flung the roll over the wall, took hold of the twisted sheet and let himself down.

It might have been that the strip of linen broke under the strain of his weight; that his hands were so badly flayed or his arms so weakened, they were incapable of sustaining him; or perhaps he thought he had reached the ground and relaxed his grip. Cellini couldn't remember. Whatever the reason, he fell; and in falling, struck his head against the ground. He lost consciousness.

Dawn was beginning to gray the sky when he revived. The fresh morning breeze was playing over him, tickling his face. It made him sleepy. It would have been even more enjoyable, imagined the bedewed and dulled goldsmith, whose senses were not yet fully recovered, if they hadn't cut off his head. And what was he doing in Purgatory? Lying still, feeling that gentle breeze waft over him, he mulled over these important topics for some time. Then, in a flash, it all came back to him.

With a weary groan he lifted the two leaden weights he had for hands to the place where his head should have been. He felt nothing but a pringling sensation, as if ten thousand pins were stuck in him. The two lead weights came away covered with blood. His eyes looked at them blankly. He must be suffering from a head wound. His fingers searched the spot. No pain. No feeling. He concluded that his was a very hard, very thick skull, and that it was high time he stood up like a man.

He tried to do that—and fell over on his face. His right leg was not co-operating as it should. He glanced down at it stupidly and saw that the foot was folded over, like one of the hinges he had removed from his cell door. The leg was broken near the ankle.

At the moment these were all minor considerations. He was out of Sant' Angelo . . . Indeed, he was out of Rome. The important thing to do now, broken leg or no, was to stay out of the castle and get back inside the city, where he had friends. Angela's instructions were forgotten, blotted out of his mind by the fall.

Pulling out the poniard, he cut a piece of linen and bound up his leg and foot, wiped the blood from his head and face, and began crawling on all fours to the Castello Gate two hundred paces away.

It took him a long time to reach it, and a much shorter period to discover that the Gate door was locked.

No longer dismayed by any circumstance, Cellini began rooting around the lower edge of the door. His mind functioned more by reflex than from any conscious effort on his part. He knew what he was doing without knowing why. There was a rock under the door. Using the dagger he dug around it until he dislodged the boulder and a quantity of rubble sufficient to pull himself painfully through the hole. The place was deserted. He began crawling into the city.

The stray dogs that night and day loitered around all the city gates, came awake to dispute the entry of this strange quadruped into their domain. They attacked in force, snapped savagely, withdrew and prepared for another onslaught. Cellini was ready for that one. He slashed out viciously. One of the larger mongrels set up a howl fit to rouse the city and limped off, followed by all the others.

Once again the goldsmith began creeping in the direction of Santa Maria della Traspontina. The gray of dawn lighted the city by the time he had dragged himself to the street leading to that church. The danger of discovery was now acute. He turned into the street, clenching his teeth on the pain, and headed for St. Peter's.

A water carrier was plodding along the cobbled way, leading his bucket-laden donkey. Cellini yelled to him for help.

The man walked slowly over. His glance held a great deal of uncertainty. This fellow crawling along the street was bleeding. There was a drawn dagger in his hand, and there was blood on it! He didn't know whether to yell, or run, or what.

"I am a poor unfortunate youth," gasped the goldsmith, "who broke a leg while escaping through a window. An affair of the heart, you understand? Her husband . . ." a hand flicked in a gesture of grim certainty "... if he should find me he will hack me to pieces. For Christ's sake, my good man, I implore you, take me up and carry me to the terrace of St. Peter's. Do that and I will give you a gold crown." He drew the coin from his purse, which he had taken the precaution to keep well filled.

"A gold crown!" The *acquaiuolo's* eyes bulged out as his fingers speared at the coin.

After a careful testing of the metal with his teeth, he pocketed it, hitched the goldsmith on his back and toted him to the raised terrace of the new cathedral. He deposited his charge there and quickly ran back to his donkey. It was the easiest and largest wage he had ever earned.

As he waited for the water carrier to move out of sight, Cellini looked around desperately. It was now fully light, and he began to recall something about waiting for someone. There was not a soul in sight. To wait there and face certain discovery and recapture was pointless. He resumed his crawl, this time in the direction of the Borgo Vecchio. He had powerful friends in that section of the city.

He had taken the first painful pull when Angela turned into the piazza, looking around as wildly and as desperately as he had done a moment before. She saw him, smothered a cry, and began waving frantically. Then she ran to him.

"Your head! It's covered with blood! Oh, Neutino, my love!" She pulled off a scarf she wore and quickly bound it around his head. "We saw the sheets dangling from the tower, but we couldn't find you!" She was panting, laughing and crying, all at once. "I am nearly mad with fear. I thought you had been taken—slain! Why didn't you wait as I wrote you to?"

The goldsmith looked up at her, patting her arm. "My dream. My Angela. Why didn't I wait? . . . I don't know . . . don't remember . . ." He struggled to rise.

"No! Lie quietly. Your leg . . . Here they are!"

Three men ran up, all of them D'Este retainers. They said not a word, threw a cloak over him, lifted him carefully, and quickly carried him down off the terrace into a dark twisting little side street. One of them whistled. A cart lumbered up, covered over in the manner of an enclosed litter. Felice was sitting in front, managing two sleek mules. The Este courtier, Luigi Alamanni, sprang down and beckoned to the waiting servants.

"Quickly," he ordered.

"Be careful of his leg," Angela implored. "It is broken."

She helped them lift her lover into the enclosed wagon and climbed in beside him. Messer Alamanni looked on while she kissed him fervently.

"So, then, *maestro,* you are free." He peered closely at Cellini, then gestured to one of the servants who promptly filled a cup from a flask and handed it up. "Mona Angela here has seen to everything. There will be a leech to attend you when you reach your destination, I promise it." He looked up at Felice. "Be off quickly. And have no fear. There will be sufficient guards." He stepped back.

Felice jerked at the reins and started off toward the Porta Palata.

"Where are we going?" asked Cellini. Angela was hugging him in an ecstasy of delight.

"To Tivoli," Felice answered. "My lord Cardinal has a villa there. Angela has packed all your belongings. They are under you. My dear, there is a bottle and cups under the seat."

Angela pulled out a huge straw-braided jug and three cups, filled and passed them around. She sipped and then sighed happily.

"There you can rest, and recover from your hurts. Then we shall go to France, in the service of the King. It is a triumph!"

Cellini smiled back at her. His head ached dully, but he was no longer befuddled. The haze had cleared. He reached back and pulled the curtain flap aside. The rays of the early morning sun were glinting off the embattled keep of Sant' Angelo, softening the outlines of its grim tower. A bitter look came to his eyes as he gazed at the massive ramparts. The vein at his temple swelled and began to pulse softly and rhythmically.

Angela's soft black tresses gleamed as she lifted her head from his shoulder and looked up at him.

"What is it, *carino?*" she asked tenderly, watching his tense face with concern. "Now that you are free, and mine once more, why do you look so grim?"

The goldsmith's answering smile twisted at the corners. "You speak true, my lovely one. To be free of that place and find myself here holding you close is a happiness that lies beyond the power of words to express. But believe me, my own," he bit out, his voice hardening and taking on a steely edge, "whatever I have left of worldly goods—all that I own—I would gladly give up in return for one little favor."

"What is that, Neutino?"

Cellini's hot eyes wandered out again in the direction of the Rome he was leaving behind. "I'd give it all," he repeated harshly. "Everything—for just one crack at the bastards who put me in there!"

Angela smiled. Her Neutino would never change.